Warehouse

Frances Hamblin

Published in 2014 by FeedARead.com Publishing – Arts
Council funded

Copyright © Frances Hamblin

First Edition

The author has asserted her moral right under the Copyright,
Designs and Patents Act, 1988, to be identified as the author
of this work.

A CIP catalogue record for this title is available from the
British Library.

Chapter 1

November. A clear bright sky. Even in the heart of the city the stars were strong enough to outshine the pools of bromine orange streetlight. Later there would be frost. A gaunt square building, burnt umber behind the violet white arches of its lighted windows, stood solid in the deep night sky. For a hundred and fifty years the brick warehouse had been rooted there, beside the huge flint church, its match in age, while the rest of the street had changed, one pub to a house, gardens to concrete flags, empty shops to let. And on the field opposite was a girls' secondary school, stabbing saw-toothed 60's architecture with a spinney of 90's repair scaffolding sprouting from its low flat roof.

Just discernible on the worn bricks between the third and fourth floors of the old warehouse, a flaky painted message in metre-high letters read: **NO 1 WAREHOUSE.**

In the still air nine o'clock cried out faintly from the Guildhall clock some miles away and shortly afterwards a scramble of activity issued from the swing doors of the girls' school as the evening classes discharged, and the students' chattering vapourised in the icy still chill. Marc emerged with a small group. They huddled towards the gates and out onto the street. In the windows of the warehouse opposite they could see the keep-fit women gathering up their mats and towels, struggling into sweaters and coats.

Suddenly from above the keep fit room there came a violent vibrating THUD like a muffled explosion deep within the building. The passers-by outside peered into the windows, curious, or scuttled away in alarm.

The keep-fit women stopped, staring stupidly, herd-like, upwards at the ceiling, outwards to the window, frozen in anticipation of the inevitable collapse of the building. But when, out of this vacuum lasting only seconds, no collapse came, activity tentatively began to resume, in a slow-motion born of suspense. Then they began to hurry away.

*   *   *   *   *

"Christallmigh'ywhatthefuckwasat?" Joe, bolt upright in his armchair, had felt the shock wave of something violent from below.

His wrinkly old wife stirred in her customary post-prandial snooze in front of the telly enough to say,

"Watch ya language, there's ladies present."

"But didn't you 'ear it? That godawful explosion!.... 'ere maybe it's them bombers, terrorists!...or someone's gas blew up? Come on Rose, there'll be a fire!.. it's dahnstairs. It'll come up 'ere, come on Rose we best get out!"

Joe was pacing about now, picking things up and putting them down in a panic of indecision about what valuables to take. There were none anyway. He settled on a photo of the grandchildren. Rose would not be moved. She had heard something, but said it was on the telly. So Joe grabbed his coat and cap and went out without her. She was probably right, she usually was. But a nervous man like Joe, thin and wiry with years of worry, kept his grip on the world by his own over-reaction to it.

It was freezing on the stairs and the stone steps sent a chill right up through his stiff old frame through the soles of his slippers to his quivering shoulders. As he drew level with the floor below, he realised that the noise had come from Lilly's flat. That was cause for concern because he knew for sure Lilly was out. He'd heard the front door earlier. They'd have to break the door down. The thought of some diversionary excitement almost overrode Joe's fears for his own safety. He sniffed for the smell of smoke. Was sure he could smell it.

The clattering of steel-tipped heels taking the stairs two by two reassured Joe that someone else was coming to help. Bernard (nice boy) rose into view. Sensing an audience was near, Bernard slowed his pace, and smoothed his way up the staircase; sharp-cut hair coming into view first, slick, shiny jacket sliding into view, rigid trouser creases above gleaming shoes.

"Oh it's you," Joe welcomed him like a stinking wet fish.

2

"D'you hear that bang?"

*　　　*　　　*　　　*　　　*

All that evening Oliver had been trying to persuade Bernard to let him stay. Oliver was jealous that he had to live at home and Bernard had broken away.

They were hunched on the broken sofa - Gran's old brown draylon. Because of its cracked frame it was so close to the ground you could never get comfortable sitting on it. It was all right for lying down on though, for a solitary night of beer, junk food and a video. Bernard wouldn't part with it even if he could afford to. It reminded him of gran and the uncomplicated way in which she had always favoured him over all her other grandchildren.

"Just tonight? Clare and I have nowhere else to go." Oliver was using his pathetic voice.

"Not Clare! She back on the scene? Thought you couldn't stand the sight of her!"

"Last week's news. Anyway she's a screw, and mum won't have her in the house. We would bring round a takeaway," he tempted. "For three," he added.

"Nope, not after last time." Bernard remembered the row that had woken the neighbours. The shrieking of a woman in Bernard's flat had confused them. They, having observed only one person, Oliver, as a frequent visitor, had pruriently elevated him to the status of Bernard's lover, thrilled to be scandalised by the exoticism of a gay neighbour. It amused Bernard not to let on that they were brothers.

"Go on," wheedled Oliver. "A bottle of vino.... alright, two, and half a bottle of Powers.....your favourite."

The creep! thought Bernard feeling himself weakening. The elder brother, he had always given way to Oliver's manipulative side. Instilled in him by both parents (both younger children in their own families) was the belief that the younger should be looked after by the elder, and that whatever harm befell the younger child was implicitly the fault of the elder. The psychological "help" that this responsibility

3

had forced Bernard to seek, had been part of the reason why he had succeeded in getting this housing association flat in the first place.

"You're not having my bed!" he warned.

Knowing he had won, Oliver didn't respond to that - but secretly thought it might be arranged later. Last time, Bernard had got so drunk that he'd fallen asleep on the floor and it had seemed silly to let the bed stay empty. This time though, he vowed to himself, he and Clare would not leave telltale traces of their bodily fluids on the sheets. Bernard had been quite within his rights to get annoyed about that.

"Thanks bruv. Be round about 7, OK?"

And they were, on the dot. But the aroma of tandoori from a brown paper bag and the clanking of bottles in the off license bag, softened Bernard into welcoming host. He had no other plans anyway.

A cosy threesome draped themselves around the mismatched room. Bernard was asserting his proprietorship by needlessly lounging along the whole of the sofa, carefully arranging his trouser creases as he stretched out his legs. Clare and Oliver were forced to spread their food out on the floor. Gratitude and the expectation of passion ahead made them uncomplaining. Anyway, they could exchange covert smiles of lust and heighten their anticipation with secret fingertips of touch.

One of the most exciting freedoms of being independent for Bernard was eating wherever he liked, not using utensils and not clearing up until he felt like it. They had been brought up in an atmosphere rigid with table manners, eating by the clock, cloth napkins and heavy guilt for food left uneaten - and the ensuing nervous indigestion.

It would stand him in good stead in the future.

As she licked tandoori sauce from her fingers and nibbled it from under her nails, Clare looked around the room for something nice to say to Bernard. She felt sorry for him, assuming him to be lonely; and appreciative that he was letting them stay here. Anyway being full of curry and slopping with wine inside made her want to delay sex with Ollie until she'd digested a bit.

4

Beer went better with curry, must remember next time.

"When d'you do all them paintings then, Bernie? I've never seen you do any here."

"School and college, foundation course I did in Reading, couple of years ago."

"Why don't you do no more then, you're really good at it, ain't 'e, Ollie? I like that one there with the shoe."

Everyone who came into the flat liked the pencil drawing of a stiletto-heeled shoe. The finish of the graphite was uncannily shiny; it was realistic to a surreal degree, being about twice life-sized.

"Mmm," was all Bernard could say. He could not be bothered to explain to this bleached bimbo why the shoe was the least important of all the many pieces of artwork pinned and stuck to the walls. It had been a simple exercise.

"Who was she then, the woman who kicked her shoe off for you, so sexy like that, eh?" Clare had lapsed into skittish mood, teasing because she too, had assumed, probably from his lack of girlfriends, that Bernard was gay. Bernard recognized the signs. There was a conspiratorial playfulness that women adopted when they thought a man was gay. It seemed to give them licence to take liberties, push the boundaries, enjoy the pretence of closeness and chumminess. See how far they could go. There was an element of 'surely he can't really resist me?' Fag hags.

But at least she had looked beyond the picture itself and a spark of interest blinked on in Bernard as he decided to reply.

"No one, it was just an drawing exercise, the teacher brought it in."

Determined to keep on being nice, Clare looked round and noticed for the first time a huge variety of pictures. One canvas, made three-dimensional by layers upon layers of worked paint, caught her eye. Great zigzags of stark angry red were slashed by scars of lightening white and a heavy outline of black, spiralled into a suppurating trickle of bilious green. Clare roused herself to go closer and look.

Bernard knew what she was going to say next. She was going to ask him what it was. Why did people always think an

5

abstract painting had to *be* something? It had to represent something or they felt they couldn't understand it, and if they couldn't understand it they couldn't like it.

"Christ you were angry when you painted that, I c'n feel the paint trying to get out and come and get me. I couldn't live wiv that. It'd be like living wiv my dad again. He was always furious, red in the face and wan'ing to hit us. Killed 'im in the end, 'eart attack."

Clare's account was so matter-of-fact that Bernard could hardly believe that she had in a few words so completely got the message of this painting. He felt exposed and thought he might take it off the wall later. But he began to change he way he felt about Clare.

It would be several years before he got the opportunity to explain to Clare that this painting had been the first he had done since leaving college. The psychologist he had been seeing because of his chronic lack of self-esteem and depression, despite good exam results, had thought him to be suppressing anger. That the anger he had been trying to deny had been at his own brother for a lifetime of being responsible for him, playing second fiddle to him. Sylvia, the psychologist, had supplied him with the paints, old unused oils from her own school days. He had done the painting in two days without eating or sleeping. He had never looked back. Had never seen her since.

The food gone and the whiskey started, Bernard began to feel magnanimous. Before the lovers could begin to make him feel unwanted, as they surely would when their thoughts turned to the carnal - soon, Bernard judged - he found himself saying:

"You can have my bed, if you like. I've got to pop out for a bit."

It wasn't true, but he didn't want to stay around listening to her screeching and groaning. She really was the noisiest screw ever. Perhaps she faked. Bernard smiled at the thought of this happening to his oh so successful, full-of-his-own-prowess-in-bed, bint-puller extraordinaire brother.

When the noises from the bedroom were reaching a crescendo that made Bernard down his last shot quickly, he

6

stood up. He was surprisingly steady after the wine and almost half of the whiskey. Muffled Jumping Jack Flash from the aerobics class below suddenly stopped mid-chorus, signalling the end of the class, about nine o'clock... Jumping Jack Flash, it's a gas, gas, gas, (God how old was that teacher?) when....
BOOOOOOOM

*   *   *   *   *

Pearl lived with her mother. She was 32. She had been kept in bed most of her adult life. They had been living in this housing association flat for six years. Pearl smelt. The old ladyish smell of the unwashed, the fetid flesh that chafed and chapped, the sores that sometimes oozed, the remains of food dribbled and spilled, the grubby clothes, all created an aura within which Pearl, unaware, existed. Beyond the sofa bed, which was her world, the sickly smell of British sherry hung in the nicotine air. That was when Pearl's mother was at home. Mostly she was out and she would leave Pearl propped on cushions in front of the TV, having checked that she didn't need the toilet, making sure there was a feeder mug of milky drink nearby and an old nappy for her to wipe her dribbles and nose (which she never bothered to do, or perhaps had never been able to), having also checked that the one bar fire was on and the crocheted blanket wrapped round her legs, Lilly would feel free to leave.

Lilly felt she had done everything possible for the difficult daughter who had been born this way to spite her. Her only solace was the pub, where almost no one knew about Pearl. In the early days Lilly had made an effort to learn a language that they could share, signs and word boards and finger spelling. But her energy had quickly run out after Ted had run out on the two of them. The drink had been the only way to lift her spirits and now at least she was tolerant and patient with Pearl, trying to anticipate her immediate needs. Lilly blocked out of her mind and out of their lives, all the tasks that seemed too difficult. Shifting Pearl for anything beyond the toilet chair had become too much for her, so sheets and clothes were rarely changed. And it was amazing,

Lilly consoled herself, how after a certain time these things didn't seem to get any grubbier or smellier. It was not that it didn't occur to Lilly to take Pearl for an outing, but in her day a disability in the family was something to be ashamed of, and she never liked attention or being marked out from the crowd for any reason, let alone as the pusher of a wheelchair. But she was not heartless, so Lilly drank to forget her guilt.

Anger had been welling up in Pearl for a long time. She did not recognise it. But she had started to cry, almost constantly. Not sobbing, but a silent weeping that had tightened her chest. With it came a physical strength that she had never felt before in her imposed passivity. Out of the blue one day she began to hear the television. It had always been a noisesome thing, a bright colour box, colours whose names she did not know. But on this day, the noise filtered through the crust of wax in Pearl's ears, where previously no expert had been able to establish whether sound could penetrate or not. What Pearl perceived did not please her. Every time her mother switched the machine on before going out, Pearl wished it off. If Lilly understood Pearl's agitated gestures of protest she did not let on. She couldn't bear to leave the child alone in silence. She believed the television was company for her.

That Thursday evening, Pearl's frustration suddenly granted her a supernatural strength. An explosion of muscle inside, without warning, jerked her briefly free of the bed. She lurched forward and smacked her furious outstretched arms and flailing hands into the flickering TV screen. The violence of the impact sent it reeling from its spindly legs. It crashed to the floor with an ear-shattering boom and an explosive flash of bursting glass.

Chapter 2

After the explosion, something began to swim about in Pearl's ears. She noticed a wallowing, swooshing noise and wanted to move away from it. She jerked her head. It bumped across the sticky lino. The small movement was caught as a flutter on a shiny piece of fractured television screen. Pearl's attention shot to it. She clearly saw her eye, floor-level, bright with the reflection of the electric bulb, staring back at her.

She shut her eye. It went away. She blinked again and again to see the miracle of her own eye. She was afraid to move more in case she lost the feeling of contact.

Pearl began to feel the cold of the floor. She noticed the sensation of her cheek, the chill pressing into it, and the contrast of the warm, pleasant feeling of the liquid that was trickling out of her ear. Her motionless fingertips shot her a violent message of pain. She shrieked and observed, not knowing it belonged to her, her bloody hand grinding into the floor. With an searing effort of will, something in Pearl's brain, something never consciously used before, tapped into the line of communication that stopped the palm from grinding the shards of broken glass into the hard floor. And Pearl suddenly knew that the hand was hers. Pearl's hand. And she knew she had made it stop moving, and in doing so, caused the pain of it to ease a little.

Her cheek relaxed into the grime, spittle transferring the taste of an unidentifiable ancient sweetness from the floor on to her tongue. She pushed her tongue out for more, briefly fascinated at the new sensation. Battering inside Pearl's head was an uneven weight, with jagged edges that splintered and cracked against the lining of her skull. The din of it abruptly stopped and the noise she then heard, she knew at once was people coming. Then she let everything slip away. All the new feeling and first-time thoughts slipped away. People coming….the muscles relaxed…the tongue lolled, she felt herself returning to the emptiness. Glazing over. Nobody in. The constant vacant state of waiting, always waiting for people coming. But though she closed her eyes, her brain did not, this time, shut down. She felt the rise of panic from her guts, she heard the wail of fear and knew for the first time the sound of her own voice.

Never again would she know the peace of the empty nothingness of those days, months and years of incarceration. From this day forward, from the moment of the accident, she would always be intensely aware of every second of the grubby, cloying, needful boundaries of her life, and her unique ability to express them.

Footsteps had stopped outside the door, banging and shouting started. But they didn't come in. Pearl listened, paralysed, fearful but willing them to come in. Why didn't they? She knew nothing of keys and deadlocks. Was her mother there? She could smell smoke. Not the familiar smoke of cigarettes, but an acrid, choking smoke that began to fill her eyes.

*   *   *   *   *

Though the cold was closing in fast, the stragglers from the evening classes at the girls' school stopped to watch the fire appliance arrive and waited to see where it was for, secretly both desiring and dreading the worst. Cloaked in curiosity, shoulders forgot to shiver. A second siren announced the approach of another. But the banshee wail drew in its wake a blue flashing ambulance.

Still waiting at the bus-stop, a group of middle-aged English class students stood with Marc. They were spellbound by him. He was exotic, a tall athletic young Frenchman, whose hair was plaited in a jolly jack tar pigtail, which would have suited the naval history of the town, except that it was white blond.

Marc didn't seem to notice their admiration and gawped into the unworldly blue interior of the ambulance, wondering that he had never seen the inside of one in France. Were they different?

Most of the dance class had left. Anxious not to be there when the building collapsed, they joked. But most shared a burden of guilt - family commitments - and were barely

10

allowed out without a trail of small children. Must be getting back, you don't know what he's like if I'm late.

The tutor dithered, both an ambulance and a fire appliance were here now. How far did her responsibility to the building stretch? Was she perhaps in the position of greatest authority here, with regard to the safety of the building? It belonged to a housing association. Were the residents all disabled, she worried?

In the small crowd, no one spoke. The rising cloud of condensation from their collective warmth dispersed, as breaths were held. All attention was concentrated on the entrance to the flats, those steep stone steps, down which a story of human tragedy was about unfold.

"Look!" A shriek went up and eyes followed the pointing finger. A sheet of yellow flame lit up the window of the second floor flat, throwing out a warm glow like a merry bonfire into the November night.

"The curtains are on fire!" And the heat from them burst the pane in its frame, ejecting a belly of red flame to shoot up, free, up to disappear into the black sky leaving the sound of glass tinkling onto the pavement below. And then the fire was gone, snuffed by the swift, gloved hands of the Thursday evening watch with sprayed foam and fire blankets.

The sound of clattering announced the difficult approach of the stretcher down the treacherous stone steps and the banging double doors revealed Pearl, an unmoving mound shrouded in a cellular blanket.

Sensing doom, many of the bystanders looked away, then following the path of their gaze disappeared into the night.

A figure suddenly peeled off from the back of the group and raced back along the road. Tracey, a member of the dance class had left her watch behind in the confusion caused by the commotion from upstairs. She followed the image of it in her head.....carefully placed on a classroom chair. She ran blind, hoping to catch the teacher before she locked up for the night. She bumped into someone at the bus stop, "Sorry!" And then realising that the bulky sports bag was inhibiting her speed, she dropped it.

"Can you keep an eye on my bag?" she shouted to the stranger and ran on without waiting for agreement.

Intermittent faces flashed blue from the bus queue in the revolving light from the ambulance roof, but Tracey had no time to notice the covered mound of Pearl. To avoid the ambulance, she cut sharply across the road in front of the fire appliance, not looking beyond it for traffic approaching from behind.

The screech of brakes and scorching smell of tyres reached her before the sound of metal impacting into lamppost. The shattering of the windscreen glass and crunch of plastic bumper, robbed her of her resolve. She stopped, turned and fled before the stricken driver, already unnerved by the emergency vehicles, could stagger sobbing, shocked, clear of the broken, smoking car. She ran away from the crash she had caused, before the on-lookers could take in what had happened.

From a distance as she was propelled down the road on Bernard's arm, where he had retrieved her from the 'Battle of Trafalgar', Pearl's mother, Lilly, saw the car hit something. So did Bernard. He saw the woman pounding away. Even in the poor orange streetlight he had seen her, a mature, short, chubby woman, like an evil twisted child quitting the scene of the accident she had caused.

Lilly was seized by a confusion that would never leave her. How could Bernard from upstairs have known, before it happened, that Pearl was in an accident? How did Bernard know about Pearl at all? Lilly had just seen the accident for herself. How could he have known before it happened? Because there was Pearl, already in the back of the ambulance.....but Lilly had seen the accident! And Bernard had come 10 minutes earlier to tell her in the pub. An unpleasant thought popped into Lilly's head. Through the alcoholic fuddle, she searched the faces on the pavement for her neighbours.

The neighbours had known nothing of Pearl. They now knew quite a lot about Pearl. Lilly felt the sharp fingers of accusation, the unanswerable questions, busybody Joe, crabby old Rose. Though neither was there.

Lilly took the first impulsive, decisive action she had taken in years. She turned and walked away. A bus drew up. She got on it with the evening class students. She didn't know any of them. Bernard ran up. He hammered desperately on the window. Lilly looked away.

She never came back.

* * * * *

Because Lilly had gone, Pearl was now alone, she had no one. Why did Bernard feel he should accompany Pearl to hospital? Just following the action through? Filling in time because it was too early to go home yet? (Oliver and Clare in his bed). Curiosity? Caring?

Bernard straightened his trouser cuffs where they had become hooked in his boot tops as he sat on the bus following the ambulance up to Casualty. He pulled the jacket collar up for warmth and shrugged the sleeves down over his sharp cuffs. At a rational level he knew. Making this journey would probably be a mistake, might lead him to a turning point in his life. He felt these moments on the bus would be the last moments of this life. A sense of premonition gripped him.

He tried to see out through the window, looking for some sign by which to mark the portent of the journey. Nothing could penetrate the reflective inside of the glass, dribbling where he had swept aside the condensation. Only his own slightly anxious face peered streakily back at him. The traffic slowed then stopped alongside a pub. Its neon lighted name flickered uncertainly, bright enough to shine in. It was The Coal Exchange. The middle six letters were blanked out, broken.

The change.

* * * * *

The screaming and the siren merged in Pearl's head. One thing she knew. Neither noise was coming from her. These noises were in her head now, replacing the fuzzy buzzing that had always been there before. In detached interest she heeded

13

the unpleasant pain in her hands. With her eyes open, she could see white softness, grey softness and something white and hard. With her eyes shut she could see the fuzzy black/pink that she was now aware had always been there. Within her body she could feel her innards rolling about, rubbing against the inside of her outsides. One thing she knew. At last. She was. This was what it was like to be her.

Chapter 3

On the Brillo-pad carpet, in the middle of the floor, a dark-haired woman knelt. The squatness of her stature and the squareness of her shoulders meant she occupied a neat cube of space, her lowered, dark-haired head its rolling lid. Tears were streaming down her face. Her emotion was so intense it seemed to inhabit a place outside of herself, to have an independent existence beyond her. She had worked so hard to be here, to have developed so well, to have sloughed off years of shit, to have buried all the damage. Now here she was, 32, having overcome the last hurdle, she was overwhelmed. The journey here had been everything. And now arrival, so long and painfully awaited was the opening ugly jaws of a terrifying abyss. Her tears poured into it.

Through the distortion of water a bare, white-walled room wobbled. The pitted, grey, polystyrene ceiling tiles pressed down on her. The scratchy brillo pushed up from below trying to fuse with the bare skin of her knees.

"What am I doing here?" she suddenly found herself shrieking.

The tears were blinked away There was no escape from the Blu-tac stains blobbed randomly about the colourless plaster, the coarse-woven brown blanket tucked into the narrow wooden cot, formica drawers, chipped shelves, black-topped desk, graffiti inefficiently erased by scouring, one brown wooden armed chair, no chair suitable for the desk.

She jumped up and threw open the two windows. It was a corner room, with windows on adjacent walls. And the relief of a through breeze calmed her. But a sudden knock on the door made her jump and she bashed her head on the frame of the opened window.

Muttering curses, rubbing her head, she crossed the room, through the lobby which housed a wardrobe, still empty, and a wash basin. She opened the door. A child was standing there. Six foot three with the beardless face and ginger curls of a five-year-old. He was her next-door neighbour, holding a toothbrush. She was stunned by the surreal apparition.

"I've not brought any toothpaste, can I borrow some?"

It was the one thing she had always maintained, her teeth. She had never been without toothbrush and toothpaste, though many's the time she had to nick them. Anything to keep a clean mouth.

The pink herbal krameria toothpaste she offered him, was met with disbelief. He really didn't believe it was actually toothpaste, but a childish prank to get him to put paint or something even more unpleasant in his mouth, so she could laugh at his expense. Her realisation of his disbelief made her jaw drop. She mutely pointed to the minute English print, last in a collection of languages from Urdu, through Arabic, to Danish. This verified that the tube did indeed contain nothing more harmful than toothpaste. Abashed, he took a tiny, suspicious smidgeon of the unappetising puce paste, sniffed it and tasted it, pulling a pained face.

"It keeps mouth ulcers away," she felt obliged to defend it.

"I don't have mouth ulcers."

"Well, you won't get them now will you."

Did she shut the door rudely on him or had he already turned away, she wondered? Did it matter? Did she care?

*   *   *   *   *

For the rest of the afternoon Tracey stayed in her room in the halls of residence She moved from the bed to the rough coconut matting floor, to the armchair. She watched the way the sun moved round from one window to the other, illuminating first the deepening green of a chestnut tree, wearying now of summer, and then the red of a Victorian villa opposite, whose warm brickwork bronzed in the lowering light. Once she picked up her holdall and then put it down irresolute.

The only thing unpacked was the toothpaste.

A deep, paralysing calm settled on her. Her breathing was shallow, her limbs heavy, she sank back on the bed to allowing herself to become part of these new ordered, alien surroundings.

16

Some time later she was woken by the sound of movement outside in the corridor. Then a tap on her door. Reluctantly she roused herself. Gingerknob was there looking both sheepish and bold.

"It's supper time, thought you might have forgotten."

Suspecting that he was a newcomer himself and that he wanted more than anything not to go down alone to face the dining hall full of strangers, Tracey asked if he would mind if she accompanied him.

"OK then." He replied his voice nonchalant, his face relieved. " I'm Mike, by the way."

"By the way", a huge and ever-growing anonymous family.

Mike Bytheway knew exactly where to go. He'd done a thorough recce. He was careful to emulate the food collecting behaviour of the people in front, ending up with fish, which he didn't like (but would eat anyway) because the server didn't understand his northern accent. To his embarrassment, mixed with admiration Tracey spent an age interrogating the servers about the ingredients of almost everything, while Mike's fish became less and less appetising with the passage of time.

"Why d'you ask all those questions?"

"So I make an impression, Miguel."

Mike was irritated at being called Miguel But because he didn't mention it at the time, Tracey never knew and continued to call him Miguel. She would introduce him as Miguel, she would refer to him as Miguel. He never asked why. The moment for protest passed with the initial instance. As time passed the name stuck.

Young, thin, willowy, unformed, ginger-haired, soft-spoken Mike would eventually become, by 22, Miguel, an auburn-haired bruiser, a man with presence, president of the Students' Union.

Tracey was swept along on an orderly tide of deadlines, timetables, mealtimes, drinking up times, such as she had never before known existed. She threw herself into everything, she was appalled at how difficult the work was, at how much assumed knowledge and how many assumed skills were expected of her. Without Miguel, and his recent knowledge of school, essays, research techniques, stationery suppliers and computer skills, she might have sunk.

But it was exciting. All new. The life experience and self-confidence she exuded made her more powerful than she could ever have anticipated. She readily became a bit of a guru to younger less worldly students.

She kept her room as it had been on that first day, never fully unpacking, never erecting posters of idols, never installing computer, CD player or even a radio. Her only mark on the room was the accumulation of new books (where did she get the money?) which she would donate to others on request, as if they didn't really belong to her, but were just passing through her hands until the usefulness of their contents had been wrung dry. This suited her image of placelessness, a wanderer, a mere visitor on earth, a restless soul. It impressed many of her young fellow students.

Only one thing bothered Tracey, her size! Though she had always declared that it didn't, fat being a feminist issue, she was fond of quoting. She was very short and stout, but without the twee charm of a little teapot. The sedentary life of halls and the two meals a day, when in a previous existence she had often eaten nothing, were making her clothes tight.

One morning she was made breathless by the walk from the shower back down the hall to her room and came to a decision. Fate had thrust into her line of vision an unavoidable poster in the halls' foyer – with information about new keep-fit classes at a reduced rate with extra reductions for students. On Thursday evenings at the old Warehouse No1. Sounded an unbelievably clichéd, trendy address. She was prepared, determined even, to be unimpressed. But equally determined to go. Alone. None of her friends needed to know about this.

On the morning of her resolve she went in search of specific details about the place. As she was passing the mail pigeon-holes in the foyer, delaying so as not to be seen examining the poster, she noticed a letter aslant in the "A" box. She knew it could not be for her. No one knew she was here. But curiosity and the urge to procrastinate the fitness project propelled her to the rear of the desk, just in case, just to check.

She couldn't believe that the name on the envelope, in a youngster's handwriting, was hers. No one knew she was there. She had no family, not now. A cruel thought flashed across her brain to be dismissed before the pain could start. No, Paul's writing can not be like that now, not at 28. How instantly she recalled how old he would be now, though she hasn't seen him since he was six.

Fitness forgotten, Tracey carried the envelope away.

"Hiya, Tracey! TRACEY! You in there?" A group of floor mates were, trying to get through. Tracey shook herself into the moment, the letter still unopened.

"Got a love letter?"

Tracey hadn't meant to retort with such a vicious mind-your-own-damn-business look and the ensuing guilt obliged her to give in to the pressure of skiving friends and join them for coffee. They told her all about a new health and fitness club "The Warehouse" with opening offers and special rates for students. The route from the coffee lounge to the front door of the union wove past the bar. It had begun to rain. The letter was safe in Tracey's pocket. The company was good, each subsequent drink improved the crack as did each new friend that joined them. A joint pact was made, all would be there the next Thursday for keep fit. Tracey knew that they, young and fit already, who had spent the evening lamenting huge stomachs (that were in fact invisible to the naked eye) would probably not bother. She knew she would.

Tracey hadn't forgotten about the letter and it was late that night, alone in her room that she first had an opportunity to think about it. As she tore the triangle flap, thinking of some stranger's tongue licking there; as the seal was broken, the knowledge seeped out like a miasma onto her fingertips. She felt it soak into her skin. She knew! Her hands began to shake She sat heavily on the bed, letting the envelope fall as the strength in her fingers ebbed. It glared up at her, the adult hand-written readdress beside the scratched child-like script. Collusion between them and a powerful signal of her exclusion. Social Services, they were the only people who knew. No one else.

At last, a letter. Painfully, shaking, she folded the letter open, flattening it on the bed, at first, unable to see it, wide-eyed to stem the crying that threatened.

56, Cousins Place
Salisbury
Wilts

Dear?

I'm not sure what to call you. I've waited a long time to get the courage to write this letter.

I hope you know who I am. I've passed 8GCSEs 2Bs,4As and 2 A*. My "A" level choices are not quite sorted out yet because I want to do Art as well as Biology, Maths and Physics I decided I want to find out about you now before I get stuck into "A" levels. Mum and Dad have told me a bit. I'm short and got black hair, like you. Maybe yours is grey now. I'm glad you always said you wanted to meet me one day and I know you always made sure I would be able to find you. I have a million questions to ask. At least I think I have, I'm not sure whether I want them answered or not. I hope you get this letter soon. Now I have written it, I would like you to write to me please.

From,
Darron (White)

Chapter 4

Marc was staring up at the dark window on the first floor where a second before the boom, he had seen a flash of light. Certain that someone inside there must now be in trouble and feeling that he should do something, he glanced up and down the street. He saw other observers moving away. They did not want to get involved. And some approaching, gawping at the show. His teeth began to chatter. Nerves? The November cold? Tension in his jaw? He didn't know. Val was hanging on his every move, watching his face.

The fire appliance arrived first in a scream of sirens. The ambulance shortly behind, the second siren teeth-janglingly at odds with the first. The two paramedics jumped out and were met at the steps by the fire fighters, who, it seemed to Marc quite unnecessarily, took charge, long-winded instructions issuing from their breathing tubes in muffled shouts.

The paramedics backed off, acquiescent before the masterful authority of the axe-wielding heroes. Marc saw that there was no longer any sign of the fire, it had balled up and shot off to bloom away in the night sky. He wished the ambulance crew on, there was someone in there hurt. He judged the massive padded figures of the fire crew arrogant, wasting time. He expelled a snort of satisfaction when they were forced back by the keep-fit women pushing down the steps, breath clouding round their heads, laden with holdalls, sports bags and rolled exercise mats groping their way down, a collective dithering making them awkward, wondering whether to get involved, not wanting to appear nosy. With a quick look round, the two medics dodged immediately through the street door still banging after the fire crew, clearly refusing to wait. They knew someone was hurt and people die in seconds.

A short dark person bumped into Marc.

"Sorry!" she barely looked at him "Oh, God I've forgotten my watch," she continued.

"Er can you keep an eye on my bag a minute?"

"Comment?" He struggled to understand. "Er, what you say…ing?"

Hearing his accent, Tracey briefly looked up at him suddenly alert. He was suddenly interesting, another foreigner to add to her collection. Tracey found any accent different from her own exciting, but a foreign accent. Irresistible.

"Please can you keep an eye on my bag, while I run back for my watch, is that OK?" And the smacking weight of it landed on Marc's foot.

Her voice left a condensing trail in the air as Tracey turned quickly to retrace her steps hoping to stop the dance teacher from locking the doors on the now silent hall.

Marc struggled unsuccessfully with the idea of "I on my bag", but had caught the idea of "watch". He obediently waited and watched the strange woman's bag. Marc was originally from a rural region of France so he did not connect the recent sound of an explosion with the risk of an unattended bag.

After rushing away from him, the woman ran across the road behind the ambulance. Suddenly a car was coming towards her. Its lights silhouetted her stocky body, an unintentional spotlight glimpse of a flitting black-attired stage-hand, caught in a flash that could dramatically, irrevocably change the whole scene. A screech of brakes, a swerve of tyres and the sickening crunch of metal followed by scattered glass as the car hit, not the strange woman, but a lamppost. Marc's breath was released in a tortuous series of spasms, his heart raced. Tracy stopped motionless. The driver struggled out of her car sobbing, shaking. Tracy turned and ran. Marc remembered the bag on his foot, kicked it away slightly, then picked it up to follow her.

Marc had to follow. She had forgotten her bag. He had to return it. He dogged Tracey's footsteps along the pavement, rushing, rustling through the crisp leaves of a dry autumn.

*   *   *   *   *

The Museum Gardens was a doubly mis-named pub. There was no museum and no garden. It was a Victorian pub consisting of one huge room, a long bar almost the width of the building fronting onto the busy main road opposite the girls' school. The atmosphere inside relied on darkness punctuated by pinpoints of year-round coloured fairy lights reflected off the neat rows of glasses, brass beer pumps and down at the far end, the shiny steel and plastic electronic gear of a band.

The only useful light was the rhomboid of butter yellow which illuminated the bright green of the pool table. Marc was enchanted by it. Most pubs he had visited in his two weeks in England had had all the atmosphere of a hospital waiting room. He stood at the bar beside Tracy, catching his breath. She looked at him, unsure. Not happy to have been followed. Ashamed to have been observed leaving the scene of an accident, an accident caused by her. Then Marc drops the bag at her feet.

"Why you running....... away the accident?" he asked, disingenuously.

Sam the barman had just expended a large portion of his evening's underpaid energy in sorting out the complex drinks order of an evening class of foreign students. Hearing Marc's broken English, he was not quite rude enough to turn away but didn't try to disguise the heavy sigh. He focused in bored irritation on Tracey. She immediately deduced that perhaps he fancied her and perked up.

As she opened her mouth to order, just getting out the words: "A pint of Ringwood and a.........?" turning to Marc to ask what he wanted, a deafening crash of percussion drowned her out.

The band was amateurish, unmusical, unoriginal but too loud to ignore. Even Tracey, a native English speaker had difficulty communicating with the barman now.

"Nothing like difficulty in getting served to give you a lovely thirst," she shouted in Marc's ear, spraying froth. He nodded, not understanding, not caring because he was entranced, thought the band were really good. Then a string snapped on one of the guitars. It could have made no difference to the noise they were making, Tracey thought but the guitarist had to stop – prima donna in an artistic emergency. Tracey welcomed the silence, a chance to talk to Marc. He wasted it by going to phone his girlfriend to come and experience the exciting pub he had discovered.

Isabelle arrived very quickly, too quickly, as if she had been waiting for his call. She was sleek. Long, sleek dark hair, sleek, smooth, cheekbones, sleek, straight, thin body, smoothened by sleek, black, satin jeans and a sleek, fitted, black velour sweater. She was exactly the sort of woman, girl really, that short, chubby Tracey hated on sight.

But Isabelle was so open and friendly and hard to dislike. Her excitement at having a chance to practise her English, her pleasure that Marc had found an English friend by himself, and her constant amusement at Tracey's jokey conversation, warmed Tracey to her. But Isabelle's praise of Tracey's French flattering the envy out of her.

It would be no surprise that Isabelle went on later to join the diplomatic service as the French ambassador to Washington D.C.

"Il y avait quelque chose tres amusant ce soir Eh bien, je suis alle au college et j'ai demande au conciege, 'Where is English class?' Il me l'a dit, et je suis arrive dans une classe avec des anglais qui ne comprend ni lire ni ecrire."

"Marc, you must try to speak English," Isabelle reprimanded him, in her almost faultless received pronunciation.

"Eh, OK, one's student, Val, 50 years woman, she don' like this 'air," he pulled his waist-length blond plait round his shoulder to indicate his hair. "But she like me." Tracey had not noticed it before, it was a bit shocking when the.fashion was for the "number one", 5 millimetre-long razor haircuts, or shaven heads.

"One student ….um?….Thorn? called he, he driving in….." here Marc does the self-propelled hand action of a wheelchair, "and two more, er," here he made Asian eyes with his forefingers. Did he mean Downs' Syndrome? Tracey was pondering when the loose, noisy group at the next table disgorged one member who approached them.

"Hello, I couldn't help noticing you are French."

24

"Not me,'" said Tracey, "born and bred in Portsmouth, me. What about you?"

"No," the black-haired girl answered, laughing, "but in Vietnam there is tradition French with some peoples."

Because of her attraction to foreigners, Tracey had of course noticed the large group at the next table.

"Your group looks like an evening class."

"Yes, we learning English in the school", (pointing outside) "we have nice teacher, very funny, she says um pub is er, English culture, right."

"Do you like English beer?"

The reply takes the form of an exaggerated grimace of dislike. They are all listening now, and laugh.

"It's warm, sour and no gas," Isabelle encapsulated the three foreigners' feelings.

"An acquired taste, I'm still acquiring it, that's why I have to practise so much." Tracey swilled half her pint in one dramatic swallow. The others all winced impressed.

"Acquired means?" asked the Vietnamese woman.

As Isabelle was translating for Marc, Tracey started to explain in English to the Vietnamese student, who waved her quiet with friendly smile and turned instead to the French translation, preferring to trust to Isabelle's language skills.

The group and the trio shuffled chairs, rearranged tables and sprawled the width of the bar. They exchanged foreigners' criticisms of England. Isabel made sure that Marc got specific directions for this English class so that when he came again next week, he would attend the right class. She wondered how he would manage without her. Imagine going to a class for adult slow learners by mistake - and then staying there till the end. God, what was wrong with the teacher, he didn't notice Marc was French?

"And, we saw an accident, well, heard one really, an explosion. That's where we bumped into each other, eh, Marc?" Tracey was saying, keen to get her version in first.

Isabelle pricked up her ears She was very curious about the explosion. Maybe it was a 'bomb' in the building. One of her tutors at the university was from Northern Ireland. He had been telling the class about the conflict there. Isabel had suddenly become very interested in Northern Ireland; the tutor was a dark, wiry, attractive man with brooding eyes, a gravelly voice, enchanting, accent and amusing English. She thought he was very sexy. Could have listened to him all day.

"Maybe it's the IRA bomb, maybe it will be in the news," Isabelle sounded quite excited. She would like to be able to impress her Irish tutor with her involvement in the incident.

Conversation was abruptly strangled by the band starting up again. For Tracey there was no point in staying. Her thoughts jumped ahead, to her cosy, centrally-heated room in the halls of residence and with a jolt she saw again the desk and on it the letter, tucked away again in its envelope. Waiting for her response. Now, so many hours on, the years of fearing this letter, of its possible contents, had been replaced by a powerful sense of relief. It had contained no recriminations, no loud call for guilt. Tracey felt she might be able to sit down and consider a reply.

She got up to leave.

On the threshold of the pub two men were standing. Tracey followed their gaze. One was young, clean-shaven, neat and sharp, the other an old man, nervous gestures, head sunk into his shoulders. They looked along the road to where Tracey was amazed and appalled to see the flashing blue lights of a fire tender. Outside WAREHOUSE NO 1

Still there! Surely the emergency was over by now. Through their dragon breath conversation Tracey understood that the younger man had just returned from the hospital where he had been with the accident victim.

"Just popped aht for a pin'," the old man, Joe, was explaining to Bernard. "Need a bit of a calmin' dahn when the flat below you gets blown up. An' the bleedin' noise when them firemen was breakin' dahn the door to gerr'er aht. I reckon vat's what thems doin' nah, sortin' aht, makin' sife they calls it. Fought they was 'ere for a bomb or someink, but nah, it was only the telly, y'know, wot exploded, wot a racket! They're just checkin' t' make sure its sife."

Fussing to adjust her toggles, gloves and scarf, fiddling time to study the scene, Tracey was relieved to see the crashed

26

car had gone, was not there to confront her, to reinforce her guilt. When she moved smoothly off the step and walked away, neither man seemed to notice.

"'Ere, mate, oo was she then?" Joe was asking Bernard's opinion. "You lives there too doncha, ''swell as me? Oo was the fat bird in Lilly's flat then? An wot d'ya spoze happened to ole Lilly, buggrin' off like tha'?"

Bernard pulled his attention away from the fire tender.

"I've never seen her before, and the flat she came out of, well, we all thought there was only old Lilly in there, you know Lilly, don't you? Rose and she are friends I think. We all thought Lilly was living there alone, and drinking alone too, in The Eagle," Bernard stops, feeling he may have said too much.

"Right, Lilly's place! That's right. Reckon she was keeping that fat bird up there, prisoner or someink?" Joe sniggers.

"I think...... maybe it's her daughter, you know, a little bastard from the past, keeping her hidden, which would be quite easy with a disabled child. And now Lilly's disappeared. And do you know, I have a feeling she'll never be back. Don't quite know why. And, that "fat bird"'s up in hospital. You want to come and visit tomorrow?"

Joe didn't hear the last part. His lips moved with the astonishing thought, "Old Lilly, A daugh'er!..... keepin' 'er secret all that time...... Nah. Yer 'avin' me on, ain't ya?"

Chapter 5

The clipboard was still clattering gently where the nurse had hurriedly hooked it on to the bed rail just as Bernard was coming down the ward. He glanced at it. Still no name and beside the address, Flat 4, Warehouse Buildings, St Mary's Road, was a question mark. He looked at the slumped figure in the bed, a clearly defined hump beneath the white blanket. And sat down to wait.

Johnson, Jackson, Johnston, Johnstone. Lilly's name was something like that. Bernard tried to visualise it on an envelope, at the front door, but found he was no clearer. There was no evidence to support his theory that the nameless unidentified woman in the bed was Lilly's daughter. Just a hunch. Who else could she be? He could not imagine anyone keeping another human being's existence a secret unless they felt in some way responsible or to blame. Only a parent would, or an abuser….no, not Lilly. He could imagine his own mother disowning him, especially if he hadn't been "normal". She would've left him for the state to care for though. He wondered when Lilly would come back.

Bernard tried asking himself why he was there, sitting by a stranger's bedside. Mostly, it was that he was shocked not to have known about Lilly's living arrangements. He prided himself on knowing his neighbours' business. To have missed such a fundamental aspect of one of his fellow resident's lives, was unsettling, it threatened his security and sense of belonging to the Warehouse No1 community. It threatened his feeling of being in control of his life - always precarious, incidents like this made him feel it was slipping away. And also he felt a pang of guilt, in some way responsible for Lilly shoving off like that. If he'd left her in the pub a bit longer, she'd have been well-gone instead of only half-cut and might not have reacted so hastily. He felt responsible for having turned her world upside down, when she had always been kind to him. She had always been supportive of him, defended him against the vitriol and prejudice of the others in the building. He wanted to do the right thing by Lilly.

Pearl stirred, opened an eye. Bernard leant down towards her face. He was sure she could see him.

"What's you name?" he was not sure she could hear him. Her face registered no change. But when he moved away, her eyes followed him. Then she began to cry. Tears streamed across the bridge of her nose, down the creases of her face into the pillow. But her expression remained unchanged. Alarmed Bernard pressed the buzzer.

No-one came.

He bent to wipe away the tears with a tissue from the bedside locker. Pearl seemed to struggle.

"What's your name?" he couldn't think of any other way to ask. But he really needed to know and he wished with a colossal empathetic effort for her to be able to tell him her name. For her to be identified, with luck as being connected to Lilly.

"What's your name?" he began to hear a note of desperation in his own voice.

Then he saw her mouth move. Was she trying to say something? He wanted to help her sit up, but he dared not interrupt her in case he missed what she might be trying to say. He was gripped by the urgent need to hear it, to understand.

She opened her mouth and the lower jaw, blackened teeth jostling chaotically, went into a spasm, like a starving agitated cat watching a bird. Bernard wished it would stop. He was becoming alarmed. Was she having a fit? He pressed the buzzer again and again. He was willing the flapping jaw to stop as the woman's voice started to push through from her larynx. The noise was a stammering, she was trying to speak! A beseeching, piercing, desperate look in her eyes.

"Er…" the muscle in her jaw quivered involuntarily with the strain, "er….er….er." Eventually she had got the sound out and fell limp, exhausted by the effort. Bernard felt both elated that he had got a response and terrified that it had cost her so much.

Pearl drew in a breath and opened her mouth again. He had to get her sitting up, to try and free her jaw and make her breathing easier. He pressed the buzzer again and again, all the time keeping his eyes fixed on her face willing her silently on. Lying on her side as she was, the pillow was constricting her mouth, it was terrible to witness. This time her lower jaw wagged violently, her lips opening and shutting like a gasping fish. A slight "p", "p", "p", sound was aspirated. With a visible effort, she forced an out breath into a voiced sound:

"Per...Per....Per....Per" then fell back.

Like a light bulb pinging on, Bernard suddenly knew what she is saying.

"Pearl, Pearl, it's your name isn't it, Pearl?"......of wisdom he thought, delighted with himself, so clever, such a good detective. She didn't confirm it or even acknowledge it, except by slumping down and closing her eyes.

Bernard was so sure. So certain. So pleased with himself. He went to find the nurse to tell her his discovery, but the ancillary he met was not a native English-speaker. She was sympathetic, but uncomprehending. She wrote Pearl, as he spelt it out to her, on the clipboard. She thought he was a relative, she didn't question him, which made him not so sure.

He sat back beside the bed and his eyes swam as he considered the bandaged hands, the scratched skin of her face and the swollen blue cheek. The edge of a hospital gown was lost in the folds of her neck. Her thin, brown hair streaked the pillow, some strands dark with sweat ringed her ear and a tidemark of grime had been missed by the staff who had washed her.

"She was really good when we took out the glass. Just sat there, good as gold, never flinched. Just let us hold her hands still. It was like she couldn't feel it. There were hundreds of shards and that TV screen glass, you know from really old TVs, is so fine. I think she was in shock. The doctor thought she was one of those from Boreham House, you know, the home for learning difficulties."

At last a nurse had arrived - now that the patient had gone to sleep.

"She told me her name."

"Aren't you family then?" A long questioning look made him uncomfortable. He realised she was thinking he was some kind of pervert.

"She's got no family, I live in a flat in the same building. I never knew her name." It sounded weak.

"I was there when it happened I feel responsible, in a neighbourly way."

The nurse was still not convinced, she gave him another hard, penetrating look. Her name was Gaynor, or at least, she was wearing Gaynor's badge.

*   *   *   *   *

Clare was alone when Bernard returned to Warehouse No 1. She had been there three days now.

"Haven't you got a home to go to?"

"I told you, my dad's dead," as though that answered his question.

"So where do you live?"

"Will you teach me to draw?"

"Whooa no! you do not live here." Bernard correctly inferred from his unanswered question that she had nowhere else. He went into the bathroom. Sure enough on the windowsill, hidden behind the curtain, a large floral black toilet bag. Back in the living room, in the corner beside the speaker, yes, a neat pile of folded clothes balanced on a pair of downtrodden trainers.

"I'll get ma coat." She laughed weakly at the reference to a popular TV comedy catch phrase. The responsive smile that Bernard attempted was not convincing.

"Yeah, right, I gotta be going ," Clare jumped up. They both looked at the pile of clothes, she wondering how to get them into a bag without him watching her. That would be too pathetic. She didn't want to be thrown out, she liked him and she might really be stuck sometime. She wanted his approval, for him to like her. He saw the eyes fill with tears and turned away, cursing Oliver. Wait til he got his hands on him! He went into the kitchen to let her gather her stuff and leave with a bit of dignity.

"Bye," she called, the cheeriness not quite masking the catch in her voice.

He opened his mouth to respond, but could not trust himself not to call her back, to let her stay. After the door clicked gently to, Bernard's controlled exhalation released the tension. He slowly eased his knotted fists, opened his palms and looked down at the sharp imprint of his fingernails, four blue crescent moons, embedded there.

*   *   *   *   *

"Oh it's you again, wha'd'you want, nah?"

'Look, Joe, I was just being neighbourly, thought you might like to know about the explosion the other day."

"I know, I tol' you it was the telly!"

"Yeah, but you should see the mess the fire brigade made. Looks like a herd of elephants trampled through."

"You bin in there, then? How d'ya gerr'in?" Joe's interest is aroused.

"It was open this morning, housing association woman in there, snooping around. I don't reckon that's right, it's still Lilly's place."

"I don't think ol' Lil'll ever be back, d'ya know why? She never wanted us lot t'know bout that other one. She's too embrassed to show 'er face 'ere again. Anyway she always 'ated it 'ere always talked about getting back to 'er family, up Essex way I think. D'ya reckon that's 'er secret daughter, then, lying up the hospital? It's what I reckon."

"That was my guess, I told you that...." Bernard smiled at the old man.

"Huh?"

"Never mind. I went up the hospital again today. I think she was trying to talk to me. It's pathetic, it's really sad. I think she was trying to say her name. Sounded like "Pearl". What do you think? Ever hear Lil talk about her? You and Rose've been here the longest, and you were quite friendly."

"Don't know nothing, me. Ars' the wife if you wan'. She's indoors."

"Nah, never an inklin', crafty one that Lil, ain't she," Rose is always prepared to talk about the neighbours, "fancy,

32

'er havin' a daughter up there all that time an' us not realisin', would'ya b'lieve it?"

"What makes you think she is her daughter then?"

"Oh ye..e..e..ss, I knew she 'ad a daughter. I remember one time, she turn' round an' says to me about that she was really upset thinkin' bout someone's birthday. Well I gorrit out of 'er eventually, about the daughter. I turn' round an' I says "Wheeee" I says, " I never thought you 'ad no daughter," I knew already her ol' man'd died, see. She was Deaf and dumb, mongrol or some'ink, couldn't do nothing for 'erself. But see I always thought she was dead, or in a home like, miles away. See Lil's not from round 'ere, from up Essex way, so I natrally thought the daughter was up there or died up there. Never thought .... not for a moment. We could've 'elped aht, see, if we'd've knowed. Must've been dreadful for 'er."

"Do you want to come up to visit her with me?"

"Me, nah, I'm no good with 'em ones. 'Ain't got no patience, me. They make me go all funny...nah, not me, ma lover..... I could fancy goin' dahn for a drink now, mind. Tain't Thursday, is it? So the Museum'll be quiet tonight." Rose felt she was in a strong position for getting Bernard, the perv, to buy her a drink, having given him all this information.

"Fancy a pint, Joe?" Bernard was curious to hear if there would be any more information from Rose about Lilly, but he could not face an evening with Rose alone. If Joe were to come he'd be able to get away when he wanted.

*   *   *   *   *

"What've I done to offend you?" Tracey tried to make light of it. She was used to being the wallflower. She tried not to sound hurt. She was completely unprepared for his response.

"Run across a road, behind an ambulance, no less, and made some poor woman drive into a lamppost..... and then fucked off without so much as a bye your leave. Sound familiar?"

33

Tracey was stunned. It was true. Denial died on her opened mouth. Isabelle looked questioningly at her.

"I'll tell you later." Tracey offered limply.

Barely able to disguise the thrill of his self-righteousness, his pleasure at trumping the stupid cow, Bernard continued in an audibly steadied voice.

"Your friend here wanted to know what happened to the woman in the explosion, but I don't think his English was up to the explanation." He looked round for a volunteer to translate.

"I'm Isabelle. I'll translate."

Bernard softened, turned towards her and described in detail the state that "Pearl" was in and what he knew of her circumstances. He asked himself again through his admiring audience why he felt so responsible for her well-being, why he wanted to get through to her, why he cared what happened to her.

"She's got nobody. Nobody visits her."

"What ward is she in, I'll go and visit her." Tracey spoke. Bernard knew she was feeling guilty about the other incident, about him telling it to her straight. She was trying to make up for being such a shit on Thursday night. Trying to get in his good books. He despised her.

"What help do you think you could be?"

"Probably none, as you know I'm a pathetic person, normally given to running away from the consequences of my actions, so probably I'd be no help at all."

My god, Bernard couldn't believe this, really laying it on with a trowel. Christ she was sad. He must not let himself get worked up about her.

"I think....mm.... really good idea go hospital, Tracey." Marc had clearly not picked up on any of the nuances, of the retelling of Tracey's actions that Thursday night, of Bernard's accusation, of Tracey's need for reparation. Isabelle looked from Bernard to Tracey. Did they already know each other? Something was going on. She tried to talk to Marc. But he was carried away by Tracey's kindness wanting to visit a disabled stranger in hospital.

Bernard sank into resignation in the face of Marc's non-comprehension.

But he could not have been more wrong. Marc understood perfectly. When he had followed Tracey, brought her keep-fit bag into the pub that Thursday night, he had asked why she ran away from the car crash she had caused. Sharpened by his own history of battling against the education system, the authorities in Paris, his own parentless childhood, he had clearly picked up Tracey's fear of the authorities, the Police, any public scenes.

"She's in E 5, ward E5. Very nice to meet you, Isabelle,....?" He looked questioningly at Marc.

"Eh, my name is Marc. How d'you do?" He said in careful English.

Bernard did not look at Tracey, but got up to leave.

"When will you go?" he looked at the wall, resolving to avoid any possibility of encountering her at the hospital when he himself visited.

"Wednesday afternoon." She said quickly, it was the university sports afternoon, no lectures. She knew he never wanted to meet her there. As he was leaving, she fervently hoped she would never see him again. Stuck-up arrogant bastard. What did he know about anything? She hadn't needed to offer to go and visit the woman. She really wanted to. Simple curiosity, no sanctimonious compassion clap-trap. OK and a measure of wanting to improve her image in Isabelle's eyes. She had a feeling Marc understood.

"I'll warn the staff..... Wednesday afternoon, right?" it sounded like a threat. He certainly wouldn't be there.

*   *   *   *   *

As she stepped out of the lift in the tower block hall of residence, as she approached the anonymity of her room, as the Tracey who presented to the world, the self-confident mature student receded, her mind raced ahead to Wednesday. It was to be the most important day of her adult life, a day she had been anticipating and dreading for 16 years. But when the letter had actually arrived, she could hardly believe it. She had made the arrangement through a third party. She only had to get to Salisbury by ten in the morning of Wednesday. The thought of it was made physical, a weight descending from her brain to form a lumpy porridge in her guts, revolving and emptying like a concrete mixer. She rushed along the corridor clutching at the rough brick wall to get to the toilet. Then she remembered her promise. Wednesday, visiting the strange woman in hospital.

There was no way she'd be going to the hospital on Wednesday.

Chapter 6

It was lashing rain. Heavy, dense rain so forceful that it seemed to rise up from the pavement as well as soak from above. Tracey shook water from the front of her coat and viewed her drenched boots with disgust. Definitely letting in water.

"Lecture's cancelled," called a woman she barely recognised.....from her course? No discussion was possible as a huddle of students arrived in a flap of spraying umbrellas, stomping feet, groaning and throat-clearing, rain gusting through the open swing doors. When they were shut again, throats were caught anew in the miasma of damp wool, and the messenger had gone.

Tracey decided to check for herself. Out side the lecture theatre a disconsolate crowd milled, each unbelieving individual trying to see for themselves the contents of the notice on the door. Being so short there was no hope for Tracey.

"Can someone read out what it says," she shouted. Her lack of stature was more than made up for by her penetrating voice. An obedient hush fell and someone started to read.

"Louder please."

"Ahem "PHYSIOLOGY Apologies to all Physiology students for the 10.00 lecture Tuesday 10 November. Dr Weasel (tittering from the crowd – he really was weasel featured) sorry Teasel, is away at a conference all day. Photocopies of the notes will be given out next week. Sorry for the inconvenience." Christ you sometimes wonder why they bother with lectures....why don't they just hand out the notes at the beginning of the course?"

"'Cos we wouldn't read them?"

"He's a crap lecturer anyway......"

"How can he not have known last week about a conference, even this university doesn't organise things at that short notice...?"

A buzz of disgust hung in the air slowly becoming a pall of indecision and aimlessness. It was too early for the pub or lunch, too late to go back to bed.

Tracey wandered back towards the entrance. Though she was trying to fight it, her mind was full of Salisbury - a place she had never been, could only imagine - and the following day's meeting. To stop herself thinking about it, ward off the rising panic, she had planned to have every moment of today filled, starting with the 2-hour lecture, followed by lunch in the pub where she was sure to see friend Jane. Shopping for something to bring tomorrow and spending the evening with Miguel from next door. All planned. Now all wrecked. And the rain. It did not bode well. In fact it was a really bad omen. Tomorrow would be a disaster.

Out on the street Tracey stood, frozen like a rabbit in headlights. She had thought being outside would clear her head. The opposite was true. She could decide nothing. Go nowhere. Refusing to think "Salisbury", meant think nothing.

A bus drew up. Its destination was a little village out of the city, up over the hill. Any escape route would do. Tracey started to run across the road towards the bus and found herself pausing to look both ways for traffic. The thought that the prat Bernard would be pleased, to see her crossing safely, looking both ways, gave her enough distance from her situation to smile at herself, to re-engage with the present.

The hospital! This bus went past the hospital. Tracey didn't believe in karma, but if there was such a thing, this was it. In her anxiety about Wednesday's meeting – no don't think about it! – she had done nothing about her promise to visit the patient, Pearl.

"Queen Mary's, please." She showed her student pass. The bus driver looked sceptical, they often didn't believe thirty year olds could be students.

It was perfect. Bernard had threatened to warn them of her arrival on Wednesday. She'd pre-empt them. That would be one up to her. It would be a distraction of a few hours in this difficult day. And Bernard wouldn't be there at this time in the morning. He probably didn't plan to go until after Wednesday to find out what impression she had made, to make sure his bad opinion of her was justified. The possibility that visiting might not be allowed so early flashed through her brain. But what the hell. Karma.

*   *   *   *   *

The double flaps of flexible perspex across the end of the corridor were apparently designed for patient trolleys to be pushed through by one porter. Tracey had stood back and waited for one. They weren't designed for small people to push their way through easily. They closed on Tracey's shoulders, she had to struggle free. But they were effective in keeping the stench of hospital fluids back. As she emerged into the corridor, the smell hit her, and with it all the real and imagined horrors of hospitals leapt into her thoughts.

The reality of what might greet her at Pearl's bedside began to occur to Tracey. But she was here now, there was no going back.

E 5, where was it?

.......Xray department..... Chapel...?... Children's wards..... General wards..... Wards F1 – 5..... Tracey's footsteps were squeaky on the polished floor. She met almost no-one. The straight corridor seemed to stretch ahead endlessly. Maternity..... Oncology department....... Cafeteria...... Local artwork splodged the walls in a seemingly infinite range of greys and blacks. Designed to lift the spirits. At last one bright-coloured tapestry labelled "Designed and sewn by local community groups". Tracey swerved over for a closer look at the silver, reds and greens and warm peach colour only to recoil at the image of a green-gowned surgeon up to his elbows in bleeding entrails on an operating table, silver instruments neatly lined up alongside..... WRVS...... Wards E 6 – 8..... E? where's 5?..... No-one to ask. Then in a recess, a sign: E 5.

The double swing doors clunked behind her. Tracey looked round for a uniform. She would have to ask someone. The only information she had was the first name, Pearl. There seemed to be no staff. She stood irresolute, intensely uncomfortable, between two lines of beds. Hospital visiting, not a listed activity on her CV, was unlikely to become one.

A cough began in the second bed. It intensified, went up a register. The bed shook. Tracey felt herself start to panic. The cough went on and on, tearing through her, then, after a searing retching sound it abruptly stopped. The mound in the bed stopped moving. Stopped breathing? Where the bloodyhell was everyone?

Other noises emanated from different beds. Grunts, rasping breathing and muttering. Tracey became aware of a tiny motionless white face staring at her from a froth of white curls barely denting the pillow of a bed on the right.

"Where is everyone?" Tracey looked towards her then realised, too late, that her question implied she did not include these patients among the human family 'everyone'.

"Where are the staff?" There was no response. She went nearer, in case the old lady was deaf. Her cheeks were wet with tears. She was silently weeping. Tracey almost cried too.

"Don't cry," she said softly, pointlessly.

Then she saw Pearl. The only dark head on a pillow. It must be her. All the others were grey, white or papery yellow skin.

On the bed the clip board said "Pearl Johnston" and the address at the Warehouse.

"Can I help you?"

Every cell of Tracey's body was jolted in shock at the sudden voice behind her. She lurched upright from looking at the clipboard.

"I'm looking for Pearl."

"Well you've found her. Are you a relative?" The nurse sounded hopeful.

"No..." Tracey began to explain how she came to be there. When she finished, the nurse, either satisfied or unconcerned, turned with a non-committal "huh" to walk down the ward. She had obviously heard nothing untoward from Bernard about this strange woman coming to visit on Wednesday!

Dissected by her wide black nurse's belt, the hefty blue-checked lower half of the woman seemed to sway and roll independently of the gliding, neat blue-checked top half, as she moved from bed to bed, listening to a patient's complaint or looking at a chart.

Pearl was lying on her back and had opened her eyes. Heard them talking probably. She looked at Tracey and opened her mouth as if to speak. Her jaw wobbled, but no sound came out.

"Hello, I've come to visit you. I was at the keep-fit class when your telly exploded."

Pearl must have understood, she smiled, though not looking right at Tracey now.

"I was there when the ambulance came."

Tracey became aware of a presence behind her. Pearl was smiling harder now, over Tracey's shoulder. Her eyes were alight. Tracey jerked her head round.

She could not believe it! Bernard had crept up behind her - in his brothel-creepers.

What was he doing there at this time in the morning? He offered no explanation for his presence. Tracey refused to let herself ask.

*　　*　　*　　*　　*

For an hour Tracey felt she and Bernard were vying for Pearl's attention. There was no contest. Pearl was clearly unable to resist his masculine charms, smiling and smiling, trying to talk. That she stopped actively cutting Tracey out of her line of attention after the first few minutes was probably attributable to her awareness of Bernard's extreme dislike of Tracey, and Tracey's plainness.

Tracey, however, was not bored. It amazed and humbled her to witness Pearl's attempts at speech, at her efforts to control her limbs. She was curious about what was going on in Pearl's head, wryly thinking how much more instructive this experience was than the Physiology lecture that had been cancelled could ever have been.

"Would you like your hair washed?" Tracey asked to fill an awkward gap when no one was able to think of anything to say. She was trying to think of establishing routines. Knowing

41

how being unwell is compounded by the feeling of greasy hair, hair washing seemed a routine and manageable task. But panic suffused Pearl's face. If Tracey was unsure that Pearl understood half of what they said, she had certainly understood that.

"You'd look really sexy with lovely clean hair and a bit of make-up," Bernard cajoled. Tracey couldn't believe he was uttering what sounded almost like a come-on. Nor could she believe that he had agreed with one of her proposals, especially when Pearl had been so alarmed by the idea. There must be an ulterior motive. Here it came.

"Tracey would do it for you. You'd just have to sit in the bath. They have these cap things that go round your head so the water doesn't go in your eyes. She'd be able to wash it for you, wouldn't you Tracey?" The look he shot her was malicious. He would of course have calculated that the idea of viewing Pearl's naked body would completely repulse her. He was deliberately trying to discompose her, upset her, prove that she was worthless.

What could she do?

"Yes, I've done it lots of times with my auntie when she was living at home with us," she lied.

"Would you like to have your hair washed?" Poor Pearl must have been smitten. Another remark from Bernard about how lovely she would look was enough. She agreed.

Tracey never really thought that the staff would actually let a stranger bath a defenceless patient. But when she asked, there was a sort of unspoken pretence that she was a relative. It relieved them of some of the pressure. They simply had too many patients and a lot of the "caring" was apparently done by family. Everyone preferred it all round, according to Bernard. So knowledgeable about caring for people!

"Come on then, how will we get you down to the bathroom?" Tracey was determined no to let her unease show. Pearl didn't respond. She did not seem able to sit up without being propped. She was going to be a dead weight. Tracey suspected Bernard was building in failure for her from the start.

42

Sure enough.

"I've done a lifting course." Bernard took charge. "You'll have to help but we should be able to get her into a wheelchair. I'll go for one. See if she has any towels in her locker, shampoo and that sort of thing." Bernard in control. Expert. Done a lifting course! Shame he didn't know to address Pearl direcly – instead of talking to Tracey about her as though she wasn't actually there!

There was nothing in Pearl's locker except a bin bag of stuff, which Tracey decided not to open after the first whiff. Probably the clothes she came in wearing, still in a mess? Ugh. When she asked the nurse for shampoo, the initial reaction was near outrage.

"Patients are responsible for their own toiletries."

"But she hasn't any, even at home. Pearl has lived like this for years with no-one much to help her with these things, haven't you Pearl?..." a bit of exaggeration – which she realised reflected badly on "family."

She went on, " and I have time to help her now, you nurses are so rushed of your feet, you can't have time...and the other patients will start to complain if we don't get her smartened up."

They both looked round the ward. The idea that any of these patients would be animated enough to complain seemed ludicrous.

"Pearl will feel so much better when she's got her hair washed. It will surely help her recover."

The nurse succumbed and gave her shampoo from her own personal locker, towels from the store and some fragrant soap left by a former patient. She even supplied an unscheduled clean hospital gown.

"Shame she can't have a proper nightie."

"Or some ordinary clothes." Tracey was being radical now.

Reluctantly, Bernard had to congratulate Tracey. She thought to put on the wheelchair brake, wedge the chair between the bed and her foot, and angle it so that Pearl's bum could be swung round using her legs, feet on the floor, as a pivot. With Pearl's arm round her neck, Bernard only had to help hoist from the safety of the bed. Pearl was disappointed at being deprived of this opportunity of physical contact with Bernard.

"That was very slickly done, almost single-handed." Patronising, bastard. Tracey was strong solid muscle for the most part.

"What about the cap thing to keep the water out of her eyes." There was one hanging on a hook in the bathroom, a plastic ring elasticated which fitted snugly on Pearl's head.

"See you later." Tracey enjoyed dismissing Bernard at the bathroom door. She made a mental note of where the alarm button was and while the water thundered into the bath, began the distressing business of undressing Pearl.

At her call, by pre-arrangement, the nurse came in to help hoist Pearl into the bath. She was lowered into a sort of sling/cage/chair. Tracey was not sorry that parts of her would be impossible to reach. But such was Pearl's physical improvement over the last few days that she managed to keep her own head and shoulders still enough for shampooing. She cried piteously and Tracey wanted to stop, but there was no going back now, her head was covered in froth. Pearl's flailing limbs seemed more controlled, as though fear made her more rigid. When Tracey reached for the shower attachment, Pearl squealed. Tracey scanned the room for an alternative. A plastic measuring jug had been left on the window sill by thoughtful person, and some talc they could use later. Weighing up the chances of Pearl slipping and drowning against the need to rinse off the shampoo. Tracey said

"Keep still, I'm just reaching for the jug to rinse your hair." There was no way of knowing whether Pearl really understood.

Rinsing went without mishap and Tracey was so keen to get the whole episode over that she soaped the loose skin like an automaton, unthinking, uncritical, merely observing the areas of smooth babyish stomach skin, the pitted pores of Pearl's back and how little body hair there was.

By the time she rang for assistance with the hoist, Tracey was exhausted. She looked at Pearl in the chair, at her clean smiling face. The nurse was delighted, she brought out a comb. They powdered her and combed out her hair. Tracey found when she scrunched it up in her hand, the hair held the wave.

"You have beautiful skin and your hair's got red-highlights. It's a lovely, lovely colour."

It dried a rich dark auburn. It was glorious when the light shone on it. Pearl smiled harder. She voiced an indistinct reply. Surely she had understood what Tracey had said. Slowly it dawned on Tracey that pearl seemed to respond only when someone had eye contact with her. Was she deaf? Maybe she only recognised that someone was trying to communicate with her when she could see the movement of the mouth.

Pearl had beautiful facial skin and her features when at rest were very even. When she tried to talk, the muscular effort temporarily distorted her whole face. But as she willed Pearl to get the words out, Tracey found herself concentrating so hard on the message, that what Pearl looked like ceased to matter. Tracey simply stopped noticing.

"Ha...a...a.....ng.   Oooo.." Tracey knew this was thank you. She touched Pearl's hand.

"You look really good. Let's find a mirror."

"T t t t t t t."

"I'll take you to the toilet Pearl and you should be able to see in the mirror there." The nurse wheeled Pearl off.

Tracey was left sitting on the edge of the bath, contemplating the previously unimaginable. It was mind-numbing to consider. How could people with disabilities like Pearl's ever manage alone? If they couldn't, what privacy could they ever achieve?

Bernard found her still sitting on the bath.

"Well?"

"I'm stunned at how exhausting it is. How much work there is in simple things like moving about, going to the toilet, getting people to understand what you want. The frustration would drive you mad if the constant having everything done to you all the time didn't. What must it be like to be Pearl?"

"Indeed - she's got no-one, until or unless her mother comes back." He was looking at her. Thinking. Waiting for her to say something? Surely, she tried to read his expression, he didn't think that she should be volunteering to care for Pearl! Tracey returned his gaze carefully masking all emotion. Then deflected the subject.

"Tell me about her mother then. You knew her. I don't know any of her herstory."

"OK over a drink?" Christ what was his game?

"Better wait and say goodbye to Pearl." Tracey couldn't go off without farewell.

"Do you think she'll notice if we don't?"

Tracey was sure she would notice if Bernard didn't say goodbye, and she would be desperately upset at Bernard not seeing her clean and fragrant. After all he'd told her how nice she would look with clean shiny hair, she had only done it for him.

"We'll wait."

Pearl was thrilled to show off her shiny wavy hair to Bernard and was flirting very obviously with him. The rigours of the bath had left her shattered too. She was almost asleep when they left.

*   *   *   *   *

It was 1 o'clock. Tracey had spent two and a half hours in the most intimate circumstances with a stranger. And it might have been only two and a half minutes. But now, seeing the time pumping away, second by heavy second round the huge clock in reception Tracey was snapped violently back into this, her longest day. The day before the long-awaited meeting.

Bernard was talking about Lilly and Pearl.

"You're not listening." He accused.

"Sorry, I am interested, but now we're out of there I've remembered the really important thing on my mind. The reason I came today, not tomorrow."

"Yeah, you said you were coming Wednesday. That's why I came today, to warn them," he laughed, "I didn't like you. Thought you were a selfish prat running out into the road like a naughty kid like that. But you're alright really.

Pearl likes you. Wonder if that is her name." God would he never shut up?

"Actually, I've got to go."

"I thought you were coming for a drink…."

Certainly Tracey had nothing specifically arranged until meeting Miguel at 6. Round the corner from the hospital was a free house. They usually had a good selection of real ale in "The Barrels". She really needed a beer. Being with Pearl had given Tracey so much to think about - from the nature of simple everyday survival activities to the complexities of the human brain.

It had been both exhilarating and emotionally draining. But Tracey wasn't sure if she could sit and talk about her now. She needed time to assimilate the bombardment on her brain that Pearl had caused. But right now she had other concerns. She was also a little uncomfortable at Bernard's about face. He had been so rude and unpleasant to her, now this sudden change.

"Come on just a half, it's knackering being a carer, eh?" He was clearly pleased with her performance, la de dah.

There was a fire in the grate at one end of the pub. Unusually for a city pub, the fireplace was huge, occupying the space of a large kitchen range now removed and a pile of logs waited drunkenly for their turn to be sacrificed. The smell was intoxicating. Like the beer which both Tracey and Bernard swilled back, the half stretching into several pints. They sank into a mesmeric state of well-being. Then Bernard flicked a switch,

"What's the really important thing you're doing tomorrow then? So that you had to come up the hospital today?"

And Tracey fell silent, thinking back, not wanting to at first. Memories were losened by alcohol, lost inhibitions dislodged her tongue. The mounting tension leading up to the following day had temporarily disipated in the warm safe atmosphere of the pub and the sincere face urging her to talk. She reached into her pocket and pulled something out. A crumpled letter. She passed it over. It was very short:

56 Cousins Place
Salisbury

A Sunday

Dear

I'm not sure what to call you. I've waited a long time to get the courage to write this letter.

I hope you know who I am. I've passed 8 GCSEs, 2 Bs, 4 As and 2 A*s. My A level subjects are not quite sorted out yet because I want to do Art as well as sciences. I've decided I want to find out about you before I get stuck into A levels. My parents agreed, otherwise I'd have to wait until I'm 18. They have told me a bit about you. For example I have black hair and I'm short like you. Maybe yours is grey now. I'm glad you always said you would be available to meet me one day and I know you always made sure I would be able to find you.

I have a million questions to ask. At least I think I have, I'm not sure whether I want them answered or not. I hope you get this letter soon. Now I've written it, I hope you write back to me soon.

From
Darron White

"My son," Tracey said to Bernard. "I'm meeting him tomorrow for the second time in our lives."

And Tracey found herself starting to talk.

"You don't want to here all this…."

"Nah, but I'm not ready to go home yet. It's warm in here, cold out there and I could do with a bit of entertainment. So how come you've only met your own son twice?"

"I suppose it really started 16 or 17 years ago. Or did it start with the trip to Ireland? Except I wouldn't have been that stroppy independent little cow if it hadn't been for Jonathan up-his-own-bleeding-arse Spires…."

"Graphic, thank you." Bernard sniggered.

48

"You want to hear this story? Don't interrupt!"

"So-rry! So who was he? What did Spires aspire to, that so upset you?"

"Well it wasn't him, really, though he was one real prat..........

Chapter 7

The story had no beginning, but now that she chose to look at it, so many years on, one ice clear moment thrust itself forward.

They were waiting at the traffic lights. A car drew up beside them on the inside lane. Without moving her body, the girl let her eyes wander towards it. It was red. Bright red. The right shade of bright red. A tiny seed of hope popped open inside her chest. Without showing with her body that she was interested, she strained her eyes round inside their sockets to peer into the back seat of the red saloon. There was a child inside, the right size and age, the right sort of hair. But he was looking the other way, pulling against his seat belt. The girl turned now and stared into the back of his head, willing him to look round. It was a power he could not resist. His face swivelled into view. Disappointment contracted into a knot gripping the girl's throat. It was not her brother. The furious glare she subjected the five-year-old stranger to made his face crumple into tearful misery.

She was glad. She was jubilant that she had the power to make the boy cry. He deserved to suffer. He was not her brother.

The woman in the driver's seat glanced round at the boy, concerned, as the red car, the wrong red car, followed it's filter light off to the left.

It had happened so often over the past few years. Tracey would suddenly glimpse a child who reminded her of her brother Paul. Thinking it might be Paul, was an automatic response. At a conscious level, she had tried to make herself stop looking out for him. Tried to make herself believe he was living on the other side of the world. Tried to stop thinking of him at all. Even after all this time, and after hours of rationalising to herself that it would be impossible to just bump into him by coincidence, she could not control this response. She knew that he would not look like the five-year-old she remembered. He would be nine now and quite different.

Jonathan Spires stopped watching Tracey as the traffic lights changed and he let the car move forward, all his concentration on driving through the crowded street ahead.

Feeling the scrutiny lifted from her, Tracey relaxed very slightly. But she kept her body rigid with dislike, her face was blank and closed. Her teeth clamped, her jaw tense. When he spoke, she neither looked towards him nor replied.

"Look, Tracey, I know how you feel, you're angry with me for coming to get you. But it is my job, you are my responsibility.......(then, lightening his voice) in loco parentis, do you remember asking me what that meant when I first met you." Hoping this shared memory would soften the fact of his role as social worker. "I know how much you wanted to escape. I know it doesn't look like it to you at the moment, but I'm on your side, I really am here to help you. We'll get something sorted out."

When he said that, that he wanted to help her, she felt nausea revolve in her stomach and a contemptuous laugh started up her throat only to stick there unexpressed. It was a hard bitter lump. She couldn't swallow. He was paid to "care". Did he think she was too stupid to realise that? "Caring" was his job. He hadn't chosen to care for her, she'd just been the next name on his list. How could she believe in his "caring" if it wasn't freely given, if he hadn't chosen her. There was nothing about her that would make him care any differently for her than all the others on his caseload. His "caring" took away from Tracey any residual sense of her own individuality and specialness. His presence made her feel more like an unwanted nobody than any one else's could have.

Tracey longed for the journey to be over. Usually travelling would make her feel secure. In transit nothing could be expected of you except that you wait quietly until you arrived. And with time on your hands and that magic sense of motion Tracey would indulge in the most exotic of her many fantasies. But today, because she had been obliged to sit in the front of the car with Jon, she could not escape his constant surveillance, pleasantness, anxiety to please. His concern interfered with her ability to dream. And Tracey was finding it increasingly difficult to get off into her dream world these days. As she got older, hard reality impinged on her awareness more and more insistently. She was being forced into self-awareness and the ability to escape into her dream world was becoming more and more illusive.

The car smelled new, but Jon didn't look after it. There was evidence of anxious children in transit; gobs of chewing gum, a piece of upholstery picked by nervous fingers, foot prints and scuff marks, chocolate and crisp wrappers and a faint smell of vomit. There were signs of Jon's stress too, though Tracey observed them with elemental disgust; a snowy film of dandruff from the scurfy psoriasis on his hands covered the gear shift. He should have had an automatic.

Then Jon did a strange thing. He got out a cigarette packet and asked Tracey to get a cigarette out for him.

"Do you want one?" he asked. If it was a trick, trying to catch her out, she didn't care. She took one. He said nothing more.

For the past year he had been castigating her for smoking. He had been constantly bailing her out of trouble at her many children's homes for smoking. She allowed herself a smile of triumph. But she didn't enjoy the cigarette, carefully stubbing it out half way through to save for later.

Feeling suddenly brave and reckless, Tracey decided that at the next red traffic lights she would jump out of the car and run. She carefully and unobtrusively gathered her shoulder bag together in a tight grip in her right hand, having first felt through it for the purse with the £53. Then she fumbled her left hand until it connected with the door handle. She glanced casually round as though sight-seeing, to ensure that the lock on the passenger door was up. The wry thought hit her that it would have been much easier to escape form the back seat of the car.......oh, no, she then remembered, there were child-locks on the rear doors, precisely to prevent such an escape. From the back it would have been impossible. It became vital that she take the opportunity that fate had so kindly laid before her. In the crowded London streets, Jon would never be able to find her. He would not be able to stop the car to pursue her because of the volume of traffic. As if to reinforce her resolve, the sun slewed out from behind the overcast city sky and beckoned her on. And a gift from god came as they stopped at a red light beside a piece of pavement unobstructed by parked cars, kept free by double yellow lines. She would be able to run straight onto the pavement from here. But she would have to time it right so that Jon would not stop be able to stop the car there and follow her.

The flowing traffic opposite slowed, indicating a change to green was imminent on their side. Jon engaged first gear. In one swift movement, Tracey opened the car door, jumped out and slammed it behind her

She ran back the way they had come, dodging between the shoppers. Not for an instant did she look back.

Tracey ran, eyes front, steadfast in her decision never to look back again. She was so short, she was quickly lost in the crowd. Her round thighs pumped hard in the tight legs of her jeans, she clutched her bag to her chest to anchor her breasts, too large for a 15 year old, an uncomfortable curse, a cause of constant teasing for any child who lived in a children's home. Because she was well-covered in flesh – puppyfat they all called it – Tracey knew better, she could remember her mother - the exertion soon left her breathless. She slowed her pace, walking fast now. Panting hard. Consciously composing herself, the redness in her round face and the anxiety in her blue eyes subsided. She forced her breathing down and wiped the trickle of sweat that was running into her eye, dislodging the piece of her short spiky dark hair that was designed to cover her cow's lick.

As she walked, Tracey felt she was leaving everything behind - the world of social workers, children's homes and her whole disjointed life. With a spark she recalled that the following day August 2nd would be her fifteenth birthday. She would spend it back in Portsmouth with her friends and then go off for good. That was the last place they would think of looking for her, she rationalised to herself.

But the real truth was she had nowhere else to go.

Knowing Portsmouth was west, she judged from the afternoon sun, now shining warmly, which way to go. Elated by the freedom, the sense of adventure and her own fearlessness, she followed the London pavements in roughly that direction.

*   *   *   *   *

"Tim.......TIM!......." a hoarse urgent whisper, loud enough for him to hear if he was there, not so loud that the rest of the hostel would hear. Tracey was perched on the concrete path on tiptoe directing her voice upwards towards the open window. Everything in the building on this side was dark. The full moon re-landscaped the garden, monochrome grotesque - luckily for Tracey, it had made it negotiable without accident or noise.

Tracey had run away from here, The Lodge, Clarendon Avenue, only the previous morning, gladly leaving the Victorian chaos of passages, mezzanines, servants' rooms and the shared dormitories with no privacy; happily escaping the neurotic repetitive behaviour of fearful children, the dead existence of children with nothing to live for, the terrible silence of a few clashing with the noisy, manic cheerfulness of others. Few were what she would regard as normal. She had run to Leytonstone, to Gary's. Gary had left The Lodge, two weeks before, his mum had taken him back when she got married again and moved into a proper house. In Leytonstone. He had given them all his new address, saying proprietorially,

"Come and visit any time." He was so proud and happy to be going back to his mum, so thrilled that she wanted him.

When Tracey had arrived there mid-morning, all pleased with herself for negotiating the journey alone, Gary's mum, while seeming to make her welcome, had snuck off and got straight on the phone to the children's home back in Pompey. It had taken Jon Spires, Tracey's social worker, just four hours to come and collect her. And it had taken Tracey half an hour to give him the slip in London. Since then it had taken her eight hours to walk and hitch back. Back to Portsmouth. Now she was outside her old "home" again.

Tim would let her in to sleep in the alcove no-one ever looked in and the next night she and Tim would gather a gang of them down on the beach with crisps and white cider and maybe samosas from the Indian, where it was easy to nick, and they would celebrate her birthday. And it was going to be brilliant. They'd smoke themselves hoarse and maybe go skinny dipping, if the moonlight was stretched out along the surface of the sea making that magic silver path it made, she often swam along that path and imagined swimming away forever into the deep black nothing of the night.

Tim was there. And the following night, they did have a brilliant time on the beach. They watched the dark horizon slip and the red ellipse of the moon emerge, still full. It inched free, floating up onto the black sea, and bled a rippling trail to their toes beckoning them. Tracey had never swum the red path of the moon before. It was magical, almost mystical as she strode into the water, careless of the sharp gravel under her bare feet. Always fearless, the cider freed a recklessness that pushed her further and further from the shore. Exotic beasts reared up, dripping red in the moonlight as the horizon pulled her on. The faint lapping of the waves onto the distant beach receded until that became the imagined world. The only reality was here. Her body was transformed now, light and graceful, strong and buoyant in the seawater. She rolled over to float on her back, a mirroring star. Above in the hollow night sky a million stars struggled for her attention, first one brighter, then another, they had surely never been seen by anyone before. She began to give them names: ....Mellicent.... Spartick...... Polonium...... Fentinulous...... Branticle....

Then a faint sound blew over to her,

"....Trace.....where....are....you....
Traceeeee.....Trace......."

The dream was broken. Tracey righted herself and looked, a dim figure on the shore was running back and forth. It was a long way away. She began to swim leisurely back.

Tim was frantic. The others had gone home, bored waiting. He thought she had drowned.

She wrapped herself in her towel, shivering now in the night air. Then they snuggled together in the blanket they'd brought, to wait for the sun to come up, watching for the

55

dawn. Competing to see who would spot the emerging horizon first, spot the very moment when the lightening sky began its separation from the sea. They sat for a long time. There was nothing to say. Then Tracey began:

"Look at that, lazy waves surge and fall......sounds like the applause of a distant audience.......for the magnificent display of a silver dawn."

"Ah yes I can hear the shingle, politely clapping." Tim added. "That's sheer poemtry," he said in a Pam Ayres west country accent, "and we're just two tiny pebbles on the beach," he laughed.

That was when he told her.

"I've joined the army."

Her briefly wonderful world fell apart. Tim had been the most constant element in it for four years. He knew all her secrets. He was the nearest thing she had to family.

"They'll send you away."

"That's what I want."

"Fighting the IRA in Northern Ireland?"

An aching quiet gripped them both. For Tim there was no other way to express the sweet sense of relief, the irresistible happiness with which he would escape a miserable childhood. The army would be different. He would not be overlooked like he had been as a child, no one could bully and hurt him, he had strategies in mind for dealing with the hard men he knew would be there. He expected that the rigid structured life would probably suit him. There was security to be found in the safety of routine, a substitute for a family.

Nothing could have adequately expressed Tracey's complex reaction to Tim's announcement. The betrayal she felt - that he had made such a momentous decision without discussing it with her! What an idiot she had been to think that he felt anything for her! So now she knew exactly how unimportant she was to him, while she saw him as a brother to her.

Tracey felt herself shrivel. All those rejections she had shared with him and the lies she had let him tell to keep himself buoyed up, trying to convince himself that he was someone, had a place in the world, belonged to and was loved by his mother. Had he forgotten? Well bully for him. But she hadn't.

She remembered when he first came to Clarendon Avenue. He had been such a runt. Much smaller than she, with a pinched, tight-lipped face like an old man and blond hair that never lay flat and was the cause of continual teasing. Between bath nights his hair would became gradually more and more stiff with his soap and water attempts to control it. His black-rimmed glasses always needed mending and by the end of the year when the optician's appointment was due, there would be more sellotape, inexpertly applied by himself, than frame. And he had a small-framed bony body drawn permanently in at the shoulder blades, ready, either to turn away from abuse if possible, or take it like a man if it was unavoidable.

Tracey could never forget that fat slag of a mother of his arriving with a trail of toddlers and a baby in a pram. Tim was so excited. His mother had come for him. At last, she was going to take him home with her. Seeing her come up the road, he whirled into a frenzy of chaotic packing.

Intellectually Tracey believed that Tim could see that this woman who was his mother was nothing but sluttish, filthy and foul-mouthed. But in her absence he sometimes chose not to believe what he must have known to be true, creating instead a false image of her as youthfully beautiful, well-dressed and softly spoken. At other times he made up elaborate excuses for her. Describing in convincing detail how the boiler had broken and she'd been unable to have a bath. How that new shampoo, and he would name a brand from a TV advertisement, had given her an allergic reaction, so she couldn't wash her hair. How she'd given all her good clothes to a sister-in-law going to the states on holiday. But mostly he described how well she looked after all his little brothers, giving them the best food. She was such a good cook. All this lying he could do without blanching, even down to her downtrodden heels, she was saving her good ones for Sundays. Sundays! For going to church!

But that day when his mother had come to Clarendon Road, Tracey watched as it emerged that not only had she not come for him, she refused to even see Tim. She had come only to bring the next little boy, Tim's half-brother, for them to care for. He was four. She thumped him down in the middle of the hall floor, with two carrier bags. She screamed at the duty staff, only a trainee on at the time, when the poor woman tried to remonstrate:

"YOU deal with the fucking little bleeder! I ain't doin no more for 'im. He's a fucking nuisance, never does as he's told, little bastard. Miserable little fucker, just like his bruvver, wot you've go' 'ere. AIN'T YOU?" she suddenly shouted into his face, at which he cringed away and began a terrified but muted sobbing. "YOU's the bleedin experts ain't ya? You can 'ave 'im."

A toddler with cherubic blond curls had left go of the pram and, feeling released from the attention of his mother by her preoccupation with his brother, was wandering down the corridor:

"ETHAN!" she suddenly screeched at him, "GERR'ERE!!" He returned guiltily, damp showing through the pants of his dungarees and clung onto the pram handle.

"D'you want to see Tim?" the reasonable request was intended to stall the mother to give time for the manager to be found.

"You're fucking jokin' int cha?" and she skiddadled, leaving a forlorn four year old.

From half way down the stairs, Tracey had witnessed this exchange. Later in the kitchen, she had been there as Martha was talking with the kitchen porter about Tim's mother.

"That woman should be sterilised!" this was shocking from a devout Maltese catholic. "You know what she does, that dirty woman, she has the sex with anyone, sailors, I think and you know why? She just wants to get more and more babies. You know why? I think it turns her on like she randy old she cat. And when the babies ain't babies no more, she don't want them. She only loves the babies and when they grow a bit she just throws them away. You know how many she haves? SIX already."

Tracey had never relayed Martha's opinion of his mother to Tim. The little half brother had been fostered. Two more of them had been in Clarendon Avenue briefly. Now sitting here with Tim on a beach at dawn, a beach, which had become chilly and bleak, Tracey wanted to tell him. She wanted to hurt him, just to make him feel something, anything, any emotion, to connect him to her.

All these years together and it seemed as though she had left no mark on him, not the smallest soft spot in his heart, not the tiniest scratch on his soul. The outpourings of the anguished eleven year old he had been, the tears he'd cried that she had absorbed, the comfort she had given. How could he have forgotten?

But of course, after only a moment, she realised. She knew he had forgotten nothing. But the strength he had finally found to make this move, move on, join the army, move away, had cost him a whole lifetime of emotion. He'd bottled it, corked it, and pressurised it into some kind of energy and drawn from it the power he needed to grow up. She realised she was one of the few people who could destroy it. Tracey knew she could undermine him with one reminder of his pathetic childhood. She could destroy him, have him in her control. Suddenly knowing this, was alarming. But Tracey had her own moving on to do, she was not interested in having Tim in her power.

The split second between acknowledging she had this power and relinquishing it, left a vacuum flooding with confusion. Chunks of the past shot up, a muddle of cruel, tender and funny moments. The intensity expressed itself as tears. Tracey cried and cried, unable to explain to Tim, who wearily, gently held her close and rocked her to and fro.

They had sex then. Tracey had never done it before. It was the saddest thing. She cried again. Perhaps he did. He was 17.

Belfast

The ferry cut through the flat silver grey water of Belfast Lough. On deck, as near to the prow as possible, stood a small figure huddled in a long blue anorak, hands thrust in pockets, both determined to keep balance in defiance of the swell of the boat and to belie the unease rising inside. Tracey's short dark hair flapped about as the breeze switched round from one point to another, adding to the wavering of her resolve. She watched as fields on either side began to close in. As the banks rose to meet the boat, they became more populated. Houses, streets, then the massive skeleton of the refinery loomed through the grey dawn light. Factory and warehouse walls were suddenly smacked by the dazzling pink spotlight of sun as it rose. The bow wave threw up two curls edged in pink lace, scrolling away from the concave sides of the boat, arrowing out from the bulkheads, making the wake. Screeching seagulls circled on the salty air, arcs of pink or purple as they swooped across the sun. Ahead, the mass of Belfast was hunkered down, ready to begin unfurling for the day. As Tracey looked to the north bank she saw the red sunlight flash onto the south-east facing windows, a few at first then more and more, as though lighting fairy lights in honour of her arrival. To the south the huge, menacing, black struts of cranes squared off the sky above the shipyards.

Suddenly all the magic of anticipation filled Tracey. The dawning of a new adventure, the rising sun, burning off her doubts along with the morning mist. Of course she was doing the right thing and if not, interesting things would happen. They always did.

The innocence of youth and the self-reliance of a disjointed childhood gave her courage, courage and a sense of her own immortality made her reckless, reckless even for her own safety.

*   *   *   *   *

Belfast was not as she had imagined. There had been no conscious picture in her head, but news photos always showed bombsites. The reality was a dignified, though soot-grimed, Victorian city with imposing public buildings. Coming up from the docks Tracey had glimpsed down a street on her left the Pisa-ish list of the Albert clock tower. In the centre of the main square, The City Hall was a huge domed wedding cake on its own green plot and facing it were buildings blackened by smoke and age in many different styles. An insurance company occupied a baronial style sandstone building with arched windows, turrets and towers. There was a blue and white painted theatre and elegant Edwardian department stores. Round the corner was the Linen Hall, with actual linenfolds carved below the sills, in sooty sandstone.

But the reality of a war-torn city soon became apparent as workers began to come into the city. Tracey noticed the barriers across every street. The turnstile gates. The warning notices. Now uniformed men and women arrived in armoured-plated Landrovers, accompanied by dark green clad police officers with sub-machine guns casually slung over one shoulder, held loosely, but at the ready, in black-gloved hands. Then a military vehicle arrived and a small group of maroon-bereted soldiers in camouflage fatigues jumped out. The soldiers were tense. Held their weapons tightly, constantly looked about them, nervous, watchful, suspicious. Tim's face was not among them. Though it was difficult to be sure, they were all blacked up like bad minstrels. It was sickening sight to see all that firepower. Those soldiers did not look like they felt at home here, as though they were the enemy, cautiously treading a foreign land. They did not speak to each other, nor the police. They moved off in twos and threes, one walking backwards, the barrels of their weapons arcing from side to side, sweeping the street a few yards at a time. Down the street of shops, security guards were just now letting in workers one at a time and locking the door behind each.

Tracey watched as pedestrians were frisked, passively submitting to being felt all over by uniformed strangers. An armed police officer strode up and down the aisle of a bus, where it was detained at the barrier. Tracey could envisage the barrel of his gun waving from side to side, touching some of the passengers. She did not want to go through a barrier and be frisked, but perhaps she was already in some kind of larger enclosure and would have to be searched to get out. What were they looking for? People wouldn't be so stupid as to carry bombs around the streets would they? Tracey had no idea what might go on in the heads of bombers. In her head was only one thought, how was she going to find Tim? Morning dragged into afternoon.

"TOY –EE!" A loud shout nearby made her jump. A small boy with a news bag had appeared close beside her. He kept repeating the chant exchanging newspapers for handfuls of coins, few of which he stopped to count. Other boys arrived. Each had his pitch. Tracey strained to understand what the strange word was. Her eyes intent on one child's mouth, trying to read his lips, she stepped on the corner of one of the many cracked flags in the pavement and tripped. As the flagstone smacked back down into its place, a fountain of muddy water splashed up soaking her jeans to the calf. It wasn't even raining.

Tracey finally deciphered the call of the newsboys as "TULLY" but couldn't work out the connection between 'tully' and 'newspaper' or its name, 'Belfast Telegraph'. But she bought one to see if there was any adverts or information about contacts for the army. Nothing.

One fearless child darted in and out of the traffic tapping on vehicle windows, stuffing in newspapers. The alien air of the streets being inhabited by these strange beings, was quickly compounded by a chattering, squealing, rushing noise and menacing, darkened sky as millions of starlings swarmed home to roost crowding to the ledges and crevices of the ornate Victorian buildings.

*　　*　　*　　*　　*

It was a scruffy-looking young man with waist-length blond hair and a beard who was the first person to speak to Tracey. It was dark and she was standing on a street corner with no idea what to do or where to go next. After a day wandering, looking for something like an army recruiting booth, like they had in Portsmouth, or a police station or a notice or sign post that might help; after a day in which she had not even passed a post office where she might ask, with only a hot dog and tea from a stand; listening to the foreign accents around her, Tracey had been unable to find the right moment to approach anyone with her enquiry, certainly not people in uniform their arms full of guns. After such a day, Tracey was overwhelmed to be spoken to. But this man also had an incomprehensible accent. When she couldn't respond, he became concerned.

"Whi ya from and whit's ya neame?" after several repetitions she got it.

What the young man heard back was:

"I'm Tricey Orllsop from Pawtsmouth."

"Chrrist, ye'rre English. You a shtudent herre?" She realised he sounded Scottish not Irish. He was. Doing Agriculture at the university, going to get his own hemp farm eventually, risking a joke.

He was very alarmed at her being out on the streets after dark, alone, English, so young. What made him really twitchy was that she was looking for a soldier boyfriend. He did not want the hassle of her. But he could not in all conscience leave her here to be picked up by the police later as they patrolled.

"Don'ch'ye know there's a currfew. The city centre's lawcked n barrrred 'til marnin' noo."

"I'll find somewhere to kip, I've done it before." She was getting use to his accent now.

"Not whirr therre's a warr oen, wee girrl. Ye better come wi me. Jus' don' talk, O. Kee."

The house fronted straight on to the street. In the dark hall, he turned and whispered to stay there and not say a word. He went into the front room where the noise of the telly couldn't mask the tones of outrage and disgust expressed by at least two other voices. Quietly Tracey hoisted her backpack and reached for the latch. She didn't want to cause trouble.

She had just got the door open and was easing herself out when she was caught in a bright triangle of light from the living room door.

"Whirr ye off ta? C'mon in an' let's have some teee."

"What about the others? Don't sound like they want me 'ere."

"Norrr.., it's not that. It's jus thirr worried, same's me. These 'rre dangerous times. Thirr jus worried aboot ye. C'mon."

On the faces of the two other young men, lounging on a plastic sofa, with mugs of tea in their hands as they detached their attention from the screen and looked up at Tracey was undisguised shock. She blanched, wondered if she had dirt on her face, reached up to see if her nose was bleeding, as it was prone to do, glanced at the Scotsman. He was laughing. One of them explained that Jimmy usually brought home bimbos, all the girls fancied him, Jesus knows why. Then realising that he had hurt her feelings (she was no bimbo), he went on to say she was just a little kid and shouldn't be out wandering the streets. So, he thought that was less offensive! But Tracey couldn't afford to care. She had hardly sat down all day. She collapsed on a wonky arm chair, her backpack at her feet. There was a coal fire blazing and after the tea and a piece (bread, marg and jam) the others paid no further attention to her. So she dozed off.

*   *   *   *   *

Because of the initial anxiety of the three young housemates when their number was increased to include Tracey, she quickly made herself noticeably useful. Keenly aware that this was a convenient stop-gap while she found out what to do next in her search for Tim, she tidied up the communal parts of the house where people hung about most, kept washing up and bleaching the sink so the ancient ceramic gleamed white and the cracks became invisible. It was a Belfast sink – did they have them in Manchester or Portsmouth, or were they Manchester sinks or Portsmouth sinks there? - You could get in up to your elbows, but it was hard to find a plug to fit it properly these days, Ray told her. Of the three of them, Ray was the most often at home. Since finishing his degree, he'd only had a few jobs. He wanted to be an actor. But he couldn't get enough work to get an Equity card, without an

Equity card no-one would offer him a decent role. Catch 22, he called it. Ray had only been in a couple of local TV commercials as a "member of the public".

Tracey never cleaned the toilet, using it as briefly as possible herself and thinking that if they kept using it in that disgusting state, they must either be unaware of its caked on shite, or they didn't care, in which case they'd be unlikely to notice if she cleaned it, so she was damned if she would. There were limits! However she always volunteered to run errands, making sure she never had the money to buy anything herself. If anyone said "who's making the tea?" she always jumped up to oblige. In exchange she got a free meal every night – which she sometimes cooked, and as much bread and tea during the day as was available. This meant she did not have to dip into her savings or get involved in the hassle of changing her dole office to Northern Ireland. She'd told them at home she was going on holiday. So she should have a nice lump waiting when she got back.

Joining the library was Tracey's only concession to permanence; after writing herself a letter at University Street to prove she lived there, joke! That way, when the rest had gone to bed or were out drinking she could lie on the sofa and read. The sofa's metamorphosis into bed could only happen after the witching hour, which was whenever the others were all tucked up safely in their own beds, fast asleep. The library was also her source of information about where Tim might be found.

Tracey had been given an address that she had written to when Tim had first been posted here five weeks earlier. But it was an army address, it made no sense to her with its list of letters and numbers. There was no way of matching it to a place on the ground. The address belonged to a whole camp. Tim had never replied since he had been in the North. He wasn't a keen letter writer, but he had written to her during his basic training and his first posting to Rheindahlen. He had only been there six months when his unit had been posted to Northern Ireland. Tracey had not seen him for over a year. And in his five weeks here, nothing.

The kind librarian was sympathetic. Assuming Tracey to be a girlfriend, she explained that there would be no hope of finding the whereabouts of a soldier, unless she were a relative, no hope of ever tracking him down. It was all to do with security. Soldiers were targets.

Tracey had already lost one brother, Paul, she was not about to lose Tim. In her head, Tim was promoted to brother.

Using the BFPO address she had been given, Tracey carefully constructed a letter to Tim. In the first instance she would assume he was able to receive and read letters. Tracey had the idea that his letters might be read by superior officers, censored before being given to him. So she had to write a letter that would let him know that she was now his "sister" and that she'd come to Northern Ireland to visit him so that she would be able to get in to see him wherever he was.

September 19th

Dear Tim,

Thanks for your last letter from Germany. I'm glad you're back from Germany, now. At least I assume you are though I haven't heard from you since you went to Northern Ireland, so I was getting a bit worried. I thought it would be easier to keep in contact as it's part of Britain, and I can get over to see you now because there are some other members of our family that I can stay with, some aunts and uncles on my dad's side that you probably don't know about. Because you and I don't really have exactly the same family, do we? It's because we have different fathers of course that we have different last names. Our family was not just those of us who lived together in the big house in Clarendon Avenue. I am over in Belfast now and I want to come and visit you. They said I should be allowed to see you because of course I am your sister. So can you write to me at the address below and explain how we can meet up?

Til I hear from you, soon I hope,
Lots of luv bruv,
Tracey XXXXX

66

Would he think she'd gone off her head? To her the letter sounded weird, but she couldn't think how else to phrase it and if he didn't write back she was just going to have to go looking for him from one army camp to another. If she could crack the code of where they were.

Although Ray never seemed to mind Tracey being around, always ready to talk, describing the delights of Belfast and the rest of Northern Ireland to her, entertaining her with acting stories, she felt Jimmy and Patsy were beginning to get irritated. The house in University Street had no heating and it had begun to get cold during the day. Ray and Tracey put on more clothes and lit the fire, but hanging about the house not doing anything physical left them shivering. Tracey decided she would give Tim one more week to reply before going direct to where she thought he might be. The BFPO address she had was – an eavesdropper in the library had told her – in a small place romantically named Ballykelly. That would be her next stop. She had looked it up on the map, found the bus route and where the bus departed from behind the Europa Hotel.

The Crown Bar was right opposite the Europa and Tracey and Ray were spending an afternoon keeping warm there, he, sitting over one pint of Guinness, making it last, counting the sips, she laboriously breaking each crisp into four and eating each a nibble at a time. The poverty game had an added frisson. The barman had his eye on them, biding his time until a genuine customer or regular might come in and their glasses were empty. Then he would come into the snug and ask them what else they were having, like a waiter. He never actually had to point out that another customer was waiting for a seat, if they didn't mind, because they always got up to leave anyway. He knew they were broke.

The Crown, really was amazing. Tracey could believe that nothing had changed there in 100 years except that by slow degrees the decoration had gradually gained the rich patina of nicotine. They occupied a snug, a secluded enclosure of warm, worn wood, a table down the centre and bench seats down each side. One bench was still upholstered in leather, its smoothened edge glistening with the polish of hundreds of trouser seats and outdoor coats. Across the barside end of the snug, a wooden door swung like a saloon door in the centre of the wooden partition. Set into it were panes of ornate frosted glass, intricate floral patterns of clear glass laced round scrolled borders and looped in some, the name of a spirit...brandy....gin...Underfoot were small square tiles with bright mosaic borders and across the wide streetside frontage of the pub, stained-glass windows obscured the grey daylight and gave the interior the rich dimly-lit mystery of a hallowed place. Then when the outdoor dark descended, inside, pools of soft diffuse light could be seen hanging in the smoky atmosphere. Originally gas, the globes of etched yellow glass marked each carved pillar of the bar and being reflected many times in the bevelled mirrors behind, were often distorted to amber or ruby by the whisky and port bottles arranged there.

One afternoon when Tim's week had elapsed and Tracey and Ray's luck had run out in the Crown, Tracey nipped across to the bus station and jotted down convenient times of buses to Ballykelly. She was not going to lose another "brother". She was determined to find Tim.

*   *   *   *   *

The familiar whiff of damp walls greeted Tracey as she let herself in through the chipped front door. She had come back to pack up for the last leg of her search for Tim. Without realising it, the 11 days she had spent living here had become a comfortable habit. Now that she was moving on, its myriad attributes took on a poignancy that caught at her nose, in her throat, brought a swell of tears to her eyes. Sentimental about a bunch of blokes who had never invited her and would not miss her, and a house that would only be improved by demolition. Most valuable of all was the experience of independence; pleasing herself; accountable to no-one; only doing others' bidding when she chose or it was judicious to do so; learning to relate to others, get the best out of people; and simply being accepted as she was. On the table she left a link to her other life, her life in Portsmouth; her name and address at the hostel in Clarendon Avenue. As she propped the used envelope against a jamjar of Michaelmass daisies that she'd gathered from in a crack in the flagstones in the backyard where they grew unbidden, Tracey laughed. She knew the envelope would fall on the floor, be kicked about there for a bit, become illegible with dirt and perhaps even, if a miracle occurred, finally be swept up with the rubbish and ditched. She knew none of them would ever contact her, it was for herself that she left a line of communication. She didn't want to cut the traces. She had had a good time. She left a bottle of Mundies for them as a thank you. No idea whether they liked it, but everything else was so expensive. It took her a few minutes to clear up her things, pack them neatly and tidy up. She was pleased with the sense that it was as though she had never been there. There were still 40 minutes til the bus. Why didn't Ray come? She wanted to say goodbye. He was such good fun, he'd taught her a lot. At quarter to she had to go. Leaving her key beside the note, she cast a last look round at the cobwebbed ceiling – she couldn't reach it, the grubby beige emulsion over wood-chip walls, a poster of Fleetwood Mac and the tiled mantelpiece and table wiped clean, the dishes all put away, the ashtrays emptied....... maybe they would miss her – but only as a maid! Ray didn't arrive and though she scoured the faces she met on the way to the bus station, she did not see him.

The blue and white Ulsterbus was throbbing, raring to go in a rising haze of black diesel fumes when Tracey boarded. Picking a seat halfway down, the back was full of smokers, and she had given up, too expensive, she slung her backpack in then squeezed in past it to the window seat. No-one could come and talk to her now, no room. She wanted time to think. Think about being upset about not seeing Ray that last time. Think about meeting up with Tim. Allowing the possibility that she might not find him at all. Trying not to think about what direction her life might next take.

Drizzle dimmed the window, then strengthened into pelting rain. The light inside the bus was brighter than the daylight, so little of the passing country was revealed to Tracey. The journey lent itself to introspection.

In Limavady, she had to change buses. Limavady what a name! Didn't sound Irish...did it? It took forever and a day to get there, she had no library books, she had returned them all, not wanting to leave her housemates with a fine and she was half way through "Of Mice and Men". The people in it were so poor and that big "eejit" – as they say in the North - with his puppy. She amused herself imagining a happy ending, but knew it was going to be tragic. Tracey had an empathy with the tragic side of life, that's why the librarian had introduced her to Steinbeck.

With every bump in the road, every deceleration or change of gear, another thought would pop in Tracey's head sewing seeds of panic. What would she say when she got to the barracks? Would they even speak to her at all? Would Tim be there?

Changing buses in Limavady was uneventful. A little bent farmer took her arm to guide her along. He was even shorter than she, happy to be of service. He was going that way himself, he said, about to board the bus after her. She was relieved when he was hailed by a friend and called away by the offer of a lift. And turned quickly towards the window in case he should want his friend to include her in his generosity. A thread of instinctive self-preservation inside told her it would be better that no-one knew she was heading for the British army barracks, no matter what their feelings about the presence of the army in Northern Ireland.

The weather had cleared and watery sun lit up the bog coloured river Roe as the bus crossed over the bridge on the Derry road. One wooded bank was tight with trees just showing the burnt tinge of autumn. And below, young cattle on the flood plain fattened themselves on grass which was a real emerald green in the afternoon light.

A middle-aged man behind, all friendly, thinking she was a foreign student perhaps, leaned over the back of her seat and pointed out the ancient ring of beech trees, she looked towards it, but couldn't think of a conversational response, then he indicated the river Foyle just glimpsable over a gate. She asked him to tell her when they arrived at

Ballykelly, he said he would, but stopped talking to her then and turned to the window.

The bus dropped her off outside a fence. A tall fence surmounted by vicious curls of razor wire. Beyond it, rose streets of solid grey/yellow brick houses and double-storied blocks, not very old, square and functional-looking. They didn't look like barracks, more a council house estate. Tracey walked along the fence towards the gate. It had a double tier of barriers, gate houses on either side with soldiers on guard just visible inside them. Cameras on poles watched her arrival. She slowed, running over her opening line again. As she drew near a soldier stepped out and pointed his gun at her, and looked up and down the road. He'd seen her get off the bus.

"Can I help you?" he didn't sound as aggressive as he looked. He had a northern accent, Manchester maybe?

"I've come to see my brother."

Was it her imagination, or did he relax a bit when she spoke?

"Can I see your clearance then?"

What was he talking about?

"I don't know anything about that….." she began, but he had his hand on a buzzer instantly and almost at once another soldier appeared. Officious icy eyes trapped Tracey in their scary ice-blue glare. He looked murderous. She was the object of this attack. Already emotional, she felt two responses fizz up to her head. She almost opened her mouth to shout back at this ugly stranger, but the muzzle of the gun had been raised, so the other response spilled forth, as tears. Tracey was furious with herself. She blinked hard, recovered, then, to cover her confusion, she babbled,

"Look, my brother, well, half-brother actually" - the two soldiers exchanged looks – "used to write to me all the time when he was in Germany. Then he got posted here," – was it her imagination or were they looking at her abdomen? They thought she was lying, thought she was pregnant and trying to trap a squaddie – "I wrote to him to tell him I was coming, but I never had a reply. His name's Tim Henderson, Private. Can you see if he's here? Please."

"No. Not without some authorisation."

Ray had said it would be like this. She would have to rely on appealing to their better natures, there was no other hope.

After pleading and explaining, discribing her difficult journey here, inventing a sick mother, lying that she was booked on the ferry tomorrow night, laying claim to a college place she didn't have....anything to look respectable, believable and NOT desperate, an officer (well, he had stripes on his arm, Sergeant?) passed by and enquired what was going on. He looked at Tracey and saw a sad young girl.

"What was the name?"

He took the soldier inside. Several minutes later, they emerged. It was not long enough for a genuine check, no further questions about the spelling of his name, date of birth.

"You do know these are married quarters?" the nicer one said. "Is your brother married?" He saw from her face it was a question she had not considered. If the man she was seeking had been married, he had not told her. Whoever he was, the soldier knew he was not her brother.

"He's not here, I'm sorry." He sounded genuinely sorry for her.

"Where has he gone?" she knew they hadn't even checked.

"I'm not allowed to say, I can't even say if he was here at all. But I can tell you he is definitely not here now."

The senior soldier walked away. The soldier with the gun waved her away with its barrel. The cruel one marched away.

Tracey had no choice but to believe them. As she turned away she saw a small sign inside the gate "MARRIED QUARTERS". They were right, Tim wouldn't have been here anyway. The soldiers here were all married.

Another brother lost to her. Tracey just stood.

Chapter 8

The battered white Mercedes drew up beside Tracey. At first she didn't notice, just stood there, rain dripping from her nose, making the tears indistinguishable - if there were any — she couldn't even tell if she was crying.

And it was lashing with rain. Just what she might expect in Ireland. She was standing outside the barracks. Jack would not have noticed her except for the rucksack.

"Look at the poor wee'un, and that 'quge rucksack on her back. And in the teeming rain." Jack muttered to himself to reinforce his decision to stop to offer her a lift.

Even though she was standing right outside the army barracks and Jack knew all about girls who stood outside a barracks…he never meant to look out for them, but somehow he always did see them, girls like that. But this one was different. A glimpse of the face under the black fringe showed such a picture of misery. This was the second time Jack had been round, giving it about 20 minutes so if she was waiting on someone they would have fetched her by then. But no, there she was still standing there. As he slowed up, no traffic behind, he thought he could see the tears streaming.

"The poor wee thing," and then he realised, "sure, she's only a teenager, a wee'un." But by then he had stopped. She never looked over, just kept her eyes in the distance somewhere. He leaned over and rolled down the window:

"Y'all right 'nere hey? D'yse want a lift."

She made no response. No response at all. And there was Jack so with the rain coming in through the window and soaking his good upholstery.

"Hey you missus, d'yse want a lift? 'Tis true I'm neither sugar nor salt, nor I won't melt, but I'm getting soaked here."

This time she looked up and then hoisted off the rucksack, opened the back door, shoved it in dripping wet across the back seat and, with an enormous effort, wearily climbed in the front seat. Tracey didn't speak. Then she wiped the sleeve across her face, never looking at Jack and just shut her eyes.

"Where d'yse want to go to, hey? I'm away into Derry after I've dropped off some supplies up the lane there."

"Derry?" she'd spoke at last "yeah, fine Derry." Then she slid down, with her eyes shut, turned her head from him.

"That's right, sure, you have a wee snooze. Ye're obviously done in."

Jack drove up McIlhenny's boreen to drop off the calf nuts. The potholes and gravel, splashing through puddles as big as the loch - thinking he would get young Don to clean the wheel arches come the weekend. And all the time he was humping and bumping the bags out of the back, she never moved, nor spoke. Missus Mac asked about her. Jack was pleased at her interest.

That story would be all round town come market day. Jack and a strange young girl. That would set tongues wagging, right enough! There was little enough scandal round there. Jack was always glad to be of service, good old Jack the lad. In his young days he had run three women at the one time. He began to tell McIlhenny in the shelter of the barn as they shared a cigarette.

"I mind the time Marty Mc Greggor, sure she was a real cracker, she caught me with Margie Malloy, me with my trousers half mast, her with no top on, lovely tits she had, but she'd a face on her like a hatchet. That was down by the river. 'Twas the summer of 67 or 68. She gave me such a kick up the bare arse. Right enough, we were suppose to be engaged.... then didn't Catherine Burke chance along the towpath and wasn't she best friends with that Veronica I'd been chatting up at the dance? Christ almighty Jesus the ructions from that. That was a summer and a half all right. Never had me trousers up. Them boys up the country, could never un'erstand it. But it was the patter. You'd to talk yeer way into them girls' knickers. This wee girl'll get the tongues wagging.Nowadays there's little enough gossip with me, right 'nough, eh Mac? Nor yourself!"

"What'll ye do wi' her?"

"I'll drop her off, just on the run-in to Derry, 'nere. Probably never see her again, sure I won't."

74

Chapter 9

Children in the street were gathered at doorways or bouncing ball against house walls. Until, at the irritated shouts of the occupants, they dispersed, howling with laughter. Twilight is long in the north and as often happened, the damp day had rolled away leaving a sunny evening. On such an evening, children could forget their unofficial, fear-inspired curfew, and were giggling and squabbling over the French skipping elastic, over who had been kissed in the playground. They were linked by common experience, common culture, a common language, rich with the imagery of the saints. Some windowsills were without tiny statues of the veiled virgin bravely peeping out from behind the lace, but even so a strict Catholic presence prevailed.

This street was the last inhabited street of the area. Beyond, up the hill, dereliction had begun to claim the housing that had once been mixed. Only brave or stupid children explored these haunted badlands now. Most stayed away. They revelled at a safe distance in the horror stories they scared each other with, fed by the passing of ratty hobos and groups of older kids, out of their heads, up-to-no-good, carrying alcohol, glue, drugs. The street was the main thoroughfare up to this no-man's land.

A small dark child saw them first. She said nothing, but quietly took her brother's hand and crossed to their house. Their silent departure alerted the others who disappeared in a hush, leaving the street empty for the group of girls starting raucously up the hill.

There were five of them, clanking bottles, slugging from them as they exaggeratedly fell about, shouting and singing, not as paralytic as they wanted the street to believe, feeling safe and assertive on their home territory, all except one. She was hunched into her duffle coat, trailing a little, staggering a lot. They were trying to include her, calling encouragement back to her. First one, then another went into a house, shouting farewell until at the top of the hill, Jo, the straggler, was alone. She didn't live here, didn't belong with them. They were babies, indulging in make-believe, following a drama in which only she was a serious player. Her shoulders relaxed, the tension went from her huddled figure, but she still wobbled about without apparent purpose. Then when she felt herself to be out of sight she pulled herself up and seemed to find a focus, which steadied her feet enough for her to begin to hurry. She arrived at the house she was looking for, an empty house, better preserved than the others, its glass and doors intact, not yet boarded up and on an inner street not frequented by passers-by, rarely patrolled by security forces. Swaying a little, she shouldered the front door open, securing it again with the weight of her hip. Safe in her jeans pocket, she had pleasure all wrapped up carefully in a man-sized tissue.

But it did not go right and from having been so anxious one minute to be alone to enjoy the pleasure, she suddenly found herself very anxious not to be alone. Scared to be alone, starting to choke, snorting shorter and shorter panicky breaths through flared nostrils, needing help. Held an out-breath, talked to herself, a fuddled inner conversation.

"Swallow. You bastard! Swallow. Down the throat. Won't go…. Must! Then it'll be better. Would you go down the fucking throat! Rasping, gagging. A choking wheeze. No, not the asthma! Shouldn't've done 'em all at the one time. Christ, so dry. Reach for cider bottle in the pocket. Shake it. Empty. No water here. So sore…fire…...like swallowing marbles, grating and grinding against each other. Did it for a bet once, in the school playground. Then slowly, down, they start to go…. but no relief. Down, gouging out a scorching gash of pain……like swallowing a pyramid, a huge obstructing lump there, deep pain, every breath shallower. Stuck there, halfway. Now the saliva comes, can't swallow, won't. Gagging. Don't fucking throw up, that'd be a ten spot wasted. Gorge rises, nausea scalding vomit rushing up behind. Mouth full of saliva, jaws ready to throw up, gulping, gulping. Massage throat, then thorax, ease it on down, down, start digesting. Be better soon. Nothing to push it down, no water, no beer, no cider. Swollen tongue like a gritted winter road. No tap working here in hell. Chin up, stroke down along the throat, dirty chewed fingers pressing gullet, like when the cat had pleurisy, stroke the pills down her throat, made her swallow them down. Then it's gone and slowly the pit of the stomach begins to warm, radiate, welcome waves rippling out. Cannot believe this is not a physical reaction to the chemical. The sensation, seeping through, osmosis, pore to pore, cell to cell, bit by bit, good feeling conquering bad………."

Calm at last. Jo looked out. Sooty grime diffused yellow evening sunlight pushing through cracked panes, rain-stained; hanging there in air thick with demolition dust, where motes danced before a backdrop of black streaky mould, wallpaper browned off with age. Distant corners of the room disappeared, retreated into a blackness cast by the blinding blocks of setting sun, tingeing gold now. Her feet slid as the muscles relaxed, knees collapsed, toe caps mushroomed out, catching the blush of pink spotlight, elongating away up the chimney, blush pink grapefruit smiled a half-segmented smile, pulling away, up and away, her shoulders fell, tongue lolled, rolled, and a thread of silk spittle bright shiny red catching the sun as it went. Then her senses sapped away, the thoughts went…. flying….. out…….. the…….. window…….. eyelids unfurled, recurled, lowered, raised, lowered, covering bulging eyeballs, sweet treacle-black peace arrived and obliterated the tickle of a rat's whiskers on a bare-skinned ankle.

Not so sweet was the dirty green shadowy dawn; the swollen tongue, glued to lips and palate; encrusted eyelashes sharp points of pain, shots of agony up through a twisted wrist, bent beneath her slumped body, a pyramid of pain. AW, fucking CHRIST! Jo saw the dark stain, both legs lying in the dust made mud. And then the smell. Fucking SHAT myself as well. Tears loosened the eye scum. Where the fuck was everyone, "Why'm alone?" she croaked. This was the pits. Condemned house, chips of brick, slivers of glass, fucking broken crap everywhere. She had to escape. Who would look at her now, let alone lend her a shot or a tab or scrounge her some money? No one! No way! She had to get cleaned up before she could go to find a friend. A friend. Clarried, wet stinking jeans plastered to crawling legflesh in the freezing air. Suddenly awareness of a freezing stare, Jo looked round to where a dark dwarf was peering round the edge of the peeling door. Jo was too spaced to react, to jump, to feel surprise.

"Christ! The smell! You are disgusting."

"A fucking Cockney-accented dwarf, making personal remarks about a stranger's personal hygiene." Jo thought but felt too ill to protest. However dimly, she recognised this as potential help arrived.

"Gi's a harnd 'n'ere wi' yous?" Jo lifted a limp hand weakly.

"You gotta be facking jokin'. I'm not touching you in that state." Jo dropped back exhausted, her head fell forward, her chin slid into a patch of vomit on her collar.

When Tracey had sneaked into the abandoned house the previous night, she had observed the slumbering body of a stranger in the downstairs room. She had smelt nothing suspicious; not the pungent sweet Muscatty smell of 'British' sherry, nor the sickly heavy vanilla smell of heroin nor the Aramaic incense of a spliff, or even tobacco, she had believed her fellow traveller was no more than that, and as a result had felt safer in her borrowed shelter, easier in her stolen sleep. She hadn't known that something had been swallowed. Odourless, smell-less, it must have been some kind of tabs. She could've woken up in residence with a corpse.

"Don't go, how'm I gonna get cleaned up?"

"I'm not your bleeding mother."

"Ye're right 'n'ere, I'm her wee dote."

Jo began to shiver. The shivering increased to a violent trembling.

"Cccchrist I'm ffffocking starvin'. You ggggot a blanket?"

"Can't eat that!"

"Starving wi cccold, y'eejit ye. (Focking foreigners.)"

In spite of her sense of self-preservation, her urge to get away, Tracey was beginning to weaken, to feel she should help this fellow human. Just because the predicament that this person was in was of her own choosing, didn't mean she was any less humanly in need.

Tracey sighed and moved in through the door, stepping cautiously between the piles of rubble.

"What's your name then?" she said as levelly as she could, trying not to inhale too deeply, keeping her tongue pressed to the roof of her mouth to prevent the stench going down into her lungs. Jo's teeth were chattering less violently now that help was at hand and she began to relax.

"Mind your own fffocking business...... Jesus, Mary and Jjjoseph, you are one ugly bitch, but," she said conversationally, as she struggled to focus on Tracey.

Tracey sucked in a short tight-lipped breath and turned away, kicking the broken bricks aside now, stumbling angry, hurt, uncaring of the raised dust. In the hall she hoisted up her backpack and slammed the heavy street door behind her. A panel fell out clattering into the early morning silence, only to set off a wailing and keening from within, which quickly crescendoed into a screaming lamentation..... "focking ugly dwarf Cockney bitch".

In the railway station buffet there was an all-day breakfast for £1.50. As much as you could eat. They still had a conversion table on the wall from £sd to pounds and pence for the old timers who went there. They were out in force today. Yesterday must've been pension day. Thursday. Several of the old people smiled warmly at Tracey. She began to feel conspicuous, out of place, too young, but determined not to leave until she was full. This was a true Ulster fry, white pudding, black pudding, potato bread, pancake, as well as l bacon, egg, sausage, tomato, mushrooms tea, and bread and butter. Heart attack on a plate. It would last her all day. She folded several pieces of bread and butter into a napkin for later, just in case!

A misty autumn morning was blossoming into bright yellow sunshine as Tracey, her full stomach sloshing, struck out over the two-tier bridge over the river, swollen with floodwater. The blue latticed ironwork threw rhythmic shadows across her path. Exposed, in the open now, Tracey glanced around to check that her night companion hadn't followed her. Looking across to the walls of Derry, softened now by the morning sunshine, she could hardly credit the repulsion it had inspired the previous night, when stabbing spires and bullying warehouses had shouldered each other upwards into a black, saw-edged skyline torn raggedly from the steely sheet of drizzle. It had been raining iron filings. Yet now, the menace was unimaginable, consigned to the night.

She thought of her futile quest. Tim was not here. No-one she knew was here. There was nothing here for her. Where next?

The Landrover crawled past. Warship grey. Slits in the grey metal windscreen couldn't afford much of a view. Barb-tipped barrels of sub-machine guns, wrapped incongruously in collandar-holed gunmetal, thrust into the morning air. They covered every compass point, chest height. Tracey's chest tightened, her breathing increased. She looked, careful not to stare, straight ahead. She kept her pace, though her boots were filling with lead. When it had passed, she didn't ease up. Every footstep shouted "Look at me, I'm English. I'm the enemy." It was a fucking war zone. She wanted out of there. At the next junction she headed towards the Gallic-looking names on the signpost, aiming to leave the north in search of what she hoped might be peace across the border. This was the border, right?

"Graighnan." Unpronounceable, unknown, as good a destination as any. It was signposted off to the left. At the turn, she stood back to let a vehicle pass, looking nonchalantly away over the fields so as not to look at it for fear it might be army or police.

"Where ye headed?" A jolly weather-scarred face under a grimy flat cap grinned through the wound down window.

"Is it the fort at Graighnan ye're after? I can run yous there if you want. Sure, amn't I headed that way mysen."

Tracey was free, she had no itinerary. Fed up walking, she jumped in, sat back and relaxed. Some miles on he stopped the car.

"'N'ere ye are now, destination Greenan! Y'all have a nice day!" he added in American.

Graighnan. A round chapel, modern with an off-set spire for funnelling up the prayers that were a bit off-set? The flat irregular stones of its construction looked as though they'd been gathered from the surrounding hillsides, large, rough-hewn blocks were interspersed with naturally splintered rocks.

80

In the car park, one blue vehicle sat randomly abandoned without regard to the scored parking plan. A track led up beyond it, signposted in fancy writing it invited Tracey up the hill. Tired carrying the backpack, she stuffed it under a hedge. Buoyant without it, she almost ran, up to where the green ridge met the blue sky.

As the ground levelled out across the field, she saw a broad, low strip of masonry. The ancient tapering, curved stone wall rose, its top a scraggy fringe of wind-dried summer gentians and grass. It was a ring fort. It seemed to circle the hill like a crown. When she got close it rose 30 feet above her. Through the curtain wall, an arched gateway let her into the circle of grassy turf inside and curved steps lifted her up towards the top of the fortress walls. Lichen pitted the stone, blood red, bright white, mustard yellow, the palest turquoise; brilliant green moss almost shimmering; the sparkle of quartz; the shine of split copper-green slate. It was so vivid that a permanent image of the moment was imprinted onto Tracey's brain. The unearthly colours, burned into her retinas like developing film; the smell of the air; the lightness of her limbs; a moment of pure sensation, permanently captured. At the top, the wind snatched away her breath and pulled tears from watering eyes. She could see forever, round the world and right back to her own back . Across hills, down to the sea, following a silver river, a muddy estuary. Miles and miles at the top of the world. Horizons of fading cloud and the distant, slow, grinding of the mauve mountains.

"Take me now." She whispered to the wind, laughing, reaching out, measuring her wingspan, wanting to jump, almost elated enough to take flight.

On the wind that funnelled up the path, Tracey caught a whiff of cigarette smoke.

"Christ, me backpack!" There wasn't anything of value in it, except all the warmth and protection she would need on an autumn evening sleeping rough. And her toothbrush; wherever she was she could not sleep without clean teeth.

She couldn't believe anyone was about. Not here. Everything around had seemed to belong only to her. Then she remembered the car. Blue, randomly parked, in the church car park. My god, they'd have the security forces out by now. Tracey imagined a fleet of khaki landrovers, several bomb disposal teams, walky-talkies, a camera crew form Ulster TV, a BBC journalist all lining up a controlled explosion on her innocent backpack. She hurried down the hill.

The woman had been looking at the backpack, but turned sharply at the sound of Tracey's approach. She sighed in relief.

"'Zis yours? Thank the lord for that. I was thinking I would have to phone the police."

Tracey bent and hooked her arm through one shoulder strap, ready to hoist it onto her back, then stopped.

"You're English."

"And you."

An awkward pause ensued. A very English pause. Too much said already, no prying allowed. Then the senior woman took the lead.

"You're very young and English to wandering so near - bandit country." (She paused to choose her description of the area). Tracey could think of no reply.

"Sorry to scare you with my backpack." Did it sound sarcastic?

"You're lucky I hadn't got round to phoning the bomb squad."

"Yes, it was stupid, I am sorry, really. But there was nobody here and it just got so heavy and I wanted to go up to see the..." she didn't know what it was.

"The fort? It's great isn't it? So wild up there, such a vantage point. You can see why they built a lookout up there."

History. This was neutral ground, safe ground.

The woman was Eileen. Not English, but back from 35 years living in the home counties where she'd almost lost her accent. Thin, grey and with skin etched by more than age. Tracey declined a cigarette.

"It's nice to have a chat and a fag. They don't let me smoke indoors. Where you headed next? Come back and have a bite of lunch, on your way?" Eileen was astonished to hear herself say this. She had had no intention of continuing the acquaintance, let alone inviting the wee girl for lunch. It was only ham and potatoes. But she couldn't withdraw it now. She was about to say something like, 'but I'm sure you've got a deadline' or 'but you're probably vegetarian' to convey the subtle message that she wasn't really expecting her to say yes, when Tracey spoke first.

"My mother taught me never to accept gifts from strangers.......(she smiled, Eileen smiled encouragingly back, thinking she would decline) but that'd be lovely, yes please." Tracey's smile was her best feature. It made people warm to her, trust her, like her. Lunch, after that breakfast, never rains but it pours, she thought, though the fresh air had made her peckish.

"Hop in then," Eileen tried to sound more enthusiastic than she felt. Shae, her husband, was always telling her not to do things on impulse, worried that she might find herself in trouble. He would not be best pleased at the rash action of inviting a total stranger, English into the bargain, into their already precarious domicile.

The chemical smell of new plastic had been intensified by the sun beating on the parked car. Shiny blue. In Tracey's experience, this was the smell of a social worker's car. How come they always seemed to have new cars? Jon Spires. A different life. If he could see her now. It was so good to be here.

On the back seat was a sectioned plastic box. Cans of polish, bottles of window cleaner, bleach, rolls of cloth, jars of gumption, were obsessively arranged in order of size, their labels all lined up, facing out. A damp mop, its head in a bucket on the floor, a broom, and a dry mop, their handles carefully aligned, stood to attention against the rear passenger door.

Tracey knew about cleaning fluids. She'd been look-out for housemates sniffing the range for a high, back in the basement in Clarendon Avenue. She never indulged herself, but didn't want mates to get in trouble. It was a way of storing up favours that she could call in later when she needed them.

83

Wasn't it unlikely that a cleaner would have a brand new car though?

Eileen seemed to read her mind.

"The regular cleaner's in hospital. I'm filling in. My biggest problem is that I don't have the key to the cupboard. It was murder cleaning with my own stuff from home, you need an industrial mop for those floors."

"Is it well paid? I need a job …. running out of money fast."

"We don't get paid at all for cleaning this church. It's a labour of love. The usual cleaner's doing it all the time at the moment as penance for her son. He's on the blank…….." Eileen abruptly stopped mid-word. Tracey knew what she had been going to say, "blanket". Something she should never talk about, certainly not to a stranger. The anxious occupants of University Street had each taken the time to explain their understanding of the troubles to her. They discussed every news item, every new atrocity. They wanted her to stay out of the way and be completely clear about why she should.

Eileen quickly swerved onto a new safe topic.

"Would you look at the kestrel there? So still. How do they stay like that for so long, just hanging in mid-air? And in this wind."

They watched it swoop out of sight before Eileen started the car.

Tracey was happy, even though the trail for Tim had fizzled out and the search would have to be postponed. There was nothing more she could do about it here in Northern Ireland. Today, she'd been to the top of the world. And it wasn't even lunch time.

The late September sun shone warmly and a warm motherly woman was taking her to a warm home for lunch. And she could escape whenever she wanted. Just at this moment all was right with the world. When Tracey was happy, she prattled. By the time they turned into a farm track through a propped aluminium gate, Eileen knew Tracey's story. No incriminating details, no emotional comment, but the gist of her disjointed life.

Apart from what she could judge with her eyes, Tracey knew only three things about Eileen. Her son had been killed in a bomb. Her daughter in law had committed suicide and Eileen had come back from England to run the farm and bring up her orphaned grandson.

As the car drew into the farmyard, Tomas reluctantly looked up from an absorbing game on the doorstep. Tracey had never seen such a black-haired, white-faced child. His dark eyes trapped her in an unblinking stare as she got out of the car. Unsmiling, he did not greet his grandmother.

"Granda's burnt the taters."

He was four or five and too beautiful for life on earth. Tracey was choked. She'd seen a couple of kids like this in care. Not as beautiful perhaps. But your heart just bled for them.

"It would make your heart bleed," Eileen muttered, looking at Tracey as she blinked away a tear.

Tracey looked at Tomas' game. Pebbles from the gravel driveway were lined up on the concrete step in a rigorous order of size, largest through to smallest. There was a whole series of lines, each exactly matching. He was on about the eleventh. Tracey watched as he carefully placed the next pebble, his fingers only just dexterous enough for the task. No irritation when one was knocked slightly out of line, just a patient replacing. It looked like ranks of soldiers, battalions, a whole army.

"They soldiers?"

There was a pause while Tom struggled to understand her accent. When he realised what she had said, he replied "Yes, English sojars. The whole of the army's here."

Could he identify an English accent? Probably, with his grandmother around. He finished a line then counted them up. Then he stood up as if to admire his handiwork. Suddenly his face contorted and he flung his foot out in fury, kicking and scuffing until all were consigned back to the dust of the driveway.

He went silently inside, leaving Tracey slightly shocked and almost wanting to giggle. Eileen was watching.

"He does that almost every day. He won't talk about it. I don't know, I'm done just trying to puzzle it out for myself.....but he was there with his mum- in a shop. The bomb went off down the street where Donal, that's my son, was parked waiting for them. See, you're not allowed to leave a car unattended. The army were the first to arrive on the scene, after the bomb, cordoning off, bossing about, not letting them go near where the damaged car was with his dad inside. I think maybe he thinks the soldiers did it. He's certainly got it in for the British army now."

When, at lunch, Tom picked up his plate, tongue clenched between teeth in concentration, and wobbled it carefully round to sit by Tracey, she was astonished, but apart from a brief glance of welcome towards the empty chair beside her, she didn't react.

"Pass no heed," Eileen hissed to his grandfather, seeing him open his mouth in surprise.

"Lovely potatoes," Tracey looked serious, then smiled sideways at Tom.

"Granda burnted 'em," Tomas laughed.

Later Eileen described how he had barely laughed, barely spoken, been withdrawn and intense and solitary for the previous long year. School was looming. He should have gone to nursery this September. But he had screamed and panicked when they took him there. And sobbed so hard when they left him for the morning that he gave himself laryngitis. He was voiceless for a fortnight. The doctor was alarmed, thought he had become an elective mute. Luckily he was wrong about that. Said to leave the nursery for a bit. But how long could they do that?

After the meal Tracey instructed Tom, in a business-like way,

"Show me round your farm, then."

He took her hand and led her away.

They asked her plans. Though Eileen knew she had none, was free. And Tom seemed to be so taken with her. Also there was work on the farm. Their help was away at his mother's funeral in Wexford. They'd given him the week to sort out her things, as he was the only son. But it was a bad week. They had seven cows coming into season and the AI man on standby.

Tomas chose Tracey to do his bedtime story. It was only the afternoon. She had no intention of being there at bedtime. He snuggled up to her on the sofa to choose the book they might read. Tracey was cuddly, children and animals were attracted to her. She was also apprehensive. Although she was flattered by Tom's fondness, she knew it would quickly become cloying. The sooner she left, the better. The longer she stayed, the harder he would make it for her to go. She recognised something in him, she had seen so many little boys lost in so many homes. It was a void that he would fill up with her and all her attention. She was a safe outsider, a newcomer who brought no baggage. In his present chaotic world he was still too busy punishing everybody, including himself. Tracey knew if she let him, Tomas might quickly become dependent on her.

When she went to tell Eileen that she would be off now, Eileen stalled her with the polite ploy of just "a wee cuppa scald for the road". Returning with the tea from the scullery with her husband in tow, they sat her down at the table. Tracey began to get nervous, cast about for her backpack. It was conveniently near the door, ready for a swift exit.

"Look, we've a wee proposition," Tracey looked straight ahead. There was no way she wanted to be Tomas' minder. "We're real short-staffed this week. Johnny, that's our help, he's away for a funeral, his mother, god rest her....." There was a pause while the enormity of this sadness sank in.

"But," Eileen took over, "we've seven cows coming into heat. They'll be for the AI man sometime this week. But someone has to be here, available most of the time, to sort it out. Ideally, you have to get it within 12 hours or so of peak fertility, or it could be a waste of money."

"Excuse me," Tracey couldn't reconcile her preconception that they would be asking her to look after Tomas, with what she was now hearing, "What's an AI man?"

"Artificial Insemination, you know, where you buy sperm from a sperm bank, you know, like, if you don't have a bull of your own." Tracey's mind did somersaults, thinking back along the possible method of production of sperm and adjusting to the preposterous idea that they wanted her to somehow organise the insemination of cows! She couldn't believe it. Tomas didn't feature.

Her mind boggled and she began to giggle. The only time she had ever heard about such a thing as artificial insemination, was a discussion she remembered with Tim. But that was about men, blokes, humans donating to sperm banks. Tim had heard about the stacks of free dirty magazines they used. He had wanted to volunteer. She had laughed so hard, he'd never mentioned it again. But the idea of bulls flicking through mags full of sexy cows to get an erection made her roar. "How - do they - do it?" she eventually spluttered.

The husband and wife exchanged looks. It was so much a part of their way of life it simply didn't strike them as funny.

"Sorry, but do they have cow girlie mags? So the bull looks at them and gets all turned on?" One set of eyebrows was frowning in puzzlement, the other was raised in shock. Tracey realised that she had begun to get onto an unsettling theme. She tried to keep a straight face, "no, really, how can you get a bull turned on?" Then it dawned on Tracey that this might be something they preferred not to think too much about. But she couldn't really believe it, not when it was farmers talking about animals, surely!

"I'm not really sure," Shea had decided to deal seriously with the question, "I know they use a machine with a cow hide on it and I think they impregnate it (Tracey tried not to snigger at his choice of word) with the smell of a cow on heat. And then they have a tickling stick of course."

"Like Ken Dodd?" Tracey was off again.

"I s'pose it is funny really," but though smiling hard in empathy with Tracey, Eileen wasn't actually laughing.

Shea moved matter-of-factly on. "If you want a particular breed, you know, this is the best way - we like to get what's good for beef, but then if you have heifer calves, you need them to be good milkers too. Heifers don't put on as much meat for beef."

Tracey was getting lost. "Right, I see...." she said, clearly not. "What's a heifer? And," she suddenly remembered the proposition, "what was the proposition?"

"We had thought you might like to work for us for the week. I know you're looking for some work." Eileen sounded surprised that Tracey hadn't guessed.

"But, but," Tracey couldn't get the expletive out, "I don't know one end of a cow from another."

"You don't need to, the AI man'll know. And the cows aren't in the byre at mucking out time. Mind you, maybe....." Shea paused, thinking it over, "maybe it's not such a brilliant idea. People who aren't used to it, townies for example (mock snide aside) can't take the hard physical labour, nor the smell at mucking out time."

Tracey's face was eloquent with horror, "What, mucking out cow shit!"

"That's farm work, I'm afraid. I used to work in an expensive boutique full of clothes for country gentlewomen. A far cry! Not to worry. I don't blame you." Eileen was shushing her husband with her hand.

In the silence that slumped down round them, Tracey could feel their disappointment and resignation. Eileen wouldn't catch her eye.

"I'll be getting back to my nice warm work then, in the nice warm cow shed," and the old man rose. "It was a pleasure meeting you, ye're a wee dote, and shouldn't ye be going home to your mammy anyways. But, god willing ye'll pass this way again. Good bye and god bless."

"It's getting late, won't ye just stay tonight?" Eileen said, "It's too late to go looking for somewhere to stay now." Again she had found herself making an involuntarily offer, as though someone inside was controlling her. The Good Samaritan?

Despite Tracey's instinct to quit she was thwarted by her own stupid need to prove herself. She could muck out as well as the next man or woman. Why shouldn't she muck out farm animals? She was no smooth-handed townie. And it certainly wasn't beneath her.

They gave her a spare bedroom and promised to pay her at the end of the week. There followed eight idyllic pastoral days of hard physical labour. She was useless at it. They had to come behind her and remind her. "Shut the gate." "Don't let the unfertilised cows in with the others." "There's a feed dispenser empty."

But it was good to be on a farm. There were piglets. Outdoor smells, silage, hay barns, where Tom and Tracey romped. She, the more uninhibited child. He, having to push himself into acts of abandonment, whooping as he jumped from the top of a hayrick, learning how to have fun.

"When do you start school?"

"Never! I'm not going 'n'ere. I'm staying here wi' yous."

"I've got to go actually. I have to go to school, in England. I'm going to be a vet so that I can look after pigs like yours." The lie was so easy.

"When I'm the farmer, will you come and be my vet?"

"I surely will, pardner."

Leaving was going to be easier than she had thought. But now the decision was made, and Tom was primed, she had to go. While she packed, she instructed him to write down his address so she could send him a postcard of The Victory when she got back to Portsmouth.

"Can I visit you there?" he asked.

Tracey had herself faced too many false hopes in her brief childhood to lie about this to him. Tom might be constantly waiting for an invitation if she said yes. And it would never come. Though she would follow through on the postcard.

"I don't have my own house there. I live in a children's home."

Tom was wide-eyed. He couldn't believe it. Realisation grew. He knew what a children's home was. He'd overheard grown-up conversations. A children's home, the very sound of it, terrifying, formless, unimaginable and because of that, one of his darkest, unvoiced fears. Wasn't Tracey too big for a children's home? To him she was an adult. He stepped back, shocked. Maybe she was a Wendy. He'd seen Peter Pan and he knew all about children in Limbo. Limbo, children's homes and Never-never Land were one and the same to him. And they had one terrifying thing in common, children separated from their mothers and fathers. He whispered,

"Are your mammy and daddy dead too?"

"Yes, I think so." It was the simplest response.

*   *   *   *   *

It was almost October now. The days were rapidly shortening. Tracey wouldn't be able to sleep out much now without shelter, the dew was too heavy. She got a lift to Strabane with Eileen. There she met up again with Brian and Julie in the square, slithery with market day cow shit. That's how she had first met them, literally bumping into them, skiting about in the shite, them all laughing. That had been there the previous week, when she had gone into town for market day. This week they had arranged to meet and drink a few pints of Guinness in a bar on the square, rowdy with the festive air of market day.

Tracey didn't like the Guinness at first, but it was traditional. And after the first half a pint, it slid down so easily that when it was time to go, they had to help her out of the pub, and then hold her, laughing, while she was sick.

It seemed to Tracey, alternately swooning and concentrating on staying upright, fighting to stop the orange points of newly lit streetlamps from swirling nauseously round her head, that after only a moment's deliberation the kind couple decided they should take her home.

"It's your fault, ye moron ye! Why d'ye keep buying it for her? If she's sick in ma Da's car, they'll be ructions!"

"She'll be fine soon, but we can't just leave the wee girl here in this state. And it's not ya Da's car any more," he added gently. She shot him a pained look and her eyes filled with tears.

Half an hour of heated dispute left Julie and Brian in a nervous icy silence. They'd thought Tracey would have sobered in the time they'd spent arguing, but if anything she was worse. Every time she opened her mouth now it was a toss up between whether Tracey would spew out a stream of Guinness or drunken profanity in her ever-crescendoing

English voice. They bundled her into the car and asked her where she lived.

When Tracey was able to focus on the question, she pointed to the back pack, "That's my home," she slurred.

Bernard and Julie exchanged a look of undisguised horror. What had they done? More to the point, what had she done? Who was she on the run from?

Julie was from Coleraine. She was blond and pretty and sounded Scottish.

Julie's mother was very nervous at the prospect of having Tracey in the house; a little housing association house with three minute bedrooms where she had brought up nine children. Julie took it up as a personal challenge, a vendetta against her mother's repressive matriarchy, to keep Tracey there as long as possible; keeping Tracey an uncomfortable piggy in the middle.

Julie's mother would not let Brian in the house.

"Bree-an, why meake such a bug deal o' the pronunciation, what's wrong wi' good old fashioned "Brian"? I'm tellin' ye, there's trouble where he is." She could see nothing good in him. Which, Tracey could have told her, made him more desirable to Julie.

At Julie's insistence, Tracey stayed there for two nights, on a put-u-up on Julie's bedroom floor, listening to Julie's frustrations, the contradictions of her life. One sister married to a soldier in Germany, two married to unemployed men in the town. One knocked about by her husband. Nephews and nieces not much younger than she. Her father recently dead. She was nineteen. Tracey had arrived from nowhere, with no history, no connections, no opinions, no prejudices. The perfect companion for a fearful, directionless young woman trying to reconcile a desire to defy convention and escape her narrow life,with the powerful pull of generations of expected behaviour. Tracey symbolised both the promise of a better life elsewhere and the dangers that could befall a lonely girl. There was no real contest. Julie had none of the personal resources necessary for escape. She was marking time until fate would deal her a hand that would keep her here in the bosom of her family, something that would leave her unable to escape and with the perfect excuse for staying, something she could blame forever which would cover up her cowardice. Tracey understood Julie perfectly. She wondered whether Julie would be forced into giving fate a helping hand, by finding a job, or getting pregnant perhaps, or whether fate would get there first putting her mother into declining health or striking one of her sisters with a disability.

Tracey found herself creeping round the house, being helpful, obsequiously attentive to Mrs Brown's continual complaining. If it wasn't the weather, it was life without a man, useless and all though he'd been when alive; the grizzling and selfishness of her grandchildren was a recurrent topic, but seeing them walk past her house from school without calling in upset her; the delivery men, coal, bread and milk, were all out to swindle her, but the flirtatious way she greeted them all belied it; and the tender way she cared for Julie, her youngest, wanting to keep her at home, was at odds with her fulminations on the wasted opportunities Julie had let slip through her fingers.

It was the third afternoon of her stay in Coleraine. The peace was shattered by the loud approach of a motorbike engine. Brian, so proud, a new bike, Kawasaki green, had arrived in well-worn leathers and a scratched helmet, a spare over his arm, for Julie. The insurance from the last accident had come through at last.

Julie's mother and Julie fought loudly on the doorstep. Julie, careless of the neighbours, was shrieking her outrage. Her mother, firmly refusing to allow her on the bike, was holding on to her wrist, harder and harder. Julie finally wrenched away, flouncing down the road, hair clutched back out of her eyes, head down, mortified, furious. Brian called out to her.

"And you can fuck right away off," she turned to shout back at him.

"And up yours, wi' a whitewash brush," he muttered.

Julie's mother held her hands over her eyes. Tracey could see the tears. Her anxieties were a genuine fear for her daughter's safety, combined with incomprehension of Julie's position, and her general inability to cope with this daughter.

When she turned back from wiping her eyes, defiant, mistrusting, she said,

"Whyn't yous two go off and have youselves a nice day."

She didn't care about them. These two young people were symptoms of Julie's malaise, but she saw it wasn't their fault. Mrs Brown tried to tell herself they were part of Julie's personal protest, a justified protest against a hopeless future, cultures adrift, a country torn in two.

In the bar later, Brian's mates either refused to speak to Tracey at all,

"I hiate you, ye're English." Or they humoured her.

They all admired him for landing Julie. She was universally accepted as the sexiest woman in the town. She was his "little prod", or was he hers? When they walked in the bar, conversation hushed. Then little huddles would develop. Tracey was always excluded from these huddles and drawn into some peripheral meaningless banter where she was the butt of racist jokes against the English. Today there was Brian's new bike as a distraction for all to share. So Tracey stopped listening, trying instead to imagine being in Julie's position. So angry at such a loving mother. A mother who was there. Had never left.

Tracey's sense of her own mother, was a marshmallow memory, floating about ever more ethereally in a painful vacuum. She felt the familiar maudlin swell and looked round the dim interior of the bar for a distraction from "mother", which had become a solid emotion in her throat, which might result embarrassingly in tears.

A godsend had just walked in. Kieran. She'd seen him before, the other night. Every woman's dream. He was a stunner. Two-eggs-in-a-basket buttocks. She watched him surreptitiously. So comfortable in a body admired or envied by everyone, sometimes both. His easy body language. So aware that one smile or wink could dissolve any woman, any age. And then he looked over. And caught Tracey's eye. Smiled that smile. She couldn't believe it. She tried to hold his look, but couldn't, had to look away, down into her drink When she looked up again, he was still smiling at her and winked. She wriggled about on her bar stool, trying not to, and then giving in to imagining his hands on her skin. Sex with him.

As Kieran moved towards her she became aware of Brian talking about defining moments of his life. A small group had formed around her part of the bar, drawn to where Kieran was heading. He was like that, charismatic.

"A throbbing machine between your leather-clad thighs, hey! Vrrrrrrooooom, a real defining moment, eh Brian? Or maybe, more on the lines of milky white thighs for ye, Tracey, eh?"

Brian in his earnest way did not rise to this, nor to her amazement, considering how well respected he was for it in present company, did he claim the successful wooing of Julie to be his defining moment. He went up in her estimation, though all there would have thought it wet if he had. He plummeted again when announcing it was the original purchase of a motorbike that had defined his life.

Others competed for attention. Conspicuous by its absence was any mention of experiences personal, political or religious. Tracey knew she wouldn't be, but Kieran was asked. While he paused to think, Tracey felt he was not deciding what to say, she felt there was a clear defining moment in his life. He seemed to be deciding whether it would be appropriate or safe to tell it in present company.

"I mind it was my birthday. 8th March 1966. I was eight years of age. My parents took me down to Dublin for the day. A wee treat, like. Just me, ma brothers hadn't to go. It was my special day, just. We drove down, me Da'd the new car, well, new ta us anyways. The blue Zephir. Into the city we went, all singing, we'd some great crack on the way down. "God's own country," me Ma'd always say when we were down south. In them days you could drive right on down O'Connell Street, like; yous were right in the heart of the city. But this time, it was cordoned off and the Garda everywhere. There was a sense of excitement, you know, but no-one could tell us rightly what was going on. Didn't seem to know. We were stopped in the traffic, but we could see along O'Connell Street. 'Twas deserted. Pavements empty, not a soul about. Eerie, you know. There was the GPO looking grand, you could see the whole of the façade, especially with no cars on the street. Then there was the Nelson Pillar and I was just saying to me Da "What's Nelson to we Irish?" when "BOOM" there was this huge explosion.......You couldn't see what it was at first. Then when the dust cleared a bit you could see the pillar, Nelson's Pillar, was just a stump, Nelson was blown right off his pillar, couldn't believe it at first, kept thinking the dust would clear a bit more and we'd be able to see him up there like normal. But no, he was bombed off, gone, just leaving the stunted bit of the pillar and the base, like. Nelson, the Englishman, toppled off his Irish pedestal. And there was debris for hundreds of yards around. There was a hushed silence, then some people started to cheer. And me Da says real quiet like, "That's 50 years since the Easter Rising today. This very day." It'd been in his mind all along. I didn't know what he was talkin' about. Sure wasn't it momentous on my birthday. Significant somehow. You know when you're a kid things take on a significance they don't really deserve. Anyway it gave me an unnatural interest in the man, Nelson. It was only later I learned me da was a republican. When he left us all, the bastard, left me ma to fend for herself, look after us all......and she was from Unionist stock." This last was a quiet addendum almost to himself.

There was a hushed silence in the bar.

"1966, you say," old Tom was nodding, changing the subject, neutralising the charged atmosphere, finding a common, a safe, topic with no political overtones. Something that would unite them all.

"Sure, wasn't that the year....."

The whole bar, enormously relieved as the tension broke, all joined in raucously "......that...England won the world cup!"

"And didn't they just make sure we all knew it!"

"And here, they're still living on the one glory now."

"Amn't I tired hearing it." Laughter was sweet at the expense of the English on the football field. When it came to sport, no customer in the bar identified with the English.

A quick babble started up. An unspoken local code protected Kieran from being asked exactly why the blowing up of Nelson's Pillar had been the defining moment of his life. No one in this bar would risk pursuing any line of questioning that might lead to a sensitive, political public discussion. It would be the height of bad manners. Kieran's family background was well-known. Everyone except Tracey knew him to be cavalier, careless of his own safety, a big mouth, and consequently perhaps a dangerous man to be associated too closely with.

"So tell us why....?" But Tracey didn't get the question out.

"Whisht, would you," Brian whispered fiercely. Tracey didn't continue. It wasn't that Brian had told her not to, she didn't really care. She was only continuing the conversation to keep Kieran near. She just wanted to detain him so she could admire his body and fantasise. But he moved away, not interested in the resumed bike conversation.

"Valve, torque, acceleration, fuel consumption," all safe topics, but no interest to Tracey, not requiring her attention, she was free to slaver. A round was ordered and the group dispersed along the bar to claim their drinks.

"When're you away back over?" Kieran had suddenly come up behind her. He spoke very quietly. She could feel his breath on her neck. The sweet smell off his breath of the second or third pint of beer. Tracey went limp at the knees and wet at the cottonlined gusset. She turned to face him. Black curly hair, strong empathetic eyebrows, a concerned frown and an intense frank stare that left her feeling thrillingly naked.

"Haven't decided."

"Thought I might come with ye, I've a few things to do on the mainland. Not been over in years. I've an aunt in Birmingham. Be nice to see her. We could travel over together."

This sounded so unlikely, she almost laughed. He bought her a drink. She hung on his every word. He said how he didn't like skinny women, like Julie. Tracey had wondered why the gorgeous Kieran hadn't got her instead of the homely Brian. He told her he liked tits. Tracey's one sexy feature was her big bosom. She hated the inconvenience of it, but men always did look her right in the chest, straight down the cleavage. Kieran reached across and brushed his fingers across her left nipple. Even through the thickness of a sweatshirt, you could see it jump to attention. Tracey was helpless and enjoying herself. Kieran was in control and enjoying teasing her.

"In case we don't get to travel together, whyn't ye give me yere address over 'n'ere and I'll look ye'up."

"I don't have an address."

"What!" his face lit up with interest, "ye've no fixed abode, footloose and fancy free?" Kieran was becoming more and more interested.

"Well a children's home's my sort of base."

He could hardly contain his eyebrows from shooting up. He was impressed. If he'd said 'better and better' he couldn't been more explicit about how pleased he was with her or her situation. She didn't understand. He couldn't like big tits that much surely. Could he? She wrote down the address in Clarendon Avenue. Southsea. Portsmouth.

"Portsmouth, eh? That's brilliant. And what a coincidence, a very interesting place for a man with my interests."

Tracey was puzzled until Kieran explained again about his passion for Admiral Lord Nelson. Kieran knew everything about the naval hero. His relationship to Mrs Hamilton, the battle of the Nile, Trafalgar, "Kismet Hardy". He knew far more than Tracey. He enjoyed taking the piss out of her for knowing so little of the history of her own home town.

"Have you ever been to Portsmouth?" she asked. How could he know so much about Nelson without having been to Portsmouth? The thought that the two of them may have occupied the same space at the same time, at some stage in the past, was oddly exciting and seemed to give their current meeting a romantic significance.

"Have you?" He retorted sarcastically, "so ignorant of your own local hero, the greatest naval hero of all time! No I've never been, not yet," and he patted the address "I'd like to see the old bugger's warship. Still there isn't it? The

Victory? In the dockyard, behind the golden gate knobs? It'd be great to see it."

Brian was coming towards them, looking suspicious. Surely it couldn't be? Was he jealous?

Kieran whispered quickly before Brian drew level, "I'll meet you here tomorrow lunchtime to talk about the trip. Don't let on 'til the others. It's our secret, would n'a want my girlfriend to find out." He winked surreptitiously, then turned to greet Brian.

"Our secret", that blew it. A Sunday uncle phrase. Now she knew there was something peculiar about it, perhaps something really peculiar about him. Though Tracey had no idea what it might be. She'd always beaten the dodgy geysers at their own game before. She could ask for the address back, but then he'd be suspicious; anyway Brian was here now and he didn't need to know anything about it, certainly not how stupid she'd been to give Kieran her address. She wouldn't say anything to Kieran. She just wouldn't be here tomorrow. Simple. Sad though, he was tasty. But even the tasty guys, perhaps more so the tasty ones, could be perverts. Perhaps it was because it was always so easy for them to get laid, that they had to invent some kind of perversion to get off on. Weird.

"I'll see yous," and Kieran was off.

"What did he want?"

"Likes my big tits."

Brian looked amazed, then laughed. He was attractive when he laughed, though Tracey knew she couldn't trust her own judgement, she was still turned on from her proximity to the sex-god Kieran.

"It's a gri-ate afternoon, I've got a good place to show you, c'mon." And Brian took her hand.

*   *   *   *   *

The noise of the motorbike had stopped reverberating in her ears, and the crunch of the sharp screed underfoot became audible. Tracey paused to look around her, but it was not the view of rocky rolling uplands sweeping down to the sea that pulled her up short. It was the eerie sound, a deep whistling, an unearthly moaning.

Even the rise and fall of the stiff wind, which greedily snatched away every word they tried to say to each other and buffeted their dysfunctional ears, could not mask the haunting sound. It seemed to be inside Tracey's skull, reverberating through her sinuses.

Tall spindly towers supported sails which moved with mesmerising smoothness. They didn't seem to be disrupted by the gusting breeze. As she watched, Tracey found she could not avert her gaze from following each of the three sails in turn. She shut her eyes, but the unremitting sound penetrated and behind her eyes the propeller-like blades kept turning. Perhaps a little drunk still, Tracey felt a conspiracy in her own head disorientating her. She snapped her eyes open quickly to avoid stumbling with nausea.

There were about 20 windmills dotted over the bleak moor, a sparse white forest so tall so out of scale with the ground-hugging blueberry scrub that it was as if the two bikers had arrived from another planet. No one was about. There was no human presence, no sign of it, except an abandoned pile of builders' sand and the pristine paint not yet weathered. It was as though people had just left, or been assumed into the wide grey limitless sky.

"It's like we just landed from space, so weird......weirdly beautiful. Like, you know someone's been here, but they've deserted, as though it's set to blow up any minute." Tracey had to shout directly into Brian's ear.

Brian gave Tracey a wry look. She was forever saying inappropriate things, making unfortunate references, forgetting the sensitivities of her whereabouts, treading where angels fear to tread. And all in her damning English accent. And sometimes he suspected she knew well what she was doing, as though she was carrying out her own personal reconciliation campaign.

"Well this is Nor'n Ireland, things've been known to blow up here. Brian smiled as Tracey shrugged. She didn't care about putting her foot in it. She enjoyed playing the innocent abroad, and sometimes wasn't. She asked people in

100

pubs if they were catholic or protestant. She had even introduced two strangers by their different religions. Tracey in her alien naivety had need of neither tolerance nor understanding. Brian would be glad when she moved on, but she had been fun. He was sure she would move on now. She wouldn't go back to Julie's. That episode was clearly over. He would offer her a lift into Belfast for the ferry. She would refuse. Brian felt she was pushing her luck staying on. There was nothing for her here. She would never belong. But then she believed that there was nowhere that she did belong.

Chapter 10

"Get your fat black bastarding backside over here, you moron." A hissed shout.

Wilson ignored it.

"Where the fuck are you, bastard?"

Wilson strolled into view. He bent down and whispered in his comrade's ear,

"You know this is enemy territory. Keep your bleeding voice down, or they'll all know we're here and bring their grannies over to dance on our bodies when they've finished massacring us."

Hickson was scared. He was a recent arrival. He was nervous. Wilson's sangfroid, his calmness only exacerbated Hickson's feelings of cowardice.

"Where've you been?"

"Looking for a picturesque place to crap, I've found one."

"It might be boobytrapped."

"What a way to go."

"You can't go, it's against regulations."

"I'll risk the court martial. It may take me twenty minutes. Don't start anything without me."

"The other patrol'll be back soon, they'll know you're AWOL."

"0523 it is now. They will be back at 0600. I'll be back before then. I'll be near enough to come running if anything happens, even with me kacks down, eh?"

"Don't leave me alone"

"Fucking wise up, enjoy this b-e-a-u-tiful morning. And don'f follow me, I hate to be disturbed."

A fine mist hung in the wisps over the dewy grass that shone his boots better than anything he could've done for drill. The sun, a heavy red ellipse, heaved itself above the horizon to hang a moment irresolute before sending blushing fingers into the hedges, disturbing creatures, rousing birds. Over on his right, a barn, black and spindly legged, curved corrugated roof astride stacks of bales, was full to the rafters. The nook he had chosen in a loop of hedge around the field, faced into the sun. As he did up his fatigues, he could hardly see for the golden images burnt into his eyes. He left the belt til he could see the catch properly. Hoisting his weapon, he turned back towards the nervous Hickson.

The way the sun struck the hay made it shine like gold. Perhaps to spite Hickson, Wilson veered off to take a closer look at the barn, wanting to breathe in the hay. The barn was not packed solid. There was a corridor down the middle. He peered in as the sun illuminated it for him. He stepped out of his own shadow and a spotlight fell on to the red mound of.....a moment's panic, a body? a boobytrap?

He blinked, remaining calm, trying to clear his sunblind vision.

A sleeping bag.

And in it, as he approached, he saw a sleeper. One perfect bare white breast was visible where the T-shirt had rucked up and an arm had been thrown out of the protection of the bag. He could never have imagined a fantasy as good as this. Compelled, he had to keep coming nearer. He reached down and loosened his fly as the erection rose and hardened. The noise of his hand against gunmetal roused the girl. She would scream. He reached down quickly, she turned, opened her eyes, and smiled.

"I was dreaming about you." She said, flitting in and out of her dreams had been, Kieran.

"And I you."

She reached out her hand, languorous with sleep and wanting sex. He knelt beside her, pushing away the gun. She finished opening his fly and gasped at the size, the shiny, black, taut penis. She'd never really seen an adult erection by choice before. It was so beautiful, powerful and yet made him helpless with need. She ran a fingernail down to his root. He shuddered and split second pearls of sweat popped out on his forehead. He touched her breast, bent to kiss her nipple. Lifted off her clothes. The chill goose pimples increased her thrill.

"I never knew a woman so wet," he said with admiration.

"And so silky smooth inside, like this," his fingers were there.

"And up here, right inside, nice and bumpy, to get a good grip on a big cock."

Then Tracey did scream. She had never come like this before. He had found places inside she had never found for herself.

"I don't have any rubbers here honey, but I just got to put this cock in, just a couple of thrusts should do it, I'm so horny, then out. I won't leave any inside you. That OK?"

She reached down to help him. Eased down his pants, so he could balance on his knees. Reached through to grasp his balls one hand barely big enough for each.

"But I'm too small for it." Tracy realised.

"No, no, just a little at a time."

The tip of his penis found its own way, Tracey dropped open her legs. The tip rubbed, the space it needed widening, in a bit, a little more. She relaxed, she opened. Her wetness soaked everything. He couldn't get it all in. At its limit she squeaked with pain. He withdrew a bit and apologised, holding it back, setting up a rhythm. Suddenly she peaked again, lifted her buttocks and came hard down on him.

"Christ!" and he pulled back instantly. She watched his penis come out of her and a fountain spurted from him, his eyes rolled, he gripped her arms, shuddering his knees collapsed under him.

"I haven't come like that in years."

"Did we get it all out? I think we did. No thanks to you. Why'd you come down on me like that, you knew I was trying not to come."

"Couldn't help it, sorry."

Tracey wasn't sorry. She never knew it could be like that. So good.

"You better have my address, just in case."

"No I had a fallopian tube infection, I'm probably not fertile anyway."

"I got to get back, I'm Ben Wilson, who're you?"

"Gloria."

"Amen."

104

"He kissed her tenderly on the cheek. "You are so beautiful."

She smiled. He went. She lay there savouring the feeling, infused with warmth. Then dozed off. When she woke, she knew it had really happened from the damp, pungent smell they had made together, but the memory was already dreamlike, surreal, part of another existence. Pounding energy and bubbles of joy jumped through her veins.

*   *   *   *   *

"Grand morning, there."

"Brilliant."

"Sure, tis a dream of a mornin'."

"And for the time of year."

"You'd never believe it was October."

Everyone she met had a friendly word for Tracey. She knew she must have a fixed smile. She couldn't have shaken it off, if she'd wanted. They must read it in my face. I had sex. I had sex. Yes Yes Yes. I had sex.

The bakers' bread was hot. Tea would've been nice to wash it down, but she was down to her last £15. The emergency fund. And she still had to get back to Belfast for the night boat. A seventy mile bus journey would eat into that. Was there a bus from Draperstown? Where was Draperstown?

A neat elderly woman smiled at her as she sat on the bench tearing lumps off the bread. Her small white dog stopped in his tracks at Tracey's feet. What giveaway smell was she exuding? He cocked his head on one side, looked up at her, and peed on her boot.

"Oh I'm So So Sorry. Whatever can've got into hum? He never did the likes o that before."

"Oh so it must not be my fault, then." Tracey retorted with a cheeky smile. Where did that come from? She wouldn't normally have answered anyone back like that, especially a stranger. She felt good. Strong. Filled with sense of freedom and with it assertive self-confidence. It was as though giving up her search for her brothers, first Paul and then Tim, had released her. She was free. She had finally relinquished her need for any Paul or Tim. The process that had started on top of the world at Graignan fort had now been completed. Tracey felt she needed no one.

Dog owners never confess to any of their dogs' previous misdeeds. They always say, "oh he's never done that before" the inference being that the bite or attack or killing is the victim's fault. He's never eaten a child before, well not whole. Tracey began to giggle. The old woman looked concerned.

Och, wee girl, I'm so sorry. Jamie, why'd ye do that dirty thung? Would ye like a wee cuppa tea? That's ma wee house, there just fernenst the post office."

"That'd be lovely," Tracey swiped at her boot with a tissue.

"Here, I'll do that."

Tracey stood up to prevent an embarrassing scene, an old lady grovelling at her feet and hoisted the bag. The woman set off. Tracey followed, her soiled toe close to the white-ish hairy rump, hoping for an opportunity to help it along. Jamie kept glancing round, nervously.

It was good strong Ulster tea.

"Just what the doctor ordered, thanks."

And homemade cake, a vast range. Who did these lone women feed all their homemade cakes to, when passing Traceys weren't around? The old woman read her mind again.

"The postman always calls for a cuppa. His favourite's the Dundee. My husband was fro, Dundee, but he never liked the cake. Then the window cleaner likes the shortbread. My sister comes on a Wednesday from Maghera. I make the almond slices fresh on a Tuesday for her. And my neighbour's wee lad loves the wee buns. And it's a "wee bunse" to make them. We always have that wee joke. I mind the time he was born...was it? It can't have been 18 years ago."

Tracey stifled a snort at the thought of the wee lad enjoying that wee joke, as he downed pints of lager on a Friday night.

"I think you're an excellent cake maker. Maybe even exceptional. A million times better than my mum. And thanks a million, that's set me up really well." Full to bursting, Tracey surreptitiously slipped a last mouthful to the dog, not wanting to offend by leaving anything on her plate. But an empty plate was an invitation to have more pressed on her. No, no please no. Tracey was touched by the old woman's generosity. It was true Irish hospitality. And you'd never get the like in the south of England.

"Have you seen the Giant's Causeway yet, on your tour round?"

"No, not yet." It sounded familiar, but Tracey had no idea what it was.

"Och, you should. They say it's getting damaged by all the visitors. You want to go now, before they close it off liek your Stonehenge. Oh and the bridge, it's a good day today, it'll be open. Now what's that its name is? Over the water, a slatted bridge. I never did it meself, yet. No head for heights."

"I went to Griaghnan fort," Tracey volunteered. She'd created the impression she was a touring student, so had to have toured something.

"Oh, right."

Not well received. Too pagan perhaps?

"Carrick something."

"W'as 'at, Ma?"

The two women jumped. A large middle-aged man stood in the doorway holding the dog against his round belly with one hand. Sprouts of grey body hair tufted between the stressed buttons of his shirt. The dog licked his face, slavishly, whimpering slightly with pleasure. Tracey cringed. Time to go.

"The rope bridge, you know, what's it called? Carrick-a-........"

"Rede, Carrick-a-rede is it."

"We have a tourist here, visiting Northern Ireland (and god knows we could do with a few more tourists here) that hasn't been across that bridge. Nor been to the Giant's Causeway, I'm telling you."

"Well it'd be my pleasure to take you on a wee run up there today. We could do both in the Merc if we set out pronto. I've nothing else on, now I've seen to the cattle."

He fancied a little jaunt on this unseasonably sunny day. He liked showing off beautiful Northern Ireland, he was saddened by the bad press and the badness which kept bubbling up. It kept tourists away. For him it was the only place on earth. He'd given England and Australia a go, as a young man, no, this was the only place on earth for him.

Their hospitality was becoming oppressive. Why so friendly to a total stranger. Surely not just because of the dog pee. Things began to close in. Why were they being so nice? Panic rose. Why was Tracey so ungrateful?

"That's really good of you, but there's loads of things I haven't seen yet, so I'll be back. I'm planning my next trip already in fact."

That awoke real interest.

"When'll that be then, next summer maybe? Easter's usually nice. You could bring a friend. Now you'll promise to drop in here when you come won't you?"

"Right now I have to get to Belfast for the ferry."

"But it's now til the evening, or have they changed the timetable?"

"No, the evening, you're right." Tracey's willpower was seeping away.

"I'll just change out of my work clothes and I'll run ye up. There's a few things need there anyway and we've time to do the Antrim coast road. It's a small detour, but worth it. You'll love that."

How could she be so churlish and snub this enthusiasm, this generosity. It seemed so genuine, Tracey dismissed instantly the suspicious thought tht this man could have anything but honourable intentions.

"That's Jeffrey, my son. Such a good boy. He went to work in England, for a couple of years, on that power station, Dungeness is it? Then he tried Sydney. But he's much happier at home with me."

108

It was hard to believe but seemed to be true. All these mothers she'd met, not one of them anything like Tracey's. But who knew what secrets they may hide.

When he reappeared, washed, in clean shirt, large enough thank god, despite his gut he wasn't a bad-looking man. The sort you'd be happy to have for a father. His boyish exuberance at the proposed trip infected Tracey. She didn't believe he had any funny ideas, anyway she could handle it.

"Well if you're sure I'm not putting you out, Jeffrey.....I'd really appreciate the lift. My mum's expecting me tomorrow in Portsmouth, she'll be so pleased when I tell her how kind you've all been. Her family is Irish, she always talked about Irish hospitality." It was a rule back at the lodge, especially with Sunday uncles, always to say someone was expecting you at a certain time. They'd think twice before doing you in, if they thought you'd be missed.

Tracey had given in to the pressure of kindness, the kindness of strangers. It would save her from spending her cash and a drive along the coast sounded great.

The perfect guide, Jeffery pointed out every landmark. When it was subjective interest only, like the first dance he'd been to, the first place he'd sold a heifer, he mentioned it in passing and waited to see if Tracey bit before elaborating. He couldn't refrain from a detailed account of the best car he'd bought. It was a Vauxhall Viva, second owner, 7,000 on the clock, £275, and all because the woman selling wanted him to have her dead husband's car, almost a bequest. Jimmy Boyle had offered her £310, he knew for a fact, but he'd never let on to this very day, though they drank together every Friday night.

There wasn't time for the walk around the Giant's Causeway, but there was time for a quick look, along the path through the gap and round the first bend. She'd be able to get the gist of it there, the flavour of what a miraculous construction it was. For construction it was, built by god himself for their entertainment.

They drew into the car park. Such a careful driver, so neatly slotted into a space. And found themselves surrounded by.......Ferraris. Eight identical low-slung red machines, flattened there into the parking grids, one yellow slab and a black one, well camouflaged on the softening, black tarmac. Tracey was impressed, once Jeffery told her what they were and how many thousands of pounds was parked there. She didn't think they were pretty. Menacing if anything. A bunch of jolly people lounged on the wall of the visitor centre. All sunglasses, tight designer jeans and dyed hair in a pall of cigarette smoke. Tracey could hear their accents. She cringed, fake uppercrust English and Essex jarred uncomfortably. She wished she had been Irish.

They got out of the car, avoiding the stares and comments of the loud group. Sugar daddy! Maybe just daddy!

"Have you got a camera?" one of them asked Tracey.

"No." Her voice was flat.

"I have," volunteered Jeffery, eager to smooth any ruffles.

"Go and get it, then." There was a "my good man" understood, if not said.

When Jeffery returned with the instamatic, the man said: "OK bring it over here and you can get a photo of yourselves sitting in my Ferrari."

Tracey couldn't believe it.

"What! You are one sick tosser! Go wank in your wank machine....." she would have gone on, but Jeffery pulled her away. By the time they'd got to the official path they were in stitches, holding each other for support.

"What in Christ's name did he think? We're a pair of school kids want a photo to remember that eejit by? And his money."

"He doesn't know we know...shhhhh....but we know most people hire them for the day. And they come over here 'cos they think the starving poverty-stricken Irishmen will be impressed, and be much too thick to know......they hired it for the day."

"I'm ashamed to be English...........WOW! I see what you mean about the rocks."

They had rounded the bend and a pavement of uneven rock had come into view, waves splashing over the seaward side. Each component of rock was a hexagonal column. It

110

fitted its neighbour exactly, like a jigsaw. But each was a different height from its neighbour, not as dramatic as organ pipes, more like crazy paving through a vertical plane. Tracey trod gleefully from one level to the next, hollows smoothed by wave action, chips lost from corners, slimy seaweed slippery underfoot. Jeffery pointed out the landmarks. There was a formation called 'the organ' consisting of a row of hexagonal columns arranged much like church organ pipes, wedge into the cliff face.

"It's incredible. Really incredible! I'll have to come back, I promise I will and walk round the top path next time."

Jeffery was delighted that she was impressed.

In the comfortable old Merc again Tracey sat back gazing out at the sunny autumn landscape. The purple Sperrin mountains way off to the right. And there really were the forty shades of green, in the patches of paddock, swathes of green grazing, split by neat pleats of the still-green hawthorn hedge. In a stubbled field awaiting the plough, on a dome of land, columns of beech trees were crowned with the red and gold of the turning season. In her search for Tim she had found so much. A whole country and a diverse people.

Tracey knew that returning to England would mean cutting the last tie, it would mean giving up the search for Tim and all that that represented. The search had for so long been her only goal. It had been her focus in an otherwise aimless life. Everything in her life had previously seemed incomprehensible, fundamentally meaningless. And within that, the search for Tim had been one of the only stable elements. It had been her excuse, a reason for deferment of deciding what she would do with her life, what she wanted, where she would go. But now she felt free and strong, grown up, able to move on, enriched by her odyssey. Life and time were all she had. All she needed.

Chapter 11

Pearl opened her eyes. But the sudden brightness of vision, pushed back her initial sense on waking, smell, a pleasant smell. She had awoken with the smell of flowers in her nose. She shut her eyes again. There was the smell again, but illusive. Flowers. It was on her left, very near, she struggled to locate it, breathing in deeply. She opened her eyes again, looking far over to the left, widening her eyes, stretching her eyeballs round. On white she could see something dark. It was her own hair, smelling of flowers. She smiled. Near the top of her head, light came, with something moving, wafting there. But right in front of her eyes, what? She tried to focus. Flat white, hard-edged. At its edge, a plastic water jug - on its side? With its orange lid flap. And a blue shape, some letters written down it. Pearl knew from this evidence that she was lying down on her side, flat. And consequently helpless. She tried to move. A shudder of muscle left her exhausted, but in the same position. She began to panic. Pearl knew someone must have put her in this position. For as long as she could remember she had never lain down on her side like this. Her mother had always propped her up to sit, or slid her down to lie on her back.

Pearl could hear movement somewhere near. She grunted loudly, forcing air up her throat, she sent out a calling noise. She looked round the other way, to her right, the direction that would eventually turn her over onto her back. With a huge effort, she threw all her strength into twisting her head round to follow her eyes. She thought of the right shoulder and willed it over backwards. Then she thought of the left shoulder and tried to shrug it under and pull it free. Her own body weight helped and she was half over. Her right arm fell back, pulling her further over. Her body and legs remained pinned. But now at least she could see into part of the room. There was a bed and someone walking by. Pearl was familiar with the ward now.

"Ahhh…" Pearl shouted a guttural sound asking for help.

Soft footsteps approached.

"Morning, Pearl, hey, you've moved by yourself. Are you comfortable?"

"Nnnnn....oh!"

"Will I help you turn you over?"

"Nnnnnn.....oh!"

"Sit up?"

Pearl nodded and smiled, "Mmmmmm," she made her assent clear. Pearl had learned that this nurse, the skinny one, though kind, was impatient with patients. She would only wait a moment or two for Pearl to speak. She did not understand that Pearl knew precisely what words she wanted to use and that she wanted to show that she could use the same language as those around her, a language of sentences and expression where every word had its place. Pearl's perception was that she could do it. The time it took her to get the words out, the minutes she spent working up to one small word, an 'and' or 'the', sped by for her because of the effort it took. But this nurse did not understand and wished someone would teach Pearl a form of shorthand. Why did she have to include every 'if', 'and' and 'but'? Nothing made her more irritated than waiting for a gem that would turn out to be (to her mind) a completely redundant 'please' or 'thank you'. Somewhere in Pearl's past was a strong thread of politeness training. She was keen to show she knew how to be polite. This nurse spoke to Pearl in monosyllables in the subconscious hope that she would do the same. But Pearl only picked up on her impatience and her anxiety to be always somewhere else, or for it to be someone else's job to be dealing with Pearl.

"I'll get Gaynor to help us."

With one under each armpit it was easy. Pearl indicated her drink, which clamped between her two hands she could hold just still enough to suck on the straw. Pearl sat watching the ward, waiting for breakfast.

After breakfast would come the physiotherapy, in the pool, lifting weights, breathing, tensing and relaxing. Saying 'hello' to parts of her body, trying to connect what happened to them, with what went on in her head. Then, a long sleep until lunch. After lunch Teresa, the volunteer, came to show her pictures and tell her stories.

For four days the routine had been the same but the food had been wonderfully different each time. Pearl was more than anything determined to learn how to feed herself. She loved the taste of the food, but was frustrated by her inability to get it into her mouth and soft enough to go down her throat.

*   *   *   *   *

"But we have no record of this patient."

"Strictly speaking Pearl Johnston (I wonder if that is her name?) isn't a patient, there's nothing medically wrong with her that wouldn't be covered by an assessment of her disabilities. The cuts on her hands are healing. The bruise on her face has reached the yellow stage. People don't get a hospital bed for cuts and bruises, nothing's even broken,"

"Except her home and care arrangements….."

"That's social services responsibility. Not ours."

"Has a full assessment of her disabilities been done yet?"

"I don't think so,"

"We can make it our responsibility to do that can't we? We can do that here on E5 because that's what we do with stroke patients."

"But she isn't a stroke patient. We are funded for them. We are not funded for cases such as Pearl's."

"But we have the facilities here. And they're underused."

"I cannot authorise it, we won't get funding for it here, she'll have to go to Braeburn Lodge for that."

"If she goes there, she'll be festering for weeks, you know what it's like there."

"But they have the facilities to care for her there, we don't."

"That's all she'll get, there, fed and washed. I firmly believe from the way she's been responding here, that if she continues to get the right physio and stimulation now - which we are giving her here - she'll make rapid progress. She'll be able to move on to sheltered accommodation. That's got to be the best thing, surely you must agree. If she goes over there and has to wait, she'll sink into a passive depression like before the accident. I think the accident might be what's shocked her into this current period of activity and motivation. She is trying so hard. If you could see her in action, she is so determined."

"I can't fund it. I don't have the staff to care for her. I've had complaints from some of them already. And here," pushing a letter under his nose," Mrs Scott's daughter has complained that too much time is spent on Pearl at the expense of the other patients. Even the families have noticed. It's my job to deal with this. I can't fund it."

"Won't. Pearl's family isn't going to give you any trouble. There'll be no complaints from them. She's easy for you to ignore."

"That's where you're wrong, she is impossible to ignore, too many of the staff are interested in her and the geriatric patient's are losing out. Look, I'm sorry Howard, it's not on."

"OK , I've an idea, I still have that bursary to set up a research project. It's in my gift and I've been umming and ahhhing for ages about where best to spend the money. I have a student in mind. Pearl will be my patient. I'll take her onto my own personal caseload. All you have to do is turn a blind eye to her continued presence here til I can set it up officially and then, if you would please, sanction the use of our equipment here, which we'll arrange around your timetable. What do you say? Come on Zara, give me that."

"God, you really are a determined man, Howard."

"No, I'm just a doctor, seeing an opportunity to help a patient improve. I'm not an administrator. I don't care about the funding. That's why I couldn't do your job….and you couldn't do mine."

"Yes, I'm a heartless old bitch. Won't you need to get her written consent to be part of the research?" Her parting shot, wishing him well in his endeavour! He knew she was annoyed that he had dared to cross her, but more annoyed that he had trumped her. She couldn't in all conscience stop him if his research fund covered it. He wondered if she would be pedantic and petty-minded enough to bill him for the use of the equipment. Her terror that something might be slipping from her personal control would probably make her want to do it, if it were not for the fact that she could be almost guaranteed to forget about it in a couple of days. She was one of those people who felt they have to do everyone else's job as well as their own because she believed no one else could be trusted to do theirs properly. She would overburden herself so much that she often couldn't even remember the tasks she had set others to do. Consequently, most of what she threatened could be ignored until at least the third time of mentioning. Her desk was groaning with memos – more unnecessary work she couldn't keep on top of - from staff who had been forced to keep records of and send her copies of every conversation. She panicked if she did not have her hand on the joy stick at all times but didn't seem to realise that the way she worked meant that she was incapable of controlling anything effectively.

Zara painstakingly slotted her papers into her sectioned bag, to show how well-organised she was and stood up to go.

Tracey stepped back round the corner out of sight. She had stopped to listen when she had heard Pearl's name and witnessed the whole conversation which had taken place in the nurses' station, the door open throughout for any passer-by to hear. Such was their sensitivity to the patients on this ward and their families.

As Zara's self-confident heels clacked out of earshot, Tracey heard Howard repeat under his breath,

"A heartless old bitch indeed."

She scuttled quickly past the nurse's station on her way to visit Pearl.

What was going to happen to Pearl then? This was all new ground for Tracey. Until a few days ago she hadn't known anything about hospitals or disabled people. She'd only come here to spite Bernard. Travelling down the corridor that first time, hadn't she sworn to herself that hospital visiting would never be on her CV under voluntary work? And here she was. But so much had happened in the last few days.

Pearl was asleep when she arrived. Tracey lowered herself quietly into the straight-backed orthopaedic chair by the bed. It was so comfortable, even for a short-arse like her, with the extra cushion Pearl used. And conducive to reflection.

It didn't sound too good to Tracey that Pearl should be the subject of someone's research. On the other hand, it seemed that Mr Howard, apprentice deity, Chapman, consultant in neurology no less, had his heart in the right place. He seemed to be saying that he only thought of the research route as the best, or perhaps only, route for some sort of rehabilitation for Pearl. If he was to be believed and her eavesdropping was accurate. And as he said, she was making such amazing progress, communicating and moving, using muscles, making demands. It would be a shame to lose the impetus for that. She couldn't wait to talk to Bernard about it. It was weird, but they were a bit like a pair of long lost siblings to Pearl, staggering their visits, putting in time helping her with the physiotherapy exercises and talking, bringing her things. Siblings? or perhaps a pair of mismatched parents.

Parents! Mother. Tracey resigned herself, wearily, to the memory. She let it surface, again. It was constantly jostling with all the everyday stuff these days, just behind her eyes it seemed, since every time she closed them, she saw him.

Stocky and strong-looking, a bit short for his age. Tight black curls, not afro, more Irish-looking black curls. And dark, the skin of a Greek fisherboy at the end of summer. Dark hazel eyes in a wide face, even featured and a neat nose, sensitive lips, a huge smile. He had greeted her with that huge smile, white teeth too big for his jaw as yet.

She had seen that smile before. Fleetingly. Once.

From across the concourse on Salisbury station, she had seen him, known it was him. Seen him arrive with a tall middle-aged man. As they parted he had indicated the café where he would watch the rendezvous. She had left a photo of herself with social services. Darron knew who he was looking for. As soon as he spotted her, he moved towards her, armed with that smile.

How could he smile so warmly? At her? Probably it was a sign of how secure and happy he was. Perhaps he thought her funny. She was so short and plain and rather round, with her chopped black hair, loose T-shirt and big boots. Surely she cut a comic rather than a maternal figure.

No, more likely, his powerful smile helped settle his nervous stomach.

Pearl stirred and Tracey prepared to give her the new sports drink she had brought, in a dazzling triangular pyramid, boasting vitamins and bursting with energisers, and not a word about quenching thirst. But Pearl relaxed again and slept on.

Tracey continued her bedside vigil, but under Tracey's wavering gaze, Pearl's face, so pretty in sleep, became transformed into Darron's. Had his parents ever had to sit like this at his sick bed? She felt her face crease into that embarrassed smile she used to disguise an awkward situation. She, the neglectful child mother, they, doing her job. The thought crystallised. It was at this moment that Tracey felt a little part of her inside die, a canker of hatred she had incubated for nearly 30 years just withered and died. She had despised her own mother for as long as she could remember and in this exact moment she was abruptly deprived of her justification for it. How could she not understand her mother's inability to bring up her own child. Here she was pretending she could be a responsible friend to Pearl.

Be honest, Tracey, here was another nine day wonder on its way! It would be the same with Darron. She was thrilled to be reunited, but would she have what it took to sustain a relationship? She had inherited this terrible flaw from her own mother. They were as bad as each other.

If Darron's brilliant smile was, like Tracey's, a nervous response to any awkward situation, it seemed to be the only thing that he had inherited that from her. He had inherited nothing else that she could recognise as coming from her. Though she was dark-haired, she was blue-eyed with the whitest of Celtic skin. His dark skin came from his dad, his teeth too. Maybe his shortness was her fault, but was his dad short? She wouldn't know, she had never stood up beside him. All she could remember was his smile and the most exciting part of course.

Then Pearl woke, smiling. She moved her head round to see Tracey. Tracey said 'Hi!' and waited for Pearl to open the conversation.

"'elp…me…si'….up….p..lea…." Pearl had so much more upper body strength now that Tracey, on her own, could just about manage to help her up.

The physiotherapist had been teaching her to breathe out each word, so her speech, though hesitant, was more recognisable as speech and consequently had become more comprehensible. Enunciation was still unclear and would be for as long as Pearl's jaw and tongue remained out of her control.

They had fun with the triangular drink. Tracey had thought it would be easy to grip. But it was hopeless. They both got into a giggling sticky mess. It was the first time she had seen Pearl so girlishly happy.

*   *   *   *   *

The letter Darron had written to Tracey asking for the meeting had increased by 25% her mementos of him. He had asked her for any mementos she might have of his origins. He particularly wanted a picture of his birth dad. He wanted to talk about him. Tracey felt terrible. By way of answer she said she would see what she could come up with, just playing for time and wanting to make another appointment to see him, anxious not to lose him again. His adopted father was clearly not happy that they should meet again. She had watched them from the concourse that first time, when they returned, watched their conversation through the café window, the father's body language. It must have been really hard for him. But Darron touched his hand, his shoulders bent forward, his head down, caring, reassuring. What had he been saying…..?

"Don't worry, you know you and mum will always be my true parents." Or,

"I'm to write when I'm ready to see her again. She's going to bring me a couple of things, that's all. But I wanted to tell you first before arranging it. It'll be the last time I see her. My curiosity about her is satisfied now."

                    *   *   *   *   *

Pearl still slept and Tracey had no more time. She crept out,
then returned to leave Bernard a scribbled note on Pearl's
bedside table:

"Meet you tonight in the Museum (pub!) I'm meeting
Isabelle and Marc there at 7.30. I've got some news for you –
Tracey."

                    *   *   *   *   *

Under the bed in her room Tracey kept her life. She slid it
out. It was all contained in a miniature cardboard suitcase.

A knock on the door stayed her thumbs on the catches.

"Come in, it's not locked." It never was.

"Hi!" a ginger haired gangly man slid round the door
and shut it behind him.

"Miguel, hi. How're doing?"

"Fine, whatch'ye got there then?"

"A little brown cardboard suitcase!"

"Yes, OK. I've never seen one so small, it's sweet.
Where d'ye get it?"

"It's a family heirloom. Correction it's the family
heirloom."

"Tell me more?"

"You're joking, right?"

"No." He wasn't.

"Well, of course my greatest inheritance is the family
ivory......my teeth!" Tracey snapped them together for him,
"my mother's side. And I've treasured them ever since,"

"Yeah, right, I know all about the special toothpaste!"

"OK...... the suitcase. Stop me when it gets boring,"
she drew a deep, dramatic breath. "It was given to me by my
grandmother not long before she died. (Violins) I must've
been about three at the time.... When me and my mum used
to go round to Granny's flat, it was the only thing there that I
really enjoyed playing with. I remember I could open the
catches by myself. I used to lift out some little books that were

120

in it, probably diaries, then some papers tied with that hairy string that you could unravel into horse's tails…."

"What?"

"You know? Oh, never mind. Then there was a box of beads and some teaspoons in those special cases. Like souvenirs. Yeah? Then after I'd taken them all out, I used to put them all back in again. Bored yet? Then I would repeat the game for hours while my mother pretended not to be crying and Granny struggled to breathe. Then one day the suitcase wasn't there. I asked and asked. But neither of them listened. I cried and shouted and tugged. They shushed and pushed me away. Then, as we were leaving, Granny gave me the suitcase and told me I could take it home with me. I was instantly mollified, I remember, I was so excited on the bus, but mum warned against opening it till we got home. I clutched it possessively to my little chest all the way. It was nearly as big as me then. The anticipation is as poignant to me now, as it was nearly 30 years ago, you know. When we got home, before the front door had closed, I laid it on the floor and unclicked the fastenings, I lifted the lid……and I could not believe it. It was empty. I shrieked with disappointment and mum came, she momentarily forgot her own miseries and I think she was as surprised as I was. I asked her where all the things had gone. I've invented a new word for that feeling."

"What's that?"

"Anticipointment."

"Impressive!……..for a three year old!"

"No, wise guy, I've invented it since! Well I think I invented it, but of course we all know nothing's really original, don't we? I remember what she said, she said, "It's yours to put your own things in now." She must've realised the old woman's mistake, Granny thought it was the suitcase, not the contents that were important to her "littleTracey". Mum told me later, she had a suspicion my Auntie Jackie got the contents. She was always Granny's favourite. Anyway I remember to this day what I said, I howled it actually, "I ha'n't got no own things.""

"Oh wow, what a sad story."

"Do you think I actually remember saying those words? I feel as though I do. Or has it become my memory just through constant repetition in my head. You know, like photos of yourself as a baby, that you can't possibly actually remember, but feel as though you can because the photo makes it so familiar. I think a photo can make you have a "memory" of somewhere even if you've never been there, especially if you visit it in a dream."

How prophetic that three year old was, thought Tracey.

So what's in the sweet ickle suitcase now?" asked Miguel.

"Birth certificate, that sort of thing. What did you actually come for?"

"Borrow something,"

"Yeah, OK, what?"

"Can't remember now!"

"You'll be back then, when you do," effectively dismissing him. She needed to get the things for Darron.

As he turned to go, she opened the suitcase. Did he really suddenly remember what he wanted? Or was it just curiosity about the contents of the case? At the door he turned back.

"I remembered,"

Tracey slammed the lid down, almost guiltily. The draught wafted a yellowed newspaper cutting out of the case and onto the carpet beside her. She picked it up and drew it to her chest so he would not see it. But he had seen the headline:

GIRL SETS FIRE TO HER SCHOOL

"File paper, that's what I wanted to borrow." Miguel pretended not to have seen.

"Not newspaper? Or a box of matches? Look, I know you saw it, and now you want to know the story."

"None of my business."

"But you'll keep wondering and imagining a worse story than it is, if I don't tell you." Tracey waved the cutting. "It was my sister, actually." Tracey found it hard to lie to people she respected. She judged whether people were worthy of her trust by whether she would be able to lie to them - not a foolproof method. Miguel, an honest, straightforward, uncomplicated person always knew when people were lying to him. He didn't always let on.

"You don't have to tell me anything. I'm not even curious. But," he knelt down and looked in her eyes, "it is about you isn't it? You don't have a sister."

Limply, she handed the cutting over. It included the date. Miguel quickly calculated it was 18 years old.

A 15 year old schoolgirl was helping Police with their enquiries last night after fire destroyed the main hall and four classrooms at West Borough Special School, Travis Road, Southmere. Fire fighters fought the blaze for four hours before finally gaining control.

One member of the fire fighting team is suffering from the effects of smoke inhalation due to noxious fumes from plastic computer casings. The east wing of the building was completely gutted by the flames, which could be seen from five miles away.

Mr Tim Casey, headteacher, said he was sickened and shocked by the news.

"Luckily the caretaker does not live on site, so he was not in danger. But we have recently installed a new computer suite. It is totally destroyed. We don't know for certain what caused the blaze, but there is a possibility that it was an arson attack. I cannot say how upset I am at this appalling news."

But while the headteacher was being interviewed by reporters, the news came in that a 15-year-old pupil from the school, who cannot be identified for legal reasons, had given herself up to police. She had previously telephoned this newspaper to make the following statement:

"I'm destroying them, just like they've all destroyed me. I'm nobody. I have no qualifications. I was sent to this school for bad behaviour when I was ten and they never gave me a chance to improve myself. They always made me feel I was stupid and useless. I never got to use those new computers. They told me I did not have the aptitude to learn."

"I don't want to talk about it."
Miguel handed it back, "I don't want to hear about it. That girl then is not the same as you now."
He bent and kissed her cheek.
"Anyway, I was 14 not 15, I think."
"File paper?" he reminded her.
Tracey pursed her lips to suppress the rising tears at his kindness, and managed to laugh,
"Buy your own, you scrounging bastard! First toothpaste, then change for table football, then it was.......a thesaurus? And a whole load of other things, now file paper....." Tracey laughed off the emotion he had sparked.
"See, that's true friends."
In the few weeks she had known him, he had become as close to her as a – she hardly dared acknowledge it to herself – a brother. Another brother. Another in the long line of replacements for Paul.

*   *   *   *   *

The only colour in the garden was the litter which had blown in under the gate, turquoise and green crisp packets and red chocolate wrappers blossomed. Even the evergreen leaves were a murky mud colour reflecting the grey afternoon light. The doorbell only worked when Tracey rotated the button and it made a thin connection which fizzed into the house, thin and unconfident.
Tracey was nervous, as nervous as she could ever remember being. She glanced up and down the road. Any distraction from the difficult exchange ahead. Next door's forecourt was a winter parody of a Mediterranean patio, terracotta pots, with sad cordalines and wispy palms. The other side was a concreted dogs' toilet. She was relieved that the dark shape behind the glass front door was clearly Darron. He opened the door.

"Come and meet my friends."

In the living room, silently heavy with her arrival, there were four boys ranging from three-ish to 16, an odd grouping of "friends".

A female voice, nightclub dark, called from the kitchen. "Hello."

"It's OK Mrs Kidd, it's for me." Darron sounded confident. He felt safe here. He was in charge. Tracey, the parent, was the junior player.

Tracey did not want to talk to Darron in company, so they sat awkwardly in silence for a while. She felt no urge to engage with this family, though she told herself it may be a sort of test. A cat walked round her legs and the youngest child broke the tension, asking her did she have a cat. They chatted. Then one by one the boys left except the eldest.

"This is Thomas, he's like me, you know, adopted. That's how we met at a sort of club. And he's my friend, that's why he said you could come here to meet me. You know my dad, I mean Brian (not my birth dad) doesn't like me to see you."

"I can understand that." Tracey suddenly realised that there was much that she could not understand. How was this Darron her lost baby? It was impossible to reconcile the two in her head and make them one individual. This young man was the angry, squawling, purple infant they had made her suckle. He had always been there, hiding inside her. She felt queasy.

Realising that Thomas was staying, she launched into the purpose of the visit.

"I haven't got much for you. They thought it best if I gave everything to your adoptive parents. What do you know about me?" She had no idea where to start, how much to tell.

"You were in care, that's all I know." He was being very cautious. "What about my birth dad?"

"He was a soldier. He was black and very handsome," she bit off the comparison, 'like you', that shot to mind.

"He was very proud of his uniform, shiniest boots you ever saw," this was pathetic, Tracey was unable to stop herself from drivelling out details that pointed more and more to a one-night stand with a total stranger. "He was a corporal, but the others didn't like him because he was black and because they were afraid and he never was. That's what he told me anyway." Darron would never know she was making it up. He would find it difficult to believe that they exchanged only half a dozen words and those all specific to their activity at the time.

"What was his name?" She had anticipated this and prepared a name, Charles Stanley.

"Wesley." Tracey couldn't believe she had said "Wesley". Where had it come from? Perhaps it was his name, perhaps he had told her, but in the heat of the moment it hadn't registered.

"Wesley what?"

"I........." She couldn't say Stanley. Wesley Stanley! No one would believe that.

"You don't know." His voice was flat with – disapproval? Disappointment? Determination not to reveal any emotion? Tracey understood why Thomas had to be there, staring at the floor, but listening intently.

"No. I only knew him a short while. I was on a quest at the time looking for my......brother. I didn't have time to - I wasn't capable of - making relationships with people. I was still trying to piece my family together. Your father was very kind to me. He made me feel valued and beautiful."

Why had she said that? Did she want Darron to feel something for her? How could he feel anything except dislike. How easily dislike would become disgust. He was certainly not smiling now. He had only one purpose, one piece of business to deal with.

"So," quickly changing the subject, "how tall was he?"

"Average. Because I'm so short, I'm not a very good judge, but he wasn't specially tall. He had really good muscle tone, very strong, a wonderful smile, just like yours," this time she couldn't stop the comparison slipping out.

"What about hereditary diseases, illnesses?"

The bluntness of his question shocked her. The implications of the question left her breathless. "I've no idea."

"What about you?"

126

"Sorry, no idea, about my own family either. I haven't gone down with anything yet. I'll let you know, if...." She heard her voice, it sounded bitter. What right had she to be bitter. "Why, have you........?" her voice trailed off. It was none of her business. He ignored her.

"Did he look healthy?"

"I can honestly say, I've never met a fitter man. I never saw him drink alcohol or smoke, he cared about his health."

"Where was he from?"

"London," what did it matter? He had a London accent? The bigger the place, the less likely Darron was to look for him."

"Did he know about me?"

"No, of course not," why did she say that?

"Why of course not? Was he married?"

"He didn't say, but looking back, I think he probably was." She felt herself wanting Darron's sympathy? Tracey felt pathetic, small, wormlike, worthless - and shrinking. All those feelings she had been familiar with throughout her young life and which she had only recently shaken off.

"Dirty bastard." Did Darron mean him or her?

Tracey opened her mouth to correct or modify the prevarication, but couldn't. What did it matter? There was no possibility of Darron ever tracing his father.

"I have some photos of my family. But none of him or his family I'm afraid. Would you like to see them? And I've got this."

Tracey leafed through her bag and brought out an A4 envelope. Inside were a few photos, but it was the small white tattered piece of folded paper that she passed him.

"What is it?" He did not reach out for it, but eyed it suspiciously.

Tracey gingerly unfolded the paper and passed him a piece of pale blue plastic. He did not want to take it, but overcame his urge to recoil. A lump rose in his throat. He felt ill. When he looked at it, he was none the wiser. It was a tiny band with holes and a stud fastening. It widened out to accommodate a clear plastic label on which was written in faded biro "Baby Allsop". When he read it, he knew it must be from the maternity hospital where he was born. His tag. It was a piece of rubbish. She'd kept it for 17 years. It was pathetic, sentimental. It made him feel angry with her, but also very, very sad. He did not want to think what she must have been feeling then. But here was tangible evidence of her pain and regret. He wanted more than anything to reject this thinking. He wanted to throw the nasty bit of rubbish back at her, to reject her, like she had rejected him. But inside he knew she had been faced with no other choice. Darron experienced, as he had so often over the years, the terrifying, certain knowledge that his very existence was a minor miracle. That unreal sensation tingled through him, he tried to push it back. It was such a huge feeling he was afraid it would blow the top of his head off if he gave it free rein.

The miracle was that he out of so many millions, had not fallen under the shadow of the abortionist's knife. And, in front of him now was the one person who could answer his question "Why am I here?" It was knowledge he would never be ready to deal with.

"And," Tracey was holding something else, small like a pen top. When he looked up and she saw how pale and shaken he looked, she withdrew her hand. Was it all too much for him? Or not enough, just revolting and pathetic and inadequate?

"I'm going to put the kettle on." Both started, they'd forgotten about Thomas.

"It's revolting really," Tracey said after the door had closed, "this is the clip that was on your umbilical cord. That I kept it is a sign of what a sad, mad, disgusting, pathetic old woman I am." She was smiling. Trying to be funny.

Gritting his teeth, Darron held out his hand. There was nothing he wanted less than to hold the gruesome grip, with its serrations and…..No, Please NO, what was on it? A bit of blackened gunge - his blood where it had mingled with hers? He felt faint. But he held it briefly because he knew he would always regret it if he hadn't. When it lay in his hand what he felt was not the mingling of their blood, but his utter, desolate, final, separation from her. He passed both mementos back. He couldn't speak.

"Don't you want them?" she asked. But she saw that he didn't. That the whole thing had horrified him. That she had totally misjudged everything. Again. Another mistake.

There was no hope of recovering the situation. She put the envelope away without showing him the photos. She rose to go, calling down the hall towards the kitchen where she could hear Thomas.

"Sorry Thomas, I've just realised the time, I've got to go. I'll have to say no to the tea. Thanks anyway."

"That's alright. Bye then."

"Bye Darron." There was no point in apologising to him. Communication between them was impossible because her rehabilitation was impossible. She was unforgivable.

*   *   *   *   *

By the time Bernard arrived, Marc was well away, rocking to the band, slopping "ze 'orrible English warm beer" around him. Isabelle was looking fed up. Considering how rude Marc was about the beer, he managed to consume a lot of it. They were very hard up, both of them living on the money she earned working anti-social hours at the ferry port. She was supporting Marc in supposedly learning English so he could get a job. He had found the right English class at last and found himself to be an instant hit; one of only three men, by far the youngest, sporting a long blond pigtail, a hippy jacket and the sunniest smile east of Frank Sinatra. He was basking in this scholastic popularity, having been expelled from all his schools in France, a Camusian non-conformist. His English was improving so rapidly that Isabelle was discomforted by it. He did all the talking in shops now. He spoke to strangers and had made more English-speaking friends than she had even met in her closed world of the ferry marshalling yard where everyone spoke French. She was the one doing a degree in English, trying to fit in this one year at the local university with the ferry job. A one year course where all the other students were foreign and the only native English speakers were the lecturers; and she only respected one of them, and he was Irish always talking about the "troubles" – a very good teacher though and really quite attractive. Marc was supposed to be the non-academic no-hoper. It was through her relationship with him that Isabelle's need for the bizarre, rebellious side of life was satisfied. Things in Portsmouth were not going as she had planned.

"Woahh, my friend, Bernarrrr, how you doing, man?" Isabelle raised her eyes in disgust at Marc's effusive shouted greeting in the fake American accent. Tracey smiled at her across the pounding noise, empathetic. There was no point in talking until the break.

"Fine," Bernard hollered back, "what ab...... " suddenly the music stopped, as Bernard found himself yelling "OUT....", luckily everyone's ears were ringing, no one heard Bernard shout for the band to be put out, "....... you?" he finished in a normal voice.

"I'm good, but Isabelle's fed up, she's wanting me to get the job."

She scowled.

"Hi, Bernard." Tracey attempted to lighten the atmosphere, but he interpreted it as an invitation and moved in beside her, eager to hear the news she had promised in her note, which was going to be hard in such a loud place.

Isabelle was left isolated as Marc strolled off to talk to the others from his English class. A beautiful Vietnamese girl was especially attentive, Rosa the Spanish woman vied for him. Tracey felt Isabelle seething and moved away to avoid the sparks. It was not her problem. And anyway she wanted to talk about Pearl. A ping of a thrill zinged through her that Bernard preferred to talk to her now, rather than the exquisite Isabelle. So different from that first time.

Then the music stopped and a temporary hush fell while they waited for the band to announce the break. Tracey could not ignore Isabelle now and leaned over to talk. The Vietnamese woman, sensitive and kind, saw and rallied the group to move over. Scraping chairs and clutching drinks they gathered round Isabelle unselfconsciously admiring her, French clothes, immaculate make-up. How lucky Marc was to have such a beautiful girlfriend.

Turning back to Bernard, Tracey had an opportunity now to tell him what she had overheard about Pearl, "You'll never believe it one of the people I heard was the top dog admin woman. Her name is Zara. God call me an inverted snob...."

"Inverted snob!" Bernard indulged her.

"Hi, hi, hi, you'll..... How're doing?" Oliver and Clare fell into their corner of the bar, already drunk.

"How d'you get in that state so early in the evening?"

"Not me." Ollie was sober.

He wasn't pleased with Clare, she was doing this kind of thing far too often nowadays. He was starting to get fed up with her, embarrassed at her determination to be as often and as totally out of her head as possible. It was difficult for him. Oliver liked to proclaim himself an anarchist. Let everyone do her own thing. He was also a both scared and envious. Clare really had no sense of self preservation, she did not care about her own safety. There was nothing she would not try. He, on the other hand, underneath the bravado, was fearful and conservative.

"Bernard, how're you?" Clare threw herself at him.

"What've been on? Not mixing poisons I hope."

"Been to give blood," greeted with a chorus of gasps, "no, I was sober then. It's my civic duty. Nothing to do with the head rush if you do it on an empty stomach and then get straight down the pub."

Ollie pushed at her sleeve to show the plasters as evidence. "Gerroff, bastard!"

A Korean woman from Marc's English class, normally very shy and completely silent when they were out together had had half a pint of lager. Her inhibitions were reduced.

"What is you-r b-lood g'oup?" She said in careful English. Her class mates quickly recovered their shock at her speaking.

"O pos'tive."

"Oh I knew it! That is so in-ter-est-ing. You are an O pos-I-tive type of person."

The whole group looked at her questioningly.

"Oh! Maybe in England is different. In Korea we say if you O positive you are strong person, someone like the ....boss. You don't have this in Engalnd?"

"In England we're nearly all O positive, so that accounts for everything, the empire, the patronising, the subjugation of the underdog," Ollie was fascinated.

"In Korea everyone is A blood group. Only a few O."

"What blood group are you, Tracey?" The conversation was breaking up, Bernard was making small talk.

"No idea, never given blood. In Belfast they used to give the students a free pint of Guinness in exchange for a pint of blood."

"When did you go to Belfast?" Isabelle was really interested in Northern Ireland, since her only good lecturer was from there.

"Long ago. It's the most exotic place I've been too. Never been to Tenerife, Costa Brava, France."

"No! Really?" Isabelle who as a child had travelled the world with her civil servant father, from one French embassy to another, was astonished.

"That's normal, in Portsmouth actually. I've never been in an aeroplane. I haven't got a passport."

Tracey looked beseechingly at Bernard. She still hadn't relayed her news.

"The wind's gone out of my sails now. Me, so parochial, Pearl, such a small problem, when you are surrounded by the world perspective."

"Come on, tell." Bernard encouraged her.

Tracey related as much detail as she could recall of the conversation between the hospital administrator and the consultant on Pearl's ward.

"I don't like the thought of her being experimented on, someone's guinea pig." Tracey finished.

"Best thing for her if she's going to carry on improving though. Let's be pragmatic about this. I'd like to talk to what's'is name?"

"Howard Chapman."

"And volunteer to support them. If they know I'm a friend of hers and I'm pushy and keen, they might be more careful with her. I could really help her."

Tracey was a bit disappointed that he was talking in the first person. She had thought they were in this together. But mulling it over, she realised she didn't know him at all. She had no reason to suppose he would be including her in anything. This was the first time he had articulated his intention to take a serious interest in Pearl's future. Tracey had not given Pearl's long term future a thought. Just because he was impressed at how she coped with Pearl did not mean the negative feelings he had had about her on the night of the accident had been erased. Her feelings of closeness towards him were based solely on the fact that she had confided in him about Darron. But that was all one-way. She felt stupid. He wanted nothing from her. She had nothing at all to offer him. He didn't want sex with her (of course, she was ugly and he was gorgeous and probably gay). She didn't have any material things he could share, no car, no comfortable place, no money, no culinary skills, no friends in interesting jobs. They'd never discussed politics or art or music. The only certain thing was what they did not in common – a taste in clothes. Tracey looked at his well-creased trousers and snappy jacket. All he needed was a pencil moustache and he would look like a spiv.

Bernard saw the look. Tracey looked hostile. He was confused. Until this moment he had thought he understood her. How she had hated him criticising her over the accident, when she had acted so selfishly. That she had probably ruled out even the possibility of fancying him - he knew she would consider him out of her league. How she had then needed to prove herself to him over Pearl. How she had confided in him about Darron. He thought she really liked him. But now she was narrowing her eyes and looking – fierce. Bernard had been wondering whether to share with Tracey an idea he was incubating for Pearl's future. He knew it was a mad idea but the more he thought about it, the more it seemed the right thing to do.

"Do you have a lot of time on your hands then, for looking after paraplegics?" There was a wounding tone in Tracey's voice.

Bernard decided to make light of it, "Yep, finished college, unemployed, except cash in hand bar and waiting work…….. waiting to find my metier."

"I'd like to help Pearl as well." She sounded softer now. But Bernard wasn't sure he could trust himself to judge.

"Have you time, with your course? And Darron?"

It sounded like a rejection to Tracey, but it could have been the start of an invitation. As Bernard was about to carry on, the band started up again in full force. Marc had been ignoring Isabelle again and she had finally lost her rag. She pushed past Tracey to go and drag Marc away. Her furious swinging shoulder bag swiped at a half empty glass. Tracey's reactions were swift, she steadied it, but not before a large dollop of beer had slopped into Bernard's lap. He jumped up as one scalded. His best chinos. He swore, cursing Isabelle to hell. She, oblivious in the deafening racket of the stage and her own boiling rage, was gone.

Tracey was beside herself, clutching her stomach with laughter. Nothing is funnier than seeing a dignified man so proud of his appearance, lose dignity in such a way. What she felt when he finally began to laugh with her was genuine affection.

"You'll have to go and change, you can't have people think you've pissed yourself." He knew it was a challenge. She would piss herself if he did go home to change, such a nancy boy who couldn't stand a dribble of beer. He wanted nothing more than to change and regain his immaculate image.

"What the hell! Let's get rat-arsed. What you having?" It was hard for him to relax, let go. Looking at Bernard, Tracey realised it would be a slow process for Bernard to be able to confide in anyone, to really trust anyone, to let his guard down. He was making an effort. She smiled encouragingly.

"Pint of Thumper, please."

Chapter 12

The meeting was about Tracey Allsop. Charles shared the lift with Susan Milhouse. They had met before at her appointment the previous semester. They had not seen much of each other since, so there was plenty of ground to cover, catching up to do on the machinations of the faculty. Conversation came easily.

When they reached the room booked for the meeting, they found a note from the other two tutors due to attend, to say they wouldn't be able to make it.

With an exasperated sigh, Susan dumped the pile of books she was carrying onto the teaching table. It was then that Charles observed that she was pregnant. An inward snigger almost escaped him as he envisaged the prof's undoubted but unvoiceable disgust at having appointed a lecturer only to have her off on maternity leave within six months. Steam would be coming out of his ears.

It was especially ironic that one other member of the interview panel had been certain that the prof had insisted on her not only for her academic record, her publications list and teaching ability, but also for her good legs, winning smile and long dark hair.

"I'm glad you think it's funny." Susan was more annoyed, seeing him smile.

"Sorry? Oh, no, it's just that it's typical," Charles answered. "Shouldn't you be putting your feet up?"

She shot him a look that would have withered couch grass.

He pulled a chair round so that he could sit in the space opposite her.

"Well, we can sort out Miss Allsop without them, can't we?" he began.

But he couldn't take his eyes off her abdomen. There was something exciting about a pregnancy. Already a father of three, Charles never tired of the beauty and mystery of a pregnant woman. He really wanted to talk to Susan about it. But he barely knew her and he had blown it with his patronising remark about putting her feet up.

Susan's arms were folded neatly across the top of her rounded stomach. It moulded snugly into the knitted fabric of her tunic top, while her leggings showed every muscle of her thighs. Charles found it impossible not to imagine her naked.

"Do you mind if we sit round at the table?" he asked. "Then I can spread out my file more easily." This was a pretext for getting her to move up to the table, just so he didn't have to look at her bump. He rummaged convincingly in his bag.

When the fecundity was tucked under the table out of sight, he hoped he would stop being distracted by it. By a fluke, Tracey's essay was on top of the papers he produced.

"We don't need to go through the essay itself now do we?" Susan was hoping for a short meeting.

"It was so appallingly written that there can be no doubt the woman needs some kind of help. God! It's not even written in sentences. The spelling is, well, imaginative and the structure, logic, argument, non-existent. Don't you agree? Isn't this just the challenge for the new study skills set-up? Miss Allsop should certainly test their mettle. It would take me hours to go through this lot. And that must be what we're paying them for." Charles said. Was the undertone scathing or sarcastic? It was expected that academic staff would despise something as mundane as 'study skills'. What was a university doing accepting students onto undergraduate programmes when they could not string a sentence together?

"I thought you were intending to boycott the study skills - a 'gross misuse of faculty funds', I seem to remember seeing on the memo,"

Susan's tone of voice was tart, but barely concealed her pleasure that it had been his suggestion to use the new system. Her new system. She had assumed he would wait, spin it out, eventually forcing her to declare it the only option, promoting her own idea, an opportunity to silently gloat that she had extracted funds from the tight-fisted finance department. She didn't stop to question his motives for the apparent U-turn, enjoying instead a brief moment of smugness.

"Great idea! Study skills programme it is! Actually I think Tracey is very vulnerable, and maybe a bit sensitive.

136

We'll have to be careful how we handle this. Just being referred might destroy her self-esteem."

"That sounds preposterous, I thought the whole point was that you give the special tuition, improve the academic skills and the resulting effect, as well as gaining the skills themselves of course, is an improvement in self confidence. These will be the wonderful self-assured scholars who will take our university forward into academe in the 21st century. That's why they have such a grandiose title. 'Academic Writing Turorials' – more like basic literacy in Miss Allsop's case." Now surely Charles was taking the piss. A less arrogant man would have been withered by the fierce, narrowed-eyed look of contempt Susan leaned forward and aggressively impaled him with.

"Right well, I'll officially refer her to you, you can arrange it all. Just keep me informed. Oh, and no bill." He laughed. But he felt her enmity and wanted to escape. Was delighted to have off-loaded Tracey Allsop.

As she straightened up, getting ready to leave, there was a further moment of awkwardness between them. Susan's swollen stomach stuck briefly beneath the table, lifting it slightly and she fell back into her chair with a clumsy wobble, an involuntary exhalation. He concentrated intently on the contents of his briefcase, hoping she would think he hadn't noticed - the lost dignity.

He turned at the door to bid her farewell. Her mouth was open to speak. But as he watched, her face changed suddenly into a magical, delighted smile. Her hand moved down to her stomach, smoothing the visibly undulating mound.

"Christ! It's doing somersaults. God, what is it doing in there? It's never felt like this before. Rather alarming. Do you think it's alright?"

Suddenly he was the expert. Must be her first, he thought.

"Of course it is. The baby will be fine, just animated by our riveting exchange!" Unable to disguise his interest, he moved towards her.

"Here," she said, holding her hand out to him, "feel it. It's amazing."

And before either of them could reflect, she was offering him her belly, and he had his hand on it too, feeling so clearly through the thin jersey material, a swirl of heels or elbows, jabbing and jumping then gradually subsiding and coming to rest.

"That is so exciting. I never managed to catch any of my children as active as that, in utero. Mary would tell me when they were very lively, but by the time I got my hand there they'd always settled down......Thank you.....for letting me...."

Charles avoided her gaze as he gathered his things once more. Susan avoided his too. She couldn't bear for him to see her eyes, stretched wide open to prevent the tears forming.

*   *   *   *   *

Tracey knocked. Dr Susan Milhouse called her in. The office was sparse, the air chill with brief, temporary occupancy, contrasting dramatically with the warm blob of maternity that was Susan; rotund, fluffy in pink cashmere, flushed with increased blood flow, happy with anticipation. In the 6 or so weeks since Tracey had seen her, Susan had altered from an intimidating, respected and elevated Doctor of Philosophy in Social History to nothing more than a large pregnancy. Tracey instantly relaxed, her fears fled in the face of this biological levelling. It would be easy for her to take control of the meeting.

"Hi, I bet you get fed up with people asking when it's due," she started.

"No, actually. My colleagues are all determined to act as though it's not there. It's a bit disappointing really. I suppose they think it's more professional. The office staff are really sweet, but you can tell they don't like to ask, and the students are either all gooey-eyed or totally embarrassed, as though it was their mother pregnant. Since you ask, or rather avoided asking, it's due in another three weeks. But I feel so well I

138

decided to work on as long as possible so as to have more time with it after it's born."

"Good idea. Funny how we always say "it". What do you think it will be?"

"A girl, called Fiachra."

"Irish connection, eh?"

"Her gandfather."

"It'll be a boy actually, or that's what my Chinese friends would say. Because the lump is all out in front like a football. They say if you can't see that you're pregnant from the back view, it's a boy, if the weight has gone on all round it's a girl."

"I haven't even thought of a boy's name."

"It's probably wrong......Anyway, I came about the essay. I noticed that everyone else has had theirs back, so there must be something remarkable about mine. I'm fairly sure it isn't that your keeping it back as a piece of brilliance to show the others," Tracey laughed, "I bet it's really bad, eh?"

Susan indicated the chair.

"Oh no, so bad I'll need to sit down." Tracey tried to tell herself to stop prattling. She feared the worst now and as usual covered her anxiety with prattle. She pulled her copy of the essay out of her bag. Susan had hers on the desk. As far as Tracey could see, it was not covered in red pen.

"It's clear that you have done a lot of research. You know a phenomenal amount about Social Policy in the period." Since her meeting with Charles, Susan had now read Tracey's work very carefully. "That's actually where the problem lies with your essay. You seem to have read everything on the book list and then tried to incorporate it all in the essay. A superhuman effort more suited to research for a PhD perhaps, but far more than was actually required for the first semester. Spare a thought for us, the poor markers, who do have homes to go to......"

Susan laughed, "and stay within your word count. Probably the most difficult thing in studying is when you've got really interested in something and you want to include it all. It's horrible to have to leave stuff out. It all seems relevant to you, but may not be relevant to the question. Let's look at the title. Tell me, what is it asking you to do?"

The unhurried, quiet confidence in Susan's voice and her gentle, encouraging approach, allowed Tracey to think about the essay. To realise that she had misunderstood the task. Though this was mortifying, Susan made her believe that it was an easy mistake to make and one that she could easily rectify.

During their exchange, the pregnancy had disappeared from the room, only to reappear abruptly when the hour was up and they rose to leave. Tracey now felt embarrassed that she had chatted so familiarly with Susan about the baby, and she opened her mouth to apologise. But there were no words for what she wanted to say and anyway it to refer to it again would be to compound the problem.

"I suppose you won't be around for the next semester. I don't want to be selfish, but I'll miss you. It was really helpful to me, talking to you today."

"If I find I'm a useless mother, I'll be back before anyone has time to miss me." She was joking, but it triggered an exchange about mothers, so personal and intense that Tracey didn't notice her hand clutching the doorknob until she tried to release the stiffened claw it had become. Susan didn't notice her ankles visibly swelling where she stood. Tracey told Susan about her own mother and Susan unburdened herself of her anxieties, her sense of inadequacy and her fury at the whole world's dismissal of her fears.

There was a pause as Tracey lifted her foot to retreat, a pause before goodbyes, but it was pregnant with things unsaid.

Tracey did not tell Susan the story of Darron, though it rose in her throat, fighting to be told. She wanted to tell about the pregnant teenager, refusing to have an abortion; the pressure to do so from her key worker and doctor; the unexpected support of Martha, the Maltese cook, whose whole life had been overshadowed by the abortion she had been forced to have as a teenager, sent in disgrace from Mosta to England to a strange English family. But Tracey divulged nothing.

140

And Susan. She opened her mouth, just stopping herself from telling Tracey that her baby had no real father. That she was not the happily married woman that everyone assumed she was; that she had chosen to become a single parent, despite having no qualms about abortion, having in fact previously terminated a pregnancy; that the child's father knew nothing about it; but worse, that she had cynically planned it without his knowledge.

The child's father, a colleague in the college where Susan had previously worked, was married. The affair had thriven for several years, she on the Pill. He always declaring he would leave his wife when the children were old enough. Then he had been invited to study and teach abroad on sabbatical for a year. He could so easily have taken her. They could have lived as husband and wife in Senegal, the people back home none-the-wiser - but he had surprised everyone by taking his wife and family. In the jagged jigsaw of snatched moments together, the sum total of her emotional life, they had always planned that his sabbatical year would be their special year together. All blown apart by this massive betrayal.

Susan's anguish had been the more distressing because she couldn't shout it from the rooftops and tear her hair in public. Worse still, it became clear he had been exorcising Susan to save his marriage. She knew in an instant that he would always deny her. Out of the ashes of her grief, fury and bitterness, two new emotions grew. Where the powerful maternal urge came from she had no idea, but she was drowning in a surge of hormones, so often pooh-poohed in now gloating friends. The desire for a baby was so overwhelming and debilitating it invaded every waking moment, and much of her dreamtime. It seemed too strong to have been caused merely by the sudden withdrawal of her opportunity to conceive, the progenitor having skipped the country - or, so she rationalised to herself. And the feeling would not abate. The other emotion new to Susan, was the powerful urge to hurt the bastard, after he had betrayed her so despicably - to hurt the bastard with a bastard, was hardly a conscious decision, but one of very few weapons open to her.

When he had walked back into the department one year later, she had been ready for him. Sweetness and light, skilfully disguising the nurtured hurt, delighted to see him again, keen to go for a drink, just like old friends and hear all about it. He was weak. She played upon his ego, he was so easily flattered. She was coy, deploying a mere dusting of guilt, "I've so missed you, it's been so dull without you."

Then she watched her cycle, and waited through a couple of days for signs of fertile mucus. As they fucked - he was so weak, it was so easy - she felt at last the satisfaction of fertile seed spurting inside her, a poignant pleasure sharpened by him not knowing. She had lain still a long time to let the magic happen. She never doubted that it would. For the first week after her missed period, she revelled in not telling him, in his not knowing. A budget cut in their department offered staff an incentive payment to 'retire early', a good omen. Susan resigned.

Relaxed, confident and inspired, she had romped through the job interview here at Portsmouth, answering questions more brilliantly than she could ever have hoped. And in her handbag, all along, the pregnancy test kit. Her hand, still warm from the professor's congratulatory clasp, fumbled with the cellophane wrapper. But as the positive result emerged, Susan found herself welcoming the baby as her own and shutting its father out of their lives. In that tense moment of watching the colour change, the need to punish him, to make him suffer, had subtly changed. Her strength would be drawn from keeping him ignorant. This baby was hers, and only hers. She briefly gave thanks for his genetic contribution - brains and good looks (but what if it got her brains and looks?) - then thought no more about him, happily writing him out of the script.

But none of this did she actually tell to Tracey, tempted though she was to unburden herself to someone. Even her closest friends didn't know. She couldn't be sure of the support of a single one of them. So Susan reiterated to Tracey her apprehension about childbirth, about becoming a mother; blessing her own mother and mothers in general.

142

As she was finally leaving Tracey was thinking about Lilly, Pearl's mother, and somewhere in the conversation, Susan had ignited an ember of guilt, making Tracey feel an unfamiliar sense of responsibility towards her own mother. For Susan there was no relationship as fundamental, as important as that between mother and child. And then Tracey couldn't believe it was her own voice promising Susan that she would search for her estranged mother. This was a search she had never previously considered. From the moment she had been taken into care, Tracey had never felt the absence of her mother as a lacking in her life; this was no unresolved business that had been clamouring to be dealt with, but something she never thought of, experiencing it as a dull dormant hatred originating from that moment when she had decided she never wanted to see the old cow again, 23 years before.

And then that old familiar feeling, long repressed, surfaced. Tracey rushed out of the room. It had never been for herself that she had hated her mother. The choking twin hands of pity and hate gripped her throat as she pelted down the stairs. It had always been for her little brother, Paul. His pathetic little face rose like a genie from the past. That little 5 year old who had been welded to his mother from birth, who had screamed at being detached for his first day at school, a premonition. Then, only weeks later, how he had stood and wept and wept and wept, terrifying Tracey with his rigid inability to move, rooted to the spot, just inside the front door, exactly where she had told him about the note, the note from their mother telling them that she had gone. In his school uniform, too big for him, still new, his tie darkening as the tears soaked it, the white shirt starting to stick to his chest.

When she had told him, he had believed her instantly, though it was her habit to tease him about his babyish attachment to his mummy. When she had reached over to comfort him, to try and make him stop, to come in the kitchen for a biscuit, he screamed as though she was his worst nightmare - as though it was all her fault. Eventually he had crumpled just where he had stood, collapsed on the floor, and his breathing had gone all noisy and he had begun to gasp and she thought he was going to die. She had heard of people dying of grief. She took hold of herself and sat close by and forced herself to think of the story they had made up together about their teddy bears. She started to tell it and he, exhausted, couldn't help but listen. His breathing evened, he shut his eyes. And when they got to the happy ever after ending, she continued in a soothing voice, unnervingly mature for her nine year old lips. "Paul and Tracey lived happily ever after because Tracey looked after him and cooked his dinners and met him from school and read him stories and was never mean to him again."

This memory that Tracey was forced to watch, like a well worn home movie not seen for more than 20 years, was as vivid as ever. But how did it end? It ended at the beginning, with the sound of her father's key. The film cut abruptly there and all that remained was the sense of relief, mixed with the incongruous knowledge that it was the first time she could remember being glad to see her father come home.

The sound of her father's key in the lock. A sound that would normally have them all scuttling out of sight until they knew his mood. A sound that would signal her mother's nervous scan of the house to make sure it was tidy, kicking a stray shoe under the sofa to be retrieved later. The signal for her to adopt a bright smile onto the freshly lipsticked lips, smooth down her sleeves, straighten her skirt. He wasn't going to let his wife let herself go, no make-up and slovenly clothes. He refused to come home to a mess or miserable people. Tracey well remembered the time he had come in when she and Paul were fighting, their mother tearing her hair and toys and pens scattered everywhere. He thundered that he could show them what a mess really was and how miserable they could be, if that was the way they wanted to live. He stamped on their toys, but being designed to be safe for babies, only one plastic plane could be crushed with a satisfying crunch. He ground the felt tips into the carpet, some snapped and swirls of colour appeared - later when Tracey first saw a Jackson Pollock, she recognised the beige carpet of her childhood as a canvas for an embryonic Jackson Pollock. Still raging her father had turned to their mother and swiped her cheek with the back of his hand, knocking her onto the floor.

144

Tracey had been about 6. She had never seen a grown up hit another grown up. She could remember the shock and her understanding, even then, that this was not been an isolated occasion. From the calm way her mother recovered herself and started to clear up the mess, little Tracey had known it was not the first time. But she was as angry with her mother for being so meek, not standing up for herself, as she was with her father for hitting her.

And where was Paul now?

*   *   *   *   *

"I got a dressing down for my essay."

".....a dressing gown?"

"No, you deaf bugger, a dressing DOWN." Tracey looked skywards appealing to a higher authority for support.

"Careful what you say, some of my best friends are deaf," Bernard countered.

"Yeah, and my gran's the queen of Sheba."

"Sophisticated imagery!" Bernard, sarcastic, "No, really, I was at a funeral for an old deaf guy last week."

In her head Tracey had started to play the conversation about her terrible essay. "Don't you want to know about my essay?" She didn't say it though, because he obviously wasn't interested and she wasn't sure she was any more.

"Why, you expecting a mention in the will?"

"Cynical bitch, actually he did leave me something. He used to drink in the same pub as Lilly and he gave me this." In his hand he held out a latch key.

"Yeah, so what is it?"

"A key, der! To a front door?......looks almost identical to mine?......come on Trace......! Use your brain!"

"It's never the key to Lilly's flat? Bernard you're a genius. Hey, we can move Pearl back in there then, without consulting the authorities."

Bernard couldn't believe it had been this easy. Having had the idea himself, he didn't want it to be his all responsibility, he wanted someone else to suggest it and then it would be their responsibility.

"That's a brilliant idea. Do you think it'll work? I mean how could it be done? We need the housing association to believe Lilly's still a resident, which of course she might be again. I wonder if it's OK for offspring to retain their home, as in, the home of their parent, even after the parent has left?"

"Dunno, but I think the biggest problem is how would she be looked after. She needs care all the time and even if this researcher gets his/her teeth into Pearl, they aren't going to want to do the toileting, feeding and that, are they?" Ever practical, Tracey could see this side of Pearl falling to well-meaning volunteers. Bernard may believe she still felt she had something to prove in that department. But there were limits. She had enough on her plate, too much in fact, to consider taking on the role of more than a friend to Pearl. With a full timetable Tracey only had a few hours here and there and Wednesday afternoons free.

"There are home helps and such like. We, no, I'll find out about that stuff. Will you still come and visit. I think you are very important to Pearl. She looks up to you."

"Well, she fancies you!"

"Oh no, don't say that." Bernard sounded really distressed.

Tracey did not understand how this could be unsettling for Bernard. He was such a popinjay, so good looking, had clearly worked hard to cultivate his sartorial elegance (and neuroses), how could he think anything other than that every woman fancied him?

"But all women fancy you, present company excepted," Tracey asked herself if she did actually have a wee notion of him, and really thought not.

"Let's go and look at the place now we have the key. It'll be awful now the fire brigade's been in. They usually leave a terrible mess," with his usual defence mechanism about anything a bit personal, Bernard had changed the subject.

In the housing association block, Tracey had never ventured further than the ground floor for her keep fit class. Only ever been there on Thursdays, except that one Friday, of course, to retrieve her watch.

146

The building loomed square, dark and foreboding in the early December twilight contrasting with the imposing flint structure of the church next door garish in its orange floodlight. The lettering **WAREHOUSE NO1** was barely discernible, but Bernard began telling her the story: about the other warehouses; one was bonded and had been raided constantly by the neighbours; the original one having started life as a factory mill. He was the veritable expert on local history.

Bernard's leather soles scuffed on the stone steps. Tracey's feet were silent in rubber. A red door opened on the landing below Pearl's.

"Oh, sorry, didn't know you had company." Joe stood in his tartan slippers, his shirt tail untucked, his glasses only hooked over one ear, one of the arms twisted out of shape. He peered hard through the lenses as if he couldn't believe his eyes.

"Where's ya boyfriend then?" He leered mischievously. Tracey stared hard at him. Bernard began to laugh.

"You mean my brother?"

"Yeah.......right!"

"This is my friend Tracey. Didn't you two meet in the pub?"

"I saw you there." Tracey confirmed, disinclined to give anything away.

"Joe and his wife Rose probably know more about Pearl and Lilly than anyone else."

Joe's ears pricked up. Was something going on? Why they were here together? He made to follow them up the stairs, curious. He had the feeling they were going into Lilly's flat, though how they would have got a key he couldn't imagine. And Joe felt he had a proprietorial right to be involved in anything that concerned Lilly. Bernard did not stop at Lilly's door, Tracey didn't know which it was anyway, he lead her on up to his flat. Joe, disappointed, trailed back home.

When they were inside the front door, Tracey looked around, amazed. There was a smell of pine cleaning fluid, the carpet was hoovered, the furniture, though a curious assemblage of new, old, renewed, recovered or disguised under a throw, was all colour-co-ordinated around warm autumnal shades, and it was tidy.

"Where's all the mess from the telly?" she gasped.

"Christ, this is my place." Bernard, though horrified that Tracey could think that his place could have been the disgusting scruffy old Lilly's, laughed. "I came up here because I don't want old nosey parker below to know we have Lilly's key. He'll never leave us alone and he'll certainly be no help in looking after Pearl, you can bet your life. We'll have to get Rose on board first in that department anyway. They're so competitive, if she thinks he knew about it before her, she'll have nothing to do with the scheme. But we need her to take a neighbourly interest in Pearl."

"You seem to have them right off pat. Do you make snap judgements about everyone like this?" Tracey looked mock scandalised.

"Only when it's needed. I'm right about them though. You could make a fortune on betting that she will always do the opposite to him, only no one would give you decent odds. I once amused myself by telling Joe to ask Rose down to the pub. Of course she said, no. Then I asked her. She came like a shot."

"That's easy, you twit! Of course she'd go with a nice young man like you. Anyway, she'd go with you cos you'd buy her a drink, Joe wouldn't, he'd make her go up to the bar and if he went up to the bar, you can bet it would be her money! ......Nice place, what's the view like?"

Tracey switched off the light and went over to the window overlooking the old factory yard, now a car park and beyond, strips of dark city back gardens. To the right, the church loomed orange, patched with black by the silhouettes of foliage not trapped in the floodlight. A stripe of sunset pink in the green western sky, was pierced by the spire. To the left, dark had already claimed the east of the city and a sliver of moon was white with the promise of frost. Below, bright yellow windows leapt into the night and in them, teasing glimpses of kitchen life flitted.

Tracey felt the warmth of Bernard's body arrive beside her. For a heart-wrenching second, she thought he was going to put his arm round her. She was furious with her increased pulse, she was furious that in this moment, if she had been anyone else, he would have. His upper arm collided with her shoulder. It was as if she had been electrocuted, but keen to disguise it, she moved smoothly away and with barely a fumble, snapped on the light.

"Where's the kettle?" Across the safe space of the room she looked enquiringly at him. Was she imagining it? Or was he a bit misty-eyed? "Kitchen of course."

"It's a great.... CHRIST!"

The kitchen door had resisted. Behind it a girl lay sprawled across the floor.

"CLARE!" Bernard was there. He crouched, reached down, about to pull her up.

"No, let's make sure it's not a neck injury or anything. If we move her, we might kill her."

*   *   *   *   *

After sitting a long time in the office she had never attempted to stamp her personality on, Susan phoned to speak to Charles. He was not there. She left a message.

"I spoke to Tracey Allsop this afternoon, you remember, about the essay? When I saw you last, I hadn't actually read it. But now I have and....I'm really not sure if she'll be able to continue with the course. I'd be surprised if Study Skills can do anything in the three hours they can offer; she doesn't even speak grammatically, how can she ever learn to write English if she can't spot a grammatical error? I'll talk to you about it later."

Chapter 13

"Look what I've brought you!" Tracey waved a disposable shower cap. "And...." She thrust a box of, also disposable, surgical rubber gloves under his nose. She had been delighted to see Bernard still wearing his immaculately pressed trousers. In paint-spattered jeans and sweater, an ancient spotted headscarf, Tracey's clothes were appropriate to the task ahead. She had had a small bet with herself that his wouldn't be.

"Thanks, so kind," was all he said, smiling, without taking them. "Shall we get on with the job?"

It was a struggle, but Tracey overcame the urge to say, "You can't do it dressed like that!" He was a grown man and she wasn't his mother.

They had thought the electricity might have been cut off, but the switch responded and a low wattage bulb in a cracked plastic shade hanging from the centre of the yellowed artex ceiling gave them enough light to scan the damage. Nothing had been cleared up, though there was no evidence that the fire brigade had made it worse. A drift of glass granules had been pushed to one side, among them, were some really sharp shards of silvery-dark glass too. Tracey recalled the dismantling of dumped televisions from her street-wise childhood. If she remembered correctly there was granular screen glass and then the fine blown glass of the tube. That was what had caused the explosion, or implosion probably, as there was a vacuum inside it. She'd never heard a noise as loud before, perhaps it had resonated in the bare walled flat. The shell of the television lay splintered in one corner, its spindly legs akimbo with tiny hinged brass feet bent up in mid air. A long curved smear streaked with browned blood indicated where Pearl had fallen onto the filthy lino. Her day bed was a heap of grubby blankets and from it Pearl's unwashed smell still emanated, even above the stale charred smell of the burnt curtains and melted paintwork. Above both these, another savoury fishy smell rose which began to cut their throats.

"What is that appalling stench?"

Tracey knew. "It's the smell of years of dirt burning on light bulbs in ancient plastic shades."

"Ugh, you seem very certain." Bernard was so fastidious.

Through the ceiling, they heard a thud from the floor of the flat above, Bernard's flat.

"Do you think she'll be alright?" Tracey had not wanted to come down here now that Clare was upstairs needing help, but the minute his brother Oliver had arrived, Bernard had insisted they leave them to it. Luckily they had not phoned the ambulance first, as Tracey had wanted. But Tracey felt deflated, it had taken the thrill out of investigating Pearl's home of umpteen years.

"Of course she will! I'm just relieved Ollie knew about the antidepressants. You do know that these days, you have to pay for an ambulance if it turns out not to have been an emergency!"

"But that's what I mean, she ought to go to hospital and be checked out."

"Look if he's sure there were only 10 and she had seven on her, she's only taken three."

"But we don't know how much alcohol she'd drunk and it might be enough for a fatal combination."

"There was less than half a bottle of whisky there. Anyway she was conscious when we left. She was even beginning to focus. Oliver can walk her about. And that was a great idea of yours to give her salt water, she puked quite a lot. That's all they do in hospital anyway."

"You just don't want to get the bent pharmacist in trouble handing out illegal drugs. Might be useful in the future, eh? But you don't know what else she might've done before she came to your place. She might've been snorting cocaine all afternoon for all we know."

"No, stop worrying, god, you're not her mother!" Bernard paused as he realised there may be an implied gibe.

"I can tell you that she had been cleaning up until she decided to sit down and drink the whisky. Hence the cleaning box still out on the counter, the smell of pine etc. (Christ knows why, that's another story! And I'll kill Ollie for giving her the key!) The cloth even felt warm still where she'd used it. True, she'd swallowed a lot of whisky in a short time, probably on an empty stomach, except for the pills. Must've just suddenly hit her, BAM. Amazing she had the presence of mind to put the glass down before she fell. Such a tidy tart."

Ah, thought Tracey, he doesn't like her. "I'll just pop up and see the tart. It's gone a bit quiet."

"You are neurotic! Don't make any noise when you go! I don't want old Joe up here."

On her return, Tracey found Bernard had started filling the industrial black bin bags. She shook her head in amazement, unable to hide a smirk.

"What's so funny?"

"Nothing."

Bernard was wearing a spotless white boiler suit. On his head, a brand new baseball cap, looking incongruous on him, with the peak turned self-consciously and too precisely to the centre of the back of his head. His hands were safe in heavy-duty black rubber gloves, which extended up to his elbows. Tracey recognised those sort gloves from her weeks on the farm in Northern Ireland.

"Christ, have you been to an agricultural outfitters? Surely you can't just buy AI gloves in Lo-cost can you?"

"AI? What are you talking about?"

"Those gloves could get a cow excited!"

"I won't reward you with asking how you know what a cow might like!"

"They're used by men called artificial inseminators to impregnate cows – you know, on farms? In the country, grass cows sheep tractors etc? They shove their whole arm up a cow's vagina, then pull the trigger on the applicator and heh presto a new Fresian or Hereford or whatever."

"You are obsessed with sex, you know that?"

"Have to talk about it, don't get any." It was funny, even though it was true.

Bernard must have brought all his purpose-designed protection down with him when he came. No wonder he had not been impressed with her disposable shower cap. He was doing everything at arm's length in order to avoid any contact between his person and his surroundings. Only the soles of his shoes and the fingers of his black gloves shared an interface with this alien world. He even breathed in an exaggerated way, as though partially closing his throat would help filter out the particles of filth.

"I think you're right, she'll be fine. Ollie said he got her conscious enough for a conversation and now he's letting her sleep. Her breathing's fine. He's staying with her." Bernard wasn't really interested, but the reason he didn't respond was fear of having to inhale too deeply.

There was a lot of work to do and if Tracey didn't interfere, she knew Bernard would throw out everything in his desperate fastidiousness, regardless of whether it would be cleanable and useful. And he would never get on with the really difficult work, scrubbing the soot off.

The fire had licked black triangles across the ceiling, scorched cracked patterns like the glaze on ancient delft and delicately misted everything else with a dusting of soot like black icing sugar on a Halloween cake. The wallpaper would have to be stripped, but luckily only off the window wall. They wanted Pearl to move in and live here. They couldn't afford to completely refurbish the place.

"Look, you can't throw that out, it's probably a family heirloom." Tracey plucked a Charles and Diana mug from the bin bag.

"It's cracked! Revolting!" Bernard snatched it from her and thrust it under her nose. It was filthy and there was a blackened crack from rim to base. "That crack'll be teeming with bacteria. Ugh, ugh, ugh!"

"OK, ok, don't shove it under my nose, then. But Pearl may need some of this stuff to trigger her memories, or just as keepsakes." Who were they to come in and dictate what should stay and what should go?

"That is precisely what we have done. We have appointed ourselves as judges of what we will allow to stay and what should go." Bernard was unapologetic and Tracey realised that he was not enjoying this work. The filth really repelled him.

In the bathroom black mould scored a heavy black line where each surface abutted the next, outlining every plane like a child's drawing. In corners a jellied growth of suppurating orange fungus oozed, and spots of white, grey, black and green mould were spattered randomly over everything including the mirror of a medicine cupboard.

"I'll get a screwdriver," Bernard went into the other room to rummage in the bag of implements and cleaning equipment they had brought.

"What for?" Tracey was mildly puzzled. She was trying to prize the cupboard door open.

"Don't do that!" Bernard shrieked when he returned, "I'm going to unscrew the whole thing, and we can drop it straight in the bin. Look, it's just suspended by those two screws at the top." But the door suddenly sprang open under Tracey's fiddling fingers.

The unhealthy antiseptic smell that rolled out slapped Tracey unexpectedly on the nose and shot her back into the past. She was briefly paralysed by it, and Bernard peered round to see what was up. "You alright? What's in there?"

"A leaking Germoline tube squashed into the hinge and a bottle of TCP with the top loose. You know how evocative smells are? That's taken me right back, way back - to a holiday in Wales. A bunch of us got chosen to go on this outward boundy thing staying in a massive stone mansion in a place called.....Dolgellau, was it? It looked like a prison when we first arrived in the minibus. Talking of smells, we never got rid of the smell of Karen Perry's sick. She puked all the way."

"How old were you?" Bernard was unscrewing the cupboard, Tracey's mind was elsewhere, he reckoned he could chuck it out and she would probably not notice.

"I don't know, eleven? twelve? Anyway, they decided to give me the very best room. A room of my own. I was always saying I wanted a room of my own, you know, in the home. So I was really pleased. But then when I saw it, it had a black iron bed that made me think of hospitals, though I'd never been in one (from pictures I suppose) with a gruesome, hideous crucifix above it (I'd never heard of Catholics then) and it was so graphically carved, you could see tears and blood dripping down and the big bleeding cut open in his side.

"But far worse than that, was the medicine chest on the wall. Without the doors even being open you could smell that horrible sickly smell of disinfectant and antiseptic. It was terrifying. And I couldn't admit that it scared me of course." Tracey drifted into a reverie.

"Did you manage to get any sleep at all?" Bernard was looking her in the eye, and talking to cover what his hands were swiftly and deftly doing – putting the cupboard in a bin bag and tying the top.

"Not much. But that was because of the crocodile."

"Crocodile?" Bernard was curious now.

"Yes. It was really, really dark out there in the countryside at night, and the staff would never let you leave any lights on, so I kept the curtains open for whatever starlight or moon there was, But of course I had to keep turned away from the scary medicine chest and the bloody Jesus, which meant I was facing a piece of wall. Well the plaster was really old and uneven, they'd just painted over all the bumps and cracks, I suppose, and it made all eerie shapes in the dim light. There was this one bit right by my pillow like the snout of a crocodile, with two big nostrils and some jaggedy top teeth 'cos it had its mouth wide open and then on up a corrugated snout to a huge bulging eye. And it was coming towards me where I lay in bed. Even when I tried sleeping upside down, I knew it was still coming for me."

Bernard was laughing, "A terrible holiday then?"

"No, it was brilliant apart from that. There was a stream we dammed and squelchy bogs, oh, and frogs, and little fish,"

"Minnows and sticklebacks?"

"No idea, and loads of trees to climb. They let us go anywhere as long as we came back at the meal bell. I was tired though. I stayed up really late, so as not to be alone in that room, which meant helping with chores, laying up for breakfast and…. Christ I'd completely forgotten this – setting mousetraps. I got really good at that. Then of course I was always first up in the morning, but couldn't go into the kitchen to make myself tea or anything for fear of finding dead mice in the traps!"

"Ahhhh, poor you." Bernard was keeping her talking, surreptitiously sneaking things into the bin bags, sure she was too lost in her past to see the passing of.......three tons of ancient newspapers, mostly The Sun, The People, The News of the World, but a couple of Private Eyes, dating back to........NO! he must not be tempted himself. It was all rubbish.

"Talking of which, let's have some. Tea, not dead mice."

"Don't think I didn't notice you throw out the bathroom cabinet."

*   *   *   *   *

Much later, having left seven black bin bags by the dustbins in the yard at Warehouse No 1, Tracey was back in the warmth and safety of her student halls room. She flopped out across her bed. A mug of tea was heat-printing a ring on the book where she'd put it to cool on the desk of her centrally-heated, self-contained student study bedroom. Wearily, she lifted up to eyelevel the envelopes of the mail she'd brought up from the foyer. A letter from the halls' association reminded her she would be expected to be out of her room by 15th December or pay the extra £35 a week to stay for the vacation. She groaned, the high spirits of her evening's achievement in Pearl's flat evaporated. She had completely forgotten about this part of the accommodation agreement and unlike everyone else here, had no other home to go to. £35 wasn't bad, but she hadn't budgeted for it and of course there would be no catering, so that meant buying food as well. Three weeks!

It was late. She decided to call at her old home, the hostel in Clarendon Avenue, in the morning. Maybe Martha would put her up for a bit. She'd kipped there before in Martha's tiny flat. She always called there at Christmastime anyway, to collect Christmas mail. They never seemed to mind her using their address. And she had moved around so often over the years that it was her only anchor point. Social Services used it as a contact address and the hostel manager had permission to give out any of her temporary addresses should anything come from them.

She had always lived in hope that Paul would be traced or Darron would be ready to meet her, so it had always been important that she should be traceable. She smiled. At the age of 32 one of those had finally come true, but only the more recent one. Perhaps it was time to give up on Paul and forget him completely. In a moment of self-indulgence Tracey followed her thoughts. What could she do at Christmas for Darron? She couldn't buy him anything he wouldn't already be getting. A party? Trip to a concert? Tracey liked the violent, manic dancing at the university concerts, even if half of them were 'E'-ed out and all of them were half her age. Wouldn't Darron, 17, like that kind of stuff?

No, not with her, it would simply be embarrassing for him.

The maudlin mood of inadequacy was still with Tracey as she trudged through puddles and fought the sea wind, turning at last into Clarendon Avenue into a squall of freezing rain. Martha opened the door and embraced her as a mother would. Tracey burst into tears and over tea in the huge kitchen, Martha guessed that Tracey had met up with Darron at last.

"And, see, so much better for you! My baby's dead." And she shook her head in a doleful, but melodramatic way, as she had been doing over the dead baby for 40 years. Martha's accent was as strong as ever and her tears as wet. Tracey leaned in and smoothed them away with her thumb and changed the subject.

"He got really good GCSEs! Don't know where he got the brains."

"That'll be the black soldier! Always underestimated, immigrants in this country. What with all the white supremacy!"

Tracey coughed, "Just down to him, eh?"

"No, no you're really brainy, everyone knows that......got to university, eh!" Martha pinched her cheek like a chubby baby and laughed.

The year's worth of gossip was punctuated by Martha's shuffled trips to the pantry or the cooker or the freezer, or her frantic chopping of carrots and whizzing food processor. Her slippers were shiny with age, use, and spills. No trace of their original colour remained, but Tracey now knew better than to buy her new ones for Christmas. Twice before, she'd given slippers, been thanked profusely and then never seen the new ones worn. By lunchtime the smell of the evening's Eve's pudding was almost too much for Tracey. She was starving.

"Can I have a taste when it's cooked?"

"You're not eleven now, young lady!" Tracey sniggered, "Anyway you wouldn't like it without custard, you always loved custard."

"Comfort food. Oh, can I make some now?"

Martha couldn't refuse, but she did protest, "This is no time for custard, it's only elevenses time." But she passed over a saucepan and directed Tracey to the pantry for custard powder.

"Any mail for me?"

"If there is, it'll be in the office. Dragon-breath is very good about that sort of thing, always keeps it locked up. What are you doing for Christmas? Don't suppose you'll be going to Tim's." Martha snorted.

"You are one cruel old bitch, reminding me of that," laughed Tracey.

"Like you forgotten about the kids there! What! Wasn't it the little one put cat food in your bed? And then the other one peed on your lap watching TV, or was it the other way round? And then the row, on Christmas morning, her throwing potato peelings and him slipping up on them, then she threw the Rice Krispies and the packet was open, it was like snow falling and you laughed and started singing "White Christmas" and she told you to "LEAVE MY HOUSE IMMEDIATELY!" Oh yes I remember all about it. I tell you, it was really funny when he came to see us in the spring, I had to pretend I didn't know nothing about it. And he told me the

158

same story and because I knew it, I couldn't laugh, you know, it's not so funny the second time. Then I said about the cat food and he didn't even know, so I let the cat out of the bag, you already told me. I hope he's not mad at you for telling me. You know he always so defensive of that wife of his."

"He'll get over it. He still doing the tourists up at Bovington?" Tracey was unconcerned. It had been the biggest mistake of her life agreeing to go for Christmas to stay with Tim. His jealous, neurotic wife clearly did not believe in the sibling nature of their relationship. She watched them constantly with suspicious eyes. As the tension mounted, Tracey had longed for some excuse to leave. Being ordered out had been a relief. She had packed immediately allowing no time for a change of mind and was out of the house in half an hour, only regretting the expense of the presents and the difficulty of finding public transport back to Portsmouth on Christmas day.

A year on, it was a funny memory. She wasn't so desperate for Christmas accommodation that she'd risk Tim's Karen again in a hurry.

There was a letter - from Tim. It was the first since his training in Germany. The only contact she had had with him in the intervening years had been since he had married and his wife had taken on the self-aggrandising role of family correspondent - at Christmas card level, anyway. Tracey could imagine her cajoling Tim to come up with people for them to send cards to. It was a sad reflection probably that Tracey, so long forgotten, was among their number. But this envelope was addressed in Tim's own scraggy hand. Before enough time could elapse for it to feel ominous, Tracey opened it. A small robin-shaped Christmas card, such as would appeal to children, concealed a tightly-folded sheet of A4. In it, Tim explained and excused last Christmas, described the birth of their third child, whose pregnancy had made the mother unpredictable and violent at the time and what a blessing it was to have the long-awaited daughter. He went on, astonishingly, to suggest she come and visit again, but immediately afterwards, himself offered compelling reasons for her refusal. Which led him on to asking if she would meet him somewhere "for old time's sake" with a list of the dates on which he would be able to get away to meet her without his wife knowing. UGH, Tracey gave the letter straight to Martha. She had seen everything over the years.

"Best ignore it. Pretend it never arrived, should you ever see him again. I'll not tell. In the Aga?"

"Mmmm?" Tracey didn't hear. The envelope she opened next astonished her even more.

She could remember Kieran. Just. What woman could forget? Sixteen years ago he had been a heart-throb's heart-throb, black curly hair, dark soulful eyes, all the clichés! She dredged her brain for an accurate picture, but only a sense of him struggled to emerge from the grey.

He had sent her a Christmas card. Why had he sent her a Christmas card? She had given him her address. She remembered the strange exchange in the pub.

Inside the OXFAM card, dippy with penguins, was a message. Tracey was not fooled by the hurried nature of the scrawl, it seemed to be trying too hard to suggest that this out of the blue blast from the past, was merely a friendly whim. Tracey sensed that Kieran had spent some time phrasing this message. "Thinking of popping over to the mainland, hope it's OK if I look you up. Regards Kieran." Not even an: "I wonder if you remember me? Did you get my postcards?"

Arrogant bastard! He just knew she would remember him. Assumed she had been receiving the postcards. To be fair he had written her a couple of letters back then, when she had just arrived back from her trip to Ireland, using the pub as a forwarding address.

Responding to her Sunday uncle suspicions, she had only replied once care of the pub, telling him about her pregnancy, he didn't write back for ages. Thought she might take out a paternity suit probably. And then a couple of years after that he had suddenly started to send her the occasional postcard from his holidays. There was never a contact address, never a chance for her to reply. Just the odd postcard. Not regular. Once when she hadn't visited Martha for months, she'd got an incongruously sunny card from Tenerife at Christmas. One year she'd been away for eighteen months and got two together. One from New Zealand, with steaming hot mud pools on it, one from County Clare. There was never much of a message. An ironic 'wish you were here' if he was pushed, but sometimes a poetic description of something, like the view inside Mount Etna with the columns of smoke. Never a word of who he was with, friends, wife, partner, children, parents. Twice she'd reciprocated, sent him a postcard. One from Alum bay on The Island, the other from Aberdeen. But it seemed stupid to address them to a pub. Tracey came to accept the cards as unexpected whims. Perhaps he had no one else to send a holiday postcard to? Perhaps he really was simply a breast man, and stills had a notion for her big tits.

And then suddenly out of the blue, a Christmas card! A Christmas card with a deliberate message, almost a request. Tracey sucked in her stomach and her chest thrust forward. Was she attractive still to a man who liked breasts? Tracey put the card to one side thoughtfully.

The usual cards were there from Northern Ireland. One from Jeremy saying that his mother had died. She had never recovered from the death of that horrible little terrier. Tracey had written condolences to her at the time, trying to keep a straight pen, though her hand had wobbled with amusement trying to recall something nice to say when she could recall nothing about the dog except that he had, on first acquaintance, mistaken her for a lamppost. And there was a card from Eileen, telling her how well Thomas was getting on in Dublin. No girlfriend yet though.

At no time in the conversation with Martha did an opportunity arise in which Tracey could convey that she would have nowhere to go for Christmas. After her initial enquiry, which had been passed over in their remembering of "Tim's" Christmas, Martha didn't mention it again. Then as she was leaving, Tracey asked if she could leave her cards there to be put up with the children's, those for whom this was their only home, those staying over Christmas. There were usually pathetically few cards, sometimes a child had only the one from the class teacher, which would be as personal as the 30 other identical ones she would be giving out.

"Oh, that's really nice of you," then Martha fell into Tracey's trap, "But won't you want to put them up yourself at home?"

"No, I gave up the flat when I got the room in halls of residence. That's my only home now."

"Oh, right, so you will stay there over the holidays then?" It wasn't a question, more a statement that Martha had no doubt Tracey would confirm.

"Well actually no. Well that's not quite true. I can stay there but it costs more and there are no canteen facilities. And I didn't realise in time, so they may be intending to let my room for one of their conferences."

She knew Martha would instantly offer her a bed on the floor of her little flatlet. Tracey didn't feel at all ashamed of having manipulated her into it. Martha was like the mother she never had. But she wasn't her mother. Nothing could be assumed. She could not ask to stay. Neither of them, strong, independent women, would have liked the hint of dependence and need that this would have implied.

"That's really sweet of you, but I've a couple of friends who might be planning something. So I'll let you know. But I'll pop in sometime over Christmas for sure anyway."

There was a pause while Tracey thought about what she wanted to say next. "I found myself making a stupid promise to one of my tutors. I can't even remember how it came about. It was about my mother." She let this sink in for a moment. Martha was dumb-struck.

"Your mother!"

"I know, I know, the woman I love to hate."

"What did you promise? Why you talking to her about your mother? She's none of her business."

"It's a long dull story, but I promised to try and trace her."

"This tutor will never remember about it, forget it."

"Ah yes, but then I began to think about it and I think I want to, it being the season of goodwill and all."

"Baked bean tin of vipers, nest of worms, whatever. Leave sleeping dogs lie, live and let live. No, no, no I do not think it's a good idea for you."

162

"Proverb me up John! What about forgive and forget?"

"You mark my words it will end in tears."

"I can't stand another cliché," Tracey laughed, "I'm going now."

"No, I know what, I ask the crystal, OK? You remember when you was young you used to ask me bout it?"

"God, no, you old witch. Anyway it'll only answer what you want it to."

"Not if you do it yourself. I got it here." And Martha pulled open the drawer in the kitchen table and extracted from it a small jewellery box so well used, the velveteen knap had been worn shiny. Inside, around the protected hinges, the fabric was still a furry, emerald green, the crystal, no bigger than a marble had moulded a perfect semi-spherical space for itself. When Martha lifted it carefully out it spun on its grubby thread glittering from its many cut facets. In spite of herself, Tracey could not take her eyes off it, fascinated and captivated, tempted by its magic, exactly as she had been when a child. She shook her head impatiently,

"No,no,no you're spooky. You're wicked, Chuvelika the witch! Chuvelika! Chuvelika!"

Catching the reference to a favourite children's story, Martha sang sweetly, "Olenka, my child, come here, see what nice things I have for you, a gingerbread house with candy chimneys, see what the future has in store." Martha's syrupy voice was convincing. "But come see what terrible things will happen....... if you go look for your mother!" her evil cackle was equally convincing.

Martha anchored her elbow hard on the table and suspended the crystal by a length of about eight inches of its thread from between her fore finger and thumb. "Look, it's showing me 'yes', swinging very clearly from east to west. Look now, show me your 'no'. Watch, wait a little minute, yes, it's moved round, swinging north to south." Although Tracey had certainly been tempted to heed its advice in the past, had in fact over minor problems, she wanted this mumbo jumbo to have no role in her decision now.

"Put it away. I'm not looking, I'm not listening. I don't know how a devout god-fearing catholic like you, a Maltese catholic to boot, reconciles your faith to all this mystical magic. Disgraceful old woman, Father Sweeney would be ashamed of you! Just wish me luck, pray for me and light a candle for me, like any normal catholic!"

Tracey knew Martha would ask the crystal what she should do about her mother after she had gone home anyway, "and I'll see you nearer Christmas. What would you like for Christmas? A new pair of slippers?"

*　　*　　*　　*　　*

The energy drained from Martha's face. The smile fell away and as the muscle slackened, the loose skin pulled down to collect under her chin in a dewlap. In that moment she aged twenty years. In Tracey's company she could be a young woman again with a role, with a relationship, with a personality. But now at the kitchen table she was tired. She returned the crystal to its case without asking it anything and blinkered her eyes with the thick worn fingers.

This would be her forty-second year in service to children in Portsmouth, the past thirty in this very hostel. This was her home, her only home. But this year she would be 60, still fit for work, but due for retirement.

Her slippers slapped across the quarry tile floor under thick legs, a floral pinny flapped at her knees as Martha resumed the routine of the kitchen. She patted the flour bag shut, wafting away the white cloud that rose, smearing her nose with the back of her hand raised to wipe away a tear.

This was her life, these children her family. They were the replacement for her dead baby - who would be in her forties now, a mother perhaps, and she a grandmother. The sense of loss, of might-have-been, was too painful to contemplate. She daren't. But sometimes it was hard, and the future thinned out before her promising less and less and finally nothing. Her older brothers in Malta were both dead now, only her mother was alive scratching out a tortured life in the family casa, in simple defiance of the hated daughter-in-law who had inherited it.

Martha would of course have to go back there when she retired. It would be expected. And she could never afford to live here, with no property, no savings to speak of, no family, no reason to live. But living in Malta would be so difficult. She would hate the hot summers, the restrictions, the widows weeds they'd expect her to adopt. There, her life would be measured out in church cleaning rotas, lighted candles, trips to market, cooking for three dried up old women. And there would be heavy doses of envy when her nieces and nephews, grandnieces and nephews would come - and she would have no one of her own.

And then the terrifying possibility of a chance meeting with him. The father of her child. Hypocritical bastard, but still, in her head, still irresistible, still sexy. She had been so studiously kept away from him ever since. Her brief holidays so carefully arranged by her family to coincide with his annual trip to Rome. His annual trip with the disabled parishioners group. And then Martha recalled Tracey's news. She'd not got the full gist of Pearl's life, but Martha made a connection between the disabled Pearl and the too-busy Tracey and thought of a possible role for herself, sometime in the future. Tracey couldn't need Pearl or people like Pearl, she had her own Darron now. And she would finish university and get a good job. But Martha was going to need a new interest for herself, after retirement, if she were to stay here in Pompey. And some kind of income, even a carer's income. Yes, Martha would need someone like Pearl. Maybe a string of Pearls could keep the inevitability of slow death in Malta at bay.

"Martha.......Mar-tha.........MARTHA!"

A face, smeared with chocolate, beamed up at her, holding out brown sticky hands in one of which was a sucked Crunchy.

"D'you wanna bite, Martha?"

Martha looked towards the door handle. Made a mental note to wipe it before brushing past it later with the clean washing, but knowing she would forget, as she bent, smiling, towards the proffered gift.

*   *   *   *   *

Kieran's card seemed to throb, give off heat, have a super-physical presence, struggling for attention from where it was bundled up with the other mail in her bag. All through her visit to Pearl, Tracey was aware of the card. While she hung on the phone, waiting for administration at social services to co-operate, the card seemed to throb where the bag hung on her hip. As she asked how to get information about her mother, as they made an appointment for her, as she walked towards Bernard's, not even the cold wind distracted her from it. As though the words had been burned on, the message, "hope it's OK if I look you up" fizzed ominously. Why should he want to look her up? After all this time. Why did he remember her. It made no sense, gave her the jitters. Let's face it, it wasn't because of her big tits!

But Tracey was sure that he would actually come, this communication was not out of the blue. There had been something odd about their last and only private conversation, something untoward. Brian had not liked it that Kieran had talked to her, and Kieran had told her not to tell anyone he had her address. But then the two short letters she had received immediately afterwards had made no reference to their conversation or to his coming over to England. They had been completely anodyne. Now suddenly 15 years later it became important that she recall the exact details but Tracey couldn't.

When Tracey showed the card to Bernard, he thought it more strange that someone should still have an address 15 years later, than that they should suddenly use it to send a Christmas card. He couldn't see the difference between a postcard and a Christmas card. Both were anathema to him. Not part of his currency.

"Look, I haven't even got my mother's address and she lives in Portsmouth." It was the first time he'd mentioned his mother. Tracey stored it up for later. Bernard accused her of making too big a deal of the Christmas card thing.

"You just fancy him, don't you? You're just wetting your knickers to see him again and wrap your sticky legs around him, and lick his......."

166

"……throbbing manhood, engorged with lust, and run my hands through his thick curly hair and massage his heaving buttocks,"

"and feel him come down on you, thrusting into you, harder and harder, as you cry out in ecstasy……"

They made slobbering, sucking noises and panted and gasped and

"oh….oh…..oh….." and Tracey made a resounding "POP" with her finger in her cheek and they fell off the sofa laughing. "I just came."

"How was it….." Bernard was gasping so hard with laughter he could hardly speak, "how was it for you?"

"Christ this sofa's uncomfortable," Tracey, recovered, but still aching from laughing, plonked down and felt the frame, "even my own personal padding cannot block out the angular skeleton that is the essence of this sofa."

"Do not mock, that sofa is the sum total of my revered grandmama's extensive estate, bequeathed to me on her deathbed, even as her last breath rattled her off this mortal coil, along the final dark tunnel towards the light, and into the unknown."

"Come on, stop pissing about, we have a job to do." Tracey wound a Mrs Mop scarf round her head and tied it in an off-set knot. "Get the buckets and J-cloths! Man the mops! Reach for the Vallium, sorry vacuum! A gallon of disinfectant there, Surgeon Hardy, a barrel of brandy! We have decks to swab. Operation Pearl's oyster clean up! Dan-de-dan-de-dan!" And she jumped to attention the squeegee handle a rifle butt over one shoulder. "Did you get any joy from old sack-features about Pearl? Are they going to allow her home? And what about this post grad student who's going to take her on, any news?"

If Bernard had answered any of these, Tracey wouldn't have heard above their footsteps, clanking squeegees, bucket and dragging vacuum lead echoing round the stairwell as they struggled down to Pearl's flat.

"Well?" she waited for a response as Bernard got out the key.

"Shhhhh…..someone's coming in, might be Joe." After a couple of minutes breathless silence, "or, maybe not."

Tracey whispered, "I was asking if you've heard any news about Pearl. Is she getting out for Christmas? Have they got this postgrad research thingy set up yet?"

"I didn't see Chapman……only the little nursie,"

"Don't call her that!"

"Said she'd been told to get her ready for a new programme starting tomorrow and Chapman's coming to see her on Thursday. I thought I'd try and be there. Do you think you could be as well? The respectable female……yeah I remember now…..'member of the family'! You never told me you'd lied to them! Could've got me into a right mess…..except I'm such a brilliant smoothie…."

"You c'n say that again!"

"I'm such a brilliant…"

"Yeah, yeah……actually I meant to tell you about that. I did not actually lie. But you remember that foreign nurse, the one with the nice hair, not the fat-arsed one? Well she was taking down some information and when she asked if I was family, I blathered on about how our mothers had grown up together. She said 'Oh sisters?' she asked me direct. 'Not as close as sisters,' I says 'Cousins, then, so you and Pearl must be second cousins!' She was all pleased with her grasp of family relationships in English, she didn't wait for a reply. So, I didn't bother to say. Left it to fate. Sorry I forgot to mention it."

"Well I think that's why they're letting you take charge of her then. Hope they don't ask for proof. Why should they believe you?"

"Just glad to see someone, anyone, take her on I s'pose. Anyway, people always trust me." Tracey was miffed that he should be surprised that they would trust her, but mollified when he continued:

"They obviously think I'm a bit of a weirdo, taking an interest in Pearl. And it's just cause I'm a bloke. Don't they know the most evil guards in the concentration camps were women? That old scraggy ancillary was telling me at great length the other day about these sickos who can only get

168

turned on by the prospect of sex with disabled people in wheelchairs. Do you think she might have been hinting at some intended impropriety on my part?"

"Yeah, yeah, keep it in proportion. Don't get carried away. As to me being there, well, my lectures have finished, so I'll probably be free, but I'm still waiting to be summoned by Susan. Dr Susan Milhouse, to give her her full title. You remember, I told you about her? She's one of my tutors. Got to see her for another meeting about my writing skills, sorry lack of them, actually. I'll have to go whenever she calls because I think she's about to go into labour any minute. Probably won't be Thursday though. I hope I get a chance to see her a couple more times before she goes on maternity leave. She's really nice, and helpful."

"What are you rabbitting about? Pass the nozzle can you?"

"Oooo, on the nozzle already, they're right, you are a weirdo! Heh, listen, what's that?"

Bernard's thumb paused, poised over the socket switch in the skirting board. His ear was close to the wall. The wall adjoined the neighbouring flat, which had its entrance on the other stairwell at the opposite end of the building. He could hear something, too. Motionless, they listened. It was sobbing, a thin sound muffled by the partition wall, but clearly sobbing. Rapid, high-pitched sobbing, a child's sobbing.

Bernard straightened, his face sharp with concentration as he tried to place the occupants of the flat.

"That's the old man's place. I've never seen him to talk to but he shuffles in and out. And I quite often see a couple of boys being dropped off or picked up by a son or daughter. Must be one of the lads, in trouble, been misbehaving."

"I hadn't thought about anyone being there, just the other side of the wall There must be a mirror image of your stairwell their side then, with the three flats? Oh, and the big room below to match our keep fit hall. They must have heard Pearl's telly explosion as though it was in their own bedroom. Must've been terrifying. Were they amongst the crowd out on the street that night?"

"Wouldn't know." Bernard's memory of that night had crystallised into a few bleak images. The blanket-covered mound, ominous, secretive, in the oscillating blue light of the ambulance. Lilly's bleary face, white in the strip light, peering out of the steamed-up bus window. The scream of disc brakes followed by the crunch of metal and sprinkle of glass like sugar on cornflakes. The short fat woman running away. Tracey.

"Should we do something?"

Why did Tracey always feel she had to do something? Why was it her responsibility?

"Nooooo….. it's just a kid crying, they cry all the time." Bernard had done his share of crying as a child, he was sure Tracey had too. He flicked the vacuum cleaner on. It roared its agreement. He looked round to see Tracey wearing a colourless fabric lampshade from the bedroom. Its filthy tasselled fringe hung down in irregular loops. It was peppered like a colander with moth holes.

"Watch out they'll get into your brain." Bernard shouted. Tracey tried to read his lips. It looked like, "What's that? They'll get Easaw away." Tracey's interpretation was clearly rubbish and not worth pursuing with Bernard, but it satisfied a train of thought. She had noticed that Pearl could understand what was said much better if she was looking into your face. She may have been simply reading facial expressions, but Tracey had begun to think that Pearl might be lip-reading as well, that she might be deaf.

When they stood back later to survey their hard work, the flat looked sanitised. It did not look inviting. It was a large, square room. Bare windows, clean for the first time in years, looked out onto the street. Huge yellow discs with golden coronas, fortunately faded by the years, shone from the dusted wallpaper, with a faint lightening where they had carefully wiped at the grubbiest patches round light switches and doorways. The bare floorboards, had been sucked clean, and were now darkened by water but would, they hoped, dry whitened by their scrubbing. The paintwork had come up like new, the dirt having clearly protected it.

A heavy oak wardrobe (how did they get it up here?) groaned at its wax polish buffing (with pleasure?). The iron-frame bed under the window, now rust-free and gleaming, was mattressless. A scrubbed extendable table and four oak chairs were pushed aside to let the floor dry. On the table was a huge box full of ornaments, a few books, some photos and bits of delft and glass that they had found and cleaned up. The rust-coloured sofa, had revealed itself a surprising orange, showing shocking gashes of vermilion in its seams and creased elbows. In the kitchen the enamel cooker had quickly come clean, confessing that it had never been much used. And the sink had reluctantly given up its secret, emerging a blindingly shiny stainless steel. The one cupboard was now empty and bleached. After a quick vacuum, they had left the one bedroom, Lilly's, full of her things, pulling the door tight shut with a wedge of paper beneath it. In the bathroom, porcelain and tiles shone white, green-eroded chrome taps having given up globs of black mould now at least worked, the bare bulb swung, a flashing reflection across black and white floor tiles. The heavy miasma of disinfectant and bleach tore at their nostrils, but comforted the godliness of their souls.

Leaving the doors and top front window open a crack to assist the drying, Bernard and Tracey backed out onto the landing, proud, reluctant to tear themselves away from admiring the good job they had done. He checked he had the key, she reached for the door handle and pulled it shut hoisting the last bin bag out in front of her.

"OW, watch out you clumsy bugger." They didn't need to push in the timer light switch to know it was Joe. He must have been out there, lurking on the landing in the dark, listening, waiting to surprise them. He was now hopping about in pain. The bin bag had connected with his shin.

"You can give us a hand to take this lot back upstairs if you like." Bernard invited. Joe had never been in Bernard's flat and being a nosy old man, had always wanted to see inside. But currently preoccupied with the outrage of his injury he said before he could stop himself,

"I could sue for this, I think it might be broken."

"You won't make it up the stairs then, hang on there and we'll give you a hand to get back down…..and then we're off for a well-deserved pint, when we've put these things away." Bernard couldn't keep a straight face, he started to snigger.

Upstairs Tracey said, "I didn't think old Rose would be able to keep from telling him, but she's done well to keep quiet this long."

"I'm not so sure he has told him, I think he just heard us and came up to investigate."

When they delivered the grumbling Joe to his own threshold, they still hadn't explained why they were cleaning out Lilly's flat. Joe was apoplectic with curiosity and frustration at their bland comments about neighbourly actions and keeping the environment of the building up to scratch, not letting things slide, just because Lilly and Pearl were away.

They pushed him through his own front door to Rose and though they shut it, they could hear her call and him reply, breathless with the excitement of his news. They paused to listen.

" 'Ere, you'll never guess what! That slime ball Bernie and the chubby bird!!" Before he could finish, Rose interrupted.

"They're never 'aving it off together! Not 'im, he's a puffta, i'n 'e!"

"Nah, nah, you silly old cow, nuffink to do with sex, you got a one-track mind you 'ave! They bin up there cleaning."

"Cleaning! Cor that sounds saucy!........Is that all? That don't sound too scandalous!"

Good old Rose, she hadn't said anything. So far, she was still on board for her share of the community effort to rehabilitate Pearl. Bernard and Tracey crept away so as not to give away that they'd been listening at the door.

Chapter 14

Tracey peered into the room, trying to see through the encased meshing in the narrow slit of fire-proof glass. Yup, there was Marc. She tried waving surreptitiously, but he was miles, or probably kilometres, away. She could not make him look round towards the door. He did not seem to be paying attention to the lesson. She bobbed out of sight when another students noticed her.

"Ce soir, je ne m'interesse pas du lecon. Et porquoi? Parce qu'il y avait une petite petite probleme avec Isabelle. Elle voulait retourner a Paris. Mais moi, non. Je suis donc assez confortable ici, avec mes amis anglais et de la musique originale, et de la biere anglaise bitter. Mais elle, finalement, elle a decide que l'universite ne offrit pas les etudes anglaises ni les opportunites....... Oh, la la! merde, merde the teacher is calling me to do my English in class. What is it? Conversation with the intelligent Jan from Finland, best-selling author. What can I talk to him? He hates me. My long hairs upsets him. He thinks I am the same his son who has the problem with the drugs. Huh! Me! I just like am anarchist, but I know it's not really anarchist. And I never like the drugs, no, because my sister, she die of drugs. Eh Jan, how you doin' man? What you doin for Christmas, going back to the Finland. Father Christmas lives there, say Hellos to him. Jan is saying me the perfect English back. I'm not listen. My eyes floating away and then they get fixed on the room in the building. Over theres. The room is blue with the television light. It lights off the walls and furniture. I see two boys sitting beside theirself, their faces is shine with the blue light. It's like a film from the future, like aliens from Pluto. Jan is asking me how about Christmas. I don't know. Not my family Christmas. I keep looking the two boys. They look sad, sad, sad. I remember, before, I was the same sad. I from an alien world. Only I was only. Heh, the teacher looking at me now, asking, are you alright Marc? Eh eh eh. It's nothing to do with her business, good colloquial expression,eh?"

As Marc looked towards the front of the class, responding at last to the teacher, Tracey knocked firmly on the door. Marc jumped and turned round. The tutor's expression was frozen between relief and annoyance. Tracey opened the door, refusing to be intimidated.

"I'm really sorry to interrupt, but I have to speak to Marc urgently." She beckoned him out of the room. The tutor shrugged. It was the last day of term. It was a tradition that they would finish early so that she could take the students to the pub. The sooner, the better. It had been a long hard term.

The corridor was narrow, so they moved to the stairway to talk.

"I'm really sorry, I just popped up to say I can't go to the pub tonight after all, I have to go somewhere else. Somewhere really important."

Because she looked so agitated, Marc asked if there was a problem. He thought it extremely strange that she should bother to interrupt his class to come and tell him this. As a trainee anarchist, he had never taken their arrangements to meet that seriously. Didn't always bother to turn up himself.

Tracey let her gaze wander past him, as she considered whether to confide in him. He looked and followed her eyes. They were both staring into the room with the eerie light, at the two boys huddled together on a sofa, only their faces bright, and behind them, from the black corners of the room, shifting shadows, grew and fell menacingly. They looked so vulnerable. And one, the smaller, looked about 5, with a straight chopped fringe and even though she was across the street and it was dark, Tracey thought she could see his expression, tense and scared. Like Paul. So like Paul. Paul, that little brother she had not seen since he was 5 and she was 9. They'd separated him from his sister for his own good. He was to have been adopted because there was no other hope for him. They would never tell Tracey where. Eventually when she had worn them down with her insistent enquiries, they had told her that he had emigrated to Australia with his new family.

Seeing the little face watching the television opposite, reminding her of the lost Paul, of her own lost childhood. Perhaps this was the affirmation she had been waiting for, an omen.

174

"I'll be in the pub tomorrow. Don't forget to find out if Isabelle's coming on 25th."

At the mention of Isabelle, Marc's eyebrows fell, a fierce intake of breath spread his nostrils, his lips disappeared into a hard white line.

Tracey hastily retracted, "OK, OK, take it easy, you don't have to tell me at all. It'll be alright. She doesn't eat a lot by the looks of her, if she comes, she comes. Let's leave it and see. I've got to go. See you tomorrow."

A wind to cut corn swathed up the platform, flaying legs, lifting coat skirts. Tracey pulled her collar over her ears and gave thanks for warm jeans and thermal socks, pitying the office girls in their delicate shoes, stockinged calves and thin fashionable macs. She was warm, her breath still harsh and quick from hurrying. The train was late. She checked again the time, the announcement, the information screen, her ticket. She tried to control her taut nerves, to breathe easy. It was only four stops. She had brought nothing to read. No time, no point.

When it arrived, the train was almost full. Seven thirty. Still full of office workers, tired and strained-looking, Christmas time taking its toll. And one or two overalled men and women, spattered from head to toe with paint, mud, plaster, carrying lunch boxes, smudgy newspapers, looking tired but content. All gazing about them, avoiding eye contact, pretending not to notice their own reflections in the darkened windows. No one travelling far enough to bother reading. One nodding off. Tracey tried not to stare. But she needed a distraction. A man stared back. She looked away first. She was disappointed, because it had only been the jolting motion that had shifted her gaze. The smell of damp dust, warmed by bodies had just begun to pall when they drew into her station.

The staring man got off too. Tracey couldn't believe it. Surely he wasn't going to follow her, give her grief on this night of all nights. Too ironic.

To blot out thought, Tracey focused on her surroundings. Her footsteps beating a rhythm with her breath, given shape by the clouding vapour before her. The looming black hedge, pressing in; the misty pools of orange street light suspended above, emanating from the bold ingots of golden bulbs; the final disappearance of the staring man. And the address pulsating in her head.

Forty two, 42 - the answer to the galactic hitchhiker's guide question -

Worldsend - a bit too possible.

Denford - sounded too normal.

Surely this would all evaporate into a dream and Tracey would come to. From: a snooze on the bus; forty winks in front of the telly; a boring lecture; a drunken stupor. But the footsteps were real, one foot heavily in front of the other, the dewy privet leaves etched real wet patterns on her cheek, her chilly fingers tingled with impending numbness.

And there was Worldsend: a cul-de-sac of modern brick houses; each with its neat garage; its tiny matching patch of grass; its own bed of evergreen shrubs; and each guarded by a tall, thin rowan, a sentry on duty at the front kerb, standing over the parked cars, many spanking new. Every window draped, every interior light modestly diffuse. Individuality was expressed cautiously, in the twinkling Christmas lights; some were bright, multi-coloured, unashamed, garishly picking out the contours of the house; some were tastefully mono-chrome, carefully restricted to the branches of the tree; one house was emblazoned with an brilliantly illuminated Santa climbing the wall with a bulky sack. No sound could be heard from any house.

2, 4, 6, 8,.......23, 25, 27.....Where was the logic in the numbering? Tracey walked them, eventually anticipating three houses away, number 42. She slowed, nearly turning back. But forced herself on. Then paused to recall the phone call. The woman answering, puzzled, and a little frightened when nobody spoke. Tracey's finger was on the buzzer now. In a last ditch panic, she wished for there to be no reply to her ring. But, inside, a shape moved towards her, fuzzied by the privacy glass, a woman. She opened the door, looked questioningly out.

"May I come in?" Tracey's voice was thin.

"Not if you're selling something," she replied.

176

"No, nor collecting, nor signing up for obscure religions, nor carol singing."

The woman laughed, "OK. Come in then and tell me who you are and what you want. It's cold with the door open."

The woman was much taller than Tracey and quite slender, though big busted. Her coloured hair needed treating, grey roots showed. Her middle-aged face was pleasant, frowning faintly in enquiry.

In the hall Tracey blurted, "I'm Tracey Allsop. I came to find you."

The woman looked momentarily nonplussed then wobbled unsteady. Tracey knew she briefly contemplated denying any knowledge of such a person. She followed her into the front room where she flopped down on a sofa, her face no longer pleasant, but pinched, anguished drawn up at the mouth, like the throat of a toilet bag pulled tight. Or a pig's anus. Tracey continued to stand. The woman looked away. "J'accuse," said the voice in Tracey's head. She savoured the moment and the phrase.

"So often, so very often, I have imagined this moment. And each time put off the reality of trying to arrange it."

Inside Tracey screamed "LYING BITCH! If you'd wanted to you could've arranged it."

Aloud she said, "Me too," with a heaviness that hinted menace.

The woman looked sharply up. "You have every reason to hate me."

"I do."

"How did you find me?"

"You're in the bleeding phone book. Haven't changed your name or anything. I just phoned the once and, God, I knew your voice straight away."

"Why are you here?" the woman asked.

"I promised my tutor I would attempt a reconciliation. I only said it to get her off my back. Had I wanted to I could've done it years ago, you being in the phone directory an all! But then the thought took hold and, well, over the years I have come up against several very different sorts of mothers. And over the years I periodically thought, what about mine? Why go on hating, when there may be no need. Though it's a passive hatred, it's still draining. Life would be easier without it. Love or being able to love certainly would be. You can't undo the betrayal and I can't forgive what you did to Paul." The woman winced. "But I might be able to understand, as an adult, your difficulty with dad, if you can explain it. Even at the time we knew he was a tyrant." This speech was not the rehearsed speech. It flew out of Tracey's mouth as though someone else was saying it. She listened to it with dismay, so conciliatory. Why was she, the injured party, the permanently damaged human being, reaching out?

All tension suddenly left the mother. She crumpled like a starched linen suit in the rain. Sweat broke out on her forehead and fell mingling with tears. She was grey and limp. She flesh looked dead.

"Where's the kettle? We need tea." A weak finger pointed, fish mouth opened, no sound came out.

Her mother had pulled herself together and was leaning on the kitchen door as Tracey fumbled in cupboards for tea things. Gradually the mother became engaged in the task.

After several false starts she managed to say, "It'll make no difference, but I am really, really sorry. I couldn't cope with you. It wasn't just your father, though he was a bastard. I realise now that he had always been such a controlling man that there was no way I could've made it on my own with two kids. And you were so wilful, so naughty. I couldn't manage you at all. I had no will of my own at all, no decision-making skills. No skills at all, except obedience. I was totally a product of his making. I had been with him from the age of 16, remember. I couldn't function on my own. I was his rib. There was no me."

Tracey sourly thought there was plenty of "me" now. And of course it had to be his fault, and astonishingly partly hers, such a naughty child!

"Even now I'm hopeless on my own. I never married again, but it's a struggle. I got myself trained. I work in the accounts office at Bradley's."

She was talking quickly, nervously, as if Tracey would know what Bradley's was. She was looking at the clock a lot. Outside the twin beams of silent headlights swung across the window. The woman jumped. Was she expecting someone?

In answer they heard a key slide into the lock. Tracey's mother tensed. They both looked towards the door as it opened. A tall young man let himself in. A toy boy? He was wearing a pilot's uniform, the hat under his arm, a flight bag and newspaper held in one hand as he replaced the key in his pocket.

He looked at them enquiringly. But even before he spoke, Tracey knew.

He was smiling, looking expectant, waiting for an introduction, an explanation.

He looked at the older woman,

"Mum?"

Chapter 15

PR Day! The day they had all been working towards, Pearl's Release day. Outside the nurses' station, Bernard was pacing. Not so much with the anxiety of an old fashioned expectant father awaiting the result of a difficult birth, more like a father awaiting the long negotiated release from prison of a difficult child. They had all worked so hard for this and now, despite reinforcing over and over the importance of all three of them being there together to receive Pearl, Bernard found himself there alone. Anxiety and fury swelled inside him; one leaping off into an internal rage against human nature, constant only in its unreliability; the other, feeding the irrational fear that if they didn't succeed in freeing Pearl now, at this very moment, something would occur to prevent it forever.

Tracey had promised to be here. Where the fuck was she? Bernard knew they would never let him take Pearl on his own. Even the research student, Robin, was a bloke. They'd never get her out without Tracey. Tracey had so conscientiously wormed her way into their world, so convincingly set herself up as the caring 'relation', she was the one to whom Pearl was actually being handed over. See the triumph in their eyes, watching him wait, watching his anxiety rise.

Funny how some people could get off on other people's failure, how could they get so much pleasure from watching other people fail? They were the sickos. Christ, and there was Pearl, all ready and waiting, all excited, so pink and healthy-looking. He couldn't bear to look at her. He sat down beside her and held her hand, looking at his own feet. What yarn could he spin her that would be believable? He needed a moment to think.

Great, at last, there was Robin, Bernard called him over, after all, she was his patient now, well, his case study really. Robin would have to talk to Pearl for a bit and stop her fretting, while Bernard came up with a strategy to get her out.

In the minutes it took Robin to make his way the length of the corridor, Bernard looked round. All these decorations. He hated them. All this tinselly stuff dripping around, no method, no plan, scruffy old bits, rejects from other wards probably, and cotton wool blobs all over the windows! What a mess, what resemblance to snow? Never snowed there anyway. And see how it really jollied the old dears along! Didn't they look a lot happier since this mess had gone up. See them smiling and dancing! Jesus, it was all such crap! It just made their vegetative states the more noticeable, threw it into even sharper contrast. They could leave the decorations up all year for all the difference it would make to them.

This brief distraction gave Bernard's brain a space in which to disconnect his fury at Tracey for her lateness and engage in solving the problem of Tracey's absence for the purposes of taking Pearl with them now.

"Right, I know, I'll go off and pretend to phone Tracey, who must be the only person this side of Calcutta not contactable by phone! Then I'll come back and explain that she thought I was picking Pearl up with Robin and that,"

"Sorry?" Robin was in earshot and Bernard realised he had been thinking aloud. God, he was wound up! Fortunately, no one else was around.

He repeated his idea sotto voce to Robin, "I'll flannel them with your great expertise and authority. Explain how we thought we wouldn't need Tracey to sign the discharge now we have you, the professional. And I'll say she has been waiting patiently in the flat for us to arrive. Getting it all warm and cosy, to be there when Pearl arrives, to make it less alien, to make her feel secure. What do you think? Then, if they say no chance, I'll go and find the bitch, makes sense since I've borrowed the car, leave you to Pearl-sit. OK? Just hope to Christ she's in the halls still. She has to get out by the 15th. That's tomorrow, right?" Was he rambling?

*   *   *   *   *

Bernard took the stairs two at a time. The hammering on the door would've woken the dead. As it was, the Iranian guy next door put his head out and deluged Bernard with a stream of Farsi abuse. As he slammed his door, Tracey opened hers.

181

"GO AWAY!" she shouted and slammed it. The Iranian opened his for one more vicious shot. Farsi became farce. Bernard hammered and hollered.

"Tracey, how could you have forgotten Pearl?" This time when she opened the door, he jammed his foot in it.

"Get dressed!" He ordered, "Now! Pearl's waiting, with fish-features at the hospital. They won't let her out without your signature. They did this as a real favour remember. You know it's not really official..... We can't let the moment pass or they might think better of it........ Their Christmas magnanimity won't last forever. We haven't got time to wait for a court order......... we've invited half the population to lunch......... You've got to come and get Pearl." He was as desperate as he had ever been.

Bernard suddenly became aware of the blank look she met him with. Her pupils were dilated. Weren't they? She started to undress, absentmindedly. Bernard had never seen a fat woman naked before. In a detached way he observed how large her breasts were, how soft and vulnerable, how large and tender-looking the massive aureoles. He was surprised that, despite his anxiety about Pearl, he could notice these things and even more surprised that Tracey's skin was so white and smooth, creased and folded in a way that made him curious to touch it. The deft way she bent to ease her breasts into the cups of her bra, to lift them into comfort, suddenly gave him a glimpse of a new world. And he had thought himself a man of the world. He believed passionately that to be human was to be flesh in all its forms and yet half the humans in the world were like this and he had never seen it before.

Tracey looked awful. Greasy hair, black bags, empty eyes.

He spoke more gently.

"Teeth?" He'd come to know some of her obsessions. Tracey obediently went to clean them, but her hand was too limp to work properly. "Wash you face." She went through the motions. "Now sit here."

Bernard brushed her hair off her face, twisted a scarf into a loose hair band and tied it around her head. He drew a few threads of hair through to give a wispy carefree look. With a cracked pink lipstick he found by the mirror, he coloured her cheeks and lips a little and then sprayed body spray all over, hoping it would hold it all together.

"Come on, you would look the part, a real jolly momma, if only you would smile."

In the car, she began to thaw.

"Thanks. I'm sorry I forgot Pearl's move was today. I lost track."

"LOST TRACK! OK," more softly, "tell me what happened. Where did you go when you couldn't meet Marc? Why so secretive? Why didn't you tell me? I haven't seen you for days. Marc told me you called him out of his class – a bit OTT wasn't it?"

"You've got your spies out! Anyway can we just leave it now please."

She patted his thigh as he drove, thankful for his friendship.

"Thanks for coming to get me. I'd never have forgiven myself if this had failed because of me."

"Well, where were you?" Bernard did not intend to let her off the hook.

"Please! Can I tell you later? I want to focus on Pearl now. I will say I had a bit of a shock the other night and then, as is my wont, went on a bit of a bender. I think I'm fine now….and," she smiled warmly at him, "I'm really pleased to see you. (in a public school accent) You're a brick, Angela! Where d'you get the smart motor?"

"Borrowed from my dad. And there's a price to pay, which involves, literally, doing some spadework for him. He thinks I'm mad, gone right off my trolley with the Pearl thing. He wants to meet you. I said it was all your idea and I'm just helping out a friend."

"Thanks, pal! Christ, I hope it doesn't turn out to be a disaster. And all my fault." In her weakened state Tracey found plenty of room for pessimism.

"Heh, where's the fighting talk? We knew at the start that if it doesn't work out this way for Pearl, social services will have to find sheltered accommodation for her. But at least this way she might get a hostel instead of a residential place with no autonomy where she might just vegetate. We will have done our best and there will be a whole load of people who know her and who will visit and take her out......But I think it is going to work."

Trickles of brick dust still lay on the treads of the stairs where the stair lift had so recently been put in for Pearl. How Chapman had persuaded the powers that were to rush this job, no one dared ask. Rose was both delighted and irritated. She had asked for a stair lift for herself - her arthritis was increasingly disabling her – months before, with no joy. Now suddenly it had become a priority job – for the little gem, Pearl!

The collapsible wheel chair was none-the-less a major piece of equipment to lug up the stairs while Pearl was held steady on the seat of the lift. It was a three-person job, including Pearl, whose right hand grip was now nearly strong enough to almost hold her steady. Re-erecting the chair at Joe and Rose's landing, transferring Pearl into it, wheeling it round to the next flight, ejecting Pearl, strapping her onto the chair lift, up another flight, the same procedure up to her own front door, took them three quarters of an hour that first time.

By the time they got there Pearl was weeping. Frustration, discomfort, emotion or fear at being home, remembering her mother, her former life? They couldn't tell. Tracey was exhausted and ready to join Pearl in a good cry.

Bernard opened the door, pushing Pearl in first so they weren't able to see her expression, read her reaction. But they saw her body jump when she saw inside. Alarm? Fear? Pleasure? Tracey hurried round to the front of the wheel chair and crouched down for a Pearl's eye view of the room.

Martha's old bright blue curtains and the yellow wallpaper gave, Tracey thought, a sunny seaside feel to the place. The blue and yellow checked (Argos) bed cover, over which a Van Gough sunflower hung, added a cheery countrified air. The table was disguised by a primary-coloured floral oil cloth, with a Poinsettia in the centre. The floorboards had been covered in an off-cut of cushionfloor in stippled beige, a hopefully, easy-maintenance colour. Conspicuous by its absence was, the television.

Beholding all this, it was difficult for Tracey to determine Pearl's reaction.

"Let's shut the door and keep the heat in."

Pearl was opening and shutting her mouth in the way she had done before the physiotherapist had really started to work on her speech. Tracey decided she was simply speechless.

"What do you think? This is your home for the time being. Do you like it?"

"Yeah....eah...eah....sss. Beautiful." The almost perfect pronunciation stopped them all in their tracks. It was a relief to Tracey. She had insisted that they do as little as possible to the place, so that Pearl could make it her own, stamp her own taste on it. But as a result it was rather sparse. She couldn't wait to go through the box with Pearl to see if she could tell her what they were, where they had come from, who the photos were of.

"Where's....mum?" Neither Pearl nor any of them had referred to her mother until this moment. They had no answer.

"She ...dead?"

*   *   *   *   *

There was no answer when they buzzed at the street door and it was too late in the day for the tradesmen's buzzer, it had already been switched off. Bernard walked round the back. Marc crossed the road and looked up at the second floor window.

"They inside, the television working anyway," he announced when they met again on the doorstep.

They both crossed the road and called up to the window for the boys to come out. Two earnest faces appeared to watch the two young men. They looked pale and glum. They didn't communicate with each other, just stood and watched silently. One slightly taller, otherwise they were very similar, straight fringes, big eyes, pursed lips. One about five, his brother about seven.

Bernard had been looking out for the old man ever since Tracey and he had heard the crying through the wall. Though he had assured her there was nothing unusual in the crying of a child, he was himself concerned, always hating to witness another's misery. The old man had not, to Bernard's knowledge been in or out in the intervening days. They had heard the boy crying again from Pearl's flat, but when they had knocked on the wall and tied to speak to him, they had heard him leave the room and shut the door.

"Is your Grandpa up there, I've got an important message for him?" Bernard cupped his hands round his mouth and called up to them from the street. The taller shook his head. He had been able to hear, then. Marc and Bernard exchanged a look of concern.

"Will you let me in to tell you the message? You know me, I'm Bernard. I live next door." Again a shaking of the head.

On a whim, Marc began to turn cartwheels along the pavement. Bernard stood theatrically back, out of his way. Then Marc stood on his hands and walked about.

"What are you doing?" Bernard thought he'd taken leave of his senses.

Upright again Marc said, "Look at the children while I'm playing about, they will become interesting and then they will want to talk with us and they will.....um what's the word?...."

"Trust us?"

"Yep." And Marc did a series of backflips, pausing to pull faces, which he did with a skill Bernard would never have guessed at. He had known Marc's face was rubber, and now he saw his body was an elastic band to match.

Bernard turned his attention to the two boys as Marc lifted up his ponytail, holding it straight up in the air with one hand, and then mimed being dragged along by it, twisting this way and that, falling and righting himself, controlled by the hand of an invisible giant above. The boys were laughing and pointing at Marc, gabbling to each other.

"Will you come now and talk to us?" he called, falling over his own feet. "Look, you can see I need some help." Marc was miming all the time he was shouting up to them.

The bigger one pointed to Marc and nodded. He pointed to Bernard and shook his head vigorously. Then they both disappeared. The two men resumed their position on the doorstep and before he pressed the buzzer, Marc decided he should have a strategy, a reason for calling.

"What is the message for the Grandpa?"

"Oh, I don't know, I just said that to get them down………I know, say he's, no they, are all invited to the lunch."

"My God, Tracey will kill you, three more." Marc was impressively emphatic.

"I'm the one cooking I think it's in my gift to invite who I like!" Did he sound a little petulant, prima donna of the kitchen. "Anyway it's only an invitation at this stage with only two small-boy appetites really likely to be extra, huh?"

"OK dokey, on your hair be it!"

"Head!"

"No, I think I'm correct here, like in French we say, "mal aux cheveux", it means like when you drink too much alcohol,"

"Hangover?"

"Yeah, it's really mean "sick in the hair". I think Tracey will cut off your hair, or put pudding on it. So "on your hair be it" not on your head be it."

"Your acrobatics are better than your laboured jokes in English."

"Yeeeesss….?" The hissing voice of the intercom could not disguise the boy's fear.

"Is me, the Clever the Clown, can I come and say: hello, you got a banana in your ear?"

"OK, not the other one though, he'd weird."

"I'm weird! I don't do cartwheels in the street." Bernard waved a limp hand, as Marc was buzzed in by the two little boys.

Upstairs Marc found there was a security chain on the door. But when he asked politely to be let in the boys, with fumbling and clattering managed to release it. He could smell the direction of the lavatory immediately, the distinctive uric smell of three males with bad aims living together. The place was a state. Without appearing to spy, he caught sight of the detritus of several tinned meals in the kitchen. The bin overflowed onto the floor. In the living room where he sat down on an overstuffed floral sofa there were scatterings of crumbs and a couple of damp patches on the carpet. Bowls and spoons licked clean were left randomly about and under the television was a soggy-looking crust. No sign of Grandpa.

Marc began to tell the boys about his life in a Russian circus and how he had learned all his tricks and acrobatics, about the white horse he used to ride and the sparkly costume he wore. His foreign accent gave him credibility, they were rapt. He asked if they'd been to the circus. They told him in detail about one trip where the trapeze artist had fallen. They seemed to think it was very funny. They told him their names, James the elder and Matthew the younger.

Marc had just begun to feel that he had their trust enough to ask about the Grandfather when the buzzer went. The two boys froze, put their fingers to their lips, imploring him to be silent and not go to the door. Marc nodded assent. Then with huge, exaggerated movements like a cartoon character trying to make no noise, he peered quickly round the curtain.

They could just see a woman standing down by the door, stamping impatiently in the chill air. Smart, clutching an official-looking attaché case. Marc recognised the type. She had "School Inspector" written all over her self-righteous-looking back. These types had been the sworn enemies of Marc as a small boy. He drew the two boys to him, "Shhhhh....keep very quite. I'm agree with you." He whispered. They all smiled in collusion.

"She's come to get you for school, no?" he whispered. "But where is your grandpa?"

The younger child began to cry. Between sobs he started to explain. The older child said between gritted teeth: "You mustn't tell, you mustn't tell! We promised not to tell."

188

But there was no stopping Matthew. The older child sat stony faced, but down his cheeks, tears also spilled.

"Grandpa went out. He said don't open the door to NOone. And now we did cos you're here. But I don't think he's coming back."

"Course he is!" snapped his brother.

"Shh…..let's see if stinky-shoes is gone." Through the window they saw the official walking away. She turned to look up at their window. They bobbed down, just in time.

"Grandpa's not coming back!" Matthew resumed, "he said there's some tins of beans and some biscuits. You'll be alright til tomorrow. That was……umm…..a few weeks ago. He said don't touch the cooker. The heating's on. Remember to clean you teeth."

"Where did he go?"

"Out."

"But where are your mother and father? Why aren't they looking after you? Where is you home?"

Whether the blank looks were the silence of conspiracy or simply ignorance, Marc couldn't tell.

"Shall we have a go to tidying up, eh?" They joined in willingly enough and Marc had the magic touch of making a game out of everything. When the kitchen was done and and a hoover found which offered great opportunities for chasing games, Marc decided he could not face the toilet. But it bothered him that they were living in unhygienic conditions. It bothered James too.

"UGH the toilet's horrible and stinky." James complained.

"Here, put on these gloves and I'll tell you how to clean it." But of course the ineptitude of young children and the discovery of bleach drove Marc to hold his nose and do the scrubbing himself. The catharsis made him tired and generous.

"Let's go for fish and chips. You got the door key?"

James was instantly suspicious, and said, no. But it turned out he knew where the spare key was kept and when Marc convinced him that he would let him look after it and not touch it himself, they all went out. Marc persuaded them to come up with him to Bernard's to get his coat.

Tracey was there. To her amazement, when she held open her arms to him, Matthew flew over to cuddle her, sat on her lap and stuck his thumb in his mouth.

"DON'T SUCK YOUR THUMB, remember what Mum said." James shrieked at him. Guiltily he took it out.

On their way back with the fish and chips, they called into the convenience store to get a bottle of coke. There was a queue. Matthew, bored, wondered about picking things up and looking at them. He found himself behind the counter.

"Come out from there," hissed Marc.

"Hey, look," Matthew suddenly yelled, "there's Grandpa."

"Stay here for pay, James, I go see what's happening." He was alarmed at the thought that in order for Grandpa to have been behind there, he would have to be prostrate on the floor. But Matthew was pointing at a small poster, tatty round the edges, pinned up on the inside of the counter. It showed the mug shots of four men. Matthew had his forefinger jammed on the cheek of a scraggy white-haired chap with rheumy eyes.

"Look! It's Grandpa. He's famous." He was excited. The name underneath was Henry McIn...... Marc's reading in English did not yet cover Scottish names.

"What's his name?" He asked Matthew.

Matthew looked at him, astounded, then he said, slowly and carefully as though to an imbecile, "Grandpa!" and added under his breath, "Dinlo!"

"You got the money for the coke?" James was itching with curiosity, wanting to know what they had found, feeling excluded, but too cool to show it, "We're next."

"Heh, the chips will be cold, let's get out of here," Marc didn't want them to know he couldn't read.

"But what about the Grandpa thing?" James wailed.

"We'll tell you on the way home. The guy was getting angry for us being there."

On their return with fish and chips when Marc told Tracey about the Grandpa in the shop, she couldn't

190

understand what it was they had seen. She asked what the 'paper' had said. Marc admitted, behind his hand, that he didn't read very much English, but there were four men's photos on it. She promised to teach him to read.

"James, what was this thing about your grandfather? What did it say?" Tracey was keen to find out what had happened to him and reunite children with grandparent if possible. Perhaps this was a clue.

"Huh?" James tried to prize his attention away from the television screen where Liverpool were uncharacteristically getting slaughtered. "Oh, I didn't see it." He stuffed four chips in his mouth so he would be unable to answer any more questions and could concentrate on the game.

"I have to go now," Marc said to the boys "Tracey takes you back to next door to sleep. You got the key safe, James?"

Having seen the woman in the wheelchair, James was very curious about her. He asked to go down to her flat with Bernard to settle Pearl for the night, leaving Tracey alone with Matthew.

"We're having a big Christmas lunch with all our friends. You two want to come?"

"Will we have a Christmas tree? Will Father Christmas come? Can mummy come?"

"Yes, if we can find her, where is she?"

Tracey really needed Marc to go with her to the shop to identify which of the four men was the grandfather. But she was keen to get any information she could as soon as possible, so decided to go alone down to the shop just to see what the poster was about anyway. She supposed photos of the faces of unidentified corpses might be posted in shops where a wide cross section of the community would see them. She had often seen such photos of missing persons on billboards. What other reason could there be for circulating photos of citizens? Wanted for a criminal offence? No, worst thought of all, not as a paedophile?

She could not see any posters in the shop and eventually had to ask. The sales assistant at first claimed he knew nothing about it. Then when she persisted, refused point blank to co-operate. Even when she explained that there were two little

191

grandsons who had seen it and were missing their grandfather. Nothing. Then a customer, fed up at being kept waiting in the queue behind this irritating woman said: "They keep those things behind the counter pinned up there so they know not to serve them."

The sales assistant resigned himself, reached down, unstuck the Blu-tac and handed over the poster with a malicious grimace:

NOTICE
By order - CITY COUNCIL
IT IS AN OFFENCE TO SELL ALCOHOL
TO THE PEOPLE BELOW
WHO ARE HABITUAL DRUNKARDS

Below were the photos, grainy mug-shots, not what you would expect of police custody standard photography. Tracey recognised two of the faces from round the town. A third was the age of a grandfather. Henry McIntyre, white haired, weathered skin, bleary eyed, red-eye startle from the police camera flash.

*   *   *   *   *

"Well, you don't need me no more then, does ya?" Rose seemed rather keen to get away. Thinking quickly, Tracey decided that Rose was feeling de trop because both she and Bernard were still there. If her anxiety to get away was connected to not having the confidence to get on with Pearl, then the two of them would have to be left alone together for a bit to get a rapport going.

"Actually, do you think you could stop here for an hour or so, Rose? It'd be really helpful. I've got some urgent stuff to do for Christmas and it'd be so much easier in the car. And Bernard's got his dad's car today…… Oh thanks, Rose." And Tracey kissed her, leaving her on option.

"Is that alright, Bernard?" Tracey asked.

192

"Sure," but he faffed around, clearly not feeling right about leaving Pearl. It was only her second day. Robin had left at lunch time and now Tracey was proposing they left too.

"Come on. The sooner we go the sooner we can get back for a cuppa."

In the street as he opened the car for Tracey to jump in, he said, "Where to then? What's the urgent Christmas shopping? You know it's against all my principals to 'shop' for Christmas. It arrives insidiously enough without going shopping for it."

"There isn't really any shopping, you dinlo, got no money anyway. I just wanted Rose to be alone with Pearl. Get some bonding done, you know?"

"Right. So what are we going to do? Sit here and pretend?"

"Nah, we'll have to go somewhere and bring a few bags back or it'll look suspicious. And we do have to buy Pearl a few things for Christmas anyway. You got any cash?"

The overcast weather oppressed them and made them want to stay indoors. A drizzle, so fine it could only be detected as they breathed it into their lungs, made them long to be anywhere indoors. So they decided a shopping centre would be best; at least it would be warm and dry and the effrontery of tinsel and flashing lights, piped Christmas music and warring families would be entertaining when there were the two of them together to share their amusement. Then they argued about which was best, Waterlooville, Havant, the Airport, Commercial Road? But could only agree on one thing, not Commercial Road. They were driving east when a break in the clouds and an unexpected shaft of sunlight made the decision for them.

"Let's go to the beach," they said it in unison and laughed, "great shopping there!" They found themselves approaching Eastney. Winding down the lane leading to the new under-subscribed marina, past the new development where there had been such a stink not so long ago about, not on this occasion, effluent, but buried asbestos and other dumped naval rubbish.

By the time the aluminium masts of the marina were in view, the sun had stretched its lazy winter light across Eastney Lake and thrown the up-turned hulls of boats wedged on the shingle into a startling spotlight. The anchored floating boats bobbed on a full tide, their lit superstructures, wooden masts and sail-wrapped booms, bright, artificial colours in the yellow sunlight.

Crunching along the pebbles towards the ferry for Hayling Island, they watched the tide, just turned, hurtling out of the narrow neck of the channel, out to sea, whirlpools and eddies sucked and swirled, patches of deceptively smooth water, suddenly snatched away. A wire mesh held the shingle tight between large anchoring rocks, like curlers in an old woman's hairnet. Death, birds' wings, empty crab shells, dried seaweed, salt-washed condoms, cast up together, drawing uneven lines at the high tide level; hulls strained on anchor chains against the fierce current.

"All the years I've lived here, I've never been on the Hayling ferry. Been to Hayling, you know, driven round." Bernard's teeth betrayed the chill in his soul.

"D'you want to go now?"

"No way, the sun might be out, but it's still freezing. Let's go back to a nice warm shopping centre, please!"

"Wimp!" Tracey was not cold, but facing the offshore breeze. Langstone. The water, choppy under the squally weather, dark turquoise in the winter afternoon light. So many different boats, families' pride and joy, were here, fishing, sailing, escape from the estate, freedom of retirement, get away from the wife, hours with a rod or a pair of binoculars, forget unemployment, delinquent kids. And behind them into the land again, the allotments and all around wheeled the brilliant white specks of seabirds picked out in sunlight, waiting to settle in banded strips across the mud flats as they emerged, draining from the ebbing tide.

"I went lots of times, on that ferry, I mean. We used to go to sunbathe in the dunes, naked! when naked was daring! And tease all the sad old paedophiles who used to gather for a peek over the peaks. It was always so sleepy on Hayling. You had to walk miles to find an ice cream van, then the bloke

194

would be having a kip and you'd hammer on the window and he'd say come back later after siesta. Hippy he was, long hair and beads, permanent spliff. Can't believe you never went."

Tracey and the others in the hostel had a freedom not available to some. Losing that freedom was the only effective sanction that could be imposed on them for bad behaviour. They all valued the freedom so highly, that staying in line was never a problem and supporting each other in times of trouble was an automatic reflex, since freedom curtailed for one, often meant freedom curtailed for all.

"There's a children's home there, well used to be, maybe it's gone now, down on the front at Hayling there, for kids who are so screwed up they can't be allowed to stay with their families or who have no one in the world......... I nearly went there."

Bernard didn't pick up on her cue.

"My childhood was not one where we had any freedom at all. My mother, Christ, I cannot tell you. She controlled every fart and then when Ollie came along she recruited me to control him with her. Not surprisingly, he rebelled and I got it in the neck. Freedom of childhood? Don't recall any." Bernard didn't sound bitter, more amused. "It is great down here in the summer though. A few years ago I used to come here alone and just sit skimming pebbles for hours. Essential part of my therapy."

"Oh, really," Tracey knew she had sounded too interested. Bernard said no more about his past, but moved into general history. He pointed out the Mulberry harbour, a broken backed lump of concrete, described its role in the D-day landings.

Tracey passed him a flattish pebble she had found, "Can you still skim? I never could, no hand-eye co-ordination."

Bernard felt the pebble in his hand, smooth, oval, a good weight. Carefully poising his body on the back foot, he cast it into a smooth patch of water. It skimmed five times. Tracey applauded.

"When I was working in Woolies I had this boyfriend. He was a delivery guy for a car parts company. I shall never forget the first time I saw him. He drove a little van, Escort or something to do the deliveries in. Bright red with yellow writing, pretty noticeable. Not Unipart, they're red, white and blue aren't they? Anyway, I was watching him, bored by the fucking job, I expect, and he unfolded himself from the driver's seat. I couldn't believe it. There was so much of him. I went outside to look. He stood up. He was about 6 foot 4 or 5. I was then, as I am now, 5 foot on the nail, toe nail. He was a bean pole. I knew it would never work out. But it was a laugh finding out!"

"What was his name?"

"Justin. No really! And it was true, he could only just get in to places. We walked along the Hayling shore a few times. He always called it the Jersey shore. He liked it. He was a real Bruce Springsteen fan, The Boss this and The Boss that. He wanted more than anything to go to New York and New Jersey, do the Springsteen thing, comparison with his own situation, visit the landmarks. I hope he made it. Don't think so. I still see him driving around in a little Escort. He had a real feeling for Hayling Island, he saw it as Hayling Island playing New Jersey to Portsmouth's New York."

"Look across the skyline," Bernard laughed, "I've been to New York and New Jersey and lived in Portsmouth, but never walked along the Hayling shore. I'm going to make it my next mission. After Christmas shopping. Let's get Springsteen's hits for Pearl. Streets of Philadelphia, that's my all time favourite. "

"CD or tape?"

196

Chapter 16

The tablecloth was made from an old sheet unevenly stencilled all over with irregular yellow stars, green potato print holly leaves, nose prints called 'red Rudolf blobs' and hand print stars. Matthew and James had cut out the stencils with scissors, moaning that it made their thumbs sore. They had chopped potatoes with a lethal kitchen knife into shapes for the printing, terrifying everyone who dared look There had been such mess, such laughter and such discordant singing along to Phil Specter's schmultzy Christmas favourites, even the cynical Bernard joined in.

Pearl was beside herself with excitement, infected by all the festive activity in her flat. She insisted on joining in with the boys' Christmas creativity, bossing them about and trying to snatch what they were using. Tracey wasn't sure how to react. As an adult, Pearl shouldn't have been behaving like this, like a spoilt child. Yet what reference points did she have? The boys found it really odd at first, but quickly adjusted to treating her like an annoying classmate, appealing to Tracey to adjudicate, then when she refused to get involved, taking the law into their own hands, snatching things back from Pearl, who then squawked and shrieked and smacked out at them.

There was no time for Tracey to really think this through at the time. There was too much going on. She would have to shelve it and discuss with Bernard later. There were whole areas of Pearl that were unfathomed. Her personality was unknown. And huge learning and adjustment would have to happen, before Pearl could form ordinary relationships with people. She had had no opportunity to make relationships, no practice. With Tracey and Bernard, Pearl probably accepted what they did, how they made decisions for her, without question. With the boys, she was her uninhibited, raw self. Wow!

On Tracey's mind was the impending visit from the district nurse. Somehow they'd collectively come to a decision that Pearl should have a flu jab. There was no doubt it was a good idea. There was a drawback, Pearl was likely to scream the place down at being jabbed. But on the other hand a dose of the flu would be certain to put a person as vulnerable as Pearl in hospital. From there it would be an easy step to the care home. Every brush with the authorities laid them open to discovery of their irregular relationship with Pearl.

But Pearl had become their mission; their "Give disabled people an independent life!" mission. They had set themselves up to fight for Pearl's independence. Not for the first time however, Tracey found herself wondering how she had got herself into this thing. And more to the point, was this really the right thing for Pearl? Interfering busybodies all of them. A further niggle that jiggled around at the back of her mind was exactly what was Bernard's motivation in taking on Pearl? Her secret fear was that he was just like Mr Toad. He would have an idea to do something, in this case rehabilitate Pearl, and then go all out to achieve it. But when the time came that he felt it had been achieved, he would simply move on to something else. Where or with whom for support would that leave Pearl? No prizes for guessing. Tracey knew this was for life. Pearl's at least.

A combination of the door bell and another squabble over paintbrushes brought Tracey back. Matthew went to the door and the problem of unequal distribution of artistic materials was solved by Tracey, flattening a huge piece of paper in front of Pearl, as the nurse came in.

The nurse was young with long hair swinging round her shoulders. She wore trousers under a white tunic and laughed a lot which disguised the canny appraisal Tracey saw her making of the unusual situation here – wondering who the child belonged to, sizing up Bernard and her, assessing the mess, careful not to show surprise at Marc's long pigtail, or French accent and trying not to peer into the bedroom to see what another couple of people in there were up to. Despite the fact that the flat was already oppressively crowded, she accepted a cup of coffee, so at least she didn't think they were unhygienic – or perhaps she was playing for time to improve her opportunity for social detective work.

Business-like she drew a chair up beside Pearl and talking to her all the time, asking her to point out what she had been doing, she rolled up Pearl's sleeve, lifted the hypodermic from her bag, removed the cover, flicked it swiftly and jabbed it in, all in one smooth movement that took about 30 seconds. All who had been quick enough to see it, were impressed. What an operator! Pearl didn't appear to notice the jab at all.

"Why don't you have no belt round her arm then? My dad's always got to before he does the 'jection. Sometimes I have to hold it for him, to keep it tight."

The appalled hush was broken by the sound of the flush and James emerged from the bathroom. He backed away again defensively, pushed back by the silence, sensing the problem.

"Look Pearl's got 'jected like dad." Matthew offered cheerfully, "but she ain't got no belt." Still no one spoke. James' pallour whitened. Tracey recognised that the emotion rising in him was fury. He clearly knew about their dad. Matthew didn't. Matthew's big mouth was getting them into trouble again. James wanted to hurt Matthew.

"Lovely coffee, shall I put the mug in the kitchen?" Nurse to the rescue. "What's your dad, then? He in the navy?" she addressed James. It was a toss-up whether his natural politeness would win out over his urge to kill his brother.

"He's written a book, about bio.....gra...gy. Not sure what. Big kids have to read it in science at school. He's really clever, our dad." The answer was there with no real pride because James' attention was piercing his brother.

Round and round in Tracey's head went the first line from a song, "There's a hole in daddy's arm where all the money goes,"

How odd that she should know any country songs and even stranger that she, who could never remember punch lines of jokes, or names of authors or lyrics of songs, should know that this song was by John Prine and the next line was, "little pitchers have big ears, don't stop to count the years." Where in the dim back of her brain had it come from?

Shouldering her bag and walking towards the kitchen with her mug, the nurse was saying goodbye. Tracey went to stand beside James, ready to talk to him, to keep him away from Matthew, who lurked behind the table, fearful, but without any understanding of what he had done of what had occurred.

Pearl began to howl for something to fill her sheet of paper with. She banged her good hand on the table. Relieved, many hands came forward to supply her with bright colours, highlighters and lipsticks, with which to cover it.

No one heard what Tracey said to James, but after she had spoken to him, stroking his arm, imploring him with her eyes locked onto his, James took it upon himself to keep popping over to tell Pearl how good her picture was and to advise her, put a bit more of this on and a bit of that over there. His tone was loudly patronising. Tracey's head throbbed at the implications for political correctness, but sank under the weight of the promise she'd made to James, that she would explain about their dad to Matthew.

"I'd have been proud to have done that myself," Bernard said to Pearl when he saw the finished picture blu-tacked to the wall. Tracey couldn't believe. It was one thing having James patronise Pearl, but not Bernard. She gave him a hard 'what are you playing at?' stare.

"What?" he stared back at her, all innocence.

Instead of causing ructions now, Pearl submitted slavishly to all James' suggestions. He had become her creative guru. Fortunately he was flattered. He sorted out the chunkiest implements for her, easier for her to grip. He snapped the end off a paintbrush because its unbalanced length meant it kept falling frustratingly from of her hand, and he sellotaped up the splintered end. It later started a row, when Pearl became furious with Matthew for using her paintbrush - it had the colour he needed and she had not been using it at the time. Tracey sat down to try and tell her it was OK. We all share. Just ask for it back when you want it. Pearl looked away. Was it that she wouldn't hear, couldn't hear or didn't understand?

In the window stood a mangy artificial Christmas tree that had been rescued from a skip and rehabilitated by Marc. It was unevenly weighted on one side where James had

200

grabbed most of the chocolate decorations first, being more nimble fingered. The 'fairy' had been amongst Lilly's ornaments. The top of her body was china, the painted face oriental, surrounded by black silk hair rigid with glue. Her lower half, an empty stiff lace skirt, was the circular base on which she was designed to stand. She now perched drunkenly on top of the tree like an old lampshade.

"She's got no legs! She's got no bum! Nick knack paddy whack on my drum!" Matthew was delighted with the bottomless fairy. Fiddling with her truncated body, he composed more lines to his song "She's got no legs! She's got no bum! Nick knack paddy whack suck my thumb! Got no legs! Got no bum! Nick knack paddy......." as he struggled for a rhyme, Bernard interposed "....wagon goes brrrum, brrrum."

There were tiny lights were on the tree, Cut Price £7.99, one carefully placed to shine up the fairy's bum. "Up the fairy's bum, up the fairy's bum," the repetitive chant thrilled Matthew as he worked, concentrating on threading garlands of colourful scrap for the tree. He tried his songs in all the octaves in his range, playing to the gallery, enjoying his audience, loving their laughter. He accompanied himself with the jangling tree decorations made from bottle tops and crown caps and ring pulls that Clare, declaring it a triumph of recycling, had punched holes in with a skewer and strung together with old boot laces.

"I thought you said the fairy didn't have a bum, Matt." James was tired of the chanting and all the attention Matthew was getting. He draped garlands of shredded bubble wrap to reflect the coloured lights, and arranged a scattering of gold and silver flowers made from the linings of Players and B&H packets, obsessively collected for the purpose by Joe, during the preceding days. Teaching the boys how to make them had been his one role in the preparations. Bernard overheard Joe explaining to the boys more than once that it was 'fucking hard being a teacher'.

"You know," she stood back appraising the tree, "this is real art! Art of the people...." Clare was off. An anonymous sigh went up. She had already dropped a hint that someone might proclaim her bottle top shaker decorations 'art'. "Using other people's rejects, things society has discarded, as materials to express your own condition, your own alienation from the herd, your disdain for everything that they impose on you, your rejection of them and all their values, their grubby gold standards and filthy capitalism. This is art. This is really neat art." Everyone was looking at her now. Tracey agog, with mock worship; Bernard sniggering his cynical sneer; James, Pearl and Matthew following the general shift of attention to Clare.

"Bleeding commie! She off again?" Joe went back to his cigarette papers.

Oliver opened his mouth to speak, but Clare was in full throttle, "Course, we members of the Socialist Workers' Party don't believe in Christmas. It's just a capitalist plot by multinationals to subjugate the workers."

"My god, what do you know about workers, Clare? Ever met one?" They all laughed.

Tracey drew Marc aside from the mess at ask if he had time to go down to the corner shop for a positive identification of the picture of the boys' grandfather. She didn't want James to come because he could read and might be upset, and she had been unable to inconspicuously separate the two brothers and take Matthew.

"If we leave it any longer they might take down the picture. Probably have. Come on, it'll only take a few minutes." Tracey tried to understand Marc's reluctance. It was as if to know for certain would mean the boys would be taken away, which would put a stop to the fun Marc was having with them. But Tracey needed to know about the grandfather. It was the not-knowing that bothered her.

Fortunately there was a harassed assistant working that day, who was under pressure from an impatient queue, and distracted by a delivery of Christmas trees. Trunks oozed resin and spiky branches dropped needles all over the pavement where inconsiderate shoppers had spread the load of trees, rummaging through for the best. So it was easy for Tracey and Marc to sneak round the counter to look at the poster. Marc instantly pointed out the white-haired Henry McIntyre.

202

"What we do, now we know who's grandfather? I suppose tell to the police." Marc sounded resigned.

"No, we'll just look out for him. I know two of the others - well, by sight. They're permanently drunk. We often see them in the park and lying around the streets and asleep in shop doorways (often marked out by a trickle of urine, she thought). Maybe we'll find him. We won't look too hard until after Christmas, though. What do you think?"

"That's good. I want to Christmas with two children. It's really good funny."

"Really good fun." Tracey corrected him out of habit. Out of habit, he took no notice and made no attempt to repeat her correction. Marc only did this with Tracey, he listened acutely to everyone else, often putting them over corrections many times until he was satisfied he'd got it right.

They bustled past the crowd of waiting shoppers, trying to get out of the shop without spending any money. Tracey was catapulted into the street into the path of old Mary. Old Mary with her rouged cheeks and well-combed long greasy ponytail walked the streets of Portsmouth pushing a large rusty pushchair crammed with stuffed teddies and dolls and one enormous rabbit. All well dressed. They were carefully placed so as not to obstruct or sit on one another and tucked in safe and warm with baby blankets. It was generally assumed that they were her 'babies'. She would sing to her family and talk to them as they walked, stopping occasionally to check the blankets, asking them if they were all comfortable.

Marc was calling out over his shoulder to someone in the shop, "NO, you I my way! I NOT pushed you!" He stumbled through the door right into old Mary's pushchair. It went flying. Stuffed toys scattered, mingling with Christmas trees, getting under the feet of passers-by, where the concrete flags were damp and grubby with winter condensation. Tracey gasped, stooping to help Marc right the pushchair, waiting for the screeching and wailing. She assumed the old woman would become hysterical at such an appalling accident happening to her 'children'. People came over to help and hesitated irresolute, when they saw the accident had happened only to toys, bending fastidiously to lift them by one ear, disappointed, duped, feeling foolish, finding there had been no child at all.

The old woman stood by and watched for a bit with a bemused smile. Then shaking her head at the people she said to no one in particular, "Them's on'y toys you know!" and she finished stuffing the rest unceremoniously into the buggy and marching off with it. The crowd looked sheepishly at each other, then began to laugh. One voice rounded of the incident. "And a merry Christmas to one and all!"

*   *   *   *   *

In the two weeks from first contact with the boys, not only had their grandfather not returned, but no other members of their family had been to his flat or made any attempt to take responsibility for them. James eventually told them that their mother had gone away on holiday and they'd gone to their Granddad's for a couple of weeks. But on his own briefly one bedtime Matthew had described being frightened by his father and mother's fighting.

Both boys worried about the grandfather, clearly more fond of him than their parents. But if the old man had gone on a Christmas bender, if he'd had enough of two little boys, there was nothing to be done. If he didn't want to be found, he would be able to stay lost. The adults tried to reassure the boys and promised to find him after Christmas. They let them believe nothing could be done until then.

Tracey or Bernard or Marc or Clare (still desperately making herself indispensable) and even Isabelle had seen them to bed, sorted out their meals, been to the launderette. School had broken up, and the Educational Welfare Officer had stopped calling. They knew that she would probably already have started putting the care machine into action. Eventually they would have to tell someone, social services, the local authority, or try and trace the family. But no one wanted to, not yet. They were having such fun playing mummies and daddies, aunties and uncles with two real live dolls. Everyone wanted the children to be there for Christmas. Inside each one of them, but unacknowledged to each other, was a small child who had been disappointed at one childhood Christmas or another. They wanted to make this Christmas special for James and Matthew as representatives of the children they had once been, to be the cause of and share in their pleasure.

They shelved all decisions about the future until afterwards, living for each moment.

Only Pearl was resistant to the boys' charms, but they both loved and were fascinated by her, well, and her wheelchair and all the gadgets that came with her. Matthew played incessantly with the tap extensions on the basin and they had to hook the bathhoist up out of reach to stop them swinging on it.

This Christmas Eve, when Pearl's room had been decorated and she had been settled on the sofa, James started riding around in her wheelchair, three point turns, two wheel balances and wheelies. He was becoming very skilled in the small space. At first amused, Pearl began to get cross and was finally reduced to a quivering rage when he wouldn't stop. Realising he'd gone too far, James sat silently beside her and held her hand, until she was pacified.

"Bedtime," Isabelle had limited tolerance.

"But it's Christmas Eve," James was having fun.

"But Father Christmas won't come if we don't go to bed early." There was no hint of doubt in Matthew's voice. He was certain Father Christmas would come.

*   *   *   *   *

"Where's your sparkly circus suit then? I thought you were going to wear it for the party." James challenged Marc the next morning when he came for them. But he was not so much disappointed for himself as trying to distract Matthew from dwelling on the awful truth. It was hard to be five and find there was no Father Christmas. James could understand that. He had the pleasure of being the one in the know, the grownup one. At first he had enjoyed telling Matthew not to be silly, how could one fat man really fly round the whole world in one night giving every child presents? But Matthew had been so devastated, so shocked, wept so much, that James gave up explaining and just tried to sooth him.

"'Twas the night before Christmas and all through the house,

Not a creature was stirring, not even a mouse,
When Ma in her kerchief and I in my cap
Had just settled down for a long winter nap."

It was just as well James didn't know any more words, it was all about the visit of Santa Clause. His voice trailed off.

Matthew was inconsolable, until with the unsquashable optimism of youth, he rationalised to himself that past Christmases had always featured a drop from Santa. He decided James must be wrong, or just teasing. He lay awake in the dark, waiting for James' breathing to ease into the rhythm of sleep. Then he crept over and put one of James' football socks carefully on the end of James' bed. They were the biggest socks they had, but earlier when he had searched, he had been unable to find the pair. He knew what he planned to do next was not really fair. Matthew tussled with his conscience for a while, then reached for his pillow. It was a struggle to get the pillowcase off in the dark, but the effort served to reinforce his decision to put it on his own bed and not James'. Anyway, James had said he didn't think Father Christmas would come and they always got exactly the same stuff, even though at home James' stocking was a bit bigger than his – Matthew always did a careful inventory to check.

But in the morning, Christmas morning, when all the children of the western world should be happy, Matthew had woken before James and seen the flat, limp pillowcase and sock. He scuttled quickly out to remove them, afraid he would be caught having been so foolish. Though desperate with disappointment, he was determined not to show it to James. He would not let his thoughts wander in the direction of James being right, in case it made him cry. Instead he imagined his bed at home and the full stocking that might have been waiting there for him, Santa being unaware that he was not at home. But thinking of home, of his bed there, brought tears to his eyes anyway. He fought the tears by scrubbing his teeth so hard with his toothbrush that his gums bled. By the time Marc arrived he was under control. But James knew, as only a brother could, that Matthew's intense silence punctuated by the forced bright remarks meant to show he was fine, was in fact a disguise, hiding, perhaps, the worst disappointment in his life.

"Heh, I'm not dress in my sparkly suit until the real party begins, come with me and see the food we got." Marc knew too, James could tell.

As they left the building the church bells started the Christmas peal. They stood a moment, transfixed by the loudness, it wobbled their ears in their heads. The morning was still, bright and frosty and the vibrations of the brass bells seemed to shake the air like a playful puppy. The wooden slats on the belfry quivered. Disturbed rooks rose from the sycamores in a clattering of wings and sharp strident shouts of irritation.

*   *   *   *   *

By 4 o'clock it was almost dark. Four o'clock was the time that every 18th century Georgian household would have been sitting down to a dinner illuminated by candlelight. Jane Austin had only been a subsidiary subject on Tracey's university access course, but she had been infused with a hankering for those gentle, civilised times, and their preoccupation with the minutiae of domestic life. At this Christmas dinner she wanted to recreate a sense of that gracious English past.

Outside, the day, grey now after the unexpectedly sunny start, was drawing to a close as they ceremoniously lit the candles. Elegant 18th century silver tableware, symmetrically arranged on white linen, might have achieved the effect Tracey craved, even in a dismal inner city flat, but the mismatched collection of new and half burned candles lined up in jars and on saucers, on the mantelpiece, the shelf, a side table and two tea towel-covered milk crates flickering unevenly was more redolent of the black arts on all hallow's eve. A grotesque brass candelabra, perhaps formerly one of

Lilly's prized possessions, stood in the centre of the table, adding to the gothic effect.

They shut off the electricity except the Christmas tree. The boys gasped. It was magical. Pearl wept. Somewhere inside her she really did understand that this was her flat, this celebration was all in her honour.

"All we need is a crack of lightening, a gust of icy air through the flapping curtain and a boiling cauldron of snails and frogs' legs." Bernard said, "Oh, begging pardon of the French contingent."

The buzzer announced the first of their guests.

"So where's the doleful bell chiming deep in the recesses of the haunted mansion?" Tracey rose to let in Martha bearing gifts; a catering pan of Christmas pudding left over from the hostel children's lunch and a box of crackers, 12, for the boys to put round. Rose and Joe came up from downstairs with chocolate and a bottle of British port for afters. Clare, still locked into ingratiation, brought a present for everyone. Ollie brought Clare. Isabelle came - and was greeted with mutters of relief. It meant hope for Marc. She brought tiny, exquisitely wrapped, beribboned and labelled gifts. Inside each was a marzipan animal, a different one to match each personality. Marc's was a frog.

Choosing his moment, a lull in the conversation, Bernard nodded to Tracey and they reached behind the sofa, lifting out two bulky, over-stuffed mis-shapen Christmas stockings.

"One for me and one for you, Bernard." Tracey teased. " You've been good all year, haven't you? This says:" and she made a really big pantomime of struggling to read the label "To a boy who has been good all year, makes brilliant Christmas decorations, can sing like an angel, Oh, sorry, Bernard, and whose name is, I can't make it out.... Ummmmm.... it begins with MMM......Maaaa....now what is it?"

"MATTHEW!" shrieked Matthew.

"Matthew." Tracey agreed smiling to crack her cheeks.

Matthew was there, eyes wide. He received the stocking, cradled it, rocking it back and forth and shot James a fierce look of triumph.

"Father Christmas did come! See James, I told you he would. He's just a bit late 'cos he didn't know where to find us." Matthew was beside himself with relief, a large part of his happiness. How he must have wished for this to happen. How harshly his faith had been tested.

"Don't be an idiot, Matt," James did not want to lose face, in front of all these adults, he wanted them to know he knew the score, but Tracey cut him off.

"What did you get, let's see?" She was surprised at how convincingly she sounded as though she had no idea what was inside the stockings. James gave her a secret look, acknowledged the expression in her eyes and smiled. Matthew started ripping off paper to reveal an unimaginative assortment of sweets and plastic toys and comics and gimmicky socks and cartoon character mittens, cheap felt tips and coloured paper, with a coin and a Satsuma and chocolate money stuffed in the toe. Just like when Tracey had been a little kid.

"Time to check the turkey. Who's coming for a jolly good basting?" Bernard knew Clare would jump up, but he told Martha, she'd done her bit and, drink this! The port was cracked open as an aperitif and drunk from garage tumblers, since the only two wine glasses had been claimed by Matthew for himself and his brother, the sophisticates in the proceedings.

The two boys suddenly went very straight faced and nonchalantly sidled over to Pearl when they realised she was about to be moved from the sofa to the wheelchair.

As Marc helped her lower herself into it there was an ear-piercing fart. She didn't seem to notice, but Matthew and James fell about helpless with giggling, the others joined in infecting each other like a bunch of schoolkids. Except Bernard who had contributed the whoopee cushion to the stocking. He managed no more than a comradely smirk; though he entered into the spirit by passing Matthew the artificial turd, indicating with his eyebrows to place it by Joe when no one was looking.

"Ooh, oops! Stop! I'm gonna wet meself," Rose clutched her sides. "'Ere let's 'ave a go!" and she made Joe sit on the whoopee cushion, collapsing in further paroxysms of laughter as it blasted.

"Just like Grandma in Giles," Ollie was recalling a family tradition. Bernard who didn't want to remember anything from his childhood Christmases, slipped out of the door with Clare. Ollie close behind. Despite insisting that his brother was as bent as a nine-bob-note, Ollie never trusted him alone with any of his girlfriends. Or was it the girlfriends he didn't trust?

To accompany the turkey there was, by special request a bowl of baked beans. And no sprouts. The potatoes were au nature in two huge saucepans borrowed from the pub, butter optional, roast parsnips were in abundance, as were carrots in garlic, peas - must have something green - and garlic bread.

"What no stuffing?" Joe moaned.

"You can get stuffed," Bernard passed him a plate, then raising his hand to a fevered brow, cried out melodramatically "after all my hard work, slaving away in the kitchen, perfecting the culinary arts, instructing an army of sous chefs...... all I get, is.......complaints, complaints, complaints...... Oh and how is the vintage? Bouquet to your liking? A little heavy on the nose? Madam?" He addressed himself to Rose, who put on her best queen mum smile, "That's the very best Chateau nouveau brune!" Bernard declared with a little pout.

"Nah, it's Newcastle brown ya daft 'ap'orth!" Rose lifted her glass, "To the chef!" she shouted above the din. They straggled to their feet: "To the chef!"

"Put that man on the stage! Warehouse No 1 is not good enough for the likes of him. Put him in Aladdin at The King's!"

"Yes, as the dame, please as the dame, I've always wanted to be a dame."

"Like the one across the road? It could get a bit crowded in this street." Tracey nodded towards the girls' school.

210

Isabelle went into the kitchen and returned carrying a wine bottle very gingerly as though it were eggshell. Setting its base gently on the mantelpiece, she reverentially opened it. A serious, tense atmosphere fell, the hushed diners watched expectantly.

"What's she doing?" Matthew rose to try and get a better look. Marc held him back.

"We mustn't joggle her, it'll spoil the wine." Bernard told him.

"Wine! Is that all?" and he went back to eating peas one by one with his fingers and drawing patterns in the gravy on his plate.

When Isabelle stood back, Marc could see the label: 1971 Chateau Margaux. Marc, believing he had sloughed off the pretensions of French wine snobbery, was aghast. In spite of himself, he knew the value of such a wine. It would be almost unobtainable now. Not a good year, 1971 had produced very little vintage in Bordeaux. Marc did however know that this wine had been a birth gift to Isabelle from her father, to lay down for a special occasion. He didn't even know she had brought any to England. When had she done it? On her behalf, Marc was anxious that this would be an empty gesture, here in England among these everyday people. No one here would care about the vintage. And he wished he didn't, but it was in his culture and his upbringing. It was just another bottle of wine to them. He gathered the empty glasses and wiped them clean with paper towel.

Isabelle had washed and dried a large jug and placed the brightest candle beside it. With her back to them it was difficult for them all to see. But all felt the concentration with which she now, so steady handed, expertly decanted the wine. There was an ecclesiastical silence broken only by a single glug as the bottle reluctantly started to disgorge its contents. Isabelle sucked in her breath, fearing some sediment had been disturbed. Barely breathing now, she held the bottle in front of the candle. Back lit by the flame, she watched the thin red stream as it emerged from the throat of the bottle. As she poured, she could examine every drop for sediment before it ran down the smooth inside of the jug. There was a tiny sludge left in the bottom of the bottle, which she stirred into the gravy. Everyone was looking at her. Bernard read the label aloud.

"Chateau Margaux, I've only ever heard of it, never seen a bottle before. Blimey, Isabelle, im-press-ive." And he whistled his appreciation. "Well as it's been opened, I suppose we'll just have to taste it. This, my friends, may be a once in a lifetime experience. How much d'you reckon that would cost?"

Isabelle gave him a hurt look. Bernard was abashed at his display of vulgarity.

"My father said for me to save this for a special occasion. I don't think there will ever be one more special or – (she paused to search for a word) - interesting. I have made some lovely English friends here and Marc is really like an Englishman." All turned to regard Marc, his long, bony knees poking through holes in his frayed jeans, his immense proud grin, the sequinned pink Tshirt (from 'the circus', via the Age Concern charity shop) topped off by the long yellow plait. Just like a run of the mill Englishman.

"I want to share this with you all," continued Isabelle, commanding their attention again with her dark chocolate voice, flicking the sleek hair back over the squared shoulders. "We have to wait a few minutes for the wine to taste really the best, before we can drink it. We can eat while we wait. This meal is so good, Bernard." He knew she was being polite, but the others mmmmed and smacked their lips, guzzled and slobbered and rolled their eyes in appreciation, reaching to help themselves to more.

"And the gravy's really good now, too." Bernard was smiling his ingratiating smile.

"I hope the wine will live up to the turkey." Isabelle was practising a new idiomatic expression. Bernard thought she was taking the disingenuousness a bit far, but wasn't confident enough to risk a sarcastic retort.

"Oh, yukity fuck, stop the mutual admiration stuff will you two? You'll make us vomit." Clare could always be relied upon.

212

"Heh, we missed the queen's speech. She's such a lovely lady in't she?"

Rose was shouted down with a chorus of "NO".

"Oh alright, be like that, but the queen mum, now, she is a real lady now." Martha opened her mouth to speak. Tracey was interested to know whether she would agree or not, there was a lot of anti royal feeling in Malta and quite a history of socialism.

But before she had a chance:

"That old bag would have entertained Hitler in her bed, given half a chance. She partied her way through both wars, never gave a toss about your ordinary bloke in the street. Plotted against her brother-in-law's marriage, and then conducted a vendetta against them. She's only useful as an advert for gin. You know they're all real fag-hags....."

"Alright, alright, you're sounding like Clare..."

"I am Clare!"

"I propose a toast to everyone here at this table. Thank you so much for inviting me. Merry Christmas to everyone." Isabelle again, so proper, so la-di-da, so out of place.

Twelve glasses had been passed round, each with an inch of wine. A chaotic chair scraping had them all standing again, obstructing Pearl's view, she squealed protest but no one heard. Rose put her elbow in the gravy. All stood except Pearl and all chorused including Pearl, "Merry Christmas". The dribble of wine that could not be contained by Pearl's lips slipped out and stained her pink cardigan. Isabelle smiled to see it. She laughed to see Matthew's face screwed up in distaste, his hand pushing it away, and James copying Marc, sniffing for the bouquet, and Marc trying to disguise his pleasure, both at the wine and at his girlfriend's affecting performance.

For once Isabelle felt uncritically pleased with herself. She had thought this moment would help her decide. This, she believed, would be the moment when she would know what to do. This would be either valediction Portsmouth, bienvenue Paris: or the duration with Portsmouth, adieu Paris. And as she gazed across at Marc, conversing so easily in this new language, sharing anarchic jokes, playing up to little children, wiping Pearl's slobbering mouth, savouring the best French wine and eating with his fingers, she knew. After two years together, she could not contemplate life without this complex, funny man. He would never be as happy in France, with its straightjacket manners, conformity, bureaucracy, and prejudices, as he was here with these strange people, this bizarre group of misfits. Wherever he was, she would have to be. It was not a momentous decision, it was a quiet realisation.

Only Tracey heard the buzzer and rose to respond, her cocked ear listening for Darron, hoping he would come. When she had invited him he had seemed keen enough to come having heard her descriptions of the bizarre ménage she claimed to be part of. He'd worked out that she was nuts, but couldn't quite believe that the combination of people she said would be at the Christmas dinner would ever come together in real life. She made it sound like The Rocky Horror Show, Til Death us Do Part and Blue Peter rolled into one, with a paraplegic, a couple of foreigners and a pair of old biddies to round it off. That would probably make him the token wog – the reason she was so keen he should come. Shame he didn't have a deaf or blind friend to represent sensory impairment. He explained that Christmas day was the one day of the year it was impossible to get away from the family. She had sent him the train fare and a copy of the skeleton holiday timetable anyway. There were only two trains from Salisbury. If he'd caught the later one he would be arriving about now.

"Who is it?" she was breathless with anticipation.

"Kieran O'Brien. Is Tracey Allsop there? It'd freeze ya ballocks off out here. Can I come up?"

In lieu of bollocks, the balls of Tracey's feet froze to the hall floor.

"Who?" she barely whispered.

"Kieran."

When she brought the tall handsome stranger in, Bernard immediately got up and offered his chair,

"You're a bit early, I thought tall, dark strangers were supposed to come at New Year."

"No longer dark I'm afraid," Kieran responded congenially, tugging at his grey hair.

"Bernard, sit back down, you haven't finished your meal. I'll go for another chair."

Tracey went into the bathroom. Bernard sat and quickly swallowed the last of his food. Picking up his plate to show Tracey it was empty, he took it to the kitchen. She pushed the bathroom chair up to the table for Kieran anyway. Instantly Rose got up, carefully drawing her chair away from the table back towards the window and followed Bernard into the kitchen towards the comforting sound of clattering dishes.

"This is Kieran." Tracey's voice was loud enough for half the company to call back, lethargically, "Merry Christmas, Kieran."

"Merry Christmas, one and all." He produced a bottle of Jameson's and brandished it. Ollie and Clare eyed each other, both fond of whisky. Clare eyed Kieran, although nearly grey, still a very handsome man. Seeing him, Pearl was so excited that she forgot the breathing technique taught to her to help her overcome her stuttering and make her speech more clear, and got stuck with her jaw flapping, trying to push out a word.

Joe couldn't stand the tension, had to cover the embarrassing sound of Pearl's struggle.

"Nice of you to bring us a presie. Jameson's. I like that. You di'nt 'ave to you know."

"Couldn't arrive with one arm as long as the other now could I, that'd hardly've been polite. Especially on Christmas."

A noise was issuing from Pearl and they all stopped to encourage her by their attention. When it eventually came it was,

"KKKKKK....'ier....ran." She was unconsciously drooling great threads of spittle, her tongue literally hanging out. Always the charmer, Kieran went to sit beside her, pulling up Rose's vacated chair.

From the kitchen doorway, Bernard studied the man who had retained Tracey's address for 15 years. And now he was, abruptly, here, an uninvited guest at their inaugural dinner. It was beyond Bernard, incomprehensible. Maybe he'd left his wife? Suddenly got the sack? There was massive unemployment in Northern Ireland. It would be hard to get a new job, especially for a man of about, forty? Christ, ancient. Bit old for Trace.

"You superstitious like me, eh, Bernie? Don't like 13 at the table." Rose was talking too loudly above the running water. Bernard was not proud of his superstitious nature, wished he could kick the habit, and didn't want the others taking the piss.

"Nah....not really," he lied.

"Aw, come off it. I seen you rush to keep the numbers down to twelve. Nothing to be ashamed of."

"Well actually there is, it's irrational and stupid, but I can't help it. When I'm - we're – (he quickly corrected himself) - starting something new, like this business with Pearl, then, yep, I suppose I am a bit nervous that it might go wrong. Don't want to tempt fate. So the old superstitions bubble up out of nowhere. You think you've forgotten them, but they never go away. I blame my mad mother."

"Yeah, my old mum was the same. Ruined the old girl's life in the end – walkin' round a ladder, a bike come past and knocked 'er for six. Went funny in the 'ead after that. That's why I'm not much good with them ones, see, after dealing with 'er."

"What do you think, Rose, think it'll be alright as long as no one gives him dinner, eh? That would mean there'd been thirteen for dinner. The importance of the last supper was that thirteen ate together, not just sat around in the same room together." Like all superstitious people, adjusting the superstition to suit the circumstances.

On his next trip to collect dirty plates, Bernard saw Kieran was eating Christmas dinner from a pudding bowl. It was stupid to think anything of it. But it reinforced his intuitive dislike of the newcomer; the instant mistrust of one good-looking man for another and the dislike of anyone whose background was mysterious and whose motives were unclear.

The intercom went beside Bernard's ear, making him jump. He was overjoyed to be buzzing Darron up. It would make Tracey's day and she had had it hard in the last fortnight, one way and another. She deserved a break.

Wrapped up in communicating between Pearl and Kieran, she hadn't noticed the door. Her shriek when she saw Darron would have shaken the recumbent occupants of the churchyard next door.

"DARRON, you made it! Merry Christmas," gushing, hugging, embarrassing the boy, who was not too overwhelmed to greet her with,

"Merry Christmas, vaginal mum." A brief, shocked silence was broken by Rose.

" 'ere my lover, you must 'ave some dinner," and she piled a plate warm from the washing up water. "To make us fourteen. Eh, Bernie?" A puzzled look went round. Bernard turned to readjust something on the Christmas tree.

"Cool, I love baked beans." They all laughed.

"Yeah, you're right, shall I warm them up?" Tracey was serious! Darron waved her away. She sank back, slurping the wine. As Darron ate, she watched him. She found herself trying to conceal something and realised with a shock what it was, a warm 'maternal' smile.

"I'm sure they have gone cold now, shall I warm them up?" Tracey was fussing. Bernard glared at her. She sank back with a satisfied smile, and slurped the last of her wine, watching Darron eat.

"I really like that wine, Isabelle."

"You needn't get a taste for it, you're not likely to get it again. That's a once in a lifetime event." If Bernard was being deliberately heavy-handed, sounding like a husband, Tracey didn't care.

"Where's the TV?" It was eight o'clock. Matthew and James had been in Pearl's flat for eight hours before they noticed. There was no TV. It might have been the longest waking time that either had ever spent without sitting in front of a screen. Most of the candles had burned out, only a couple had been replaced and a gloom began to fall.

"Ain't you got no 'puter, Pearl?" Matthew was looking round for one.

When the communal alcohol supply ran out, they had a tea break, ate the chocolate and then started on Kieran's whiskey.

217

The drinkers in the group began to tire of playing with the two boys. Ollie's cracker hat was round his neck. Clare wore one round each black-stockinged thigh. Someone had pulled Pearl's hair into five spiky bunches with rubber bands from the crackers. Bernard's nose was lipsticked red from his Rudolf impersonation and then Kieran fell asleep.

The two boys had been taught a hand jive game in French. They then all tried to juggle beer bottles until Darron smashed one; they played consequences with the new pens from Santa; and the two small boys had been tossed and bounced, hidden and sought. All the subversive versions of all the Christmas carols they knew were sung in glorious cacophony and they competed to make up even more obscene ones.

"Heh, heh, that's reminded me. I know a r...r....r....what's the bleedin' word? A riddle, me diddle, me widdle de dee." Spoken English was slipping away from Darron. Matthew began a hysterical giggling, alarmingly impressed by the older boy. Tracey's antennae were adjusting to their combined behaviour, like any real mother.

"A wha' a wha'?" Matthew encouraged Darron.

"A riddle, it's like a sort of joke thingy. You 'ave to guess........." he had drifted off.

"Wha' ? Wha' ?" demanded Matthew.

"My first is in face, But never in fare....." there was a pause, Darron struggled to remember. "My second is in up, but never a pair.....Oh I can't remember any more....pass me a pen someone, I'll have to write it down...." He started writing it on the table cloth in black felt tip pen, scattering spent matches, streaking sooty scars across the bright hand prints, scrawling around gobs and spatters of dried wax, evidence of an afternoon of amateur pyrotechnicians in training.

It was getting late. Matthew had his thumb in his mouth. Clare and Martha elected themselves to take them home to bed. As they said goodbye, filing by everyone to hug them goodnight, and make sure they took all their presents and the crap from the crackers, James said quietly,

218

"That was the best Christmas ever. A bit like Tiny Tim's. Do you remember, in the video?"

As she was leaving, with Matthew clutching her skirt, Martha rummaged through her handbag to find an envelope, which she handed to Tracey.

"One more."

"Another of your little surprises?" Tracey hissed. "Like Kieran. I wonder who told him where I was today, eh?"

A look of beatific innocence settled on Martha's creased features. "You do fancy him, then?" She deduced from Tracey's vehemence.

"Nooooo.....that's you, you dirty-minded old woman." Tracey was smirking now. But her expression slid when she looked at the envelope. It had been readdressed, twice. One look at the postmark, and Tracey went to tear it up.

"Eh, eh, eh. Maybe there's money in it. I open it and see. If there is, I keep it so you won't be dirtied by it. OK? What you think?"

Tracey unhesitatingly handed it over. Martha opened it.

"Come on, Nana Martha," Matthew whined from the doorway.

"I'm not your Nana, you cheeky monkey. I'm too young to be a grandmother. Hey, look Tracey, yes, it's a twenty. It's mine OK?" Martha waved the note round.

"Give it to Bernard for food and drink, he spent a fortune getting everything for today," Tracey tore the card and envelope into tiny pieces and threw them in the bin. One small piece settled on the top. It retained the postmark, clear and complete, 'Denford'.

"Ahhhh," shrieked Darron, suddenly alert. Heads corkscrewed round to see what was the matter. He was pointing to the floor beside Joe's chair "A turd! Where's the f-ing dog? Oh no....." his voice trailed off as he realised sickenly it might be human.

"Heh, that's mine!" And Matthew rushed back from the door where he had been about to leave to pick it up.

"Surreal." Darron blinked slowly as if to clear his vision.

*　　*　　*　　*　　*

Afterwards, nobody could remember exactly how it happened. They had finished the whiskey, Ollie had helped Joe up with a crate of Newcastle brown he had been saving for new year. Pearl had fallen asleep and been plopped unceremoniously into bed. Only to be disturbed later when they remembered the incontinence pad.

Amid fits of undignified giggling, Tracey and Martha struggled. Although not conscious Pearl seemed to co-operate. But when they finally managed to penetrate her clothing, trying not to look too closely, held back from doing so by modesty and respect for her, neither could miss it. Blood.

Tracey was speechless, not that Pearl, like every woman should bleed, but at her own lack of forethought. It had never occurred to her that Pearl would of course menstruate. It drew her up short. She was as bad as all the others she liked to criticise, treating Pearl, anyone with learning difficulties like children, or sexless pets.

Martha had none of Tracey's misgivings. She, completely matter-of-fact, took it, as everything about the human condition, in her stride, as normal.

"You know her cycle? She due on now?" As though Tracey should have been prepared.

"Er, no this is the first time, since I've known her."

"These pads, they best for periods anyway. We just got to make sure she don't get sore."

They got it on her, during which Pearl remained unconscious, snoring heavily, the comatose sleep of someone not used to alcohol. Tracey flicked the switch of her alarm button, in anticipation of being unable to remember it later.

How it was that they all went home to their respective beds and left Kieran in Pearl's flat, no one could recall. But Boxing Day morning, when Rose let herself in to make Pearl's breakfast, there was Kieran spoon-feeding Pearl warm Weetabix. Pearl was gazing adoringly at him. A full and tied bin bag by the door bore witness to the tidying up he had done from the night before, a sign of his bid for acceptance. Every surface was scoured of candle wax, a fresh breeze through an open window chased all sign of the previous day's shenanigans. The floor was still wet from the mop.

The message seemed clear. He felt he had earned the right to be here.

"She'll get cold with that window open. She's prone to chestiness. That why we don't smoke up 'ere, see. You cold Pearl, my lover?"

Pearl shook her head, "Nnnn....ah," and opened her mouth for more Weetabix.

"Why you lettin' 'im feed you? Lost the use of your arms, all 'a sudden?"

" 'S nice." Pearl smiled.

"You will lose the use of your arms if you don't practise proper! Fancy a cuppa anyone? So where'd'ya sleep then, Kieran?"

Kieran pointed to the door of Lilly's bedroom, "I just kipped down on the spare bed in there. It was so late, by the time the party ended, it was impossible to get back to my digs. Hope that's OK, now. Pearl seemed alright with it, didn't you Pearl?"

"Yeah!" she shouted.

"I've a wee message to run. Any shops open around here today, Rose?" The way he used your first name all the time, when he'd only just met you was too intimate for Rose's liking. It was a bit intimidating, but she was also charmed by it.

"Woolies and that, places with sales starting, Allders and Debs down Southsea, I s'pose. Don't know really."

"Well, just point me in the right direction, Rose, an' I'll be off. See yous later Pearl, Rose. No misbehaving now, mind."

Later that night when Kieran went to leave Pearl's flat, she kicked up such a fuss, he agreed to stay. Tracey didn't like the situation. Especially as he went to great pains to protest that he really would have preferred to go back to his digs. So she decided it was her duty to stay too, ridiculous, since they had worked so hard an persuading Pearl that with the alarm, she was not really alone in the flat at night, there was always someone one flight of stairs away. It was like going backwards into dependency again for Pearl.

When she'd got Pearl to bed, she sat down with Kieran over a cup of tea and asked why was he here? Had she got the postcards, he asked? Yes, thanks, it was nice getting them from all over the world. And you never thought to send me one of The Victory, he chided, and me such a fan of Nelson. Or had she forgotten? No, she hadn't forgotten. But it had never occurred to her. Sorry.

Beneath their conversation was an undercurrent of teasing. He seemed to be constantly taking the piss. She was guarded. Didn't trust him. Couldn't say why. But he was still an attractive man. She wanted him to touch her.

Had he a family? She probed. Have you? And he winked. That same old come-on wink. What was it like over there in 'norn iren' these days? Seemed quite peaceful now, only isolated incidents. Omagh was the last big bomb. Wasn't that terrible? Did he still see Brian? What happened to that girlfriend of his, what was her name? Jesus, it was so long ago. Julie was it? And that awful mother of hers.

The two of them spent a couple of pleasant hours during which Tracey relaxed, slackened her guard. Kieran was funny, he could crack a joke and always think of a witty repost, he listened attentively, then followed whatever she said with a funny story of his own, about his parents or old school friends, or some strange uncles of his, or all night drinking sessions. Tracey tried to drag the conversation back to Pearl and her battle for an independent life in the flat. Kieran's responses were all agreement, but she felt he didn't understand what she was talking about; about Pearl's achievements, the self-esteem; her ability to do things herself; think for herself; but that these were all hard for her, and as her friends, they had to encourage her to do things herself, not do them for her. It was hard for everyone, watching her struggle with the kitchen door when they could so easily do it for her. But she had to be able to do it unaided when she was alone. And how quickly and easily she could sink into that old familiar state of depressed lassitude, when people did too much for her, reminding her of her uselessness and worthlessness and how safe it was to be useless and worthless. She could and must feed herself, not let Kieran do it. But

222

Kieran's only concern seemed to be that it was important for her to be able to choose her own friends.

Then there was an almost imperceptible change of tone, though Tracey didn't notice at first. With a seeming reluctance, Kieran began confiding in her about his wife. He'd wanted children and she hadn't, so guess what, they had none. He'd always wanted to be a father, would've been a good one too. Anyway, it wasn't to be. The wife ran off with a Derry woman.

"What like on a farm or in a cheese factory? Long blond plaits and two pails on a yoke?" Tracey was genuinely bemused, thought he'd said "dairy" woman.

"No, a woman from Derry, D-E-R-R-Y - which is hardly the point, Tracey. Don't ye get what I'm telling ye? She ran off with a woman!"

"It would have been OK for her to have run off with a man then? I've just realised that's an anagram of MNA, MAN. Perhaps that's where it comes from, an English/Gaelic sexual identity confusion."

"By Christ ye're one cold, unfeeling bitch. Here'm I confessing the secrets of my life and ye couldn't give a toss, could ye?"

"Oh I'm sorry, really. Somehow I got the impression it was like another of your funny stories. Apologies."

"You don't get it do you? You're still taking the piss. It's a real blow to a man's masculinity. I began to think she'd only fancied me because of something effeminate about me......It undermines your.....sexuality."

Tracey couldn't respond sympathetically, so she stayed quiet. Her own view, based on subjective observation and experience was that a lot of nonsense was talked about sexuality. She believed that sex was 90% opportunity. If a randy man fucked a sheep, it wasn't because he fancied the sheep in the first place, just that it was available (and willing!) when nothing else was. The most relevant factor was an individual's urge for sex. She's noticed that people with high sex drives spent a lot of time either wanking or talking about it – mind you, so did people at the other end of the scale, with big feelings of inadequacy.

"It was really demoralising, I couldn't get it up for six months." Kieran was unstoppable.

"Don't you think that might have been your ego, a psychological barrier, being rejected, rather than your sexuality?" Would he not get the message that she was not interested?

"Now Pearl," Tracey changed the subject, "she's an interesting case. She seems to fancy almost anyone in trousers under the age of 50. It's really hard to explain to her about useful inhibitions and, well, that sort of unacceptable behaviour, when she's just revelling in her new found freedom. But she is clearly sexually motivated. I'm not at all sure about it. Is it in fact any of my business? Isn't that an aspect of the education she needs, has a right to, if she's going to be independent?"

"Whooa....I cannot help you there. No way Jose, I'm not offering myself to Pearl for sex, not even as part of an 'education programme'. No way. It would be abuse..... of me!"

This was a massive jump to make. Tracey was floored, guffawed.

"I didn't..... for... one... moment..." She choked the words out between gasps of laughter. "........ I ....wasn't.... suggesting ... for....... one...... minute. Oh my God! How......... could you have even.......... thought it!"

Kieran was lost for words. That was a first.

"You're an experienced woman, teenage mother of one. Perhaps it is your responsibility as a friend, to sort her out. It is Darron, isn't it? He's your boy, your baby, your souvenir of Northern Ireland? Isn't he?"

When Tracey went back to Martha's she was almost reassured, leaving Kieran to sleep in Lilly's bed. She checked Pearl's alarm twice and resolved to make time to talk to her about the concept of abuse. Whatever his motives for being here, Kieran did not seem interested in abusing Pearl.

But in bed that night the thoughts that circulated in Tracey's head were that Kieran and she had talked for several hours and she still did not know why he was here, why he'd left Northern Ireland. Why at Christmastime?

Chapter 17

In the oozing warmth of not quite awoken early morning, with the sense of his body blissfully suspended somewhere east of sleep and west of the snooze alarm, the thoughts in Darron's head slowly churned, curdling into fixed impressions all the previous day's events.

"She is truly nuts. I hope to fuck I haven't inherited it, but then again, she is one unique individual. Certainly isn't boring. Tracey – what kind of name is that for a mother? Sounds like a teenage doll …… (snort) anything less like a Barbie, be hard to imagine. You're on tenterhooks the whole time, wondering what outrage she's going to get up to next. Maybe when I'm older I'll want to be like that. Then there's this weirdo. Not at all sure I wanted to sleep on his sofa. Bent as a nine bob note this one I reckon. But the alternative? a midnight trek through the cold to stay in the cook's quarters in a children's home. What a choice! Between two of my worst nightmares and on Christmas night too. He's such a prissy dresser, fingering his collar all the time, rubber gloves for the washing up. Fancy any mother calling her son Bernard. Bernie the bolt. I thought I might have to bolt last night. Hardly slept a wink, thinking he was going to come in and touch me up. Kept imagining his hands coming in under the bedclothes. Then when I did doze off, woke up with a huge stiffy. I was really jumpy. Couldn't help thinking he'd come in, but it was too good not to toss it off. Came quick though. Must remember to pick up the tissues. It was a good night at Pearl's though. Jesus! Never been so drunk. My old dears don't drink at all. Wonder if I've got a hangover? Don't think so, feeling fine, but then I'm still lying down, snug and warm, not bad this old sofa. Feel a bit of a snooze coming on."

"AHHHH! JESUS FUCKING CHRIST! ……"

"Er sorry, didn't mean to startle you. Brought you some tea. Do you want sugar?" Bernard was naked from the waist up. He looked reassuringly masculine, hairy chest, good muscle tone. Darron's eyes followed the line of hair down into the sculpted dent of his rib cage where it pointed down his abdomen and tailed into a black arrow pointing - Oh no! He had a belly button ring.

Darron shut his eyes again. "Yes, one please."

"Your mum, er, Tracey's, just rung."

"Tracey, please! No way is that head case my mum, except in the vaginal sense."

"As you so eloquently put it yesterday. Anyway she's on her way over and wants to take you to do a bit of sightseeing. It is a brilliant day, look." And Bernard whisked back the blackout curtain.

"Ahhhh….." Darron was blinded, the sun shone full in on him. "Bastard, I'm blinded."

"Will you stop shrieking like that? That's just like Tracey, you definitely are your mother's son, like it or not. Except your language. She doesn't swear, well hardly. Every other word form you's an expletive. Bet you don't talk like that at home! Bacon sarnie? Or muesli? You young people are all high-fibred veggies aren't you, animal rights and all that? But I never knew anyone who could resist the aroma of a bacon sandwich."

"Will you stop trying to categorise me, and tell me what I think? I'm an individual, with a brain who can draw my own conclusions from empirical evidence. Actually, I am not a veggie. It seems to me to be totally within the natural order of things for the human animal to be an omnivore and what's more, having the biggest frontal lobes of any species,….." (here he drew breath),

"Whale?" Darron ignored this,

"……to be dominant over other species."

"Coo, just like your mother!"

"Will you stop that!" and Darron threw a cushion, and Bernard threw it back and Darron jumped out of bed and hit him with it, then quickly picked up his mug.

"Uh, uh, uh, mind my tea." He started drinking so that Bernard, standing, cushion aloft ready to strike the next feather-weight blow, could not get him back – not without making a mess, and as Darron knew, Bernard couldn't abide a mess! Then looking down, Darron quickly crossed his legs. He was only wearing boxer shorts. And the flies were – phew -

not gaping! Finickety as ever, Bernard bent to pick up the tissues and put them in the bin.

*   *   *   *   *

The low winter sun shot brilliant pyrotechnic sparks up from the surface of the sea that cut at their eyes. Blinking and streaming, their eyes shaded with cupped hands, they pressed on eastwards towards South Parade pier.

"It was burned down when they were making 'Tommy', a film about a pinball wizard. Before your time. They rebuilt it as an exact copy, but all pastiche. It's horrible, all plastic and chip board." Tracey was being guidish.

"Not the metalwork supports, surely?" Darron was being pedantic. "Actually I have heard of Tommy because of The Who. Dad used to be a big fan. Still is, the old raver. Used to writes his own songs, all Dylan plagiarisms if you ask me."

"Bit of a poet, eh? There must be something to this nurture versus nature thing then....bit of a poet yourself as well, aren't you?"

Darron, looked over at her, screwing up his eyes against the glare, wondering if he hadn't drunk so much the day before whether his eyes would've been less painful, "Eh?"

"Or isn't it your own composition?" Tracey was unfolding a bit of scrap paper torn from.......what? The table cloth from yesterday. The memory began to swim into his head. Writing the riddle out on the Christmas tablecloth.

Tracey began to read aloud:
"My first is in face but not in fare.
My second is in up, but never a pair.
My third is in next, but can't be in exit.
My fourth is in tea. I hope that she gets it."

"Yeah right! It is original actually." There was a hint of pride in Darron's voice. "I wrote it for English. A sort of test to see if she actually read any of our homework before grading it. I have this mate who always gets Ds, no matter what he does, even if he copies me. And I always get As no matter what I do. So I tested her. I thought she would have to rap me

227

across the knuckles for this piece of filth. But no! So we concluded she never reads anything before marking it."

"Fine, good story," replied Tracey, "but there was no need to corrupt our two neighbours. Innocent little lads."

For a brief moment Darron was contrite, "Do you think they understood it then? I assumed it would be beyond them. Heh, wait a minute! Have you heard their language? I distinctly remember James referring to his mum as a cu....."

"OK, OK," Tracey shocked herself by not wanting to hear Darron say the word.

They were walking under the pier now examining the colourful trails of seaweed flapping wetly round the spindly rusted struts, a chaos of criss-crossed iron. Darron stopped to pick at the limpets. There was constant dripping and the fluttering of pigeons in and out of roosting spots was audible above the faint curling of the waves, waves too lazy or hung over this Boxing Day morning to shift their quota of shingle. Mother and son turned and crunched back along the beach in the direction of the city, going west, the sun pushing up behind them now. From this perspective, the sea was a flat Mediterranean green. As they rounded the castle, they could see the sunlight at its most acute winter angle, slapped up against the white walls of Gosport. Once, not long before, Darron had fallen in love with a beautiful girl on a holiday in Malta. For a brief moment this looked so like Malta, it could have been Malta. He was momentarily seared by the poignant memory.

On the pinkp-tarred promenade, traffic was heavy. Joggers ran off Christmas excesses. Couples arm in arm, step by step, meted out a rhythm of content. New clothes, gloves, scarves and hats, still bore the puncture marks of price tags. Children fell off new bikes, scuffed new roller blades, skidded on new skate boards, in jolly defiance of the posted bylaws. A merry throng interwoven by the multicoloured warp and weft of dog leashes, all watched protectively by the benign Alec Guinness- featured lions, smiling down indulgently from their war memorial pedestals.

Past the hovercraft, the closed kiosks, under the stumpy blue striped tower of Clarence Pier, a colourful, frivolous

228

treasure of sixties' design - the skeleton of the big wheel, and the not so big dipper were imprisoned behind spiked bars for the winter. Darron thought it funny, tacky, dated. Tracey thought nothing. It had always been like this, nothing much had changed here in 30 years.

The wind began to get up and little waves started to run in more sharply. The neck of water at the point narrowed to a couple of warships' width, pushed in by the massive stone Tudor ramparts on one side and the brick façade of HMS Dolphin on the other. The concentration of tide and current spun multiple vortexes, clearly visible in the water.

"You couldn't swim here. Look at that water! It would drag you straight down. I suppose it's too polluted anyway." Darron was stating what seemed obvious to him. Tracey looked at him and smiled. They climbed on towards the Round Tower. Suddenly there was a yell and three figures hurled themselves off the top of the ramparts, sixty feet down into the water below.

"Christ they must be mad! They'll be killed." Darron tried to peer into the water for them, but they were too far away.

Tracey pointed out the notice. "If not killed, then a £1000 fine. I was at school with a kid who did it, Jason Fry. He broke his neck, ended up a quadriplegic. Eventually he topped himself. Never found out how he managed to do it, the suicide, I mean."

"That's terrible......Look! I think I can see someone in the water."

"Well of course, it's Boxing Day, an age-old tradition."

"What! You Portsmouth people are mad. And this is confirmation as if I needed it, after yesterday. You mean jumping off the tower on Boxing Day is such a strong tradition that they have a special bylaw and huge fine, but don't bother to get down here to enforce it? So it isn't even effective!"

"No, jumping off the tower isn't the tradition, swimming is. Come on I'll take you to look at the hardened swimmers then on round to see a real Boxing Day tradition, it'll be on soon. We'll have to keep moving or we'll miss it."

Tracey led the way down a long flight of steps and they passed through an archway onto a tiny patch of beach. A small crowd was gathered there, many ancient wrinkly leathery bodies were in faded swimming togs. Some were hobbling over the pebbles down to the sea, some were emerging, shivering and goosepimpled. Several were lined up hugging the base of the wall in their towels. Then three conspicuously young men staggered out of the water.

"Look, the jumpers. Have any of them broken their necks do you think? What about a citizen's arrest?" Darron regretted the joke immediately, she might just take him seriously - and do it.

Despite her hurry, Tracey felt she had to take Darron up to the top of the Round Tower. They looked around. It was a fine view, the dockyard, the massive masts of The Victory, Nelson's flagship, and the Warrior declaring the link with an important naval past. Beyond, to the north west, the cliff on the mainland. There was a thicket of modern masts at the Camper Nicholson yard with the flat green Gosport ferry passing in front and the old red church campanile tucked between two patterned blocks of council flats. Gosport marina, the submarine tower. Out at sea, a smattering of white triangles of sail, but no commercial shipping yet today. The Isle of Wight so clear and near today, presaging rain tomorrow.

"Enough gawping at the view. Come on or we'll miss the treat."

"But Tracey, look at the time already."

"Oh, I wanted you to see the tug-o-war."

"I've seen them before. One every year at every village fete for miles around Salisbury. Yep, we excel in countryside stunts, such as the tug-of-war. There are a hundred villages, every village has a fete, every fete has a tug-o-war, my Salisbury mum loves village fetes. Work it out, until the age of 13 I was always dragged along. That's approximately 1300 tug-o-wars."

"OK, OK, OK, I get the picture," Tracey laughed, "But this is between the American and the Bridge."

"Sounds a little unbalanced. How big's the American for god's sake? I suppose it's a suspension bridge?"

"No they're two pubs,"

"Might have known, this is Portsmouth!"

"the tug-o-war is done over the water, a rope slung between two docks. It's quite a spectacle." Tracey didn't want him to go.

"My train, I'll have to go. Thanks for a great day yesterday." Darron bent to give her cheek a quick kiss. "I know the way to the station, don't walk with me. "

She couldn't watch him walk away, turned to look at the sea and console herself. "There would've been too many people there, on such a lovely day. We wouldn't been able to see anything anyway."

*   *   *   *   *

Without his company, the bright day faded. The anticlimax of Boxing Day, the pathos of being alone in the thick of this convivial crowd oppressed Tracey. Her feet took her on towards her original goal with a meandering detour around the point, past The Still and West. She played a game with herself, noticing and captioning all the people she saw, what they were doing. It was a way of trying not to think about Darron.

The feeling of being disconnected from her surroundings meant she was unprepared for what she glimpsed through the window of the Spice Island pub. At first it seemed to have no significance, Tracey had temporarily lost her points of reference. But the back of a curly grey head and beside it a head of sleek black hair...... She stopped, struck by the odd sense of familiarity, but disconcerted by the location, the heads bent together intimate, conspiratorial. She didn't know anyone who would be here at this time. The two heads bent towards each other, the sleek head lower, listening, submissive. And then she knew and pushed into the pub through the brass-handles doors, her mouth moving ready, shock forcing up outrage.

"Hiya, great day for a walk! You left Marc cooking then, Isabelle? Must be great to have someone who can cook, you know, for a partner." Did she emphasise the word partner enough? Did the sarcasm have enough weight? Tracey was being careful that there would be no chance for either of them to confide in her.

Kieran might be anxious about his sexuality, but breaking up Marc and Isabelle, Tracey couldn't stand by and watch that happen. There was a thread of honesty in Tracey, she couldn't deny being motivated as much by wanting to protect Marc as a twinge of jealousy herself. Hadn't Kieran come to see her? True he'd not made any overtures to her, no lunging for the tits he was supposed to admire. And there wasn't much breast meat on the beautiful Isabelle, with whom he seemed rather taken. Unless the tale of woe about his marriage had been a subtle come-on, preparing the way, softening Tracey up for a sympathetic cuddle. She still fancied him after all these years, but…….. Nah! She couldn't compete with Isabelle.

Had they been holding hands before she interrupted? When she looked down, they weren't.

"He has such a sexy accent, don't you think Tracey?" Isabelle's sang-froid was amazing.

"Who, Marc or Kieran here?" And then she remembered Isabelle's infatuation with her Irish lecturer. And decided to go with the innocent explanation. Isabelle couldn't resist Irish accents. Tracey could go along with that. She was attracted to anyone who wasn't from Portsmouth; collected foreign accents, languages, looks; surrounded herself with as many people unlike herself as possible.

"They're both sexy, I think. But Kieran hasn't got a blond ponytail, has he?" Tracey paused while the effect of her implication that she had a taste for Marc herself, sank in. "Kieran's really quite conventional-looking and – here she whispered loudly – and he's a mature man in his forties, past his best."

"Watch it! Watch it! There's life in the old dog yet." Kieran was jolly, perhaps glad to have been released from temptation or a potentially embarrassing situation. Much as he was clearly flattered by Isabelle's attentions, he had been party to the difficulties between her and Marc and surely couldn't want to be a pawn in that game. He had his own preoccupations.

"Who's with Pearl?" She regretted it as soon as it was out. It was not for her to dictate a roster and certainly not for her to suggest that either of them had any obligations towards Pearl. "Anyone want a drink?"

"No, I'm going back to help Marc. You coming, Kieran?" There was an awkward moment when Kieran could not read whether Isabelle's invitation was genuine or a ruse to get him to herself again. He shrugged, indicating his half empty glass, passing the baton back to her. She hesitated, then looking at Tracey said, "It's easy to get lost in Portsmouth. D'you think he'll find his way home. He's such a newcomer, I was just showing him round."

"I'll conduct him safely back for you. Are you expecting him for dinner?"

"C'mon 'nere heh! Yer talking about me as though I don't exist, but! Do I not have a say in all this?"

"Does he take sugar?" He frowned, puzzled. Isabelle and Tracey shared a private joke. The fact that they did nothing to stop the over-protective way Kieran treated Pearl, didn't prevent them from wishing he could see how patronising it was and enjoying an opportunity to give him a feeling of being in the same position himself.

"We'll be back in a couple hours then, Isabelle. And I'll join you in a half, Kieran. You buying?" Dismissed, Isabelle left. The relaxed self-confident smile on her face, gave nothing away.

*   *   *   *   *

The pavements of Portsmouth were polka-dotted in gobs of grey gum - so dense outside pubs and clubs as to conceal the tarmac beneath. And the morning after a high day or holiday, such as this, or even after a routine Saturday night, the flags were also adorned with colourful splatters and garlands of vomit.

"It's great," Tracey was enthusing, in her guiderly way, watching where she trod, "you hardly ever see dog shit on the pavements nowadays - people have become quite community-minded since they started enforcing the bylaws." Kieran glanced at her, he could detect no trace of irony.

"I think it's partly the fact that they've been gradually replacing the scruffy old flags with these parquet-laid continental paviours. Gives people a sense of civic pride." Tracey was drivelling. She was trying to keep Kieran away from Marc and Isabelle's as long as possible. His attention was so evidently not on her, nor anything she said, that she suspected he had actually wanted to consummate his liaison with Isabelle. What red-blooded man wouldn't? And he was now frustrated, perhaps annoyed.

"You alright?"

"Mmmm. I waaas hoping to get a wee close-up glimpse of the Victory. Ye know, Nelson's flagship. Though I know it won't be open today."

So astonished was Tracey at this innocent-sounding request that she stopped in her tracks. But of course, he was an Admiral Lord Nelson fan, as would anybody be who'd seen the man toppled from his pedestal, as Kieran had on his eighth birthday in Dublin. They were currently walking away from it.

"Come along'a me," Tracey was happy to oblige, to kill time, leave Marc and Isabelle alone together. "We'll take a detour across Guildhall Square and through Victoria Park. See the terrapins and rabbits."

"Ooooh, goodee gumdrops!" in his piss-take English accent.

Kieran's first sight of the Guildhall was the dark wavering image of its clocktower reflected in the wall of black windows opposite and below it an austere Queen Vic was graciously welcoming visitors with her inimical, witheringly stern stare. When he looked round at the huge chunk of brilliant white wedding cake that was the Guildhall, its stone fascia glistening like sugar crystals, it seemed too clean and new, too solid and self-consciously monumental. He preferred the wobbling reflection, imagining the tinted plate glass smashed, the rubble being bulldozed.

"It's modern, a reproduction of the original, bombed flat during the war." Tracey confirmed that it was new.

Alongside, in the tiny city park, skeletal trees made black patterns against the bright sky, a few squirrels, disturbed by the warmth of the sun scampered through them. Bare, manured beds and scraggy grass, were decorated with seasonal patches of breadcrumbs, offerings to winter birds from lonely pensioners. The ancient Burmese bell corroded gently where it hung over its stone plinth and the still fountain, a painted cast iron swan, wings erect, waited, holding the memory of water cascading to the pond below. Sluggish, golden koi moved stiffly beneath the weed in the cold black water. Reaching the gate, Tracey told Kieran to look behind him at the Zurich building. A massive multi-storey edifice of sheer, unbroken gold-black glass rose up and curved away from the shrubby edge of the park, more than doubling its size in facetted reflection.

"That's one godawful menacing-looking building," he declared.

"D'you think so? I think its brilliant and in the evening when the setting sun shines on it, it's just magnificent."

Queen Street passed in a straggling muddle of struggling businesses. Anachronistic, Dickensian gentlemens' tailors jostled with humming One-stops and empty pubs. Most premises were barred and shuttered, in line with the confidence the proprietors had in the local population, some of whom emerged and entered, booted and spurred from towering flats between crowded rows of terraced houses in the narrow streets behind.

Soon Tracey and Kieran found themselves walking in the company of the unscalable dockyard wall, stretching half the length of the road.

"Well, what do you think?" They had been surprised to find the Victory was open to visitors. Kieran had been silent most of the way round, restricting himself to responding to the guide's quips, to make him feel he was doing a good job. They were perched on a bench studying the fat-bellied side of the old tub. Bold stripes of black and ochre yellow were broken up into regular patterns by the gun emplacements, portholes merrily open to the afternoon breeze, black canon muzzles kissed by the afternoon sun. The masts rose into the blue, anchored by lattices of tarred black stays and hung with swaying rope. They could just make out the Christmas tree on the deck.

"I really can't explain."

Tracey had been expecting something anodyne, 'interesting but cramped' or 'what an appalling life' or 'do they always make that stupid crack about the block of wood nailed to the deck to mark the spot where Nelson fell – I'm not surprised with that piece of wood there?'

"Believe it or not, I used to dream of seeing this when I was a kid. Made Airfix models of it, ya know like. And I thought I'd get some sort of feeling, d'ye know what I mean. But what I've got in my head now are odd little things, the powerful smell and the red paint in the infirmary, the tiny size of the man, his bed doubling as his coffin, an all. But I never got a sense of the man. I tell you, I'm disappointed."

There was nothing Tracey could say except "I suppose all those millions of tourists have rubbed away the man himself completely by now. You should've come when you were little, maybe there'd have been a bit left still then – so long ago." He smiled, not in the mood for teasing.

*   *   *   *   *

"This room is too small."

"I'm sorry, Ms Allsop, but when I wrote inviting you to bring everyone who is involved in Pearl's care, I'd no idea there would be so many of you." Kerry had introduced herself as Kerry, also proclaimed on her lapel badge. No second name. She apparently was a social worker.

"Sorry, but what is your second name? And exactly what is your responsibility – in relation to Pearl?" Tracey wrote deliberately and laboriously on her note pad, far more than the simple 'Kerry Braithwaite, social worker' response. Situations like this were not unfamiliar to her. Tracey was

236

sharp, she knew how to get the edge on people and how to keep the advantage.

"Just as well we're not all in wheelchairs. We'd never get in." Tracey had hoped that Kieran would keep quiet. She hadn't wanted him to come, but Pearl had more or less insisted. And now here he was, the second person to speak, sticking his oar in. Christ why hadn't she talked it through with him beforehand. Of course he was right, there wasn't room for more than three people in wheelchairs in this room at any one time.

"All the meeting rooms are like this, meant to be cosy and non-threatening."

Sue, the Key worker, suggested moving the table out to make more space. Tracey rushed to help her. Now she had got the edge, and she was confident they would not sideline her, she needed to win these people over. They controlled everything that happened to Pearl now.

Rose offered to wait outside. Tracey had forced her to come, against all her protestations and now assured her that they really needed her to be there, in the meeting, please.

Recalling Rose's agitation earlier, even Tracey was beginning to have doubts.

"You know I don't get on with them disabled people, in wheelchairs and that, dribbling all the time. 'Aint got the patience, me," Pearl had repeated ad nauseam all the way up on the bus. What did she think Pearl was if not disabled? How did her role with Pearl, which she clearly enjoyed, fit in with this mass image of disability? But Tracey didn't ask. She didn't want the friendship between the two women spoiled by Rose suddenly becoming aware that Pearl was one of these disabled people who did indeed dribble a fair amount – if she hadn't noticed already. When they had arrived, she had hurried Rose hastily into the meeting room without going into the day centre where Rose's fears may have been realised.

Bernard was there of course, he'd come in the taxi with Pearl and Kieran. Rose and Tracey sat side by side, but where was Robin? The only one of them paid for any of this work, was late. His role was crucial to the whole project. He gave it Health Authority authority.

"Shall we start?" Kerry was getting irritated. Robin bounded in.

"Oh, am I late? Sorry." He clearly wasn't.

"There are a number of things to cover. Will you make notes please, Sue? Head it up 'First monthly review - 29th December' can you? Right, firstly, we need to talk about Pearl's care arrangements, how that's all going. Then there's her physiotherapy." Kerry was counting them off on her fingers. Tracey was making her own notes. "Then we have to do a review of the adaptations to the property and lastly, future plans for Pearl. Is that OK with everyone? On our side, there's been some news. We have found some information about Pearl's background."

Was it only Tracey who wondered why this woman had been addressing herself to the group and not to Pearl? Talking about her in the third person as though she weren't present. Kerry actually seemed to be avoiding eye contact with Pearl.

"Shall we go out while they tell you the information about your background?"

Tracey leaned over to ask Pearl. There was no response. She was looking blankly ahead. Oh no, don't do this to me! Don't do this to yourself! She screamed inside. Don't switch off, Pearl. Tracey undid the brake and swivelled the chair round so she was looking right in Pearl's face and waited till Pearl's eyes woke up, and Tracey could see that somebody was in. Pearl hadn't been like this since those first few times in hospital.

Tracey was scared. Was this a relapse? She repeated the question. This time Pearl answered, her jaw flapping worse than ever, for an agonising age, before she got out the words,

"Noooo……. Stay……'ere……pppp". They waited for the last word, the tension mounted, "ppplease." Thank God. Tracey reached out and took her good hand, ready to give it a wake up squeeze should she go off again.

"Well it turns out that she was born,"

Tracey interrupted and said pointedly to Pearl, "Are you listening Pearl, this is about you?"

At last, Kerry took the hint. She waited until Pearl was looking at her and started again.

238

"It looks like you were born in The Royal Northern hospital in London, Pearl - nearly a Cockney – on 16th March 1961. Your mother was Lillian Johnstone,"

"That's Lilly, your mum, who's moved out, she's not living in the flat now." Tracey interrupted, anxious that this should be clear.

"(as I was saying) she was 35 and your father was George Johnstone. You were their first child. They were living in a flat in Barnet at the time. We can't be certain that these are your records, but the birth report is certainly your mother's, if that doesn't sound contradictory. It seems likely in view of the long difficult labour, the eventual forceps delivery, which took a further three hours, that this was you being born. Those conditions would be very consistent with the birth trauma that usually results in Cerebral Palsy."

Tracey gasped. They all looked at her. This was the first time she'd heard a name applied to Pearl's condition. Had they all been talking about it and she had just missed it? No one else seemed surprised. It made her feel strangely comforted that it had such a well-known name, more manageable somehow.

Kerry continued, "But there are some health visitor's notes from the time, about you and your mum, that seem to corroborate it as well. I have some photocopies here if you want to see later."

Pearl looked suitably stunned, probably because she was in a room crammed with people, all looking at her, she was the centre of attention, she was being addressed.

Perhaps at some level she did understand that this was her identity being discussed. But it was really too much information. Tears rolled. But she was smiling.

"Sixteenth of March 1961! It's unbelievable, we're twins, Pearl." Tracey was shrieking. "I was born on 15th March 1961. I can't believe it, it can't be true."

"Keep your hair on, Tracey. Statistically it's not that unlikely. Think of all the millions of people in the world and yet there are only 365 and a quarter possible birthdays in the Gregorian calendar each year, and millions and millions of us

to share them. Chances are a few of us will share birthdays."
Kieran was being pompous, showing off.

"Yes, but the same year?"

"OK, but even there, if you take a range of say a
generation, that's 30 years, there's still only 10,000 possible
birthdays for millions and millions of people to share,"

Tracey couldn't believe it, he'd told Tracey he wouldn't
be saying anything, said he never spoke up in situations such
as this, there was still such a lot of prejudice against the Irish
in England.

"Fascinating though this is," Kerry, in control, stared
Kieran into silence, smiling a little in case he might fancy her.

"I still think it's amazing, don't you Pearl?" Tracey was
not so easily diverted from what seemed to her an astonishing
coincidence.

"Don't bother about me. Just call me an old sceptic. I'm
the worst type, a lapsed catholic sceptic." Kieran rejoined,
then catching Kerry's eye, "Oh, sorry."

"As Pearl's 'second cousin', I should have thought none
of this would be news to you, surely you should have known
all this!" Kerry said sourly, defiantly, suspiciously, looking up
from a hand-written note on the file.

The hospital bin lorry suddenly started up outside,
revving loudly before startling the occupants of the tiny room
by reversing towards their window, its warning alarm beeping.
The distraction covered the excruciating moment of panic
that any liar feels when discovered. Tracey had time to
recover.

"Yes, we are second cousins" she repeated the lie to try
and make it real for herself, "but although our mothers were
inseparable as children, they never saw each other later, ya
know, after we were born," she was on an unstoppable roll
now, all eyes on her, "there was a falling out, my dad and her
dad never....... ouch!"

"Oh, SORRY! didn't see your foot there." Bernard had
definitely, deliberately kicked her. But though looking hard
into her eyes, he was not sure she would get the message. He
was keen to stop her getting carried away with this fantasy,

knowing that the unnecessary embellishment was giving doubt to the lie rather than flesh.

"Well, anyway, I never met Lilly, cause my family moved away. And I never even knew of Pearl's existence. Did I Pearl?" Tracey added, looking at Pearl, as if she would corroborate her story.

The meeting struggled to a close. Kerry expressed reluctant satisfaction with all the arrangements except two.

"I'm a bit concerned that there is no one actually sleeping over with Pearl in the flat,"

Tracey willed all the assembled company to keep quiet. Despite all her fears to the contrary, the arrangement with Kieran really seemed to be helping Pearl progress, and it was tremendously convenient for the others in the care team. They all knew the complications and delay that would ensue if they tried officially to add Kieran to the team at this stage. Tracey stared at Pearl, wondering if she would say anything. Pearl smiled. Did she know to say nothing?

"We have these alarms, you know. Rose and Bernard are on call night about and Rose is happy to be called if it's something personal that Bernard isn't permitted to deal with. Pearl tell Kerry how you work the alarm. Yes, that one round your neck." Tracey knew Kerry wouldn't want to waste time waiting for Pearl to explain.

"No, no, that's fine thanks Pearl. I'm sure you are very good at it."

"The other question I have is about the physiotherapy. Tell me, are you a trained Physiotherapist, Robin?" The pause was eloquent.

"I'm a student of Conductive Education and have the support of Professor Chapman. And you know Pearl has agreed to take part in this research programme."

Tracey was surprised that Chapman was a professor. Robin wouldn't promote him to boost his own status? Would he? They'd only have to look him up to find out!

"I'll need to talk to you about this later, Robin. As the people responsible for Pearl's welfare, Sue and I have to be sure that what she is receiving, is appropriate and could not be harmful in any way." It was hard not to feel Kerry had taken against him. Perhaps a hidden agenda, thought Tracey, alive to every nuance. Social Services versus Health Service? Entertaining though this thought was, it may not bode well for Pearl in the long run.

Tracey didn't miss Kerry's batting eyelids and cosy smiles as they left. "She could hardly keep her hands off you, Kieran, you sexy thing."

"Oh, shut yer nyammin. Ye're just saying that to make me feel good. To repair my damaged sexuality! To reinforce my self esteem with the opposite sex." Tracey gave him a friendly thump.

"No, I did that when I told you Pearl fancies you. Anyway, what about Isabelle?" she added in a whisper.

"You are one evil bitch, sure ye are." Kieran was delighted that women found him sexy.

When at last he could get a word in, and they were safely out of earshot, Bernard opened his mouth at Tracey just as she, indignantly remembering, turned to ask him why he'd kicked her.

"Because," he hissed, "you kept on inventing more and more lies about your relationship with Pearl and it began to look really suspicious. I thought at any moment Kerry was going to rumble you and ask for some kind of proof! The only comforting thing is to know that you are such an unpractised liar. Don't you know that the more you lay it on, the more unlikely it starts to sound. There has to be a nice balance in a lie, keep it simple and then it's easier to remember it accurately."

"Bloody hell, listen to the expert! That's the first lecture I've ever had on Mendacity."

They were standing under an awning, waiting for the taxi. It proclaimed THE DAWN COMMUNITY. New dawn? Lost dawn? Darkest hour before the dawn? Tracey wondered what message this was sending out to the clients who came here everyday. To her, the word 'dawn' suggested an endless treadmill of new beginnings, with no conclusions, no possible end in sight, well, not on this planet. But her eye was caught by a plaque on the wall. Dawn had been the name of a former client. With what hope her parents must have named her.

As they were squeezing Pearl into the taxi, to the cacophonic noise of 'You Sexy Thing' blasting from the taxi radio and Pearl, squawking and bossing and upbraiding them all, Robin emerged from the building, looking pleased with himself.

"That old bag, she wanted to get me off Pearl's case, old cow...... from Kerry, d'you think? She should get back to making butter, except she'd sour the milk." He was smiling, so Tracey anticipated some *coup de gras*, some happy outcome.

"No anti-Irish remarks please!" Tracey mock scolded. She hadn't liked Kerry much either. But who'd want to be a social worker? A difficult, thankless job.

"And the sub-plot seems to have been that her daughter had tried to get involved in some completely unconnected medical research programme up in darkest Manchester, but they wouldn't fund hers, so she's annoyed that I did get funded for mine."

"Cut the paranoia and explain how this will affect Pearl."

"Ahhhhh.....well. You know she wanted to discredit me because I'm not a physiotherapist? Trumped her there with my first class honours in....da da! ....medicine from Glasgow and then I told her about my work at the sports injury clinic, where I was actually acting head for a bit. Ha! she didn't know I was a post grad medic. Then I was pleased to draw her attention to some well-respected published research (which I happen to have here in my bag) which suggests that there is a sizable proportion of physical disability made worse by the conventional methods of so-called treatment. Slapping on callipers, forcing people to be mobile in ways that distort their bodies, particularly legs and spines, can lead to worse disability in later life and other complications, heart and circulation problems, digestion etcete-ra! See, because Pearl's body is virgin territory (if you'll pardon the description), and she's had the life she's had, her muscles have been allowed to waste sort of equally, evenly. I'm hoping, as you know, that an adapted application of the conductive method might be really effective for Pearl, develop her body more evenly." This was the most animated Tracey had ever known Robin, so she resisted the temptation to take the piss. But he did sound pretty arrogant.

"Seems to be working – though I think the main motivation for progress to Pearl, is being surrounded by sexy young men. She can't wait to be running round the bed after you all." Tracey knew Robin would be shocked, but you had gee them up, these earnest young men.

"Anyway," Robin went on, "as I pointed out to merry Kerry, show me a person with a similar prognosis to Pearl's, who has suffered the regular health service interventions, and who has reached her age, and is as fit as she is. - Can't, can she!"

"Ner, ner, na, ner ner! Come on let's drag Rose away from the roses, look she's up to her nostrils in savage pruning over there, what's the matter with her, there's nothing to look at?"

Rose was admiring the patch of garden, despite the fact that it had been hacked back for winter, thinking how lovely it would be in summer.

"There's a bus due, come on, Rose."

Chapter 18

It was all over the newspapers. An explosion in a brand new shopping mall on the outskirts of Manchester killed three people and seriously injured twelve others. Hundreds more had less serious injuries. There was no warning and no one claimed responsibility. There was briefly a rumour that it was the responsibility of an Israeli gang targeting a number of Arab-owned businesses there. And at least one newspaper ran a story about an alleged insurance scam involving an unidentified property magnate who was in financial difficulties over the new development. The mall had been constructed on a disused refuse tip and official investigations focused on the possibility of an accidental explosion caused by inadequate methane gas release mechanisms.

It happened on 30th December and the shops had been full of people when the explosion occurred. A 'tragedy and an outrage', but also a miracle that so few were killed. But to Tracey and the team, shocked and sympathetic though they were, there was a surprising repercussion, a 'little local difficulty', caused simply by the explosion happening when it did.

Rose and Joe's children and grandchildren had clubbed together to buy them a new television and video for Christmas – a sop for not being invited by any of the 23 of them to spend Christmas with them, in Tracey's view.

Tracey witnessed an act of touching generosity when she came up the stairs one evening. It was Joe, leaning on the doorjamb, panting at the threshold to Pearl's flat having buzzed the door open, and at his feet, the cause of his breathless state, a heavy old television set.

To Rose and Joe it had been a gesture of pure altruistic generosity to donate their old set to Pearl. After all they could have sold it! But no, Pearl didn't have a television and who could live alone without the telly? Kieran couldn't be there all the time to keep Pearl company, brilliant friend though he was to her. In fact he had made it clear to Tracey that he was only there for a holiday, getting over his marriage break-up, between jobs, and would only be staying until the redundancy money ran out.

Tracey wasn't sure what to do. Pearl had pointedly turned away from all the television screens on the hospital ward. She had been adamant she didn't want one in the flat. If she remembered nothing else about her past life, she did seem to remember the role of the television set. Tracey didn't want, for herself or Pearl, to hurt Joe and Rose's feelings and anyway she thought there might come a time, now that Pearl was more able and could control some things herself, that she might want a television.

Better, also, that they introduced it as a useful pastime now, before Kieran showed signs of actually leaving, which he inevitably would. Better to get her accustomed to it now, it might turn out to be useful company for her when none of them were available to spend time with her. Tracey decided to play for time for Pearl and be honest with Joe.

"That's really sweet of you and Rose, Joe. But look at you, you're knackered now."

"Oooooo.....is it? Kie-ran?" Pearl called from within, sounding a bit anxious. They could hear her struggling to manoeuvre the wheelchair.

"It's only us, Tracey and Joe." Tracey called back.

"Leave it here," she said to Joe, "I'll take it in. You know, I'm just thinking......Pearl hasn't had a telly since that last one blew up. So maybe we shouldn't just spring it on her. I'll tell her about it first, so it's not a shock. Is that OK? What do you think? You look as though you could do with a cuppa after all that effort."

When she chose to, Tracey could be very firm, very certain. It would have taken a stronger man than Joe to put up a fight.

"You're right, I'm a bit puffed. I'll pop up later and see how you get on, OK?"

At first, Tracey tried to sneak it into Kieran's (how easily Lilly had been erased!) room without Pearl seeing it. But it was impossible. Pearl was right there and caught Tracey starting to lift it up from the hall floor. Tracey couldn't believe it. Pearl was pleased with the present. She wanted to watch it there and then. But there was no aerial connection now. They had removed it in the clear up process. And Tracey still didn't think it was a good idea, not just yet, not without some preparation.

She plonked the television up on the table and tried to explain about the aerial. Pearl was angry and frustrated and couldn't understand that it wouldn't work. But mollified when Tracey said she'd go for Kieran or Bernard.

There was a note on the fridge from Kieran. 'Gone for messages, back 5ish'. Tracey was a bit put out that she hadn't been told that Kieran would be out, but told herself that Bernard and Rose would be completely capable of arranging cover for Pearl without her. In fact, it was a jolt to realise that after she went back to university, most of Pearl's caring would be up to them to sort out.

Bernard was out. Tracey had a brainwave. James and Matthew! Bound to have some suitable videos. You didn't need an aerial for videos. Did you?

The noise reached her the minute she hit the street. Shouting. Bernard shouting at someone and someone shouting back. She had witnessed him swearing, being rude to people, had herself been the victim of his scathing sarcasm, but she had never heard him lose his cool like this.

"You filthy fucking perv, I'll get the fucking police onto you, you fucking dirty piece of shit. Just you wait." The woman was beside herself with fury. Her hair, scraggy and bleached was a frantic electric halo round a face, puce with rage. Eyes flaming, she slashed the air with manic hands. Her whole body shook.

As Tracey kept out of sight on the doorstep, sizing up the situation, she could see Bernard physically taking control of himself. He had stopped shouting. He relaxed his shoulders down and back, and lifted his head. She could see his fingers by his sides flex and curl. The woman ranted on a bit longer, then fell into hysterical sobbing, pulling at her hair, smearing mascara as she rubbed at her eyes. A passer by, looking fixedly ahead, shrugged himself closer into his winter collar and hurried across the road to avoid them.

"What have you done to them?" she suddenly screamed with renewed strength.

Working fast, Tracey's brain began to click into gear. She moved forward, confronting them both.

"He's been at my children, doing things to them. He had the key. He just let himself in." She was appealing to Tracey, distraught now, hiding her face in her hands.

Tracey took the opportunity to touch Bernard's arm, without the woman noticing, to indicate he was released, she would take over. He nodded his understanding but stood a moment as though uncertain what to do, until Tracey had led the woman away towards the front door.

It was closed, they didn't have the key. They buzzed up. Again and again. After a long time, a timid voice whispered through the intercom,

"Who is it?" James' voice shaky, nervous.

"It's your mum." There was no response. The woman began to weep again.

Tracey pressed again.

"It's Tracey, can I come up?"

"Is mum there?"

"Yes, we'll come up together. You can tell her all about Christmas. By the way, I don't suppose you've got a Sesame Street video I can borrow for Pearl? She's got a telly now."

"Has she?" Matthew was there now. He sounded interested.

"Open the door, can you, it's cold out here."

The woman had opened her mouth to speak. Tracey lifted her hand to silence her. The door clicked open.

Both boys had tear-stained faces. Bernard's signature rubber gloves were on the kitchen floor, where they had in haste, been discarded. The sink was still full of washing up liquid bubbles. In the terrible silence, Tracey could hear them gently popping. It didn't look much like the scene of a pederastic orgy that the boys' mother had been claiming had greeted her arrival.

"Can you find some videos for Pearl, boys, please?"

"You think you're their mother, now?" hissed the woman.

Tracey turned away and left her in the kitchen.

"What have you got then? Any Sesame Street? I'd love that, so would Pearl."

"Ohh…..what! That's baby stuff. We don't watch that. We got Terminator. And Grandad's got some videos, but we can't reach them – not allowed - An' here's James Bond. He lets me watch 15s ." James was keen, even through his recent distress, to appear grown up.

"This is more like it, The Muppets, yeah, can I borrow this for Pearl?"

Their mother was perched on a kitchen stool, at a loss, lost for words.

"Can I take it for her?" Tracey was asking the boys.

"Yes, take it!" the mother said, "leave us alone and don't come back. I've got to get them away from here," and a fresh bout of sobbing began.

"We'll come, I want to see Pearl's telly, per-lease. And we want to give her the video, ourselves." James, usually so cool and in control, sounded a bit desperate.

"No way!" shrieked the woman. "You stay here with me."

Matthew turned from his mother and said to Tracey, "What's a…… feed……..o (he paused to think)…….pile? Mum says Bernard's one."

Suddenly it dawned on the boys' mother that this woman and that monster knew each other. It must be a paedophile ring. They were probably all in it together. She rushed over to the boys and squeezed them to her.

"GET OUT OF THIS FLAT. GET OUT. GET OUT. GET OUT"

"OK, OK. But where were you at Christmas, then? Where were you for the past three weeks? Eh? Leaving two little boys alone. Shame on you." Tracey's voice was as flat and emotionless as she could manage.

"I left them with their grandfather," she wailed. "I thought they'd be safe here, away from their father, that bastard. And then (more sobbing) …. and then….. It's not enough that my father, their poor grandfather, goes out one day shopping for stuff for the boys for Christmas and dies suddenly, alone on the street and he's lying in the morgue for weeks till they identify him. It's not enough that their father left us for that effing little whore and then comes back to beat us up when she treats him like shit. But then, my boys get molested by some puffta freak. How could I know that pervert next door would worm his way into their – oh I can't bear to even think it." she wailed, weary now.

"You're wrong about Bernard, he is not a paedophile." She sounded certain, but how well did Tracey actually know him? "And (she lowered her voice) you're wrong about your own father. Wherever he went, it wasn't shopping for the boys, he planned it. Went off and left them locked in with several days' supplies."

"GET OUT GET OUT GET OUT! How dare you say wicked things about my old dad, such a sweet old man and now he's dead."

Tracey made for the door and as she opened it she asked again,

"But where were you while all this was going on?"

Bernard was there, at Pearl's. He was shaking. He had clearly been weeping. Nothing could have prepared Tracey for that. Bernard crying. It was too much to bear. Tracey felt a boiling rage rise inside her that that miserable little inadequate cow could have done this to Bernard. He was their tower of strength, their lion-heart.

They got the video working. Pearl was thrilled with The Muppets. Tracey kissed Pearl, said she'd be back with dinner in a bit and took Bernard upstairs, home.

"How could she think that? I was washing up. They were drawing. She stormed in, already angry, looking for a fight. Had her own key, you see. I was flabbergasted. Maybe I did look a bit flustered, you know, how you do when you've been surprised. But I did not have 'guilt written all over my face'. Then James grabbed Matthew and rushed him into the bedroom, you know, like it was a familiar learned response to her shouting. I dunno. Maybe she thought they were trying to hide from me. God knows what was going on in her head."

There was nothing for Tracey to say except that she knew he would never have touched them. She said she understood how he felt. And certainly she had had a lifetime of being misunderstood and unjustly blamed. But she couldn't really imagine the intensity of how this might feel, to have your kindest deeds, your most altruistic actions, twisted in such a way, not just wilfully misunderstood, but poisoned, filthied.

"You know how I feel, it's like, just by her disgusting accusation, that she has destroyed something inside me, something that was nice and sort of innocent. Something that meant that I could be with, for example those two little boys, and be just me, a kid again maybe, just relaxed, normal. You know like when you're with real friends, when you can just be somewhere and there are no innuendos, no tough-guy facades. You can forget that someone might see you and think you're a prat. It feels like she's tainted all my future contact with children. It's as though she has destroyed an innocence in me. Up until I'd met those two, I didn't know there was any innocence left in me. It wasn't like I was aware of it, you know, as such. Until that moment, until she said that. I had never, ever thought of children other than as just small people. That you treat like any other human beings, but nicer because they're not so street-wise. I suppose I'd never thought of them as objects, that could be, I dunno, in someone else's power, certainly never as sex objects...... I cannot believe it."

Then Bernard pulled Tracey down onto the sofa beside him. He needed to be comforted. He sank his face into her hair. She was intensely uncomfortable. There was barely room. This was not right. Almost buried within Tracey's soul dwelt a deep pessimism. Now she felt it threatening to erupt. Everything was going wrong.

After some time in which Tracey's leg went numb and her shoulder began to ache, but she had been unable to move without disturbing the sleeping Bernard, there was a knock. Tracey had to ease herself out of Bernard's sleeping arms, but he didn't stir. She was relieved to greet Kieran. So as to make no noise, she held the keeper back with a knife and softly pulled the door shut behind them. They went to fix the aerial for Pearl.

251

In Lilly's bedroom, looking for an alternative aerial lead, while Kieran was in the street trying to see in the near darkness if there was a connection to an aerial on the roof, Tracey had a chance to see what Kieran had done in there. He had pushed back most of the furniture and cleaned only one small area. She was shocked to see he had screwed two ignorant bolts into the doors of a substantial oak wardrobe and these were now fastened with chunky padlocks. She hurried out. It was nothing to do with her. Unless.....he was a drug dealer? Or grower, though she would have seen the tell-tail ultra violet light round the cracks of the cupboard, surely, or do they switch them off sometimes to simulate night? A secret collector of pornography? With an interest in specialist stuff perhaps? Sex with disabled people? Like the nurse had suggested to Bernard? Don't even follow that train of thought, Tracey, counselled herself. She shut the bedroom door behind her, just as Kieran returned.

"It's done, I hope. Let's give it a go."

They all cheered as the evening's children's programmes started. Pearl joined in noisily. Although the volume was turned up very high, there couldn't be too much wrong with her hearing!

Pearl was alone in the room when the 6 o'clock news came on.

Kieran and Tracey were in the kitchen peeling potatoes (to his disgust, such waste of effort, Irish people cook them in their skins, much more nutritious). They worked in companionable silence.

"I went back down to look at Nelson's ship, there, the other day. I couldn't believe it wouldn't have had more of an effect on me, you know."

"It's because he was so small. You'd seen him thrust up on his pedestal, hundreds of feet in the sky. Didn't your mammy ever tell you it's dangerous to put people on pedestals. They can't live up to it."

"I think I'll pay him a visit in Trafalgar Square. Haven't been there for years. Maybe in the next day or so."

"Oh can I come? Please, please!" Tracey was like a kid getting excited about a Sunday school outing.

252

"Have you been a good girl, then?......" Kieran asked sternly. "Though I don't know why you'd want to come at this time of year. So what happened with the boys next door, then, you never finished telling me?"

Tracey told him about the ructions next door and the uncertain fate of James and Matthew. She was glad they'd not done what Bernard had been pressing them to do – contact Social Services. A mother who was around some of the time was better than no mum. She expounded on the probable beneficial effects the mother's fright would have on her parenting behaviour. Then from the next room, they heard the explosion. And then the rising howl as Pearl panicked. They rushed in. Tracey saw it was the news item about the explosion somewhere in Manchester. She had seen the headline on a billboard earlier in the day. She had no idea it had been captured, complete, on some passer-by's new Christmas present video camera and that this shaky footage was now being broadcast to the nation and at the volume of the new telly, sounded like it could have been in the room with them.

On the screen, clouds of dust and smoke and debris falling, then a silence and then just as she got there to switch it off, the sound of people screaming. She flicked it off as quickly as she could. Kieran was crouching beside Pearl, holding her in both arms. Crooning a soothing tuneless anxious hum. There were tears in his eyes. Tracey felt a warmth towards him growing. He was just a regular compassionate bloke recovering from a broken marriage and perhaps more poignantly, a broken heart, a heart of gold. Pearl was quivering, seemingly unaware of him, her unseeing eyes transfixed by an invisible terror somewhere in the middle of the opposite wall.

Chapter 19

"Come on, Pearl, let's do some exercises," and Robin reached out for her hands. She didn't lift them towards him. How quickly he had come to expect her co-operation. How impossible it was without it. It was salutary for Robin. He had assumed that most of the rehabilitation work, most of the physical effort, had been his. How wrong he was. And he now realised for the first time how stupendous the effort must have been for her, how much of herself she had given. How much he had underestimated her personality and strength. To see it slipping away now was heart-breaking.

"No joy?" Kieran came in from the kitchen. Pearl's eyes flickered with interest. Tracey was right, Pearl probably did fancy him.

"Do you want to try?" Previously Robin had jealously guarded his control of the exercises, made nervous by the need to keep accurate records for his research. He now decided that it would be just as legitimate to record someone else practising with Pearl though. Would that be prejudicing the results? Not really, he reasoned. The emotional set-back had already totally altered the conditions of the test. Was it a fair test at the moment? No way. He just wanted to get Pearl back to where she had been before this second trauma had upset it all. When Kieran reluctantly agreed to try, Robin started a new page of records, a separate log, so that he could use this as a separate piece of research if needed or if it turned out to be a mere blip in the results he could simply write it up in his evaluation. It was aggravating though, and so avoidable. Robin indulged himself in a smug inward stream of irritation that this situation had arisen. It was not his fault. But his work had been badly set back, if not destroyed. The thought churned round and round in his head:

"Idiots. They are idiots. Crass amateurs. Well-meaning, certainly, but idiots. Mum always used to say it was one of the worst things you could say about someone. 'She's well-meaning.' Meaningless coffee morning talk I suppose. But it'll set my work back. I'm not sure if Pearl will ever recover. So much of her development is connected to her will to achieve and now she's totally relapsed. Whose bright idea was the telly anyway? And then letting her watch the news, when the only news is the Manchester bombing, just one huge explosion is all it took. Unbelievable, ironic certainly, considering that's where this all started, with an explosion on the telly, not quite so literally this time of couse. It's exactly what I'd expect, this traumatic reaction she's having. I was doing so well. OK we were doing well together. She had the use of both arms, almost equally, and the fine motor movement of the two right fingers and the thumb. She was so near to getting the manipulation and strength equally into both hands. Then she would have been able to push herself about the flat in her wheelchair unassisted. At the moment she can only go round in a circle, left. But that left hand was getting stronger and stronger. Now what's going to happen? This could set us back weeks. She may never come out of it. Look at her, just sitting. I could cry. Mind you she couldn't even sit properly when I first met her."

Kieran reached out to Pearl. After a long wait he spoke kindly.

"Hold my hands, Pearl." And she looked up at him, as though waking from a dream. Screwing up her eyes, blinking and refocusing, after a heavy pause, her jaw began to drop and vibrate, preparing for speech.

"KKKKKKie......r...nnn." Robin heaved a sigh of relief, perhaps all was not lost.

"Hold my hands, Pearl. You can do it. Do it for me." Robin winced. But with an intense struggle, something inside Pearl's chest seemed to unfurl and she moved her hands slightly upwards, almost in supplication. Kieran could bear the strain no longer and reached out further to grip her hands and lift her top body up towards him.

"That's great Pearl, you did it. Did it for me."

Robin was dismayed. Pearl did do it, but it was true she only did it for Kieran. This was exactly what the programme Robin had devised was trying to avoid. Pearl should be doing these things for herself, not to please Kieran or anyone else. The whole programme was designed and skewed to develop Pearl's capacity for self-determination. Her own willpower, a sense of her own place in the world. That was why it had been working so well, with so many and such a variety of people to support her. Pearl could so easily become dependent on one individual, Kieran in this case. The implications of this would probably be drastic. When Kieran went away, she would relapse again.

No, Kieran would not do to support Pearl's exercises. Tracey was right, Pearl was clearly in love with him. But would she co-operate at all, develop at all without that love, now that she had experienced it? Was her progress now dependent on that need to please the one she loved? Robin began to feel he was losing control. Powerless in the face of Pearl's passion and the possibility that without it she would be back to square one, no matter what the rest of them did.

Later, Kieran announced that he would be going away for a day or two. Tracey decided to move in. Martha and she had run out of things to say and they disturbed each other in their sleep. Only two more days until Tracey could have her room in halls back. She longed for the peace and quiet. And anyway she had some work to do. She hadn't even attempted any over the holiday. It had been so hectic there hadn't been a moment free.

While he was away, Pearl missed Kieran, calling out for him in the night. But during the day, she slept a lot, because being unconscious meant the time seemed to pass more quickly. Like a pining puppy. Tracey would have been concerned, except that she had a piece of writing to produce for Sarah and only two days to do it in. Sarah had sent her a message saying her baby was to be induced on the 12th January, so she wanted to get things sorted out with Tracey before then. Write anything, don't worry about the format for this first piece, she'd said. She did not say that this piece of writing was to be analysed by the academic development department and the results of their analysis would dictate whether this would not only be Tracey Allsop's first piece of writing for them but also her last ever in the university.

'PRODIGAL DAUGHTER RETURNS', or 'MOTHER WELCOMES ESTRANGED DAUGHTER' or 'REUNION WITH LONG LOST BROTHER'. Tracey started and restarted one bitter diatribe after another. But it was pathetic to want to blame Sarah for what happened, to want to force her to read it, to force her to accept some responsibility.

One day, Tracey felt she would be able to write about these things, but not yet, she wasn't ready. At the moment the wound was too fresh. Although no longer, raw, bright red and difficult to hide, it was now a clear seeping plasma of unhappiness which in due course would harden into a scab of indifference and ultimately leave only a faint scar. Thankfully, only Bernard knew anything about it. The best way.

'ODYSSEY' It would be the story of her arrival here, in the corridors of academe. The progress from orphaned schoolgirl arsonist; through Northern Ireland; along Woolworths' sweet counter, giving birth on the way; through theft to keep body and soul together; from job creation to further education; sweeping through office cleaning to administration clerk; through the open doors of the Access course, to triumph, to gain at last, a place at university!

And all the skills she had acquired en route: how to forge references; who to trust; how to work the system; how to fill in forms; how to stay out of trouble; who to use; where to ask; who to help; how to show love and be loved; and how to learn to transfer someone else's belief in you, into a belief in yourself. Once she started, the words simply flowed. It was fun.

All morning there was only one interruption. A hammering on the door revealed a gangly ginger man,

"Miguel, how lovely to see you. It's like epiphany, you're Balthazar, the last of the three wise men. How did you find me?"

"Nah, I don't think Balthazar was a wise man...."

"Stop being so earnest! I was only bluffing, I just liked the sound of the word – Balthazar – no idea who he was, maybe I made him up. Any way, how did you know where to find me? And how was Christmas with the proud, doting old folks?"

"Your old nursey told me." Miguel settled down for a chat. "Don't you remember, you gave me that address in

Clarendon Avenue? Well, I got back a bit early. Thought I'd come and see you. It was so boring at home, the old folks' incessant questions about the course. Their admiration and pride, hoiking me round their dull friends to repeat everything all over again. I know it's sweet and all that. But suffocating. And I don't deserve all that crap. It's not exactly Oxford is it? No offence. Hey, and I didn't know the halls don't open again till tomorrow!" He had apparently been starved of conversation, despite all the family attention at home.

"Are you looking for somewhere to stay the night?"

"I don't only speak to you when I want something, you know!" Miguel almost sounded hurt.

Tracey sucked in her cheeks, her eye brows were raised in amusement.

"Toothpaste, file paper, loans, washing powder……."

"OK, OK, it's true, it's true, I need you. I can't function without you," he wailed.

"Oh good, not left your sense of humour behind in Ashby-de-la-Zouche, Burton-on-the-Water or whatever picturesque piece of England spawned you!"

"No, actually I'm staying with Rob tonight. But we should all go out for a New Year bevy. You on for it?"

Tracey had a reputation to maintain. She was famous for her ability to drink large quantities of beer, remain sober and never suffer a hangover. It was almost a spectator sport, without much competition.

"I, believe it or not, have not had a boring Christmas. It has been truly hectic and I now have work to do, before Tuesday."

"What is it?" She shut the filepad before he could reach her. "Why don't you wordprocess it, much quicker?"

"No PC - good enough reason?"

"Use my laptop! Got it for Christmas. I've been dying to show it off to someone! Look, I even have a brand new floppy. You can keep the floppy, and if you don't save it on the hard disc, I'll never be able to read your purple prose." Sure enough he had it in his holdall. And he really was keen to show it off.

"Don't look over my shoulder," Tracey scolded, "just be there for when I can't do something......like spell, or write, or.....do something stupid, like what I've done now, the whole lot's disappeared!"

"What, all three sentences? You've probably just pressed page down, let's see?" He tried to peer over and reach his hands down to touch the keyboard. "I won't look at you bloody writing, woman! Look........you've got it back. Your purple prose."

Was this an accurate description of her writing?

When Pearl moved in the bed, disturbed by the noise, Miguel jumped back. Mortified, he assumed the presence of a gentleman friend, "Sorry, I thought we were alone."

They weren't. And a couple of seconds later two small boys arrived at the door with a potted yellow chrysanthemum.

"For Pearl, she can keep the video, too," said James matter-of-factly. "Our grandad's died, so we can't come to stay here ever again." The last two words were emphasised. Then Matthew started an ineffective whistle, "Look, I can whistle," to cover James' whisper as he nodded towards the stairs where Tracey could see the shadow of someone waiting, "Can we come and visit with our dad sometimes?"

"Yes, of course," Tracey whispered back.

"Hurry up, boys, or we'll miss the bus." The voice of command rang round the stairwell from below. Tracey recognised the mother's voice. The thought of their previous encounter was painful she wanted to make a move towards reconciliation. She wanted to keep in touch with the boys. As she leaned over the banisters, the highlighted head turned, a black ring of dark roots round the elastic securing the blond Pompey pompom. She chivvied the boys. Although she looked quickly away, Tracey saw the black bruised cheek and scab drying on her lip.

Her concerned curiosity was genuine, a way in, a way to make friends, "Oh dear, what happened to you?" but when, after a long pause, the question still hung, ugly in the air, Tracey knew.

"Dad hit 'er," Matthew broke the silence, matter-of-factly, twisting round to blow Tracey a chubby little fingered kiss, which might have been a touching gesture, but for his mother pulling his ear, and him emitting a theatrical screech. Matthew smiled up from under her elbow, clearly not afraid of his mother.

"Least I've got a man! And my own kids. Not like you, you dried up old bag." Tracey heard the woman leave the building before allowing herself a snort of laughter. It wasn't funny, really.

But the sight that confronted her back in the flat was.

Miguel was transfixed by Pearl, who, having woken, had struggled to sit up and was now engaging him in a one-sided conversation, which was incomprehensible to him. She was so excited at having another (young male) visitor. He, poor chap, was trapped, didn't know where to look or how to respond.

She had shuffled and heaved and pushed, finally settling back onto a pillow and rucking up her tracksuit top. Its lower hem caught on a teddy bear's nose. The teddy now looked out from her arm pit, his nose pressed into her exposed bare nipple. Pearl's obliviousness added to the comic effect for Tracey. The fact that Pearl might be mortified if she herself noticed the bare boob – this was previously uncharted territory, Pearl's capacity for humiliation – or that Tracey might not be able to control her amusement at Miguel's discomposure, meant Tracey was fit to burst.

"Here, I'll tidy the bed." Just managing to maintain a normal voice, Tracey pulled down Pearl's top for her and concealed the breast in the same motion as smoothing bedclothes and plumping cushions. "Would you like to get dressed now?"

Pearl was concentrating on Miguel.

"My name's Michael," he introduced himself, holding out his hand, his self-confidence returning.

After a bit of a pause, while she processed the cue, Pearl raised her hand and gripped Miguel's.

*　　*　　*　　*　　*

He had tried explaining, given examples, quoted case studies, but in spite of everything, Robin had failed adequately to convince Kieran of the harmful effect that Pearl's growing dependence on him would have on her in the long term. Either he did not care, enjoyed the power it gave him too much, or simply disagreed with the regime. He always paid lip service, but then went ahead and did his own thing, congratulating her, babying her, imploring her to try a difficult task 'for me Pearl, do it for me'. Robin was beginning to get really frustrated. He solicited the support of both Tracey and Bernard, who were careful to keep exercise routines impersonal and separate from the friendship/care side of their relationship. Rose was a different problem, behaving by turns either kind, sympathetic and patronising or visibly irritated. Consistent only in her inconsistency.

Robin asked himself over and over what was this interfering Irishman doing here, anyway? Where had he come from? Where did his money come from? He was never short. And he didn't work, well, not noticeably. Who was he? To Robin, he seemed to be on one level, some kind of an opportunist, up to no good, with a secret agenda of his own, and on another level, he was a massive spanner in the otherwise well-oiled research work. Tracey, Bernard and Rose, appreciating the value of Kieran in Pearl's flat and the freedom it gave them, were reluctant to take him to task on Robin's behalf. Only Tracey had qualms, but they were just a distraction from Robin's agenda. She told him she was worried about the nature of Pearl and Kieran's relationship. She just had the uneasy feeling Kieran might be taking advantage of Pearl in some way, though she couldn't think how. Pearl had no valuables, nothing to offer really and Tracey was sure there was nothing physical going on. Robin gave Tracey's anxiety no consideration at all, consigning it to the realm of repressed neurosis on her part. Probably envy, or wishful thinking. What woman wouldn't want to share a flat with the handsome Kieran?

Robin had waited two hours with Pearl after their session, which had gone badly due to Kieran's absence. He wanted to see him and get this sorted out for good. It could not go on. But seven o'clock came and no Kieran, though the note on the fridge said he'd be back in the afternoon. Robin was stuck. Tracey had gone out with some ginger boy. Bernard was out. He knew Bernard's brother Oliver was upstairs in Bernard's flat, with his girlfriend Clare. He'd greeted them on the stairs earlier. But hearing the uninhibited sounds of their copulation, he was discouraged from going to them. Marc and Isabelle had no phone and anyway seemed to be having their own problems. And Rose was not responding to the pager alarm, either because Robin had said he'd wait for Kieran or because she was out too. He knew he didn't really have ot stay, but didn't like to leave Pearl, though caring for her had never been part of his remit.

After a short sleep, Pearl had awoken, displeased to find Robin still there - a good sign because it meant she could retain information – and asked for Kieran. Robin and she shared a joyless meal of beans and eggs, which Robin had to restrain himself from feeding to Pearl, such was the mess she made unassisted. He also had difficulty withholding praise when she managed a whole mouthful without spillage. Robin did not normally get involved in this day-to-day care.

Out of breath, dishevelled and red-faced, as though from running, Kieran was in no mood to be friendly, when he finally arrived. He was not grateful to Robin for staying, thought it had been unnecessary for him to have done so, after all, Pearl was by then sound asleep. He looked about nervously, as if checking everything was as before, giving Robin the impression he thought he might have been going through his things. He almost pushed Robin out of the door, still in his coat and clutching the WHSmith's bag he had arrived with.

On the stairs, Robin met Tracey and told her Kieran was back. With the quantity of beer, the hilarious stories of Miguel's weird family and the unexpected arrival of Marc and Isabelle in the pub, she had forgotten that Kieran would be back and that she should have been going back to Martha's for her last night there before returning to the sanctuary of her cosy halls room. Now she was here, she decided not to disturb Martha, but to kip at Bernard's and maybe call on Kieran, it wasn't too late yet.

When she had left the others in the pub, she had thought that she would be able to get a bit of peace and quiet to finish her piece of writing, her autobiography, for Susan. But the minute she hit the night air, the alcohol hit her. There was no way she was sober enough to write coherently, her walking wasn't even coherent. Fine motor skills went before gross motor skills. She still had Bernard's spare key, (so he wouldn't be lying when Ollie asked for one for Clare and he said he didn't have one). She would go up there for a sleep. But as she passed Pearl's door, she stopped to listen, to see if Kieran was still up.

Inside the flat the faint noise of someone moving around the kitchen could be heard. Tracey called softly through the keyhole, "Kieran." All noise stopped. She called again. Nothing. As she was moving away, there was a clatter followed by a curse.

She wondered if it would be really rude to use her key, knowing that he was in there. Then Kieran opened the door.

"Trying to make meself a fry without disturbing Pearl." He whispered before she could speak.

But somehow, the equipment in the kitchen did not look like frying pans and eggs and the smell was not bacon, though there was a smell of something. Something she had never smelt before, with a hint of....... marzipan? Certainly not bacon. Kieran reached past her and shut the door.

"Ah, come on, what are you up to? That's not your usual Ulster fry I can smell. And I've eaten a few in my time. Smells like a cake to me. Someone's birthday?" Tracey had the playful tone of one who has spent many hours drinking. "You can tell your old friend Tracey, I'll give you a hand with the icing, oh sorry, frying pan, wasn't it? I'm Greasy Nan herself...."

If she had been sober Tracey would have seen the rising colour in Kieran's face and backed off.

"Shhhhh...... you'll wake Pearl. Actually I'm just off to bed myself."

"Thought you were making a fry? I could eat a bacon sarnie meself." And she went towards the kitchen. He dived for the handle and held it tight. Tracey went to tickle him, giggling.

Kieran suddenly thrust his face into hers snarling, in a harsh whisper, but the words that came out did not fit with the furious, desperate expression or the vicious tone of voice.

"It's a.... secret − a........ surprise, erm,.......... for Pearl, and I didn't want to tell you yet, either, but, you're not allowed to see it yet, it's a surprise. I'm making something for her..... yup, for her birthday − in March. And no it's not the cake. I'm not such an eejit as to make a cake this early on."

The snarl had gone. Had she imagined it? His face was close to hers to keep the noise low so that their whispering would not disturb Pearl. He was smiling his usual twinkling smile again. She thought he was going to, yes, he was going to kiss her. She sought out his eyes, ready. Clear and blue, so pale and the curl of grey hair that bounced down. But he didn't, it was just that she believed it for a moment and then it was gone.

"Maybe she and I can share it then, you know our birthdays are a day apart?" Tracey hurried the conversation forward to escape the mortification of having nearly reached up to kiss him. Being so short could sometimes save you - from embarrassment.

"That's right, I knew that." Kieran had recovered his usual calm, "and this'll be something really special." But the edge was still in his voice.

They were surprised to hear feet shuffling noisily to a halt outside the door and muffled voices.

"Tracey, Kieran, we're going for a curry. You coming?" Bernard's voice. Christ he must be drunk to be slurring his footsteps like that. Tracey would've liked to have seen him in that state.

"Er.....No, but would you bring us a carry-out? Your choice. We'll settle up when you come back." Kieran's voice sounded completely normal now, shifting seamlessly from near snarl to charm. But the narrowed eyes, the flared nostrils and the clenched teeth passed across his features again briefly, as the footsteps had receded. How could she have thought he was going to kiss her?

264

In that fleeting moment Tracey realised that she knew nothing about him. Unused to being concerned for her own safety, it didn't occur to her that someone else in her current situation might have been frightened. She looked steadily at him, suddenly sober but decided to maintain the playfulness. His unpredictability, the mixed messages he was giving out, were exciting.

"You are up to something," she teased, "and it's not just a birthday surprise, is it?" Tracey's brain suddenly made a leap. "You are here in Portsmouth for a reason. Hmmmm.... Now, what is it? Why did you suddenly turn up after 15 years? Appearing out of the blue on Christmas day, bearing gold, well golden whisky, like one of the three wise men? I know, you've remembered that five quid I owe you!......"

"No," he laughed "not a fictitious fiver." And his voice softened as he said, "But I have remembered something." And he reached out a hand towards her, he was so sure of her, so completely in control.

Her nipples tingled in anticipation, an anticipation remembered 15 years after the only time he had ever touched her, brushed her nipple with his hand, in that scruffy bar in Coleraine. Was it possible? Had he remembered at last that he was a tit man?

*   *   *   *   *

"I gotta take my hat off to you, you're such a smooth operator, no one ever really questions you. And if they do you just turn the question around. You just slotted right in, making yourself indispensable. All the women fall in love with you. The only person who doesn't like you, you know, is Robin. And he's thinking of doing psychiatry. Perhaps he's the only one who can see through your enigmatic front and understand what is really going on....what.....(suspense music - de, dah!) is Kieran, (de dah!) doing in godforsaken Portsmouth? Can it really be research into our famous naval hero? Will the definitive biography of A.L.N. himself be the result of this surprise visit? Has he come to sweep the female sex off their feet, especially any from France? Oh and what about Pearl?"

Tracey wasn't sure why she had gone off on this tack of "why was he here?" But having started it, it was impossible for her to stop, just as it was impossible for her to change the sarcastic tone of her delivery.

They were still hovering in the doorway of Lilly's bedroom. Pearl slept on, oblivious to what Tracey suddenly realised through the beer was tension mounting in the room. She was also aware that she was winding up the tension herself. Every time she opened her mouth it was to insinuate something snide, negative about Kieran. Sober, she may have realised that one thing that was motivating her was the snub she had felt. The implied snub of his not kissing her. It gave her a need to needle him.

"My God, Tracey, c'mon n'ere, hey. Don't be getting carried away. Ye just hold it right there, before ye say something ye may regret." Kieran said it exactly like a threat in a police soap opera, complete with phoney gangster accent, but better acting. Tracey did stop and look carefully around, something alerted her, something woke her beer-soaked brain and finally popped her hope for sex.

"Now where did I put my bag?" she said to cover her surveillance activities, looking for signs of something suspicious in the flat, knowing that she hadn't brought a bag.

"You never use a bag."

"Very observant, yes. I do sometimes use a bag, but only when I'm menstruating. That's the only time I can't carry everything in my pockets."

Hoping he would be discomforted enough not to pay too much attention to her looking round. But nothing in this room was out of place. Whatever it was, if it was anything beyond her imagination, must be in the kitchen. Maybe he really was making something. Perhaps the smell had been..... glue? Left over from the Christmas preparations? Then when Lilly's bedroom door came into her line of vision, she suddenly remembered the padlocked cupboard.

"Well, what've I done with it? My bag that is."

Pearl moved in her bed and let out a long sigh. Tracey and Kieran held their breaths. Then to disarm him further she added, "And there's nothing that looks like a surprise for

Pearl. C'mon, what is it? I know it's not really for me as well. So you can tell me. I won't tell Pearl, I promise. Perhaps it's in Lilly's bedroom?" She teased. And she was through the door before Kieran could get to it from the kitchen.

Pearl groaned in her sleep. They both froze, looking towards Pearl's bed under the window. Gradually, Tracey moved her head round to look into Lilly's room. The bedroom light was off, but light from the main room thrust a triangle of yellow into the gloom and in it, Tracey saw the cupboard doors were open, the open padlocks hanging from rings in the bolts. There were some clothes hanging there and cardboard boxes were piled up underneath.

Tracey had to think quickly. A wild, irrational, unfounded and terrible suspicion had come to her. It was impossible that it could be true, but when she trusted her instincts, Tracey often found them to be right. If she was right, then it was vital that she find some means of giving Kieran a way out. If she was wrong - and she was only too familiar with the melodramatic side of her imagination - a diversionary tactic would get her away from the situation and give her some time to think it through.

Lilly's bed was hard, as Tracey collapsed on it. Kieran was hovering by the door, ready to rush back and defend the kitchen if she should go that way, but trying to use his body as a screen between her and the contents of the cupboard.

It was her move.

"I should never have had that last pint. I suddenly feel a bit nauseous. D'you mind if I just kip here a while?" Without waiting for an answer, she lifted her legs wearily onto the bed.

"Sorry about my boots but I don't have the energy to take them off." And she pulled the edge of the quilt around her and dropped instantly off to sleep.

Kieran knew people who could do this, especially after a few pints, but he gave Tracey a good five minutes before he moved at all. She certainly seemed to be asleep. He had a lot of work to do. He didn't like to leave the cupboard unlocked with her there, but if he locked it now, she'd be sure to hear and wake and he needed time to clear the kitchen, which would probably be better done soon and with her unconscious. Although on the other hand, if she did wake, he could just send her packing off to bed upstairs in Bernard's and they could both pretend none of this had occurred. Oh, but Bernard, he remembered, was out for a curry, so she'd be hanging around here, anyway, for a bit.

It was a risk, but he decided to leave her and went to clear away his activities in the kitchen. His hand was not steady. He had never been so close to discovery before – but then had never taken any risks before. Certainly never in the seventies, even though they had worked in twos or threes, they'd never had a weak link. They'd always had the back up. Never needed to set up their own base. Always done by the back room boys – or girls mostly. But now, he had completely retired from that work, from that part of his life. He was working alone now on his own personal project, no support needed, independent, responding to a personal mission, he could not really afford to take any risks. Though here he had found himself doing just that, inevitably, he had had to. There was really no such thing as working alone. It had been a hard lesson for him to learn so late in life. At some stage other people always got involved. Having had to accept the delivery so early, such a long time before he needed it, made him nervous. And there was a new system now. He'd been out of it too long. He'd been trying it out tonight when your woman returned.

Everything about this had turned out to be different from any thing else he had ever done and different from what he had imagined. Half-planned, waiting at the back of his mind for so many years, conceived, though subconsciously at the time, as a child, it had now taken on its own momentum.

At first the chance of free accommodation with an uncommunicative spastic had seemed a godsend. But it had turned out quite differently from what he had envisaged. Kieran had inadvertently become embroiled in Pearl's situation.

As he snapped on the surgeon's gloves to pack up, resigning himself to resuming later, after Tracey'd gone, Kieran's ears were tuned in to the bedroom.

But his thoughts were with Pearl. He had never before been on the receiving end of such a love. The unquestioning, non-judging way she loved him was overwhelming.

It ought to have been a burden. Though married for several years, there had been no children. This, he thought, must be what it would be like to be loved unconditionally by your own child. His rational side told him it ought to have felt stifling and unbearable.

Thinking he knew himself, strong, independent and resistant, he couldn't understand how Pearl managed to create in him both a sense of intense well being and a sense of worthlessness. It was cloyingly sweet, addictive, a syrup that he could not step out of, he knew, without tremendous upset, mess and repercussions. Traces of that sugary glue would remain forever. He forced himself to try and think how Pearl would feel when he had to go. He tried to think where he would go when this long-awaited event had finally been staged. He tried to think what was next? He could not.

This had been a project for so long, he had never thought ahead of it. 8th March 2016. The problem was that it was still a long way off, and he was not really happy that he was being forced pre-empt it, but he had realised that it would not wait until then.

There were a million reasons why it had to be now: his own possible incapacity - his father had Parkinson's; Kieran himself would be 58 in 2016 and getting too old; a general weakening of his resolve; as he matured the obsessional fury of youth was beginning to leave him; the hand of fate putting Tracey's Portsmouth address into his hand when he was sorting through the family home after his mother's death. It had had to be this year. Thirty-year anniversary instead of the desired fifty.

The kitchen was clear. Everything was neatly packed into the shoebox, wrapped in the plastic WHS bag, which for the time being he hid in the bin where he'd put a new black bin liner. He replaced the empty milk carton and potato peelings on top. Tracey was not likely to look there. He gripped the edge of the worktop and stretched, trying to empty his mind. He thought he could hear the even breath of sleep from Lilly's, from his, bedroom. His head dropped. He examined the splodgy speckled markings on the floor tiles, letting them come into focus, then recede. What was he doing here? She was right to ask. He was mad.

No shadow fell, only a slight change in the tone of the light. He knew she was there. He gave himself a second, then looked up.

In her hands a London A-Z was open at page 61 where a patch had been highlighted in fluorescent green. Highlighted by him. Their eyes met in a sudden flash of understanding.

"Most people have novels beside the bed, or sex manuals! Course I wasn't rude enough to look under the bed." her jollity was false, too bright. She didn't mention that she had had a quick look in the boxes. Tracey wished with all her might she could now unknow what she felt sure she knew.

"Going sight-seeing then? D'you know London?"

"Like all my countrymen I worked the building sites. Is that what you meant, by site-seeing then? Looking up the buildings I've had a hand in building, my old buildings? Interesting idea. Like visiting graves."

He smiled his killing smile and Tracey suddenly knew again the way she had felt about him, the way she had fancied him as a 16 year old. In that pub with, who? Brian, the bike man. Kieran had been way out of her league. But he had come over to her, picked her out of a whole bar full of people. And now that she had remembered, the feeling was there again, and here she was, smiling, smiling, softening, melting. And knowing this was a dangerous man.

*   *   *   *   *

"Oh fucking Christ, who let us forget their takeaway?"

"That is so like you, always got to have someone to blame. We are all equally culpable. We all forgot. No one is to blame. There is no need for blame." Like us all, Oliver was at his most nauseating when self-righteous.

"On the contrary, dear bruv, there is very good reason to apportion blame," Bernard was inclined to use increasingly

270

pompous language as he grew more drunk, this was fortunately beginning to wear off, the curry having now soaked up some of the alcohol, "to know whose responsibility it was to have remembered, will be to allot that person the unenviable task of retracing his or her steps to order and effect purchase of the forgotten but promised take away. To appoint one person will be to save the group from perishing unnecessarily on this chilliest of chilly winter evenings and limit the harm to but one individual, who, after all, will be able to keep from hypothermia on the return trip by clutching the curry bag to him or herself."

"Someone shut the bastard up!"

"Bugger it, I'll go…..not, I hasten to add, because I accept responsibility for having forgotten, but because I am a decent human being, a peacemaker among men and I can't stand Bernard's convoluted crap ANY LONGER. I wish you good night and here's hoping you all have scalding hot anuses tomorrow!" Robin was about to exit dramatically left. He had turned out to be quite entertaining. They had all warmed to him this evening.

"Robin, Robin, my red-breasted friend, not so fast………As you do not live with us in Warehouse No 1, and will indeed be taking an different route home, there is no point what so ever, in your, admittedly generous and selfless gesture. Also the Indian of choice, from which we have just so recently departed is in fact not in the direction you have or are about to take, but back to the right." Bernard was drivelling again.

"You sure you know how to get home?" Clare asked Robin, really concerned, she'd never seen him drunk before.

"Sure! (hic) just testing!" Robin had had a hard few days and the strain of not assaulting Kieran, had made him ripe for a bevy. He no longer cared what happened, but meekly wandered off leaving the company, going home, south towards his flat in Ashburton Road.

"Let's all go! C'mon. Not you and Isabelle, Marc, 'cos, you're nearly home now anyway. We'll let you off. G'night, G'night."

"You want to see, really?" There was a chance that Tracey might understand. Kieran had never told anyone about this dream. It was tempting to tell and she exuded an air of having no real interest, as though she were just humouring him, which made him want to tell. And her disinterestedness made him believe that if he did tell her, she would not judge him. Added to which, he had the feeling that she had already guessed.

But Tracey had only barely remembered Kieran's disclosure in a pub conversation from 15 years before. About the most important thing that had happened to him, or the most memorable or life-changing, or something like that. And as she remembered it, though it seemed fatuous now, for him, this important event had been that he saw Nelson's Column blown up. Not the one in Trafalgar Square, it had been some minor statue in Ireland somewhere. Dublin? And she had just seen Kieran's London A-Z with Trafalgar Square highlighted. So she had made the connection between the two Nelson's columns, that's all.

She knew he was unusually interested in Nelson, for, to her incomprehensibly obscure (and, she had the impression) anti-British reasons. But then he had shown such a touching, sympathetic interest in the man Horatio Nelson on his trip round the dockyard. 'One in the eye for so-called equal opportunities these days,' Kieran had said, if she would pardon the pun, employing as admiral of the fleet, a one-armed, one-eyed, vertically challenged adulterer. And when she asked him, he had seriously considered that he himself, if he'd been around at the time and served under the great man would have drunk a toast to him from the barrel of brandy his body had been preserved in for the return voyage after he had died.

"Let's have a cuppa, I'm parched." Tracey never thought that she would find herself in any awkward situation that would entail making tea. But here it was, the only thing she could think of to diffuse the tension, a distraction to defer the imminent confession that she had apparently so pleaded for and now did not want. An normally fearless person, she was now really concerned. She understood at last that Kieran was a zealot, he had a secret mission and whatever else it was, it was going to be a big gesture, and it was not going to be legal and it might even be lethal. That he felt he could confide in her was extremely worrying. They watched each other carefully as she filled the kettle and lit the gas. He paid no attention to her actions only her reactions. They both knew if he told her, she would be involved in whatever it was in an irrevocable way, she would never be free. Perhaps that was already the case. But she did not know what he had in mind. Most terrifying of all, she suspected he didn't know what he would do about her, that this particular moment had not been part of his plan, which made everything from here on in unpredictable.

"OK."

Kieran reached into the bin and pulled out a WHS bag. A sigh of relief escaped Tracey. WHS, so innocuous, almost scholarly. He glanced once at her and began to unpack its contents. Tracey stood by, realising that her intuition, the instincts on which she relied in everything were going to be useless here. He was going to show her something. She stood by, increasingly aghast. The pulse in her chest pumped so hard she could see it when she looked down, even through the dense breast flesh and the fleece material.

"This is a bit new to me," he sounded really unsure as he began to pull the various bits from the shoebox and start to assemble them. She couldn't concentrate, couldn't take it all in, the receptors in her brain were being shut down by the rising apprehension. All Tracey caught was the impression of some kind of machine.

Kieran snapped on surgical rubber gloves.

"Well, it'll mean nothing to me. I'm your original technophobe. Why don't you explain it to me first before you show me anything? Give me a bit of background. I'll have a better chance of understanding."

Had he noticed the nervous panting in her voice, the toneless delivery to disguise the fear? The talking a lot to play for time.

"For a start," playing for time, "to start from the beginning." It seemed a neutral place to start, the place where this new dialogue, the real dialogue, began, with the highlighted A-Z. "What's the significance of Trafalgar Square?"

"Nelson," came the flat reply.

"Mmmmm, yeah?" she encouraged him.

"You mind that time, in the pub, when you were over? D'you mind that?"

"Yes, I do."

"I told you about my birthday." There were pauses where his mouth stopped issuing sound, and she could see that the tip of his tongue was working his teeth as he concentrated on keeping his too-large fingers steady in manipulating the delicate parts of the machine. "Ye know, my eighth birthday... the trip to Dublin?" Pause. "And Nelson's pillar blown up right there in front of me on my birthday.........
Me being born on the anniversary of the Easter rising. Then when I was older,.............. (tongue working) it was like a sort of sign and every time one of me compadres was," he paused, this time to choose a word, "in trouble, or I had a bit of a doubt about the Troubles, you know in general terms, I only had to think about it,............ that sign, and I knew. I was following my destiny."

Tracey breathed out slowly. Oh no. She kept silent while she worked out her response. The alcohol, almost worn off now, was enough to keep her from panicking. She had met so many people who were in the grip of an obsession, pursuing their 'personal destiny'. Following a sign. The saddest of them was a friend whose only goal from a baby-doll preoccupied childhood was to have her own baby, and who was now a childless post-menopausal woman. The stupidest was an ex-boyfriend who believed he was a kind of guru who knew what was best for everyone. The stench from his flat lead to his discovery six months after he'd topped himself. But the most dangerous was here. Kieran. In a disabled woman's kitchen, a woman for whom Tracey had taken legal responsibility was this weird man, who could only have been here because of his connection with her.

"See, d'you know what it would've been in 2016?" Kieran didn't wait for a reply. "The anniversary. It would've been the centenary of the 1916 Easter Rising. And it would have been the half centenary of Nelson being blown off his Dublin pedestal."

Tracey became nervous. The word 'blown' resonated.

"So what? You came here with some kind of plan connected to Nelson? To Trafalgar Square?"

The sheer madness of what was going through Tracey's head made her eyes swivel.

"And how is this connected to Pearl, to Portsmouth, to me?" And the dreadful truth dawned on her the certain knowledge that here, in this kitchen, he was planning to build, no, NO he was actually building it now...... the components were there, he'd kept them in the bin. Tracey faced it, saying the word in her head....... a...a....some kind of a.........bomb. He was going to blow dear old Nelson off his column in Trafalgar Square as the ultimate outcome of a childhood sign, to satisfy his personal destiny. And he had the explosive device here, in this kitchen. Now. As far as she knew, ready and primed. But then she remembered something he had said, it was all a bit new to him. Perhaps he was not really a bomber, perhaps this was his first time. Perhaps he had never made a bomb before. Maybe that's why he wanted to show her, to reassure himself. Tracey quaked.

He was sweating, though it was freezing in the kitchen now the heating had gone off. His hands were shaking with effort.

He was simply mad, psychotic.

"I'm really tired actually," Tracey yawned dramatically. "Could we talk about it in the morning?" But she knew she could not get away, there was no hope, she was clutching at nothing. There was nothing to clutch at.

"So why now?" the calm voice Tracey managed to ask this time wasting question in surprised her. "Why not wait until 2016? That's the anniversary."

"A sad tale. I'm not as able as I was, already. And me Da had Parkinson's. It's probably neurotic, but I imagine myself shaking already. By the time I'm 58, I'll maybe be too disabled to accomplish it. Then, I told you, I was made redundant this last year and then the wife thing. I dunno, it just seemed I'd not make it to the 50."

How could she escape from this madman? Get Pearl? Tell Rose and Joe?

Her next action was a response to the kick of adrenalin these thoughts for others' safety engendered.

"I think I'll be off to bed." And she bolted for the door.

He grabbed for her with one hand, the other holding something black, a tiny liquid crystal minute minder, set at? Tracey couldn't see the time on it. The walkman head phone cord shot out from the lip of the shoebox as it was knocked flying by Kieran's hand reaching to restrain her. The box slammed across the cooker, dislodging the kettle, slopping boiling water, emitting a gush of steam. She had forgotten about the tea.

Kieran's hands moved quickly toward the box, to save it, catch it before it fell. Tracey saw the blue gas flame lick the cardboard and flare along the cord. She rushed to the sink for water.

"No not water!" he shouted, as a yellow flame burst from the paper of the box. He had dropped it and was trying desperately to batter it with the towels, when,

BOOOOOOM!

*   *   *   *   *

There was such stillness, he could hear his pulse banging into the pillow, resonating through the hollow fibre filling. The rubbed texture of the pillowcase, jabbed at his unshaven cheek, the base of a birdcage had been transplanted in place of his tongue and the pulse intensified into a point of throbbing pain above one eye. Hungover. Robin was rarely hungover. He felt a little proud, if rather unwell but had enough experience to know that staying in bed would magnify the symptoms, fresh air followed by tea, then breakfast would dispel them.

Robin didn't want to be alone. There was only one place he wanted to be, one group of people who accepted him at face value, never made him feel awkward and with whom he had a clearly defined role.

He despised people who wore shades in winter, thought it pretentious, but on opening the front door onto the street facing east, wished for some himself. The low sun pierced right through his eyeball into the centre of his headache and his eyes began to stream uncontrollably. No tissues. A faint feeling of being distanced from the world accompanied him, almost a levitation, a sense of not having quite all his weight connecting with the pavement, and walls, trees and bushes seemed to recede or encroach unnervingly as he walked. He was shocked to feel his hair being combed on the way up St Andrew's Road as he was passing a wall overhung by trees, the stiff winter branches had reached down to give him a coiffure. Why had he come this route?

The diversion signs and queues of traffic should have warned him. But the blue and white police tape cordoning off St Mary's Road, seemed, at first, festive. The crowds of people gawping awoke him. But not until Robin turned the corner around the church did he even begin to realise. There, vehicles of many shapes and colours with satellite dishes and loops of wire were randomly parked across the road and where Warehouse No 1 had been was a gaping gap piled with rubble.

Robin moved up to the police tape. The jingling sound of glass being knocked from church windows. The dust filled air where hard-hatted white suits sifted through bricks and pieces of cookers and splinters of furniture and strips of wall paper. Then he saw a red patch at his feet and jumped back. Blood. But the smell that rose to his nostrils was tandoori sauce and there were the foil containers and a scattering of bright yellow rice like a wedding in any churchyard.

*   *   *   *   *

Safe in the maternity wing, Susan wearily lifted the newspaper. It was all there. With Tracey's name. A surge of almost pride rose in her, that she had known this woman, a weight of horror that she had been going to recommend her to leave her course. She reached out to her little son, hours old, asleep in his cot, tucked in tight, on his side with cellular blankets. Two tiny hands squashed together, on one the fingers flexed in sleep and she could see the wide, too wide, thumb, and the wide apart eyes flicker and rest.

Lightning Source UK Ltd.
Milton Keynes UK
UKOW02f2347101114

241416UK00005B/467/P

9 781784 079437